"Darling, I want to tell you again how sorry I am. I haven't been sane since the night you disappeared from the yacht. . . ."

With arms more powerful than she remembered, Dake half carried Reesa from the crowded room to the deck. The stars glinted silver in the night sky, and the moon traced a path over the waves, making it seem as though she could step from the boat and walk the glittering path to infinity.

"There's Orion," Reesa whispered, pointing to the constellation.

"Yes," Dake murmured. He cuddled her body in front of him so that her midnight hair blew back in his face. "I had forgotten how thick your hair was. It's like black satin."

"It's too long—"

"No. Don't cut it. It's glorious." He was silent for long minutes. "This is the best part of being at sea . . . the nights," Dake said. "It's a wonderful way to spend a honeymoon. . . ."

Reesa stiffened. "Dake, that was all thrashed out between us . . . that night. It's over."

"The hell it is," he growled.

"You have it all wrong, Dake. I'm not the same person I was. I've found a measure of . . . of stability. . . ."

"Stability? What you found was a hideout, a retreat from the world. All right, sweetheart, if that's what you want, we'll go for it, but we'll go for it together."

"No." Unable to free herself from his arms, Reesa turned around, her back to the rail.

Dake's hand reached up, his index finger touching her lips. "Don't say anymore. We'll take it a day at a time for now. . . ."

WHAT ARE *LOVESWEPT* ROMANCES?

They are stories of true romance and touching emotion. We believe those two very important ingredients are constants in our highly sensual and very believable stories in the *LOVESWEPT* line. Our goal is to give you, the reader, stories of consistently high quality that may sometimes make you laugh, sometimes make you cry, but are always fresh and creative and contain many delightful surprises within their pages.

Most romance fans read an enormous number of books. Those they truly love, they keep. Others may be traded with friends and soon forgotten. We hope that each *LOVESWEPT* romance will be a treasure—a "keeper." We will always try to publish

LOVE STORIES YOU'LL NEVER FORGET
BY AUTHORS YOU'LL ALWAYS REMEMBER

The Editors

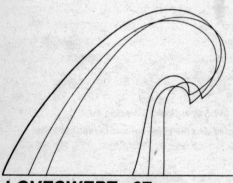

LOVESWEPT · 67

Helen Mittermeyer
Vortex

BANTAM BOOKS
TORONTO · NEW YORK · LONDON · SYDNEY · AUCKLAND

VORTEX

A Bantam Book / November 1984

LOVESWEPT and the wave device are trademarks of Bantam Books, Inc.

ISBN 0-553-21669-4

Published simultaneously in the United States and Canada

Bantam Books are published by Bantam Books, Inc. Its trademark, consisting of the words "Bantam Books" and the portrayal of a rooster, is Registered in U.S. Patent and Trademark Office and in other countries. Marca Registrada. Bantam Books, Inc., 666 Fifth Avenue, New York, New York 10103.

PRINTED IN THE UNITED STATES OF AMERICA

O   0 9 8 7 6 5 4 3 2 1

*To my mother, Mary McMahon Monteith, and
my sister, Elaine Monteith Vogt, and to Clare
and Bobby and Mark. We are a family?*

Many thanks to the fine Norwegian crew of the
M/S *Starward*, who were unfailingly courteous and
quietly efficient for the entire cruise. To Kim, Howard,
and Reid, who were gentlemen.

To Doug, Ed, and Mitch, the Dive-In Group who
were so helpful and informative not only about diving but about the care and beauty of the undersea
world. To Michael, who took time.

To Cecilia, who exchanged our money and answered our questions with a smile.

But most of all to Captain Hartvig Von Harling,
master of the *Starward* at the time of our cruise,
who with courtesy and humor told us stories of the
sea and invited us to share a part of his life, this
book is dedicated with great admiration for him and
for all others like him who undertake to master a
ship and the oceans. He is a man of warmth, charm,
and quiet efficiency.

Thank you all,
Helen Mittermeyer

One

Maria Halcon watched the passengers disembarking from the tender, all of them carrying snorkeling gear for the two hours of diving arranged for them by the Sea Dive Group. As one of the group leaders, she had arrived on the boat before the passengers to check that everything was ready for the dive. She'd also wanted to test the waters to make sure that they were clear enough for the divers, regardless of whether they were experienced or rank amateurs.

Maria waved to several of the passengers, who were trying to get her attention. This would be the first dive of the cruise, and most of them were eager to get into the warm turquoise water surrounding Saddle Cay, the small island owned by the Oslo Caribbean Line.

"Maria! Are you going to help us?" an older man called as he and his wife approached. They had confided in her the day before that they couldn't swim but still wanted to snorkel so that they could visit the undersea world of coral and marine life.

1

"Either I'll go with you, or one of the other Sea Dive instructors will." Maria smiled at Mrs. Calkins, gesturing at Dave, Arthur, and Andy, the other instructors. Maria was the only woman, and, even though her credentials were excellent, it hadn't been easy for her to get the position on board the M/S *Windward*.

"How is it that you're Spanish, Maria, but you speak English like you were American born?" Mr. Calkins asked her as the couple followed Maria from the tender docking along the white sandy beach to the spot where the dive would take place.

Maria felt her heart thud against her breastbone. She had been asked that question a few times before, but it still came as a shock. What would he say, Maria mused, if she told him she didn't know why her English was so good, that she didn't even know who she was. She believed that Halcon must be her real name, because that was the name she had been saying over and over when she was found by Miguel Aroza and pulled from the waters of the Windward Passage. She'd been sick and feverish as they traveled to Maria Island. Miguel had named her Maria after the island he called home, and had told her that Halcon must be her name because she kept calling it out in her delirium.

"Spanish was the second language in my home, Mr. Calkins. English was the first." Maria gave him her usual answer. It was the truth, in a way. Miguel was married to an American woman who spoke very good English. Maria just couldn't bring herself to explain to a stranger that she had no desire to find out who she was. A black, fearful feeling seemed to smother her every time she began to recall things in the dim past. Whatever it was that she had done, or whoever she had been, there was something that had frightened her enough to make her forget her past.

The peace of mind she had known with Liza and

Miguel was something she cherished. She had been with them on the island for three months when she decided that it was time she earned her keep. A neighbor of theirs had suggested she try to get a job with the Sea Dive program on a cruise ship. Then Consuela, the neighbor's daughter, who worked as an assistant purser for the Oslo Caribbean Line, steered her toward the dive shops on the island. With their help she got certified as a scuba instructor with emergency medical training. Now, seven months after Miguel had found her, she was a member of the diving team on the M/S *Windward*, and she shared a room with Consuela.

"Now, listen," Dave Lenser, head of the Sea Dive Group, called to the passengers standing in front of him on the beach. "We'll be going out in four groups. I'll take all of the nonswimmers and those who think they might have difficulty. The rest of you should pair up with the other instructors."

Maria was listening to Dave's spiel about diving safety and the underwater life they would see, when she sensed someone staring at her. She looked over her shoulder, her gaze sweeping the beach. Many of the passengers had elected to join the beach party just to swim, eat, and drink, and the sand was crowded. She spotted a middle-aged man scrutinizing her, his eyes fixed in narrow concentration. Coolly, she returned his look, then glanced away. She'd gotten used to the stares of the men on board the ship. Just then she felt a hand on her arm, and she turned, a polite smile on her lips. She froze when she saw the man who had been watching her.

"Look, I'm sorry for staring at you, but you look like someone I once knew. Have you ever lived in California?"

"No," Maria answered quickly. For all she knew, she might have lived in California, but since she had been found in Eastern waters, she doubted it.

The man frowned. "Boy, you could be her double.
. . ." he muttered as he moved away.

Maria felt her stomach flutter wildly.

"Hey, Maria, c'mon, your group is waiting," Andy
called.

"Coming." She tried to put the incident out of her
thoughts. Maybe she should have asked him who it
was she resembled—no doubt his ex-wife, or maybe a
girlfriend. She slipped on her fins and the orange
T-shirt that identified her as a diving instructor. She
checked her group, then fitted her mask to her head,
her swimming cap keeping her hair confined. "All
right," she announced. "Let's go out there and see
what we can find. Stick with me, please. I'll be diving
down and bringing up things for you to look at, so
stay in a group, at least for now." Maria counted her
group, then began paddling toward a coral reef about
a hundred yards from shore.

Whenever Maria dived into the colorful world below
the water's surface, she delighted in the aloneness,
the beauty, and the quiet, teeming life amidst the
undulating waves.

Today her first find was a small sea urchin. With
great care, and using the flat of her gloved hand, she
scooped up the creature and shot to the surface,
blowing her tube by throwing back her head. Lifting
her mask, and peeling off one glove so that the creature could sit on her bare hand, she showed it to her
group. She kicked her legs gently, her fins moving
back and forth to keep her afloat. "Look, this is just a
baby. You can hold him if you like, but be careful.
Those spines you see can be very painful. Remember
always to use caution in picking up anything in the
sea. Some of the corals are poisonous, and there are a
few things that can sting you. Fire coral is just that. It
will give you a very painful burnlike wound, so stay
away from it." She watched as the sea urchin was

passed from hand to hand until everyone had held it. Then she took it and released it into the water.

Maria gestured for them all to put on their masks and move slowly forward toward the reef. Only once did she have to stop to help a passenger inflate his vest for more buoyancy. Most divers preferred their vests partly deflated. That way they could move faster and dive deeper. Although the inflated vests prevented deep diving and were often cumbersome, they gave inexpert swimmers greater confidence.

To Maria's surprise, none of the divers in her group were ready to return to shore where a beach party was already in progress, the music of the steel band drifting out over the water. Enthusiasm ran high, so much so that Maria began to watch her charges closely, noting that both Mr. and Mrs. Calkins seemed to be showing fatigue.

She swam over to the elderly couple. "I think you should go in now and get something to eat and drink," Maria advised. "You don't want to overdo the first day."

The couple agreed and Maria swam with them to shore, her legs moving in lazy synchronization through the turquoise water. She glanced over her shoulder to check on the others in her group, and quickly she returned to the loose cluster of people near the reef. Pairs of divers explored the area, then one by one went ashore. When the last two emerged, Maria followed. Habit made her check the beach, then dive back into the water to check for stragglers.

A short time later she was nibbling a hot dog while Arthur described a close call with one of his group. Just then the stranger approached her again.

"Look, I don't mean to be a pest, but I do publicity for DM Productions. Does that mean anything to you?" He spoke abruptly, his gaze fixed on Maria.

Apprehension clutched at her heart. She shook her head. "I don't think I've ever met you, Mr. . . . uh . . ."

Maria clenched her back teeth to keep her face from showing the turbulent emotions that were shaking her.

"Leaman. Jasper Leaman, but everybody calls me Jazz." His smile flickered across his face, his eyes blinking nervously as he glanced at the divers clustered near Maria. "Maybe we could talk sometime?"

Maria jumped up from her seat at the picnic table, knocking over the soda.

Dave touched her arm. "Maria will be busy with the dive most of the afternoon, Mr. Leaman."

"Jazz. Call me Jazz. Everybody does." Jasper Leaman's smile flashed around the semicircle of people. "Well, maybe I'll catch you later. My wife, Janet, doesn't like swimming"—he shrugged—"so we didn't sign up for diving." He took a final, piercing look at Maria, nodded to the others, and ambled back across the beach to a blue-striped beach umbrella.

Dave looked at her. "Think it's a come-on?" Neither he nor any of the other divers knew much about Maria, except that she could handle her job.

She felt her mouth stretch to a smile, though her insides still churned. Did the man know her? Did he know what might have happened in her other life to cause the nightmarish fear that followed her day and night? "Sure," she said with a forced chuckle. "I've heard about every line in the book."

Dave, Arthur, and Andy laughed. Each of them had tried to date Maria at least once, and hadn't succeeded. Now the four were just close friends.

Maria laughed with them, but she couldn't quite smother the disquiet deep within her. She also noticed the puzzled look Dave gave her, but she knew he wouldn't pursue it. They'd all made a pact not to inquire about each other's private lives.

When they reentered the water she forgot all about Jazz Leaman and his questions. Not all of her divers returned to the water; the Calkinses chose not to, as did some of the other older divers. The ones who did required a good deal of watching though. Many had gained confidence after their first dive and now were more adventuresome, swimming out to the reef and screaming with delight when they found something interesting. Of course, when other swimmers approached, the specimen would disappear.

"Maria!" Todd Hughes, a precocious ten-year-old, called to her. "I saw a squid. He changed color." The excited boy waved to her.

Maria waved back as she kept an eye on her group. Most of the divers adhered to the safety rules, but a few got distracted and paddled off on their own, bringing a friendly reminder from Maria.

Maria was glad to get back to her cramped quarters on the ship and rinse the salt from her body. She stood under the warm water, soaping her body to remove the tanning oil that smelled of coconut and left her the golden color of a bronze goddess. Then she toweled dry her long hair and twisted its black, silky weight into a coil on top of her head.

There wasn't a full-length mirror in the cabin, but if she stretched, she could see most of her five-foot-five-inch length in the dresser mirror. Maria shrugged at her image, not overly impressed by the satiny skin, the ebony eyebrows that arched above light green eyes, and the heart-shaped face with the high prominent cheekbones of a model.

Consuela came into the room, slamming the door and letting out a loud groan. "I'm exhausted. How can I possibly tell Mrs. Soames the exact moment her postcard is going to reach her friend Mary in Wildflower, California—which is just south of Los Angeles, in case you were dying to know." Consuela threw herself down on Maria's bunk and stretched. Opening her eyes a few moments later, she surveyed her cabinmate, dressed only in plain white bikini briefs and a bra. "You know, for a gal with such a super figure, you sure wear crappy underthings!" Conseula told her in her slangy English.

Maria grinned at her. "I'm not about to spend my money the way you do. I'm saving to invest in Miguel's fishing and chartering service. I don't want to spend my life on the *Windward*, or the *Northward*, or the *Leeward*, or any of the other ships of the Oslo Caribbean Line." Maria ducked when Consuela threw a pillow at her, and laughed at her extravagant friend who spent so much money on exquisite silk lingerie. "Barney Freedling is engaged to be married, anyway, Connie," she reminded her friend gently.

"He isn't married yet," Consuela retorted. She rose up on her elbows to watch her friend pull on a pair of white cotton shorts and a ribbed cotton top. "Even with a bra on, Maria, you can't hide those breasts or those slim hips and long legs, and those perfect ankles. . . ." Consuela sighed. "You have the face and figure of a movie star. I think I hate you," she warned with a smile.

Maria laughed and threw the pillow back at her, picked up her small white purse, and waved to her friend. "See you for dinner at seven." She shut the cabin door behind her and walked down the narrow hallway, her body automatically adjusting to the roll of the ship, her movements smooth and free from the staggering gait that she'd had when she'd first embarked on the ship a few months earlier.

She'd promised to meet her friends in the Constellation Lounge for a couple of beers before dinner, but as she passed the purser's office in the ship's large lobby, she came face to face with Jazz Leaman. Maria started to turn away, but the man grasped her elbow.

"Please, Maria, I'd like to talk to you for a moment if I may."

Maria felt like jerking her arm free and walking away, but she knew the maxim of the line: Always be courteous to a passenger. "I can give you only a few minutes. I'm meeting some friends."

"Fine." Jazz Leaman took her arm and led her to a sofa in the corner. "Look, I'm not trying to make trouble for you, but I called my office in Los Angeles and told them that I'd met a woman who was almost a dead ringer for Reesa Hawke."

Dark swirls of fear clouded her sight and hearing for a moment, and Maria missed his first question. Reesa Hawke? Hawk was the English translation of *halcón*. No, it had to be a coincidence. The name Reesa Hawke meant nothing to her.

"And so I thought I had better tell you what I had done. I hope you aren't upset," he finished.

"What?" Maria tried to focus on what he was saying. What was he talking about? She shook her head, knowing all she wanted to do was to get away from Jazz Leaman. He made her nervous and uncomfortable. "No—no, I'm not upset, but I do have to go now." Maria stood, wondering if the relief she felt at leaving him showed on her face.

"Boy, that's great. I didn't want you to be angry with me, Maria. I'm not usually this pushy, but I believe in going with my hunches." Smiling, he pumped her hand, then walked away.

Maria watched his retreating back for long minutes as he crossed the carpeted lobby and headed for the casino on the next deck. "Maybe I should have asked what he did do," she mused aloud. Then she shook her head. "Leave well enough alone, lady."

"Talking to yourself?" Barney Freedling, the first officer, stood in front of her. The tall, sandy-haired Norwegian was a good-natured fellow with the reputation of being something of a lady-killer, but he had become a good friend to Maria once he understood that friendship was all she would offer him. "You must have money in the bank."

"Don't I wish." She smiled and fell into step with

him as they traversed the wide corridor and walked toward the officers' quarters. Maria would have to retrace her steps, but she wanted to speak to him. "Barney, it's none of my business, I know, but don't you think that you and Consuela should—"

"You're right, it's none of your business." Barney's smooth features tightened into harsh lines. "Consuela told me that I should go ahead with my long-standing engagement, as she intends to spend her life with a host of other men." Barney stalked away, anger stiffening his body.

Maria glared after him. "You are both stubborn—and pigheaded," she muttered, turning back the way she had come.

"Hey, Maria. That Leaman guy was looking for you," Arthur said when she entered the lounge. He slid over on the banquette to make room for her.

Maria sensed that Dave was staring at her as she turned to answer Arthur. She forced a smile. "I saw him down on Atlantic deck. You know how it is, there's always one passenger who thinks you look like Uncle Fred."

"Is that what it is?" Dave quizzed in his soft Florida drawl.

"Yup," Maria answered, reaching for the beer that Arthur offered. She took a long swallow of the cold Norwegian brew, ignoring the probing stare of the senior member of the dive team.

"Okay then." Dave began to discuss the strategy of the next day's dive.

Maria forgot Jazz Leaman as she listened with the others, picturing the rocky shore of Georgetown and the beach where they would be diving.

"Will we get some time to ourselves to dive near the wrecks?" Andy inquired, referring to the sunken vessels near East Bay and Gun Cay. Dave shrugged. "After we get the group dive over with—and there are no problems—I don't see why we can't go over to East Bay with some equipment."

Andy whooped, and the other two looked delighted. It was fun to dive near the wrecks, and since they were all checked out on scuba, it promised to be a great time.

"But only if we don't run into any snags with the passengers, and"—Dave chuckled—"don't forget the singles' party tomorrow night. Everyone goes— including you, Maria."

She made a face.

"What's the matter, sugah? Don't you enjoy feeling like a piece of raw meat thrown to the tigers?" Andy inquired, laughing.

"We don't all enjoy being live bait like you, man," Arthur said with a Jamaican lilt in his voice. Maria breathed a sigh of relief that Dave had stopped studying her so intently, and she brushed all unpleasant thoughts from her mind.

The next morning they landed at Grand Cayman Island. The waves were fairly high during the excursion, which caused a few bad moments for the inexperienced divers. Many were thrown back by the force of the waves onto the rocks and had to be helped from the water.

By the time the dive was through, Maria was exhausted and wished she hadn't promised the other divers that she'd go when they dove near the wrecks off Guy Cay. She would have preferred to beg off and attend the party on Seven Mile Beach. Somehow the thought of just loafing on the beautiful white sand seemed far more appealing.

Her fatigue faded somewhat once they'd entered the constantly changing undersea world. Right away Maria saw a giant grouper that she could have ridden like a horse. The friendly fish whisked by her in graceful undulations, dozens of smaller fish following in its wake. Maria nodded to Andy when he signaled that he wanted to dive around the wreck, and she followed, the rhythmic flutter-kick of their fins carrying them down where yellowjack and butterfly fish angled with bluestriped grunts and porkfish for space in the watery world.

By the time they had explored as much as they wanted, all of them were tired and their air supply was nearly exhausted.

They surfaced, clambered back into their small boat, and headed for shore.

Maria felt a deep fatigue as she slumped in the backseat. As usual when she was tired, depression swamped her and her mind flashed hazy images. She felt as though she were walking through a dark room where flashbulbs kept popping. She saw flickers of things, noses and eyes but no clear faces, bits of color and fabric but no one she could recognize. Instinct told her that she was remembering, that her mind was opening up like a flower, and that soon she would recall her past life. Cold perspiration dripped down her back. She kept her eyes squeezed shut when Andy spoke to her, knowing she would be unable to answer him clearly.

"Hey, sleepyhead, we're back at the dock. We'll just make the last tender if we hurry."

"All right." Maria tried to smile at Andy, but she felt so shaky, she just stared.

"Are you okay?" Arthur asked, concerned.

"Yes. Maybe I stayed down there too long."

"Maybe you did. Make sure you get some rest before dinner, promise? Remember, we have a date for the gala Singles' Stampede." Arthur grinned at her but his eyes revealed his concern.

"How could I forget? I'm putting on my cleats and shin guards the minute we return to the ship." Maria smiled, grateful that he had changed the subject. "There's the tender. Dave and Andy had better hustle." She stood on tiptoe, looking down the avenue that bordered the sea. Andy and Dave were sprinting toward them. She waved them on just as a private jet approached the landing field on the far side of the town. Its roar drowned out Arthur's shout at the other two to step on it.

Panting and laughing, Andy and Dave joined them. Then the four of them walked out onto the quay and climbed into the boat.

"We're not leaving yet. I have to wait for the people coming from the plane," the pilot of the tender informed them.

"What!" Andy groaned, still trying to catch his breath.

Dave slouched down on the seat next to Maria. "It must be one of the cruise line bigwigs. The captain wouldn't wait for anyone else."

"I didn't think he'd wait even for them," Andy muttered.

For fifteen minutes they cooled their heels, waiting for the late arrivals. Then an outislander ran up to the boat and whispered to the pilot, who grimaced.

"Ladies and gents," the pilot began apologetically. "We don't have to wait any longer. The person we were expecting took a private launch to the ship." He closed his eyes when the divers protested. "I know, I know how you feel, but you know it wasn't my fault."

"Can the complaints," Dave instructed, his eyes closed and his head against the wooden back of his seat. Soon they were alongside the *Windward* ready to board.

They went up the gangway and onto the ship, the darkness of the interior momentarily blinding them.

"So you damn well *are* on this ship. Damn your soul to hell! What were you trying to do?" The growled harshness of the words stopped all four in their tracks. They turned to face a very angry, very tall, chestnut-haired man.

Memory exploded in Maria like an incendiary bomb, stripping away the black uncertainty, ballooning the fear into reality. She reeled back, unaware that Dave's hand came out to support her. "Dake!" she choked out.

"Yes. Dake. Damn you, woman. Did you think I wouldn't find you?"

"Go away." Maria forced the words through tight lips.

"What is it? What's wrong, Maria?" Arthur asked.

"Maria? Who the hell are you calling Maria?" Dake hissed, danger sparking off him as he leaned toward the quartet who stared open-mouthed at him. "Her name is Reesa. Reese Hawke. So don't call her Maria—"

"Yes. Yes, I *am* Reesa Hawke. God, that's what I was mumbling to Miguel when he found me . . . *halcón . . . halcón . . .* meaning hawk." Words dribbled from her mouth in shocked cadences. She felt tremors course through her body as she stared at the man in front of her. "Go away. Leave me alone."

"Go? The hell I will. I spent time in jail on account of you, lady, and I want an explanation. I was accused of your murder, damn you!" Dake's words were shouted in fury.

"I don't care what you think she's done. She doesn't want you around, so get out of here." Arthur, her sweet, gentle friend, pushed his way in front of Reesa, planting himself in front of David Kennedy Masters, known as Dake Masters.

Dake inhaled, a hard smile on his face as his hands clenched and unclenched. "Get out of the way, kid, before I toss you off this ship."

"Then you'll have to take on the rest of us, because we're not letting you near Maria—Reesa." Dave spoke firmly, moving beside Arthur.

"Right," Andy joined in.

"That's enough." The deep voice of Captain Ivarsen

broke through the heavy silence. "I'll have none of this on my ship." He stepped between Dake and the others and turned to face him. "Mr. Masters, I told you when you insisted on coming aboard my ship that I would countenance no trouble with my crew. You are here at my sufferance, and as such you will obey my orders. I will not allow you to harass anyone on—"

"I'm the one being harassed. Because of her, I was arrested on a murder charge," Dake shot back. "If anyone committed a crime, she did!" Dake's arm shot out, pointing at Reesa.

For the first time in her life Reesa Hawke fainted, falling, falling, down into the black vortex.

Two

She knew the moment she opened her eyes that she
was not in the cabin she shared with Consuela.
Blinking, she tried to orient herself as memory after
memory washed over her.

"You're in the Cancún suite on Atlantic deck." Dr.
Margaret Roberts leaned over her, smiling. She was
the ship's doctor, in her late thirties, and a very good-
looking woman. Her thick blond hair was swept back
in a French twist and her blue eyes sparkled with
amusement. She lifted the stethoscope from her
neck, still gazing down at Reesa as she lay on the
king-size bed in the suite. "I was ordered to bring you
here by your fiancé—"

Reesa knew immediately who would have the nerve
to dictate to the doctor and claim to be her fiancé.
"Dake Masters is *not* my fiancé," she said in a hoarse
voice.

"No?" Margaret's eyebrows arched. "He's a very
interesting man," she mused, her eyes still on Reesa,
her hand taking her pulse.

16

"He's divorced . . . and available, I'm sure, so if—"

"I'm not available," a hard voice interjected. Dake stepped into Reesa's line of vision and next to the doctor. "Would you mind if I spoke to Miss Hawke alone?" He flashed a smile at the doctor, the dimples at each corner of his mouth a surprise on that hard-planed face.

"He also has a cleft in his chin, which means he's devious and two-faced," Reesa added, bringing both Margaret's and Dake's heads around to look at her. Dake was frowning now. Margaret looked puzzled. As she opened her mouth to speak, Reesa continued what she was saying. "You think because he has that charming smile and those dimples that he's some kind of hunk, right? Wrong. That man's a vampire. He sucks your blood!" Reesa made a loud slurping sound, her words slurring.

"It's the mild sedative I gave her . . . I think." Margaret looked from Reesa to Dake and back again.

"I fell for the dimples too. God, it's a mistake to turn your back on the buzzard." Reesa cackled, her eyelids feeling heavy. She heard the whispers from Dake and Margaret and then a door shut and footsteps returned to the bedside, but she was too sleepy to open her eyes.

"Listen to me, Rees. You are not going to pull this on me. I went through hell when I thought you were dead, and Cynthia died and . . ."

It was an effort for Reesa to open her eyes. She tried to focus on Dake's face. "Cynthia died? That's a shame. I know how much you loved your mother-in-law." Words spilled from her like jelly beans from a bag. "My goodness, what will you use now as a barrier to marriage? Join the Marines?"

"There are no excuses nor have there ever been." Dake spat the words, furious with what she was saying to him. The bitch! After all she'd done to him. Getting him arrested for her murder! Hiding out on a cruise ship while a battery of lawyers tried to get him free! "Must I remind you that neither of us wanted marriage?" He inhaled deeply. "After Cynthia's death—"

"I don't give a damn," Reesa muttered, then yawned.

"Bitch. You will give a damn. I'm not through with you." Dake's mouth tightened as he watched her sink into sleep. She was much thinner. That wonderful voluptuous shape had been pared down to svelteness. He watched for long minutes as she muttered in her sleep and thrashed for a moment on the bed. Even with the help of a tranquilizer she was restless.

When she kicked back the cover his gaze swept her body. The slender curves were twisted in sleep, one arm flung over her head, causing her breasts to tauten. The creamy whiteness of her skin above her bathing suit line drew his eye to the black silky hair arrowing between her legs.

His mouth went dry and he could feel a heat building in him. He damn well fully intended to tell her to stay lost once she signed a deposition about what had really happened to her, but her beautiful body still tempted his libido as it had always done. With the flat of his hand he pressed gently on her abdomen, the feel of her silken skin making his heart race.

"No . . . no . . . no . . . alone . . ." Reesa moaned without waking, her body jerking in rejection of what she was feverishly dreaming. "Nooo," she whimpered, her fearful body curling into the fetal position.

Dake's eyes narrowed on her. "Stop it, Rees. Wake up." He leaned over her to shake her and she slapped at his hand, whimpering again. Fear ran over his skin as she keened loudly.

"Hurt me . . . *halcón* . . . *halcón* . . ." she moaned.

"Darling, don't—don't be afraid." Dake's stomach knotted when he saw the terror on her face. Cursing, he kicked off his shoes and lay down next to her on the bed, gathering her shivering body into his arms.

At first she stiffened and pushed him away. Then she moved softly again and pressed closer to him.

In minutes she fell into a deep sleep, her fists clutching at his shirt as though she would never let him go.

Dake lay stiff as a ramrod at first, but gradually Reesa's body stirred him, filling him with a tingling warmth, releasing his body to relax. "She's so frightened," he muttered to himself, wanting to shelter her.

He had no idea when he fell asleep, but a knock on the door of the suite awakened him. Instantly alert, he glanced down at Reesa, still curled tight against him. Carefully freeing her fingers one by one, he slid out of bed without waking her, wrapping her in the soft quilt to keep her warm. He padded from the bedroom into the sitting room, closing the bedroom door behind him. He flung open the door to face Dr. Margaret Roberts. "Yes? What is it, doctor?" he brushed back his hair, aware that he sounded too abrupt. "Sorry, I just woke up."

"Yes, I can see that." Margaret assessed him in lazy amusement, bringing an answering frown from Dake. "I thought maybe Maria—I mean Reesa, would prefer to be in her own cabin." Margaret waved a hand at the Sea Dive Group standing silently behind her. "Some of the others felt—"

"I don't think so," Dake interjected smoothly. "She's sleeping soundly and I don't want to wake her. When she does wake up, I'm sure she'll decide to return to her quarters, but in the meantime—"

"She's going to the singles' party tonight," Andy said truculently.

"Singles' party?" Dake inquired, condescension in his voice.

"It's a get-together for all the single passengers, and

all the unattached members of the crew are expected to join in the fun," Margaret explained.

"If she's well enough, she'll be there," Dake said firmly. "When she awakens, doctor, I'll call you, but for now I think she needs to sleep." The finality in his voice didn't escape any of the Sea Dive Group. The angry flush on Dave's face and a tightness in Andy's lips attested to that.

"Fine," Margaret agreed, urging the others to move down the hallway. "I'll wait for your call."

Dake closed the door, his anger erupting as he turned away and slapped his fist into his hand.

"Who was it?" Reesa asked from the doorway of the bedroom, one hand rubbing her eyes.

"You should go back to bed," Dake told her.

"Don' tell wha' to do," Reesa argued sleepily. "I have to shower."

"Do what you damn well please, but—"

"I intend to!" She turned away from him, almost tripping on the down quilt she had wrapped around herself. "Where are my clothes?"

"Don't you think you should wait until you see the doctor?" Dake exploded, wanting to throw her out the nearest porthole into the ocean, yet longing to wrap her tight in the quilt and lie with her in the king-size bed. For a moment fury burgeoned in him, both at Reesa and at the ambivalence she had always aroused in him, but which seemed to have ballooned since they met again.

"I'll see the doctor at the party. She's single too," Reesa answered flippantly, taking rumpled shorts and top from her tote bag and heading for the bathroom.

When Dake saw her stagger, he knew it wasn't from the motion of the ship, but he said nothing, swallowing the angry words that rose in his throat.

When she emerged from the bathroom in her wrin-

kled, damp clothes, Reesa spoke hesitantly. "Dake
. . . thank you for . . . taking care of me. . . ."

"De nada, Señorita Teresa Martita Hawke." Dake
sneered, his mocking bow in her direction stiff with
anger.

Her chin rose. "Don't make fun of my Californio
ancestry. You know I hate that kind of slur."

"Is that what I was doing?" Dake baited her.

She inhaled. "You're still the same supercilious,
pompous ass you've always been." She slammed the
door behind her and raced down the narrow stairs to
the crew's quarters. She had seen animal fury in
Dake's eyes when she left his cabin, and she didn't
draw a calm breath until she reached her quarters.

Consuela came flying into their cabin as Reesa
emerged from the shower drying her ebony tresses.

The two women stared at each other for long
moments.

"You're a movie star . . . a television actress . . ."
Consuela cried. "You won't want to stay with us
anymore on Maria Island."

Reesa rushed to Consuela and enfolded her in her
arms. "You're my friend . . . my sister . . . my confi-
dante." Reesa felt her own throat tighten with emotion. "I won't be separated from my family—you, your
mother, Miguel and Liza and my little Miguelito—
we're family!"

The two of them cried and held each other closer.
Then Consuela pulled away from Reesa and studied
her friend intently.

"Carmen says"—Consuela referred to another
assistant purser—"that Dake Masters is a real hunk.
Is he, Maria? I mean, Reesa?"

Reesa nodded. "He's very good-looking, and he
knows it."

"Do you think I'll get to meet him?" Consuela
looked eager.

Reesa shrugged. "Now that he's on the ship at least until we reach Mexico, I'm sure you'll run into him."

"I'll make sure of it." Consuela winked broadly, making Reesa laugh.

Reesa smothered the hot, unsure feelings that tumbled her insides. She didn't give a damn who saw Dake Masters or whom he saw!

"Wear your cream-colored lace tonight," Consuela called as she went through the door into the bathroom. "I'm going to wear my pale blue. I like the way we look together in those outfits."

"You solved my dilemma, sister dear," Reesa called back. "I'm so tired, I don't care whether I wear my mask and fins tonight," she muttered to herself, sure that Consuela couldn't hear her over the noise of the shower.

The outfit she pulled from the small closet was a dressy pants ensemble in very light cotton that would do well for the balmy night below the Tropic of Cancer. Consuela's mother had made the outfit and embroidered all the decoration and made the lace on the top and pants by hand. She'd used champagne-colored thread for the flowers, the leaves, and the lace that edged the sides and neckline, so the ensemble was in various shades of cream only. The trousers were snug-fitting, like caballero pants, displaying the slender line of Reesa's hips and thighs. The outside of the pants was trimmed in champagne lace that undulated gently with every move she made. With the outfit she wore high-heeled ankle boots of soft champagne-colored suede. An Indian friend of Miguel's had tanned the leather and made the shoes. Reesa had been so taken with his fine workmanship that she had brought samples of his work on board the ship, where she and Consuela had set up a small boutique to sell his work.

It didn't take long for Consuela to dry her hair and

slip into her dress. Then the two girls struggled to see themselves in the small mirror.

"I think we look good," Consuela said, sighing. "But who can tell in this awful mirror?"

"You look wonderful in that baby-blue color; with your black hair and soft brown eyes you look like a madonna," Reesa told Consuela with admiration.

"And you look gorgeous, and sexy, and—and sophisticated." Consuela shook her head. "Why didn't we know you were somebody special . . . the way you glide when you walk, the way your hips sway so gently, your beautiful long hair the color of midnight . . ."

"Connie, I wore my hair short when I worked in movies and plays. It grew this length while I was living on Maria Island. I always meant to cut it, but—"

"Don't! We all love it. You look so . . . so Mexican, like us."

"I am a Californio, you know, descended from the Spanish just as you are, but my name, Halcon, is really Hawke. Hawke is for my English great-grandfather, who sailed around Tierra Del Fuego to California, where he met my great-grandmother and never went to sea again." Reese put her arm around her friend. "So you see, we are more like sisters than we ever knew."

Consuela hugged her back. "Yes, we are. Let's wear those beaten gold earrings and necklaces that Figueroa made. You know, with that ivory comb in your hair, pulling it all to one side, you look like a princess. You may need to beat them off with a stick tonight!"

The two of them left the small cabin laughing. If Reesa felt unusually nervous tonight, she tried to hide it from Consuela. She felt sure she'd be able to handle it. Now that her memory had returned, she recalled the many times surging crowds had made her jumpy when she attended openings. She had learned to cope, covering her uneasiness with a cool smile and a nod of her head. The gossip columns had described her as the "regal Reesa Hawke," the "empress without an empire." The disguise had been an effective one, so their sarcasm didn't bother her.

The two women could hear the steel band playing as they approached the Constellation Lounge. Already a crowd was forming and they hurried, realizing how late they were.

They joined the receiving line, getting smirks and chiding remarks from other members of the cruise staff.

"It takes longer and longer for you to fix your face, Maria," Andy called to her from his place in line.

Out of the corner of her eye Reesa saw Dave jab him in the ribs with his elbow, then heard Andy mumble, "Sorry, I forgot she was Reesa Hawke."

As soon as the last passenger went through the receiving line, Reesa broke ranks and stood in front of her three colleagues from the Sea Dive Group. "Look, all of you—I *am* Reesa Hawke." Reesa looked from one to the other, watching the mixed emotions showing on their faces. "But I had no idea who I was. Please believe that."

"I always heard that amnesia was a nebulous thing, and not a true illness," Dave said quietly as the four of them moved to a dark corner of the lounge where they could speak privately.

Reesa looked serious. "I guess people can blot unpleasantness from their minds. After the trauma of being hit on the head when I fell from the dinghy, being in the sea for a few hours in the Windward Passage . . ." She shrugged. "I guess I'm just lucky I had the sense to put on a life vest before I climbed down into the dinghy that night."

"What made you do such a thing?" Dave asked, his expression softening.

Reesa pressed her lips together to keep them from

trembling as that dark, clouds-on-the-moon night came back to her in a rush and she saw herself shrug into the life vest, tie it, then climb down the ladder on the side of the yacht. She'd clambered into the dinghy to see if she could tighten one of the hawsers that had come loose where the small boat was attached aft to the yacht. "I was alone on the deck"—after a flaming argument with Dake Masters not ten minutes before, she thought, trying to bury the picture of the two of them leaning toward each other shouting epithets— "and it was poor judgment. After what I've learned in the Sea Dive Group, I don't think I would be that stupid again." She smiled, relieved when her three friends grinned back at her, their camaraderie restored. "Anyway, I remember reaching up to the metal fastening on the back of the *Firewitch*—that was the name of the yacht—and I had the slipped hawser in my hand. I couldn't quite reach the grommet, so I stepped on the gunwale of the dinghy. My feet skidded." Perspiration broke out on her face at the memory. "I grabbed for the rope, but a wave tipped the dinghy just then and I fell. My head hit something, very hard, knocking me out, I think. When I woke next, I was coughing sea water from my mouth and I was alone in the Windward Passage and drifting fast. I think I was in the water about three hours when Miguel found me a little after dawn. I was delirious and mumbling the word *halcón, halcón,* which is why Miguel thought it was my name. I really don't know why I was saying the Spanish word for my name. . . ."

"We looked for you." Dake's deep voice broke through the murmured responses of the four members of the Sea Dive Group like a wave on the beach. He could feel the cold fear that had filled him on that night. "It wasn't until daylight that I went back to the cabin. You weren't there. Even then I wasn't alarmed. I thought you were in the other cabin. I had been drinking—more than I should have—and I thought you were sulking. I didn't check the other cabin at first. By the time I checked the yacht from stem to stern, we must have traveled twenty or thirty miles." His masklike face showed nothing, but his eyes had lost their sparkle. He inhaled several times, fighting to keep the black horror from swamping him again as it had that fateful night when he finally realized that Reesa had gone over the side. Even now, with the lady standing in front of him, he could still feel the despair that had filled him then as the yacht cruised back and forth trying to find her and coming up with nothing.

"We contacted the U.S. Coast Guard. A Cuban helicopter searched for you." He clamped his mouth shut as he felt his mouth tremble. Dake recalled radioing to the mainland and having a private flotilla of planes and boats brought in to comb the area. "I don't know how we missed talking to your friend Miguel," he muttered almost to himself. "We must have talked to everyone who had ever fished or sailed in the Windward Passage." Dake thought back to the endless searching in the body of water with treacherous currents. It ran between Cuba and Haiti, and connected the Atlantic Ocean and the Caribbean Sea.

"Miguel brought me to Maria Island as fast as he could. I was sick and delirious," Reesa pointed out, her eyes glued to Dake's tall frame, feeling the electricity that had always been between them setting her skin on fire.

For long moments the five of them stood silently, as if their thoughts had shackled them to one another. Then Arthur spoke.

"I think we're supposed to circulate among the passengers, but—would you like to dance, Mar—Reesa?"

"Please." Reesa shot her friend a grateful look. She sensed Dake's ire as she passed him, but she didn't look his way.

Consuela waved as she danced by in the arms of an attractive, dark-haired passenger who held her closely.

Reesa and Arthur glided around the dance floor in a restrained foxtrot. When she looked over Arthur's shoulder she saw Lacey Welles, one of the ship's blackjack dealers, approach Dake and invite him to dance. Reesa looked away before Dake took the blond woman into his arms. Her eye spotted a glowering Barney Freedling, his gaze locked on Consuela as she danced with the passenger.

"Barney can't have his cake and eat it too," she commented to Arthur when he followed her gaze.

He nodded. "I think he's just beginning to understand that Connie is a very special woman." He looked thoughtful. "But it's up to both of them to reach for what they want."

"True." Reesa smiled at Arthur and applauded when the music stopped. She looked across the floor to see one of the passengers pushing his way through the throng to reach her.

"Here we go," Arthur warned her as a petite redhaired woman in her twenties approached him.

"Damn the torpedos," Reesa murmured back.

"Hi, I'm Ken Stark from San Francisco, and I wondered if you would—"

"The lady's with me," Dake Masters snapped, grasping Reesa's elbow and pulling her around to face him.

"Stop that," she said, pushing back from him.

He released her just enough so that their bodies could sway to the soft rock music. "We always danced well together, not to mention a few other things we did well as a couple."

Reesa felt her face freeze over the mocking tone in his voice. "As I recall, we had decided that we didn't fit that well together. In fact, we were through . . ." She forced the words from a dry throat.

"That was then. Things change. We have a great deal to discuss, Reesa." Dake's hard body bent in sensual persuasion over hers.

"No!" Thoughts she had suppressed suddenly filled her with terror. She couldn't bear to accept the truth: that she no longer belonged to Dake Masters, that the wonderful life they had shared for five years was over. It was *that* she hadn't wanted to face, *that* she still didn't want to remember—the loneliness of her life without him. She could still recall the shock on Dake's face the time they had first made love, and her own stunned emotions as their bodies melded. He had murmured her name over and over, and whispered, "I never dreamed of anything like this . . . never."

"Come out of your fantasy, ice goddess," Dake spoke softly, using an old endearment. When they'd first lived together he and Reesa would alternate noisy arguments with stony silence. Sometimes Reesa would not speak to Dake for hours at a stretch. That was when he coined the nickname. Later, Dake would call her by the nickname when they were making love, telling her how much he loved melting the ice goddess.

"Don't call me that; I don't like it," Reesa snapped, feeling her heart twist inside her.

His arms crushed her to him until he could feel her heartbeat echoing within his own heart. Dake had never felt so torn between black rage and uncontrolled desire. Reesa seemed not to care about the agonies he'd experienced—the weeks pacing in his cell, imagining her choking, drowning, dying—without a chance to ask her forgiveness or hold her in his arms. Did she realize how many hours he had wept silently, knowing that all that he cared for had died in the Windward Passage?

"Stop it . . . stop, you're hurting me!" Reesa gasped, her fingernails digging into his chest. "Don't you think I've been through enough?" Reesa sobbed, shaken that the armor she had built around her heart since Miguel had saved her was weakening. Dake Masters was the chink in that armor. "Leave me alone, please." She tried to push herself free of him.

"No." His harsh reply was like an epithet. "Darling, I'm sorry. I know you've been to hell. . . ." Words faded away as remorse flooded him. God, if she kept shaking, her bones would fly apart! Dake led her to the side of the room, then, keeping her clasped to his side, moved forcefully through the crowd toward the exit that would take them out to the deck.

"I can't go," Reesa argued in a trembling voice. "The party . . ."

"We'll come back . . . when you calm down," Dake stated.

"Maria—I mean, Reesa, where are you going?" Consuela came up to them. She looked quickly from Reesa to Dake Masters and back. "You should stay. . . ."

"We'll be back when Reesa feels better. My name's Dake Masters." He offered his right hand without releasing his grip on Reesa's waist with his left.

Connie smiled shyly. "I know who you are."

"This is my best friend, my sister, Consuela Diego. She and her family live down the lane from us on Maria Island," Reesa said by way of introduction, her knees still a bit wobbly. She tried to free herself, but Dake's hold tightened.

"Us?" Dake ignored all the other words and seized on that one.

"Miguel and Liza and Miguelito . . ." Her voice faltered as she looked up at him, his eyes filled with a golden fire. "They're my family," Reesa finished quietly.

"You have no family, except your uncle Lionel Hawke who still runs the winery in the Napa Valley," Dake said firmly, trying to picture the people who meant so much to her that she referred to them as her family.

"Uncle Lionel! I had forgotten . . ." She put her hand over her mouth as she thought of the tall, stoop-shouldered man with the mane of white hair, whose constant carping at her to be more of a lady in the Hawke and Delgado family tradition had been a thorn in her side. It was hard to love Uncle Lionel, but he was her only blood relation. "How is he, Dake?"

"The same curmudgeon he's always been—but I think he's aged since the news of your death. You are the last in your line, and the idea of the Hawke family name dying out was a terrible blow to him."

"Yes, it would be. I must call him. . . ."

"I called him, darling," Dake said, his voice gentle.

Consuela's head snapped around to stare at him, her soft doe eyes sharpening. "Ah, maybe it would be a good idea if you got some fresh air, Reesa." Consuela urged them toward the door.

"But . . ." Reesa felt weaker than she'd been since the early days of her convalescence on Maria Island. Dake half carried her from the crowded room out to the small hallway, then through the double steel doors leading out to the deck.

Reesa took several deep breaths of the balmy night air, the muted roar of the water cascading off the hull of the *Windward* sounding like a wild Russian dance. The stars glinted silver in the night sky, and the moon traced a path over the waves, making it seem as though one could step from the side of the boat and walk the glittering path to infinity.

"There's Orion," Reesa whispered, pointing to the constellation.

"Yes," Dake murmured, his voice muted by her hair. "Darling, I want to tell you again that I'm sorry. I haven't been sane since the night you disappeared from the yacht."

"We've both talked out of turn," Reesa admitted softly.

Dake cuddled her close to him so that her midnight hair blew back in his face. "I had forgotten how thick your hair was. It's like black satin."

"It's too long—"

"No. Don't cut it. It's glorious."

There was silence for long minutes as the shimmering blue sea frothed along the side of the ship, the sweet night air lulling them into a breathless quiet.

"This is the best part of being at sea . . . the nights," Dake murmured.

"Yes. Each night you can see the honeymooners strolling the decks," Reesa said dreamily.

"It's a wonderful way to spend a honeymoon, but I think it would be better with just the two of us on the *Firewitch*."

Reesa stiffened. "Dake, that was all thrashed out between us that—that night. It's over."

"The hell it is!" he growled.

"We can't make it work, you know that. We—"

"Stop it, Reesa. We're not going to discuss this now. You still aren't well."

"Of course I'm well. I put in twelve- and fourteen-hour days," Reesa sputtered.

"You must have lost at least fifteen pounds—and you weren't fat before. I'm taking you away." Dake rushed his words as though all the plans he had ever made were erupting in his head. "I promised myself that if I ever had another chance with you, I was going to take you away and show you—"

"You have it all wrong, Dake. I'm not the same person. I have a family now, a different way of life. I don't think I can go back to the world I used to live in—at least not to live the kind of life we had together." Reesa drew a long, shuddering breath and ceased trying to break free of those strong, comforting arms. Dake made her feel so safe! Yet that was a joke, because nothing about their life together for five years had been safe, or even comforting. "No. That isn't for me. I've found a measure of—of stability."

"Stability? Hell, what you found was a hideout, a retreat from the world. All right, sweetheart, if that's what you want, we'll do it, but we do it together."

"No." Unable to free herself from the steellike grip of Dake's embrace, Reesa turned in his arms, her back to the rail. It wasn't much better; now her face was tucked under Dake's, while his hands slid from the railing to clutch her back. "I—I have choices now. I like working aboard the *Windward*. I'm going to finish out this cruise, and then . . ."

Dake's hand reached up, his index finger touching her lips. "Don't say anymore. We'll take it that far."

Reesa gave him a half-smile and acquiesced. "You still have eyes that change color with your mood," she whispered, feeling his breath mix with hers as he leaned even closer, not quite kissing her. "They always look like shiny brown rock when you're angry, like a lemony-green when you're laughing, and—"

"Very golden when I'm feeling sexy, you always said. Are they very, very golden now?"

Reesa nodded.

"Darling, come to my cabin."

She shook her head. "No. I'm not going to do that. I won't have you taking over my life anymore."

His body jerked with anger. "If anyone took over anyone's life, you took over mine. You were the one who set all the ground rules—"

"You agreed. You didn't want to risk marriage again, but didn't want me to live my life away from you," Reesa shot back.

"Damn you, I loved you. Of course I didn't want you to live your life away from me." His words shot out over the sea like fiery comets, his temper heating the already balmy air. His hungering mouth came down hard on hers.

She braced herself for that iron mouth and was staggered to feel his soft urgent lips persuading hers apart. Reesa realized her taut lips were opening and her firm resolve was collapsing under Dake's sensuous request.

He felt her response and groaned with delight, his arms coming more fully around her and clasping her to him with one hand on her nape and the other at the base of her spine. His heart hammered in his chest when he felt the sinuous wonder of her body pressed against him. Damn her, she did still love him! He could feel her body reacting to his, fitting itself to him as it had always done.

They broke apart suddenly, all but consummating their love as they stood there linked to each other by a passion that had always been a whirlpool neither of them could control.

"God, darling. I'll be taking you here on this deck," Dake said, gulping air.

"It would be like the first time we saw each other," Reesa murmured. "Do you remember how you stayed on the set to watch my love scene with Barton Stevens, even though Will had ordered the set cleared?"

"If I had seen you before that moment, other than in your pictures, I wouldn't have let you film that scene," Dake recalled fiercely, following her lead and letting the turmoil within them abate.

"If I had known that you were on the set with Will and the cameramen, I wouldn't have shot the scene. I had been guaranteed absolute privacy for the nude scene." Reesa brushed her fingertips across his chest, her breathing quieting as they talked.

"You dropped that satiny robe and I thought for a minute I had gone blind. Your skin was white lightning, your breasts and ankles so perfect, your thighs smooth and lightly muscled." Dake could feel his breath quicken as he recalled how she'd looked under the klieg lights. He had been mesmerized. "Then

Barton walked onto the set and I damn near killed him when he took you in his arms . . . put his hands on your skin." Dake clenched his fists.

Reesa laughed. "When I heard the commotion on the set I didn't realize that Will had cut and printed. I thought someone was telling me to go through the scene again."

"Your mouth fell open a mile when I rushed toward you with your robe and wrapped it around you." Dake's mouth softened in a smile, the silvery moonlight turning his chestnut hair to gleaming auburn.

Reesa felt her pulse jump into a gallop as he looked down at her with those hot golden eyes. "You said that I was never to do a nude scene again!"

"And you said who the blazes are you?"

"I'm the love of your life—you snarled that at me." Reesa gulped, torn between horror and amusement as she recalled how he had stood there and glowered at her. Then he had followed her to her dressing room, standing just outside the door when she slammed it in his face, and announcing in a loud voice that she had better accept the inevitable, that they were meant to be together. She had waited until there was a light tap at her door. Norma, the wardrobe mistress, had whispered that he had gone. She hadn't seen him again, not answering the messages he left for her at the studio, until she had seen him at Senator Wicklow's party.

It had taken him just five days after that party to convince her to move in with him. She had fallen more in love with him each day after that, even though she knew from the start that he had an aversion to marriage, that his former mother-in-law, to whom he was devoted, preferred that he didn't marry again. And so did his son. Reesa's head snapped up. "Robert! How is Robert?"

"Fine. He has grieved for you and talks of you often. I didn't tell him that I was coming to check out a report that you were alive. I didn't want to raise his hopes."

Reesa nodded, resting her head on his chest for a moment. "I love Robert." *And I always wanted him to be mine,* she admitted to herself. She had been jealous that Dake's wife had been the mother of the boy that she, Reesa, would have so loved as her own.

"He missed you and told me that he loved you very much and that he loved staying with us at our house."

Reesa nodded, knowing it was true. An eleven-year-old couldn't fake the bubbling feelings that Robert displayed whenever they were together.

Dake nuzzled under her chin, his lips gently scoring over her skin. "Darling, we both missed you . . . needed you."

The banging of the door leading to the Constellation Lounge shook them from their reverie.

"Reesa, we've got a full day tomorrow, and we're starting early," Dave called out.

"Thanks, Dave, I was just going in," Reesa answered quickly. With a fleeting kiss for Dake she hurried to her cabin, checked her gear for the morning, and crawled into bed. The moonlight streamed in, recalling to Reesa the way it glinted off Dake's hair, and she lay awake for nearly an hour before she slept.

Three

The next day the ship anchored briefly in Playa del Carmen on the coast of the Yucatán Peninsula. A tender came alongside to transport the passengers who had elected to tour the Mayan ruins at Tulum. The Sea Dive Group would be diving at a lagoon called Xalha, so Dave, Andy, Arthur, and Reesa loaded their equipment onto the tender. The sky was a dazzling cerulean blue, fluffed here and there with clouds, making it a perfect day to sight-see and to dive.

Seated next to Arthur, Reesa felt a tap on the shoulder and turned to see Mr. Calkins. "I'm surprised you will be diving, my dear. We've heard that you, ah, are a very important person—Reesa Hawke."

Reesa smiled at the anxious looks from Mr. Calkins and his wife. "I'm still a member of the Sea Dive Group, Mr. Calkins, no matter what my name is." She spoke softly, trying to keep from drawing attention to herself. She was sure that many of the passengers had heard the same news. The grapevine on the ship was lightning-fast, but still she hoped that nothing would interfere with her work as a diver. When she turned around more fully to listen to the older couple, her eyes locked with Dake's. He was sitting in the back row of the bench seats on the tender. What was he doing here? He wasn't a member of the Sea Dive Group and the Tulum tour was full, Dave had told her that. "Pardon me, Mrs. Calkins, I didn't hear what you said."

"I was wondering if you were going to stay with the diving or go back to your work on the stage."

"Don't be silly, Myra. Of course she'll go back to her acting. She was a very important person in her profession," Mr. Calkins gently chided his wife. Reesa smiled at the couple then turned around to face front.

"We couldn't expect to compete with the glitter of the cinema," Andy said in a poorly imitated English accent.

"Really, old man, I couldn't agree more," Dave concurred, in an accent even more lacerated.

"Keep looking behind you today, comedians," Reesa warned her grinning tormentors. "When I get my chance, I'm going to put you on the bottom."

"And I'll help her," Arthur said mildly.

"See, you've got trouble," Reesa threatened, grateful that none of the Sea Dive Group seemed the least bit impressed by her celebrated past.

When Reesa felt the nudge on her backside, she looked around, a smile fixed to her face. Dake! He had moved to a place just behind her. "What are you doing on the tender, Dake? You don't have tickets for the ruins or Xalha . . . or for the box lunch." Reesa's voice faltered as she saw the arrogance flash across his face. His lips curved in a smile. "How? How did you get them? There weren't any more."

"I have tickets for the ruins and for Xalha. The captain arranged them for me and he's letting me use his diving equipment."

"And you're checked out on scuba, aren't you?" Reesa asked through clenched teeth.

"I'm checked out as an instructor, as a matter of fact," he stated gently.

"Grand." Reesa looked straight ahead, feeling the blood run to her cheeks when he chuckled.

"You don't resent my presence in the dive, do you, darling?" Dake drawled.

"Certainly not. Of course we will try to keep an eye on you just as we would any other member of the Sea Dive Group." Reesa swallowed hard, wanting nothing more than to tip him off the side of the tender into the deep blue waters of the Caribbean! "I'm sure you would have had a better time if you had gone on with the ship and anchored at Cozumel Island instead of coming to the mainland with us."

"I love it when you talk like a tour guide, Reesa, but save your breath. I'll be right at your side today."

For the rest of the ride in the slow-moving tender, Reesa stared straight ahead, answering those who spoke to her in monosyllables. After they disembarked at the long quay at Playa del Carmen, they walked through the town to where the buses were waiting.

Reesa was startled when she felt Dake's hand at her back as she climbed aboard one of the buses. He guided her into a seat near the rear. "I wanted to sit with my friends," she panted, a little out of breath from being railroaded down the aisle of the vehicle at such a fast pace.

"You can see them later, when we get to the lagoon. I would like to see the ruins with you. You can explain things to me as well as a guide. I assume you've been here a few times."

"Yes, of course." Reesa forgot to tell him how high-handed she thought he was. "They're marvelous.

Every year a dig is organized by the University of Pennsylvania, and little by little and step by step much of the Mayan life as it was lived at Tulum is taking shape." Her voice had dropped to an excited whisper. "There was another dig not too far from here, but during the Second World War the United States Armed Forces built an airstrip over it, destroying the site. The airstrip isn't used anymore." Reesa grimaced. "I wonder how many digs are destroyed forever because of man's mistakes," she mused out loud, her eyes gazing at miles of dense jungle just outside the bus. José, their guide, told them that jaguars and poisonous snakes roamed wild in the trackless greenery.

"It's like another planet out there," Dake whispered, staring at the jungle. For just a moment he found himself wondering what it would be like if he and Reesa were alone here on the deserted road, near the jungle. No, it would be too frightening. He would find another way to be alone with her.

"And yet José told us that much of this jungle will be cleared away in a few years to build another resort area like Cancún."

Dake's brows arched. "Sounds like a good investment."

"Yankee go home," Reesa muttered, stiffening when she felt his arm snake around her waist and tighten.

"Perhaps you would like to make a picture down here in the impenetrable jungle?" he asked her silkily.

"You Tarzan, me Jane?" Reesa snapped.

"Darling, what a novel idea. I don't think we've ever made love in a tree."

"Quiet!" Reesa's eyes glanced to both sides, trying to discover whether or not Dake's strong voice had been overheard by anyone sitting near them.

"I've seen a few ruins on the peninsula, but I've

never been here. Tell me about it," Dake commanded, a glint in his eye.

Reesa was glad he had changed the subject. "March twenty-first, the vernal equinox, is also the Mayan new year. The Mayan people were great astronomers and they calibrated much of their lives with the stars. They held human sacrifices on the special holy days. Some young, honored person would be chosen to be put to death. . . ." Reesa's voice faded away. "But— but you know all that. You've been on several digs. You told me so."

"Yes, but I love hearing that fervency in your voice when you talk about the Maya. You care about all this, don't you?"

Arthur leaned across the aisle of the bus. "You can't help but feel something for these people, the direct descendants of those Mayas who built such a great civilization, when you've been around them as often as we are on our visits to Tulum and Xalha." The shyest of the Sea Dive Group, Arthur surprised Reesa by speaking out so forcefully. "The more you see, the more you want to learn about them."

"Arthur studies marine biology in school, but he also has an interest in archeology." Reesa smiled at her friend.

"Charming," Dake responded coldly.

"Interesting is what it is." Arthur waxed enthusiastic on one of his favorite topics. "Did you know that many people in this area are full-blooded Maya? That the Mayan language is spoken in the home around here and is carefully preserved and nurtured?" Arthur didn't seem aware of Dake's curt nod as he leaned closer, his eyes sparkling. "The Maya are descended from a yellow race, you know, and some say they are members of the Maori group from as far away as New Zealand."

"There are others who say they come from the Japanese or Chinese groups and crossed the Pacific

Ocean on their trek to the Yucatán," Dake interjected, feeling more relaxed until he noticed the smile on Reesa's face as she looked at her friend. Damn her! She could still make him as jealous as hell! She had always been able to do that, even when they'd lived together. Sometimes at a party when she would be asked to dance—Dake ground his teeth as he recalled the times he had watched the swarms of men around her—how unaffected she had seemed to be by their worshipping looks, but still . . .

Arthur continued. "I've often wondered what would have happened if the conquistadors hadn't come in 1517 and tried to dominate a people who were educated astronomers, who worshipped the stars, and had named the planet we call Venus. Do you know that the pyramids built by the Mayas and Aztecs were astronomical observatories?"

"Yes, I know about that theory," Dake said, quietly amused at Arthur's eagerness.

Dave leaned forward in his seat and put his hand over Arthur's mouth.

"Spare us any more history, Art. You should write a damn book."

"Oomph—rumph—" Arthur worked free of Dave's hand. "Maybe I will write a book someday," he said sheepishly. "Sorry, I didn't mean to run on like that."

Dake smiled. "I happen to find the Mayan civilization very interesting. I enjoy it."

"You didn't seem to at first," Reesa whispered. "You had a very supercilious look." Reesa dared to push Dake, even as she saw the thunderous expression building on his face.

"Watch it, darling. We aren't that far from the Guatemalan border. I might decide to kidnap you and run for the border," he warned with silky menace.

"Stop that," Reesa fumed, trying to still her galloping heart. It would be just like him to pull a stunt like

that! Go for it! That was Dake's maxim whenever anyone challenged him in any way. It had brought him
phenomenal success, but he had left a few dead bodies along the way, Reesa ruminated. She was torn
between fear that he might actually try to drag her
over the border and fury that he was trying to intimi-
date her.

The bus screeched to a halt and the group hastily
disembarked to gather around the guide.

". . . and so," the guide was saying as Reesa and
Dake edged into the circle of people around him,
"when the Franciscans came here they thought they
would stamp out the 'pagan' religion of the Maya by
forbidding them to speak anything but Spanish.
Only in the privacy of their homes did the Maya dare
to speak their own language."

The guide indicated that next they would tour the
great pyramidlike structure that was a Maya temple.
Some members of the Sea Dive Group helped the
older people over the rough terrain and up the
twenty-seven stone steps to the platform holding the
sacrificial table.

The staff dispersed then to wander at leisure
through the fortresslike area that covered the slope
up to a cliff top overlooking the sea. The Mayas had
chosen the location well. The cliff allowed them a panoramic view of the sea as well as of the land that gave
access to the village.

Reesa walked with two of the divers, and Dake was
constantly at her side. She wanted to consign him to
staying with the other passengers, but there was no
way to do so without causing a fuss. Dake would
cause a fuss, too, if she said a word. Hell, he would
cause a ruckus if he decided to! Reesa pressed her
lips together and trailed behind Dave and Andy, who
were taking pictures.

"Hey, Maria—I mean Reesa, Let me take one of
you." Dave whirled around, his camera up to one eye.

She felt herself caught around the middle and clamped to Dake's side. "Let me go," she grated out between clenched teeth.

"Smile, Reesa. That's a good one with the two of you."

"See, darling? Even your friends think we make a good team." Dake chuckled as Reesa smiled at the urging of her friend. Before he released her he kissed her, letting his mouth move over hers gently. It angered him that something forced him to stake his claim, even in front of the members of the Sea Dive Group, whom he knew had strictly platonic relationships with her.

"Caveman," Reesa sputtered, feeling her heart flop over like a fish tossed on shore. No way was she going to let Dake Masters into her life again! "I'm not your puppet."

"No, my love, you were never that!" He grinned down at her, but there was a steely glint in his eye. "I think I was the one jerked around, darling."

"Twaddle." Reesa took a deep breath, aware of the palpable menace radiating from him like the heat from the tarmac road they had traveled from Playa del Carmen.

"You really push your luck, Teresa Martita Delgado Hawke." A muscle quivered on his rocklike cheek, then was still. He lifted his head and looked around him. "Let's climb the steps to the sacrificial table."

She swallowed, feeling a trickle of perspiration run down from her underarm. Lord, Dake had no place here. He belonged among the Norsemen, Reesa thought. Wodin—Wodin, the god of the Vikings, that should be his god. "Ah, did you know that multiples of three were sacred to the Maya, which would account for there being twenty-seven steps instead of . . ." Her voice trailed off as she detected the wry amusement in his face.

"Come, darling." He took hold of her arm, his bland words belied by his manaclelike grip.

From experience Reesa knew that the climb up the very sheer stone stairway was not nearly as hair-raising as the trip down again. Still she leaned far forward as she climbed to keep her balance in the steep ascent.

"Not to worry, darling. I won't let you fall," Dake whispered behind her, his hand patting and caressing her backside.

"Stop," Reesa hissed, trying to swipe at him and almost losing her balance in the process.

For a moment her arms swung like windmills then she was caught around the middle and lifted straight up the last ten steps, Dake holding her tight.

One of the female passengers standing near them as they reached the sacrificial table sighed. "I wish you would do that for me, Dennis," she said.

"I ain't no macho beach boy," the man she'd called Dennis said.

Reesa chortled when she saw the blood run up Dake's neck. How he must hate that man referring to him as macho *and* a beach boy, she thought. Dake turned and looked at her, and she tried to wipe the smile from her face. She failed.

"Laughing at my expense, love?"

"Yes. And I'm not your love," she shot back.

"Yes, you are. And you shall be paid back, my angel," Dake said, his eyes shooting green sparks from their brown depths.

"Go jump in the sea." Reesa skipped behind one of the portly passengers of the *Windward*, who conscientiously ate his way through eight meals a day on the ship. "Hello, Mr. Johnson. Nice weather we're having."

"Too damn hot. No air-conditioning," Mr. Johnson panted, his pumpkinlike face beaded in sweat.

Reesa stared at the obese man. "Shall I help you

down the steps, Mr. Johnson?" She looked down at the daunting descent.

"Nope. My wife can do that."

Reesa glanced at the tall but thin and long suffering Mrs. Johnson, who had spent much of the cruise reading while her husband ate. "Ah, she doesn't look as though—"

"She can do it," Mr. Johnson insisted, gesturing to his wife to join him, then indicating that they were going back down the steps.

When Mr. Johnson gripped his lean wife, the couple seemed to teeter back and forth for a moment. "Damm it, Grace, can't you do anything right? Do you want me to fall?"

A thoughtful look passed over Grace's face, then was gone. She sighed, took her husband's arm, and approached the edge again.

"You go first, Grace. If I fall, you can catch me," Mr. Johnson announced.

"No, you'd squash her," Reesa whispered.

Mr. Johnson's head swung her way. "Did you say something, missy?"

"I said I'll get in front with Mrs. Johnson, then we can both help you down." Reesa started toward the stairs and instantly felt herself lifted straight up and back onto the platform again. She gulped and stared up into Dake's angry face.

"Damn you! Do you want to get hurt?" He thrust her behind him and looked down at Mrs. Johnson, indicating by an angry jerk of his head that she should come back.

She scrambled to obey him just like everyone always did, Reesa observed with annoyance.

"My wife can help me," Mr. Johnson said testily.

"You could help yourself if you weren't so damned overweight that you can barely move," Dake snarled back, stepping down nimbly to the third step from the top and facing the irate, red-faced Mr. Johnson. "Now, sit and come down on your backside."

"It's not dignified." Mr. Johnson's many chins quivered in outrage.

"It's a little late to worry about dignity," Dake shot back. "Now, move, or you can stay up here, because I'm not letting either of these women help you down the face of this pyramid." Dake stared narrow-eyed at the man for several seconds.

Mr. Johnson puffed himself down to a sitting position, almost bursting out of the Bermuda shorts he wore. Then one by one he lowered himself from steep step to steep step until he was at the bottom. When he stood and dusted himself off, he turned around to glare at his hapless wife. "Come on, Grace. I want to talk to you."

Mrs. Johnson swallowed. "No. Go back to the bus and sit there yourself. I'm going to the marketplace to shop. And . . . and if you think you're going to tear into me when we return to the ship, think again. Say one word and I'll get off the ship, get on a plane, and go to my sister's."

Mr. Johnson's mouth opened and closed a few times, but then he swung away, waddling toward the short tunnel that would take him out to the hill overlooking the marketplace where the buses were parked.

"Thank you, sir, for helping my husband. Aubrey has poor manners." Grace gave both Reesa and Dake a small smile and followed along behind her husband.

"Shall we do some browsing in the marketplace too, Reesa?" Dake bent over her, one hand coming up to smooth back the strands of hair that had escaped from her chignon, the balmy sea breeze blowing the tendrils around her face.

"That poor woman, living with that—"

"We create our own prisons sometimes, Reesa," Dake said, his voice redolent with annoyance.

Reesa continued to watch the retreating Mrs. Johnson. Then she swiveled his way, her chin up. "How like you to think that a woman would create that mess!"

Dake took hold of her upper arms, shaking her once. "Don't you lay that trip of me. I am not now, nor have I ever been a man who puts down women mentally, physically, or spiritually. And I damn well resent the implication!"

Reesa looked up at him, her lips slightly parted, then she nodded. "I know that. It was a cheap shot. I'm sorry. It's just that I feel pity for anyone living with an albatross." She smiled weakly.

"Still champion of the underdog, Superlady?" he drawled, his smile coating her like honey.

"What was it you said about the marketplace . . . and shopping?" She felt out of breath as he continued to watch her so intently. When she saw that strong mouth descend slowly toward hers, she decided to turn her head away. She was still deciding to look away when his lips touched hers, rose, touched again, his tongue intruding into her mouth. "Shopping . . ." she gasped when he released her mouth momentarily.

"Whatever you say, darling."

His voice was husky; the hot tropical sun glinted on his hair, bringing out the auburn highlights; his eyes seemed to glow like molten gold. He appeared to be oblivious to the people all around them.

Reesa was well aware of the sidelong glances they were receiving, but years of professional training helped her mask the agitation she was feeling. She had grown accustomed to her privacy and being out of the limelight and away from the emotional volcano that she and Dake had lived in together.

The marketplace was teeming with tourists bargaining happily with the owners of the many open-fronted shops.

Reesa wandered over to the stall where she usually stopped and greeted the proprietress, Juana Oros. "Hello, Juana. What have we today?" Reesa grinned as the round-figured woman bustled over to a line of clothing hanging from the ceiling. With a long stick she deftly unhooked a garment from the rod high above them.

"This one I 'ave been saving for you, Maria. Look at it. My cousin Margarita did this herself." She put down the wooden stick and grasped the dress, spreading it in front of her for Reesa to see.

She gasped at the incredible beauty of the hand-woven ecru-colored lace. The dress was not cotton with insets of lace. It was *all* lace, from the deep off-the-shoulder bertha to the many tiers down to the hemline. "It's beautiful! You should ask a very high price for this, Juana."

"Margarita is grateful to you for what you did for her son, and my nephew, Marquito. You take him to Cozumel and let the ship doctor look at him. She gave him the shot that fixed him and now you always send him the vita—vitamins." Juana fixed her lovely onyx eyes on Reesa. "You will take this."

"I will pay you for the dress. It is worth far more than a few vitamins!"

Dake moved forward and lifted the tag at the neck of the dress. "We'll take it."

"No . . . no, señor. Not yours, not for sale. That is why I put such high price on it." Juana looked bug-eyed at Dake.

"It's all right, Juana," he said easily. "I am with Maria, and want to pay the price for the dress for her."

"Is too much," Juana muttered, rolling her eyes at her husband, who'd come to her side.

"I am Francisco, sir. And we cannot let you pay that

much for the dress. You see, it is for Maria." He smiled at Reesa.

"I know the dress is for her, but I want to give you the price. You can share it with your cousin." Dake paid in American dollars, not pesos, and even Juana's loudly sputtered protests couldn't deter him. "This dress was made just for . . . Maria, so she will have the dress and you and your cousin will have a fair price for all the work she did."

"He's right." Reesa stepped in, hugging Juana and then Francisco. "I love the dress. Tell Margarita and Marquito that I will visit them the next time I'm here in Tulum."

A few minutes later as they walked away with Dake cradling the wrapped dress in his arms, Reesa looked up at him. "You were so kind. They can live a month on just the extra you gave them, and they didn't have to feel it was charity. Thank you."

"It wasn't such a selfless thing. I can't wait to see you in this gorgeous thing." Dake scowled for a moment. "But you had better wear a body stocking or something under it."

Reesa laughed out loud, the happy sound making heads turn. She stopped walking when she noticed that Dake wasn't at her side. When she turned and looked at him, his face was a twisted mask, his hands clenching on the wrapped package. "Dake? What is it? What's wrong?"

He swallowed convulsively. "I never thought I'd hear that sound again. I didn't even know that missing it had made such a big hole in my life until . . ." He muttered as if he weren't thinking of what he said. His neck and cheeks flushed. "Dear Lord! Reesa, your laugh was like a transfusion to me, making me come fully alive again."

Reesa whimpered his name. She hated the hot, melting feeling that galloped through her veins. She tore her gaze from his, shooting nervous glances at the people around her. When he stepped to her side and slipped his arm around her waist, she jumped, her eyes darting again to his face.

"You're right, darling, this is too public a place to say all we have to say to each other," Dake crooned, his mouth brushing her hair.

"No," Reesa squeaked.

Dake tugged her to a halt in front of a stall where onyx was sold. "No what, Reesa?" he said at last. He seized an onyx comb and brush set, studying it intently.

"We don't have anything to say to each other."

Dake's narrow gaze swiveled her way, looking from her rather white face to her entwined fingers. "You worry too much, love. Nothing unpleasant is going to happen."

"We had enough unpleasantness when we lived together." Reesa took one step backward as a sulphurously angry expression came over Dake's face.

"We were happy," he snarled.

Reesa looked at the Indian woman whose eyes resembled the onyx she was selling and tried to smile, but her face felt frozen. "I'm going back to the bus."

Dake glared at her, then rather surprisingly dismissed her with a curt nod. "I'll be along in a minute," he said, and went back to studying the wide assortment of onxy and turquoise items in front of him.

Reesa greeted the bus driver in Spanish and asked him about his family. She took her seat at the back and watched the desultory return of the other passengers as the designated time for departure for Xalha approached. She grew a little calmer in the air-conditioned bus, but when she felt the seat move next to her, she stiffened.

"Turn around, darling, I want to show you what I bought us," Dake whispered into her ear.

She intended to tell him to go to hell, but when she saw the onyx chess set he unwrapped, she gasped with delight. "It's beautiful!"

"It will be nice in our house." He grinned at her. "Maybe now you might be able to beat me."

"You didn't win all the time," Reesa protested, her chin jutting out as his smile widened.

"Oh? Did you win once?"

"More than that." Reesa pushed at him, her lips quivering with a barely repressed smile.

"Twice?"

She turned and looked out the window when she felt her control slip, a full smile curving her lips.

"Don't hide your laughter, darling. I love to hear it," Dake said, his voice stirring the fine hair on her neck.

Reesa shivered.

They both fell silent as the bus started its journey. The driver took the road to Playa del Carmen, turning off at a side road to Xalha.

Reesa closed her eyes, sinking into a light doze. She could hear the rise and fall of voices as Dave and Andy talked to Dake, and an occasional soft interjection by Arthur, though she didn't pick up any of the words.

Some of the passengers began to sing, but it didn't rouse Reesa. She sank deeper into sleep.

When she felt herself rolling she was sure she was back on the ship.

"Wake up, love. We're in Xalha," Dake whispered, his warm lips on her ear.

Reesa's eyes fluttered open. "Good morning, darling. Where did you say we were?" she blurted sleepily. Then she jerked wide awake as she heard him chuckle. "Ah, Xalha. Yes, have to get the equipment. . . ." Damn him! He knew she'd thought for one groggy moment that they were together back in the life they'd led before the accident.

"I'll carry your equipment with mine," Dake told her, amusement coloring his voice.

Reesa shook her head to clear it. "No. We carry our own!"

"C'mon, Maria—I mean Reesa." Dave grimaced as he called to her from the bus door. "Sorry. It's going to take me a while to get used to the name change," he said apologetically.

Reesa smiled at him. "Don't worry. I like the name Maria."

"Why don't we call her Hey you?" Andy offered, chortling at his attempt at humor.

"Why don't we call you donderhead?" Reesa asked sweetly. Dake's chuckle at her back as they filed slowly to the front of the bus made her pulse jump.

"I second that," Arthur offered.

"Very funny, children, but I'll bet my group finds more interesting specimens than yours," Andy challenged them.

Reesa grinned at him. "You're on!"

"Done," Arthur and Dave added in chorus.

"No cheating." Andy looked at each of his friends.

The three of them raised right hands.

"May the best man . . . or woman . . . win," Andy said, rolling his eyes at Reesa, pretending to cower when she glared at him.

They followed the people heading along the winding palm-lined path past a fish-laden section of the lagoon where swimmers were forbidden. Fish leaped from the water when people threw bits of bread.

Reesa had seen the same scene countless times, but the sight of the jewel-colored fish flashing in the sunlight never ceased to fascinate her.

"Rubies, emeralds, and diamonds couldn't sparkle more brightly," Dake whispered to Reesa.

Reesa nodded, then looked up at him and smiled. He had always been able to read her mind, to know what she was feeling.

At the swimming area the passengers in the dive program were already fastening their flippers to their feet and donning their face masks. Reesa forgot all about the beauties of the lagoon and concentrated on the safety of her brood.

Gathering ten of the Sea Dive program participants, she spoke to them before they entered the water. "We'll swim out to the island." She pointed to a rocky cluster in the middle of the lagoon about a hundred yards from shore. "We should see some interesting specimens there. After that I'll take you over to a cave on the other side of the lagoon." She gestured to the far shore, perhaps another three-hundred yards beyond the island. "If there is anyone who thinks that either the island or the cave would be too much, please tell me now. We have a group that will be diving just on this side of the lagoon near shore." Again she lifted her arm, this time to point toward a group that Dave was gathering around him. Two of her divers left the group and joined Dave's.

"I would like to go, but I think I might need help," Katie Thorpe, a woman in her middle twenties murmured. Her eyes rested on Dake, who stood next to Reesa, his mask dangling from his fingers.

"I will be glad to keep a close eye on you, Miss Thorpe," Reesa snapped, even more irritated when she heard Dake's low chuckle. "In the water, everyone!" Reesa shepherded them down the stone steps leading into the crystal-blue water, then she turned to Dake. "There's no need for someone as expert as you to stay with us. You can always go off on your own."

"Thank you, love," he drawled, taking her arm and helping her down the steps, seeming to have no trouble with the fins that were already on his feet. "I'm going to stay with you, Reesa."

Delight and anger warred in her at the thought of having him with her. "Suit yourself." She lowered herself into the water, gasping at the slight chill that preceded the welcomed warmth of the currents. She slipped her mask over her nose and mouth, then moved to the center of her group of people. Finning rapidly and smoothly through the water, she was acutely aware that Dake's powerful body stayed at her side.

It was a wonderful day for diving at Xalha. A great variety of fish abounded in the clear water; passengers who'd rented undersea cameras from the Sea Dive Group enthusiastically photographed everything in sight.

When the group had made its way around the rocky formations of the island, Reesa paused and removed her mask. She asked them if they would wait there while she dove down to a small cave to see what she could find.

Bringing her knees up to her chest, she faced down, then straightened her legs with a snap, sending her in a smooth dive toward the bottom. She patted a gentle tiger grouper, the fish almost as large as she was, and waited patiently until it cleared the entrance to the small cave. Immediately she found a sea anemone and picked it up with her hand, holding it carefully for the return to the surface. Then she saw a blur off to her left and stiffened for a moment. It was Dake; he had followed her. He gestured for her to precede him, as if he knew that her lungs were about to burst.

She shot to the surface, her head back to blow the water out of her snorkle tube, her hand still clutching the anemone.

The beautiful creature was passed—with care to keep it underwater—from person to person. When she was sure that all the members of her group were busy with the sea creature, Reesa turned to Dake. "I was just fine down there. There was no need—"

"Rees, be quiet," Dake said in silky anger.

She wanted to tell him to go to hell. Instead, she turned back to her charges and watched them as they released the sea anemone. "Let's go. Just follow me. If you become disoriented, simply follow the life line back to the shore." Reesa indicated the buoy-marked line that extended across the calm lagoon, far from the open sea.

They swam in leisurely fashion toward the other side, the tiger grouper swimming near them, angelfish waving in a graceful ballet around them, a blue parrotfish doing a water dance. Reesa was pleased that there was so much to distract her swimmers so they would not notice the growing agitation of their leader as they approached the cave. Reesa had dived down into many an opening in the sea, but she only had to stand or walk in a land cave to become almost paralyzed with fear. She had fought to overcome this as a Sea Dive instructor, even when she hadn't remembered the time she had been shut into a closet by a nanny when she was a child, coming out of the darkened area permanently fearful of being enclosed. The nanny had been fired at once by her mother, but the damage had been done.

Now, after she'd instructed her group to take a deep breath for the short distance they would have to swim underwater to enter the cave, she led them forward. When all of them were inside oohing and aahing about the interior, Reesa fought the swelling blackness of fear.

Dake shooed the divers back out of the cave quickly, saying that he was cold, then he turned to her. "C'mon, darling." He shook her gently to get her to look at him.

"I do this all the time when we come here. I'll get used to it." Reesa told him through numbed lips.

"I'm with you all the way, love. Don't be afraid."

She looked up at him, feeling the blackness ebb. She gulped, fixed her mask to her face, and swam out at his side, his hand entwined with hers.

Four

That evening while Reesa was undressing, an envelope was pushed under her door. It was an invitation for her to "a cocktail party in Mr. Masters's private suite."

She stared in the mirror, the invitation clutched in her hand. Her eyes looked more round than almond-shaped in her still-too-thin face. The last thing she needed was more of Dake Masters! Yet, how could she escape him? She had no doubt that he would search her out no matter where on the ship she chose to hide. She picked up the dress that Dake had handed her when they'd stepped off the tender and back onto the ship.

In the shower she recalled the forty-five-minute boat trip that afternoon to the island of Cozumel. Many of the passengers had sung songs; Dake had bought handmade Indian baskets and tablecloths from vendors roving the decks.

"We'll need them when we build that house you've always wanted to have in Santa Barbara overlooking the harbor. I bought the land before . . . before the accident," Dake had whispered to her.

"Things have changed!" Reesa had said firmly.

"Some things never change."

She stepped out of the shower stall and toweled her hair and body dry. Naked, she went into the tiny cabin, picked up the lace dress, and held it in front of her.

The only thing she had to wear under it was a body slip in sheerest cotton that Liza had made for her. The strapless top served as a bra, the embroidered skirt of the slip was flared and edged with tiny ruffles. Reesa loved the garment, but didn't wear it much, preferring to save the delicate marquisette. She took it from the drawer and put it on. As she pulled the lace dress over her head Consuela came into the cabin, almost hitting Reesa with the door.

"Sorry, I didn't—" Consuela paused, her mouth agape. "That's beautiful. Is that the dress Margarita made for you? She told me about it. You look like a bride!" Consuela gasped as Reesa twirled in front of her. "Oops . . . quite a bit of you shows even with the slip on."

"I was afraid of that." Reesa grimaced, looking down at herself. "I should wear this another time. Maybe I shouldn't even be bothered going to this—"

"Oh, please wear it, and please don't back out of the cocktail party," Consuela pleaded. "Both Barney and I are invited, and I want to ignore him!" She shrugged when Reesa laughed. "I've decided I am going to pretend that Barney Freedling doesn't exist."

"Good for you." Reesa looked down at herself again. "Maybe if I wear another slip under—"

"You'll do no such thing. You look gorgeous. Pile your hair on your head and wear those ivory combs the Figueroas made for you," Consuela insisted before edging into the tiny bathroom to shower.

Reesa didn't wear any jewelry except the combs, not

even earrings. She piled her hair at the crown of her head, letting curls fall from the top. She used no powder, just blush and a green eyeshadow that enhanced her eyes. The ivory combs gleamed with a richness that was a shade lighter than her dress. The champagne lace was so fine that it flared when she moved, showing the sheer slip beneath and her bare legs under that. She wore no stockings, and shoved her feet into chamois-soft high-heeled sandals the same color as the dress. Her black hair and lustrous green eyes were the only contrast, her honey-hued skin almost the color of the lace.

Consuela wore a black cotton dress edged in matching lace.

The girls laughed at the contrast.

"But we do look beautiful, I think," the unaffected Consuela observed as they pressed themselves close together to look in the mirror.

Reesa was glad of Consuela's chatter as they climbed the several staircases to the deck where Dake had a suite.

"This will be my first visit to one of the luxury suites," Consuela confided, "except when you fainted—"

Reesa interrupted. "I don't think I've ever been in one for a party anyway. Whatever it looks like, it's bound to be better than what we have."

Consuela giggled, then put her hand to her mouth, shushing both Reesa and herself as they approached the open door and heard the sound of music and conversation. "Do you think he has the steel band in there?" Consuela asked in a whisper.

"No. I'm sure that's a record or tape you hear." Reesa tried to smother the nervousness she felt, calling on her acting skills for help. She took a deep breath, gave Consuela a shaky smile, and walked into the cabin.

At once she saw Dake talking to their tall, handsome captain, Hendrik Ivarsen, both of them about the same height at six foot one inch tall. Although the captain and Dake had radically different coloring, they both possessed an awareness of themselves that went beyond conceit into self-confidence. Perhaps Dake had a more reckless attitude toward life than a ship's captain could have, but both had adventuresome glints in their eyes that would brook no challenge without a reply.

Reesa took scant interest in the others there, though she spoke to the first officer and smiled at two of the passengers she recognized.

"Oops," Consuela muttered. "The captain is looking you up and down as though you were a free dinner." She giggled. Though Hendrik Ivarsen was considered to be a gentleman, he was also known for having a propensity for the ladies.

"Not to worry," Reesa mumbled back. "The captain and I have an understanding. I don't chase him and he doesn't chase me."

The captain excused himself from talking to Dake and came toward them across the spacious sitting room of the most deluxe suite onboard the *Windward*.

She swallowed when she felt Dake's eyes rivet on her. Shivers followed as his gaze scoured her from eyebrow to ankle. She resolutely fixed her eyes on the captain.

"Maria . . . I mean, Reesa, my dear." He inclined his head in a gallant gesture. "May I say that you look stunning this evening?"

"Thank you." The words pushed themselves through her lips, which were stiff as plastic. She watched apprehensively as Dake came up behind the captain, then around him.

"And you look quite lovely too, Consuela. In fact, I think you are causing great consternation to one of my officers," the captain teased, his eyes sliding to a frozen-faced Barney Freedling, who hadn't stopped staring since Consuela arrived.

"Really? Which one?" Connie asked in a sweet voice.

There were murmurs and some laughter at that.

"Let me get you a drink, ladies." Dake eased around the captain and stepped between Reesa and Consuela, taking an elbow of each. "Excuse me," he said to the captain and two other officers who had come forward. His tone had a touch of frost in it.

Why was he angry? Reesa racked her brain. He always used that lofty, icy tone when he was angry. Dake had always been a street fighter. Swanky streets—Beacon Street, Wall Street—but still he was a street fighter. Whenever he felt threatened he came out of his corner fighting, she mused.

Dake handed her a Saratoga water with two pieces of lime in it. "You're lovely," he snarled softly, his eyes brooding over her.

Reesa stiffened. Consuela giggled, then bit her lips and was silent when Dake's gaze swung her way.

"Don't you dare snap at her." Reesa bristled.

"I wasn't snapping," Dake growled back.

"You are now," Reesa shot at him.

Consuela stood with a glass of white wine poised before her lips, her eyes sliding between the two of them.

Barney stepped to her side. "Hello, Consuela."

"Hello." Consuela barely glanced at him, her worried gaze still on Reesa and Dake.

"I would like to speak to you."

Consuela took a deep breath and faced the tall, handsome Norwegian. "Shouldn't you be writing to your fiancé? Get lost, Barney." Her breath left her in a shuddering sigh as she watched a blush rise up his face.

Dake broke his eye contact with Reesa long enough to shoot a glance at them. "Is there a problem?"

Consuela jumped and shook her head. "No problem," she muttered, her eyes on the stiff shoulders of Barney Freedling as he strode from the cabin.

Reesa took advantage of Dake's attention to Consuela to turn to speak to the captain again.

"So, all this time you were a movie star in America and no one knew it." Hendrik's eyes appraised her again in the champagne lace dress.

"Not even me." Reesa tried to smile.

"We won't be seeing you after this cruise," the captain stated.

Reesa hadn't known what she would say until the words tumbled from her lips. "No . . . no. I'll finish out the cruise, then I had better go back and explain to Liza and Miguel . . . and . . . well, I suppose I'll have to return to the States and see how many pieces I have to pick up in my life."

"I'm one of the pieces, darling," Dake said at her back, his hand closing on her waist and causing her body to arch.

She looked around and past him. "Where is Consuela?" she asked, ignoring his remark.

"She said that she was due at the purser's desk for a while to relieve someone."

"And I also have to leave, Mr. Masters. Thank you for the lovely time." The captain inclined his head first at Dake then at Reesa. "And, of course we will talk again, er, Miss Hawke." He winked at Reesa.

When the captain left, several of the staff and officers followed.

Reesa was about to join Mr. and Mrs. Calkins when she felt a hand on her arm. She looked up at Dake.

"Introduce me to your friends," Dake said, his eyes golden in the glow cast by a hanging lamp.

Reesa's heart flopped over in her chest. "All right."

There were just two other couples besides the Calkinses still in the cabin when she introduced Dake to them. "And this is Dake Masters. . . ."

"How are you?" Mrs. Calkins gushed. "So you are Maria's, I mean Reesa's, young man. How nice."

"Yes, it is." Dake clamped his arm around Reesa; his voice was sultry as he joined in the conversation that ebbed and flowed as the other two couples still left in the cabin joined them. This time it was Dake doing the introducing.

Reesa began to feel lightheaded, smiling at the others but taking no other part in the conversation. When she saw the guests moving toward the door, she walked with them until she was stopped by that steellike arm, which inched her back so that she was standing in front of Dake, pressed against his body as the others made their farewells.

Dake closed the door by reaching around Reesa. The muted clang of the steel door reverberated in the stillness.

"I can't stay," Reesa whispered, looking at the wall. "Have to work."

"I checked." Dake's mouth was on her neck, his tongue teasing into her ear. "You have no commitment this evening."

"Have to mingle with the passengers," she babbled.

"Mingle with me," Dake whispered. "I'm a passenger."

"We talked. I remember that . . . the night when . . . when . . . I fell and hit my head—"

"We were too angry, too keyed up. As usual, there were too many people around us and our privacy was minimal." His hands clenched on her body, making her wince. "Sorry, love. I don't want to hurt you. Will you listen to me for a bit?" he mouthed into her ear, the palm of his hand flat on her abdomen.

"Yes."

"Good." He shuddered a breath into her neck. "When they finally called off the search for you, I had to face another monster in my mind. There was no way to tell you that I loved you, that I didn't want us to be apart."

Reesa's throat felt sandpapery and tight. "I remember we often said we loved each other, but—"

"No buts," Dake rasped out, turning her in his arms. "We did love each other. We were happy."

Reesa shook her head.

"Are you saying we weren't happy. That we didn't love each other?" Dake held her shoulders.

"We had a strange, sophisticated love." Reesa spoke in a distracted way, as though she hadn't thought out the words issuing from her mouth. "In the world we lived in we were happy . . . but . . . but in the time I've lived as Maria Halcon, I've seen real love! And I've found I don't want a substitute—the concentrated, squeezed-into-a-can type of relationship that is always on hold while the world, the job, and other people are taken care of first." The words shocked her, maimed her. Her love for Dake was a tinsel thing? A slick plastic counterfeit? No! She looked up at him, seeing the pain in his eyes that surely showed in hers too.

He took a step back from her. "I want to love you." His voice was barely audible.

Reesa's hand rose to her cheek and found a moistness there. "I wanted that too. I wanted to be your wife. I wanted to be Robert's mother." She felt as though she might bare her soul to him as she had never done.

"We can have children."

"Without love?"

"We have love." His voice vibrated through the cabin.

"Or a reasonable facsimile thereof." Reesa found it hard to inhale. "I read that somewhere."

"Do you want to go?"

"No!" The word was wrenched from her. She didn't

even pretend to misunderstand him. "What I want, Dake, is the real thing."

"My love, that's what I want to give you." His sibilant hiss wrapped around her like a silky coil, but he made no move to touch her.

Reesa smiled, feeling sadness and amusement at the wary, angry, puzzled stance of the cocksure, superconfident Dake Masters. "If I ask the next question," she mused out loud, "it will sunder forever what we had, and maybe what we could have."

"Ask." Dave spoke through his teeth, his body crouched, his fisted hands held in front of him.

"Do you know what real love is? Even though I've lived in a house of real love, would I recognize it in my own life? Would we be like thirsty people, handing each other cups of water from a poisoned well?"

A muscle jumped next to his mouth, but other than that Dake didn't move. "You are certainly more philosophical than you once were."

"I came damned close to buying the farm," Reesa snapped at him. A tremor flickered across his face. "Maybe that's why," she whispered.

"Ah, Reesa." He took a deep breath. "Did you know that my picture ran in the L.A. *Times*? I was handcuffed to a federal marshal. I was subpoenaed as a material witness, then told by a federal prosecuting attorney that the circumstantial evidence was mounting fast that I killed you in a fury and dumped your body overboard." Dake spoke rapidly, the words like a catharsis to his sick soul. He hadn't wanted to tell her the details, but now the words poured from him, breaking apart the brick house where he had encased his spirit since Reesa had been pronounced missing and presumed dead under mysterious circumstances. "I was jailed for two weeks because at the prosecution's urging the judge didn't set bail. When I was released, after the pretrial hearing was overturned, I faced real enmity from the public, who had been convinced by the media that I was a drug-crazed—"

"Drug?" Reesa pushed the word from a dry throat.

Dake had been pacing while he talked. Now he paused. "Oh, yes. Our friend, Haddon James, had cocaine on the *Firewitch*, Oh, I knew he used it on occasion, but I didn't know he had brought any onboard for the trip."

"I didn't even know he used it." An errant thought intruded. "Does Jazz Leaman still work for him? I don't remember him, but he did say that he was a publicist for DM Productions, and Haddon James is the head of that company."

"Not anymore he isn't," Dake said abruptly, not elaborating. "And Leaman works directly for me now."

Reesa stared at his set features. His face might have been chiseled from granite, his resolve forged of iron. She sighed. There was no way to get information from Dake that he was not prepared to give. His family had power and money, but it had been Dake's own personal dynamism that had made him so successful. He'd charged through law school, through a two-year stint as a congressman from the Boston area. His father had connections, but it had been Dake's instinct and talent that had made him a producer of first-rate plays in off-Broadway productions, then onto Broadway itself. He stormed Hollywood, finding the best in the film and television industries. As she looked at him, one unalterable thought surfaced, something she had never even considered until this moment. Despite the fact that he seemed always to be in a crowd, Dake Masters was a loner. He threw punches, but he took his lumps too. How alone he must have been when he had been accused of her murder! "Go on. Tell me about what happened to you. The charges . . . everything." Reesa swallowed. "Please."

"When the FBI searched the yacht, they found the coke. Haddon told them I had supplied it to all my guests—"

"That's not true. You never used anything but a little alcohol."

"Thank you, my love," Dake grated out. "But you weren't there to tell them that, were you?"

"No." The word was barely audible.

"For a few months I was even persona non grata in the business, then things calmed down. I was able to begin work on another film, but when I was recognized by the public it was different." His attempt at a smile resulted in a downward slash in his face, no humor in the expression. "Your public was loyal, my sweet. I was attacked more than once . . . and sometimes by women."

"God," Reesa sobbed.

Dake inhaled, feeling the emotional fetters crack. "The worst was knowing that I would never see you, never talk to you, never tell you that I didn't want to be separated . . ." He took a deep, shaky breath. "I wanted to tell you that I was going to do everything in my power to marry you. Then Cynthia died and I realized that all that so-called protecting of my mother-in-law's feelings was ridiculous, that she would have understood how I felt about you, that all the barriers I put up about marriage had turned on me, buried me. I had divorced Linda before Cynthia died. I was bitter about Linda, about what she had done to Robert and me."

Dake could still recall the emptiness he felt when he had faced Linda across a courtroom and the judge announced he was free. Her face held a consummate indifference.

"Do you have a check with you?" she'd asked.

"Shut up, Linda," he had shouted before spinning around and striding from the courtroom.

"Don't forget to pick up Robert. I'm leaving for France on Saturday," she had called after him.

Dake shook himself away from the bitter memory. "One good thing," he mumbled, his eyes sliding away then back to Reesa's face. "I never had to sue for custody of Robert. I think Linda was relieved to have him off her hands except for a holiday now and then."

"He's happy with you," Reesa observed in a thready voice. "I want to see him."

"He talked about you so much." Dake's smile fell away. "Sometimes I wanted to yell at him to stop, but I didn't."

"No. Children should be able to talk out their fears and grief."

Dake nodded, then looked around the room, fixing on the twin portholes where the muted sounds of the ocean's surf penetrated the cabin.

His smile softened the craggy lines of his face. "I remembered your feelings for Robert and was going to use them if I had to."

"Devious."

He sighed, taking one step, then two, to clasp her tightly in his arms. "I'll give up my armor a small piece at a time, not in big chunks."

Reesa nodded, feeling warmth spread through her from his encircling arms. "You always told me it was smart to cover your buns in any situation." A ripple of laughter squeezed through her lips.

"Wise, aren't I?" He leaned forward, pressing his lips to her forehead, the rest of his body held away from hers.

"Canny is a better word. Canny street fighter describes you to a T," she mumbled, sliding her right foot forward so that her knee touched his calf.

"My blue-blooded family would frown at that." His lips moved along her hairline.

"Your family has a permanent frown about every-thing that isn't Back Bay and Wasp." Reesa's left foot settled a little in front of her right, so that it was between Dake's legs, and her body was now touching his from chest to thigh.

"True, but who gives a damn?" Dake could hear the tremor in his own voice as her satin body rubbed on his. "You're so tiny now." His arms tightened on her, resting at her shoulders and at the base of her spine. "How much weight did you lose?"

"About fifteen pounds, maybe a little more." Reesa lifted her head and looked up at him.

"You're crying," Dake whispered, feeling tears well up within him, too, at the realization of her emotion. "Oh, darling, darling, you were alone and hurt and I wasn't there." His voice cracked, his heart pounding against hers.

"I was so afraid when I surfaced after hitting my head. My mouth was full of water. I tried to call out. The yacht went farther and farther away. I was alone." Reesa sobbed, her hands clutching at him. "Sometimes I would sleep . . . then I'd waken. I knew I was going to die. My head hurt. Sometimes I couldn't see. I don't even remember Miguel picking me up. He said I was feverish and calling out 'halcón . . . halcón . . .' over and over again."

"Your name in Spanish." Dake leaned back from her, his smile shaky, feeling the wetness on his cheeks. "Your Californio background is more deeply imbedded than you think."

"Yes." Reesa lifted one finger to his cheek, wiping away the tear.

His face turned into her hand, kissing each finger, tasting the mild saltiness of her skin, inhaling the sweet, elusive odor that was hers alone. "God, I missed that fragrance."

"Ummm?" Reesa leaned on him, her hands digging into him as though she were running a reality check, as though she must know if he was really there, if he was really flesh and blood.

"Your body has a fragrance like no other woman's in the world. You have always excited me with the lovely odor of you that is more than soap, beyond perfume," he muttered into her temple, his breath ruffling the fine hairs there.

The ship rolled and they both compensated by bracing themselves, their bodies coming even closer together.

Reesa looked up at him, feeling her bridges crumble and fall, her instinct to escape melting at the sight of him.

"I don't want you to leave me," Dake said, his grasp on her loosening as though to give her the choice.

"I don't want to go."

"Thank you." His voice was thick. He leaned down and kissed her nose, his index finger pulling at the lace front of her dress, stretching it from her body. His eyes followed the movement, his pulse accelerating as he saw the creamy curve of her breasts beneath the sheer marquisette. "You have two very sexy garments on, lady."

"Do I?"

"You do." He eased the lace down farther on her arm, the movement pulling the sheer cotton with it, baring more of her breasts, uncovering her nipples. "Darling, I need you. . . ." Dake's voice was a croak. His mouth homed in on her breasts, the gentle sucking and pulling making his heart thud out of control. When he heard her whimper, he thought his blood would burst through his veins.

"Dake . . ." she whimpered, clutching at him when he lifted her and carried her to the king-size bed in the adjoining room in the cabin.

He set her on her feet next to the bed. "I love this dress, so I'm going to remove it very carefully, love. I don't want it crushed or torn."

"No," Reesa agreed, reeling with the love that filled her. "Margarita worked so hard on it."

"Yes," Dake concurred, his eyes riveted to her creamy skin as he lifted the dress over her head, then removed the marquisette slip. He stared at her as she stood before him in her flesh-colored briefs of inexpensive nylon. "You're too thin," he said gruffly, his hands cupping her hipbones. "What's this scar?"

"Miguel can't swim, at least he couldn't when he found me, even though he's a fisherman. He hooked me with his gaff and pulled me into the boat that way. By the time the fever broke, the wound was healing nicely." She tried to smile at Dake, to wipe away that harsh expression on his face. "Miguel can swim now. I've taught him and Liza and I'm giving lessons to Miguelito."

"Fine." He dropped to his knees. His lips grazed the jagged scar at her hip. Then he kissed her abdomen, his mouth coursing down her flesh, lingering on the imperfection.

Reesa's hands ruffled his hair, the dark coarseness an erotic massage to her skin. She bent over him, holding tight to his head, loving it when he looked up at her, his eyes a melting gold.

"Darling, you still have the same creamy satin skin that I always wanted covering mine." He buried his face in her softly muscled abdomen, his mouth open on her body. "Of course, I love all of your body, but I do prefer the untanned parts." His words were slurred.

All at once he stood, holding her around the hips so that her body rose above him, the top of his head below her chin. He looked up at her. "You're lovely." His words coiled around her like a silver bond.

"I'm tall too!" Reesa laughed huskily, knowing that her head was almost touching the cabin ceiling.

Dake growled softly, letting her slide down his aroused body, feeling her every tremor at the contact. "I want to make love to you all night long, but if you tell me no at this moment, we'll dress and go upstairs and dance."

"And that wouldn't bother you?" Reesa smiled at him, knowing him.

"Yes, damm it, it would. And I sure as hell would try to talk you out of leaving."

"That I believe," Reesa answered.

"But I damn well wouldn't hold you if you wanted to go. . . ."

"Darling." Reesa breathed the endearment more then said it, reveling in using the familiar term. "Is your bed comfortable?"

The sardonic twist to Dake's mouth was also something Reesa remembered well, but she saw relief flash in his eyes. "Not as comfortable as our bed at home." Dake referred to the monstrous round bed that they had cavorted on and loved in at their home in California.

"Shall we put this off then?" Reesa laughed at him.

"Damn, Reesa. When did you get so . . . so cool?" Dake bent down and lifted her high in his arms, then knelt on the bed, falling forward, yet swinging his body so that he was beneath her, she on top of him.

She leaned over him, her hair like wavy black velvet curtaining them. "I assure you I'm not cool."

"Dear heaven, neither am I." His guttural words were buried as he took her breast into his mouth and sucked gently and rhythmically.

Reesa clutched at him, not even aware that her nails were digging into him or that the high keening sound of satisfaction she heard was coming from her.

He ministered to her other breast, then placed tiny biting kisses over her neck and shoulder.

All the while Reesa was loving him, too, her body arching in recalled wonder as her tactile exploration of his body increased. "Dake . . . Dake!" Myriad lights exploded behind her eyes. She wanted him now.

"Not yet, precious, not yet," he crooned as he

turned her slowly onto her back, his hand and mouth not ceasing their loving rhythm on her form.

When he lifted her foot and began to kiss her instep, then the sole of her foot, Reesa could feel her head thrash from side to side, her passion building. She felt a sensual irritation with him that he wouldn't join her, yet she delighted in the mounting emotion as each nerve end tingled from his touch.

He turned her on her stomach and began a sweet journey back up her body, his fingers massaging each muscle and tendon, so that while the love tension climbed within her, her body relaxed totally, became flexible, bendable, soft, warm.

She whirled on the bed and caught at him. "I've waited long enough for you."

He chuckled, his breathing quickening at the sight of her sensually curved body at his side, her legs rubbing up and down his in silent demand for him. "I'm yours," he offered, once more sliding down her body, parting her trembling legs, his mouth in moist intrusion there, his blood pounding when he heard her moan, her body twisting beneath him.

"Dake . . ."

"Yes, darling."

"Love me," Reesa pleaded.

"I do . . . I will," Dake vowed, entering her with a soft violence that had her gasping and holding him tightly.

They spun away, the vortex taking them, enclosing them, separating them from all the world but each other, where nothing and no one could trespass.

Dake held her as they panted and breathed into each other's mouths, the culmination of love slowly waning, settling them at last on the earth that they had left together. "It was beautiful."

"Yes." Reesa opened her eyes, feeling a stinging there. "We always made love well, but there's more.

. . ." She couldn't explain something she didn't know, hadn't experienced.

"If there's more, then we'll find it together," Dake said in a fervent tone.

Reesa eased herself free of his arms and sat up. "How do we know where to look? How do we recognize it when we do find it if we don't know what we're looking for?" She gulped, her back to him.

She felt his mouth at the base of her spine, his tongue stabbing at each of the vertebrae until he reached her neck. "Dake, I mean it. I want more."

"Then you'll get more, my love."

She twisted her body so that she was facing him, mouth to mouth, nose to nose. "Dake, has it ever occurred to you that what we have between us is not the stuff that dreams are made of, that 'eternal' and 'always' don't apply to commitments like ours?"

"No. That never entered my mind."

"Yet that night when . . . when I fell into the water, we had agreed that what we had was over. You had no intention of marrying and neither had I—"

"We said too much in anger," Dake burst out. "I said that evening that nothing had changed, that I had no intention of marrying. I used the excuse of Cynthia's weak heart, as I had done before."

"You see—"

"But when you were lost, when I thought you were dead, I would have given anything to have you back so that I could have told you that I would marry you at once."

Reesa stared at him as they knelt facing each other, her eyes flitting over his sinewed body, the lighter chestnut of his chest hair arrowing to his thighs. Looking at him gave her joy. He was a beautiful man! "Don't you see? Do you hear what you're saying? I had to die for you to release yourself in your mind from the commitment you had made to others and to yourself."

"It's not like that," Dake barked, running his strong hand through his hair, mussing it like a boy. "We keep going round and round on this like damned verbal dervishes, creating dust but nothing solid."

"Spinning in a vortex," Reesa said with a dry laugh.

Dake's head shot up. "I damn well don't accept that I'm caught in a whirlpool. There is nothing on this earth I can't fight my way out of, lady."

Five

Reesa and Dake went up to the nightclub after they dressed, silence a granite barrier between them.

Reesa wanted to rail at him, to scream and shout until she won the argument with him, but she wasn't sure what the argument was about. She couldn't express herself better than she had already, and she knew that Dake didn't understand how she felt.

They had donned their clothes, eyes meeting then sliding away, mouths opening to speak then shutting again. Their breathing was asthmatic in sound; their throats worked in audible contractions.

When Dake held the cabin door for her, Reesa cleared her dry-as-dust throat. "I—I'm going up to the nightclub. We are—"

"Fine," Dake interrupted, his face like a carved totem as he gestured to her to precede him, locked his cabin, then followed her down the narrow corridor of the ship to the stairs.

They entered the nightclub and Reesa nodded at the Jamaican members of the steel band. Arthur waved to them from across the room to join some of the other members of the staff.

"Ah, my friends," Reesa said.

"I see them. I take it you want us to join them," Dake said tersely.

"No one is making you do anything," she snapped.

"Shall we battle here at the edge of the dance floor, love?" Dake asked her silkily.

"Bastard." Reesa sniffed, marching across the parquet floor at a break in the music.

They ordered drinks and Reesa introduced Dake to some of the staff that he hadn't met before, including Lacey Welles. Dr. Margaret Roberts was sitting opposite Dake on the banquette, leaning forward and engaging him in conversation.

Reesa felt as though smoke were coming out of her nose and ears as both Lacey and Margaret vied for Dake's attention. She experienced a macabre enjoyment at the thought of throwing both women off the fantail of the ship.

"Stop biting at your lower lip like that and dance with me," Arthur demanded, chuckling.

"Wonderful idea." Reesa jumped to her feet, knowing that Dake's eyes had swung toward her. She ignored him and took Arthur's arm until they reached the dance floor.

At first the band was playing a ballad, and she and Arthur wended their way in slow rhythm around the floor. Then the tempo changed and the steel band played a calypso song; the pulsating tones leaped into their bloodstream. She and Arthur danced apart, gyrating their bodies in harmony with the lovely native music of the West Indies.

"Reesa, you are one wonderful dancer, but I think that Mr. Masters is going to attach my hipbone to my jawbone if we stay out here much longer!" Arthur grinned, not the least intimidated by the glowering looks cast from the table.

"Tough. I like to dance with you." Reesa told the truth. She and Arthur often danced together when they had a chance. And the next evening, when the staff would put on a show for the passengers, she and Arthur would be doing a song-and-dance routine to a medley of Broadway tunes. Reesa's rather sultry mezzo voice was a good foil to Arthur's strong, pleasing baritone.

Many times when they had rehearsed the skit for other cruises Reesa had wondered if she had been a singer in her other life. She would smother the question as soon as it arose, not wanting to face the blackness that such speculation brought.

"Ready for tomorrow night? Should we have one quick rehearsal after the dive tomorrow?" Arthur asked when they came together to dance to a ballad.

"Yes, I'm as ready as I ever am for the shows. And yes, I think one more rehearsal couldn't hurt us." Reesa smiled at him.

"No wonder you project so well, each word sounded on its own, each syllable enunicated with precision. You *were* a professional all along."

Reesa nodded, still smiling at him. "But my voice isn't as good as yours."

"Yes, but your lyrics are crystal-clear." Arthur batted his eyes. "Now say something more that's nice about me, dahling." He grinned at her. "How am I doing? Think I'll make it in Hollywood?"

"A surefire hit." Reesa laughed. Then her eye fell on Dake sitting slouched in his chair, watching them, a sulky menace emanating from him.

When she saw Margaret pluck at his sleeve, causing Dake to turn his head her way, Reesa looked at Arthur. "How about trying our luck in the casino for a while?"

Arthur chuckled. "Blackjack?"

Reesa looked down her nose. "*Vingt-et-un*, if you please, sir."

"Of course, madam." Arthur sketched a mocking bow and gestured for her to precede him off the dance floor; they left through a door on the opposite side of the room from where they had been sitting.

Reesa risked a quick glance toward the table. Margaret still had Dake's attention.

She and Arthur walked through an area housing one-arm bandits, pausing for a minute to put five quarters into one. She lost. Arthur put five quarters in the same machine and won ten quarters. Reesa punched him lightly on the arm when he laughed with glee.

Then they entered a hushed area with baize-covered tables and high stools, the women dealers working quietly. Only the hissed instructions from the players as they asked for a card or told the dealer they would stay with what they had broke the stillness.

Arthur and Reesa took their seats, smiling at Janie Lynd, one of the English girls who worked in the casino and who was dealing blackjack that evening.

Cards had never been an absorption of Reesa's. She never lost more than she set aside just for that purpose, but still she found gambling diverting and good fun now and then.

"How much can you lose tonight?" Arthur asked her, putting a twenty-dollar bill on the table and getting chips.

"Fifteen is my limit tonight." Reesa grinned at him. "I bought a few things on shore today."

"Spendthrift." Arthur laughed, then he bit his lip. "But you really don't have to worry, do you Reesa? Don't you have . . . I mean, aren't you kind of rich?"

Reesa stared back at him. "I suppose I'm what you could call well fixed, but not rich. Still, I think of myself as Maria Halcon, girl on a budget, and I probably will until I finish this cruise." She felt a sadness. "I still have to talk to Miguel and Liza about the new

me. I don't want to be parted from them. I love them."
She gulped and turned silent, mutely accepting the
cards dealt but not really seeing either of them. "I'll
take one," she mumbled.

"Reesa," Arthur hissed. "Look at that: you've got
nineteen! You shouldn't have asked for another hit."

"Oh." Reesa gave him a limp smile and turned over
the card that Janie slid toward her. It was a two! She
had twenty-one! She stared open-mouthed at Arthur,
then laid her cards down after Janie showed hers at
eighteen.

Arthur and Reesa laughed as Janie pushed a pile of
chips toward her.

After a while the cards began to take her attention
and she forgot the sadness she was feeling at the
thought of leaving Miguel and his family.

She and Arthur lost more than they won, but neither of them went below the limit they had set themselves, so they kept on playing.

Reesa reached out to pick up the cards dealt her,
barely noticing the player who sat down on her left,
and nodded that he wished to be dealt into the game.

When the person won with ace, king, and jack, she
turned to look at him. "You! I should have known.
Cheating!" She sniffed, lifting her chin, making
Arthur gasp and Janie look at her searchingly.

Fortunately there were no other players at the table
when Janie leaned toward her and hissed, "Maria?"

Staring at her cards, Reesa couldn't seem to make
out the marks. "Ah, I'll stay with—"

"She'll take a card," Dake interjected, his honey-
sweet voice wrapping around the others.

"Play your own cards, buster." Reesa glared at him,
then picked up an ace that with her seven and two
equaled twenty. "I think I'll—"

"She's set." Dake smiled. "But I'll take one."

Reesa opened her mouth to tell him to cram himself
through a porthole, when all at once he leaned toward

her, his tongue shooting into her mouth like electric velvet. "Ahhh . . ." Reesa rolled her eyes toward Janie.

"You win again, Maria . . . I mean Reesa." Janie grinned, her glance sliding toward Dake. "Lord, I'll never get used to it!"

She pulled away from Dake's kiss. "Maria is a beautiful name. Call me that if you like." Reesa turned when she heard Lin, the Korean waiter, inquire if they would like drinks. "Yes, I would like a Jack Daniel's on the rocks. Uh, make it a double, please."

"Reesa, for Pete's sake," Arthur said from the side of his mouth.

Janie stared at her, her jaw slack. "You'll collapse like overcooked pasta, Reesa. You aren't used to the hard stuff." Janie continued to deal, but her eyes darted from Arthur to Reesa and back again.

"I'll have an orange juice," Reesa muttered. "Lots of ice . . . and vodka."

"I'll play these." Dake smiled at each of them in turn, thanking Lin for his Irish whiskey, straight up, as he'd ordered it.

Janie sipped the ginger ale that she always drank when working, Arthur sipped his Dutch beer, Reesa stared at her juice, wishing that she hadn't ordered the vodka in it. She took a hearty swallow of her drink, coughed, then grabbed for the glass of ice water next to Dake's drink.

"Acid in orange juice." Reesa croaked out the words.

"True?" Dake grinned at her watering eyes. "Drinking a double orange juice is so efficient. You won't have to order as many drinks," he mused. He studied her as she resolutely downed a great deal of vodka and orange juice in two rapid sips. She was not a drinker!

Arthur leaned forward so he could look at Dake.

"Reesa doesn't drink anything usually. It makes her sick."

Janie pursed her lips, nodding and shooting glances at Reesa, who had now swallowed most of her screwdriver.

Reesa scraped the edge of one card on the baize, signaling that she wanted another dealt to her.

"Over." Reesa inhaled a shuddering breath, looking owlishly at Janie. "I lost." She hiccupped.

"Tipsy already!" Janie's British accent was very pronounced.

"I had better get her to bed," Arthur ventured nervously.

"Dave and Andy put me to bed once . . . in their bed. . . ." Reesa announced in pear-shaped tones, knowing that Dake had turned to look at her. "I slept with them all night." Reesa nodded several times, feeling a little lightheaded, but delighted that he was irked.

"Shhh." Janie leaned toward her, putting an index finger on Reesa's lips. "What's gotten into you?"

"Quiet," Arthur whispered.

"All night? In their bed?" Dake's muted roar stopped the play at nearby tables.

"Certainly!" Reesa sunk another barb into him. "Friends take care of one another." She swung around on the stool, lifting her hand and poking her finger into Dake's chest. "They're my friends. I would do the same for them." She rose, teetered sideways, then back, then around again.

Dake caught her, lifting her to his shoulder in a fireman's carry. "I'll put her to bed."

"Ah . . ." Arthur stood, his eyes sliding around the room. The other players seemed to be concentrating on their games. "It might be better if I took her."

"Don't worry." Dake pushed his and Reesa's chips toward Arthur. "Enjoy." Then he walked from the room, Reesa's head bobbing against his back.

"Stop. I can walk." Reesa's words, slightly nasal from being upside down, reached Arthur and Janie as Dake pushed open a steel door that would take them out on deck.

"Do you think I did the right thing?" Arthur slid back on his stool, looking glumly at the chips in front of him.

"Listen, Arthur," Janie said, leaning toward him, "if I hada bloke like that chasing after me, I wouldn't want any interference from my friends."

Arthur nodded. "He does seem to care about her."

"Care about her? Cripes, he's bonkers about her, and he hates it!" Janie chuckled. "I'll play these," she informed Arthur, then proceeded to beat him.

Dake shifted Reesa's body as he walked around the almost deserted deck, the stars like myriad crystals suspended from black velvet, the moon casting a rippling silver path on the water. "Breathe deeply, darling."

"O-kay," Reesa said as he stood her in front of him. She leaned her head back on his shoulder. "I think I have spi-spinal ch—back trouble. I'm dizzy. My legs aren't working."

"They'll work in the morning." Dake soothed her, his strong arms holding her upright. "Breathe deeply."

"Great. Now you're a doctor too." She licked her dry lips. "I didn't know that."

"Take deep breaths," he instructed her, smiling into her hair. "You might have a headache tomorrow."

"From my bad back." Reesa hiccupped. "Where did that come from? I think I'm all right."

"You won't think so tomorrow," Dake muttered before telling her again to take deep breaths.

"I do keep breathing," she told him, "but it makes me dizzy."

"Bedtime," Dake intructed, smiling at a couple who walked by them, managing to put his hand over Reesa's mouth when she opened it to speak at that moment.

"Umple . . . mumphle . . ." Reesa finally bit the palm of his hand. It made him swear, but he did release her mouth. "Thank you. I don't think you realized it, but I couldn't speak." She smiled up at him. Then she threw a harpoon. "Are you going to take me to Dave and Andy's cabin? I slept there—"

"No," he barked. Her feet banged on each step as he led her down the stairs to his cabin deck.

"Ohhh," Reesa exhaled audibly. "Well, if you are intending to sleep with Consuela and me, I must tell you that you won't fit!" She beamed up at him, then frowned. "You know, I'm very glad we don't have a snorkeling class tomorrow. I'm . . . I'm not sure I'll be up to it . . . you know."

"Bet on it," Dake said crisply.

"Have you a headache? Headaches make you grumpy, I'll bet—" Reesa lifted her index finger to her temple and tapped twice there. "They always did."

"I think *you'll* be grumpy tomorrow, darling," Dake said, a hard chuckle brushing her ear.

"Not me. Wonderful disposition. Sweetheart, that's me." The motion of the ship made her stumble.

Dake supported her with one hand while he fumbled for his key, putting it into his cabin door lock. "You'll be sleeping here tonight, my sweet." He inhaled a deep breath, then hoisted her upright with an arm around her middle back and under her armpits.

"Kind of you . . ." Reesa squinted around the interior of the cabin, wishing she had an aspirin. Consuela always had aspirin! "But I'll be going." She turned somewhat unsteadily and tottered back to the doorway.

Dake caught her around the waist. "No need to get

edgy. I have no desire to make love to an inebriated woman," he said, knowing if she made one sensual move toward him, he would end up loving her. Damn her hide! She still had the power to take his control and whirl it away like dry mesquite in a desert wind.

Reesa looked up at him. "Oh? All right, but actually I was just going back to our cabin because Connie always has aspirin. Making love with you hadn't entered my mind." She licked her dry lips. "Not that it wouldn't have occurred to me at some time during the night . . . maybe." She gave him a blinding smile, seemingly unaware of the thunderous looks she was getting from him.

"I am sure I can get you aspirin." He snapped off the words like dry twigs.

"Really? That's very inno—innova—" She hic-cupped, smiled at him, and continued. "Very smart of you," she managed, beaming up at him. "Would you get it now, please? My eyes hurt ter-rib-ly."

Dake released her and she collapsed on the sofa, watching him for a moment when he went to the phone and punched out a few numbers.

Dake turned away from the phone. "The cabin steward will—" He paused, his eyes narrowing on her sprawled figure on the couch, her head thrown back, her mouth slightly open, a very low snore coming from between her lips. "You still snore if you don't sleep on your side, I see." Dake walked closer, her deep somewhat stertorous breathing reaching him. He leaned down, placing his mouth over hers, taking the low snores into him, feeling his heart begin to hammer at the contact. "Damn you . . . damn you, Reesa Hawke, I'm going to break the hold you have on me!"

He was about to lift her into his arms when there was a knock at the door. He answered it, keeping his body in the opening so that his cabin steward couldn't see into the room. "Thank you for the aspirin." Dake gave the man a ten-dollar bill, smiled, closed the door, and locked it again, putting the night bolt on. He turned to Reesa, who had now slipped sideways a bit, her mouth hanging open. "You don't look like the sexy siren that burns up the silver screen now, darling," he mumbled, approaching her, pulling her forward so that her body fell as if boneless into his arms. He lifted her and carried her to the bedroom of the suite, lowering her onto the bed, then beginning to strip her clothes from her body. "Do you know what you're doing to me, love, even though you are, clinically speaking, unconscious?" He touched her velvet skin and pulled back as though he had been burned. He bit his lip and peeled the dress from her body, then the very sheer marquisette slip. He closed his eyes for a moment, then looked back at her body, now clad only in sheer briefs. "God," he groaned, sliding her under the covers, watching her pull up her knees and take the cuddling position she almost always assumed for sleep. "This should be an interesting night for you, Masters," he lectured himself in sardonic tones.

He shed his own clothes, then, glancing at her as he went into the bathroom, he shook his head. "You've got me taking cold showers, damn you, Rees!" He flung himself into the shower stall and turned on the cold water. Gasping, he stayed under the icy stream as long as he could, then towelled and dried himself.

He switched out the light near the bathroom door and made his way to the bed by the shaft of moonlight that came in the porthole.

When the bed sank with his weight, Reesa rolled toward him, emitting purring sounds of satisfaction when she found the hard warmth of his body.

"Rees, for heaven's sake." He groaned as she wriggled against him, her warm arms encircling his middle. He tried to edge away from her, but she followed right along, digging her fingers into him when he tried to escape. Finally he gave up and enfolded her close to him. The soft growl she emitted sent his temperature soaring and almost out through the top of his head.

He was sure that he would never sleep, but the rolling of the vessel and the warmth of the woman at his side soothed him, at last sending him into a deep blackness.

He woke because he heard her moan. He looked down at the head cuddled into his shoulder. "Rees?"

"I think I'm Rees. Oh, Lord, I feel sick! My head is thumping! My stomach is . . ."

"Churning?" Dake inquired in a soft voice.

"Don't use that word!" she pronounced in sepulchral tones.

"Sorry." He smiled into her hair.

"You're not sorry." She gulped. "I hear you grinning."

"I had no idea you could hear a grin."

"You're chortling in your mind. . . . Ahhh, I'm going to be sick." She coughed, then felt herself lifted and carried to the bathroom, her head pushed down as she began to retch.

"I can't drink," she whimpered as he wiped her face with a warm wet cloth.

"No, you can't," Dake concurred.

"All the world hates a smart aleck," she grumbled, her uncertain stomach still feeling like a dinghy in a gale-force wind.

Dake laughed, lifting her into his arms, then carrying her back to the bed, where he propped her against the pillows. "I'll ring for hot tea."

"Ring for formaldehyde." Reesa gave a shaky sob, feeling more unloved and unattractive than she had ever felt in her life.

Dake chuckled, turned to the phone, barked into it, then hung up. He went back to the bed, sitting down on the side of it, noting that she winced at the movement. "You'll feel better after tea and toast."

"Aaaagh . . . don't mention food," Reesa begged.

"You'll live, darling." He leaned forward and kissed her cheek.

Her eyes fluttered open. "You look pleased that I'm dying."

"One, you are not dying. Two, I am not pleased that you are suffering from a slight hangover—"

"*Slight?*"

"Slight," he confirmed. "Remember, I've had a few in my day."

"Do I ever." Reesa shut her eyes again as pain creased her forehead. "Remember the time you dove into Senator Wicklow's pool stark naked? Then the whole next day you wandered around with an ice pack held to your forehead mumbling, 'What the hell was in that punch?' Then—"

"I felt like raising hell. I'd just finished a picture. And need I remind you that I wasn't the only one to dive into that pool without any clothes on?" He rose and went to the bathroom, returning with a wet cloth he pressed against her face.

"I remember very well now Nissa James jumped into the pool right beside you, naked as the day she was born," Reesa said crossly before groaning.

"That was the second time we met." Dake laughed, remembering how he had surfaced from the pool, looked up, and saw her jade eyes going over him, then passing on to someone else in the water. He had climbed out in front of her, forgetting he was nude, forgetting everything but those eyes and that heart-shaped face with the pale, slightly olive skin.

She had looked him up and down, cocked her head to one side, and said, "Of course." She had snapped her fingers. "You're the new centerfold that everyone is talking about." She had shrugged, looked him up and down again, and smiled. "You're not the best I've seen, but you'll . . . pass." Her drawl had crawled up his spine like an electric magnet, pulling his blood into a fast-paced rhythm, then making it sing through his veins out of control.

"You're lovely . . ." He remembered that he had murmured, ignoring an attendant who had tried to hand him a towel.

"And you're naked." Her smile had been slow in coming, but her eyes, too, had glistened with it. "Much as I enjoy beefcake, I think you should put on your clothes."

"You're not as blasé as you would like me to think," he had drawled back. "Your cheeks are a little pink. You're a bit embarrassed, lovely lady." He had leaned toward her and stroked her cheek with his index finger.

She had taken a deep breath, then looked him up and down in slow forays. "Maybe I was just hoping you'd have had a greater build. . . ."

Her spear had pierced his armor. Dake had always had a strong awareness of his looks and knew his tall, muscular body was attractive. He had been approached to model for underwear ads . . . and though he had been tempted to do it for the hell of it, he hadn't done it yet. Masking his irritation with her, he looked her up and down the same way, at last taking the towel from the attendant, wrapping it around him, and knotting it at his waist. "I assure you, I don't find you lacking in anything."

She had walked away from him then, deliberately ignoring him when he followed after her. He stood at her side when she talked to other people, not saying anything, just watching.

In no hurry, he left her to don his clothes in one of the cabanas near the pool. When he returned to the party he looked for her, but she was gone. He questioned everyone in sight until he found out where she lived. He hadn't expected to see her at the Wicklows' party, because Reesa Hawke had the reputation of being reserved—and the Wicklow parties had the reputation of being anything but. He had wanted to see her, but he hadn't pushed it with her, feeling that she still was uncomfortable with him because of their first meeting on the set.

He left the party soon after and drove all the way to Santa Barbara to the address given him by Marty Rosen, an agent who worked for the firm that represented Reesa Hawke. Marty Rosen owed him a few favors.

"Damm it, Dake, I could be tossed out of Brownlee's on my ear for giving you her address. I tell you, the lady doesn't mix with the usual Hollywood crowd," Marty had said plaintively.

"Then why was she at the party?"

"Wicklow was married to her second cousin. She was a favorite of Reesa's. The cousin died in plane crash . . . or something." Marty had shrugged. "That's how the senator gets the Latino vote. The Californio background he married into and all that. The wife's mother was a Delgado, just like Reesa Hawke's mother."

"She has a Eurasian look to her," Dake had mused. "Her almond-shaped green eyes look like the finest Oriental jade; her body is curvaceous but with the delicate bones of the East." He had grinned absentmindedly. "But her legs are strictly American— gorgeous and long!"

Marty had been scribbling on a pad. "I'll use all this when we put out her next press release."

"The hell you will!" Dake had reached out, torn the paper from the pad, and stuffed it in his pocket, ignoring Rosen's howls of indignation. "Thanks for the address."

He had gone to Santa Barbara even though it was after midnight and he lived in the opposite direction. He had driven up the curving drive to her home, noting the two Doberman pinschers on the lawn that had paced the car up the drive.

The front door had opened and Reesa had called the dogs to her. "What do you want, Mr. Masters?" she had questioned, keeping the two growling dogs in front of her.

"You," Dake had answered her in a low yet forceful voice that had carried through the perfumed night air like a shooting star.

Six

Dake shook himself from his reverie when Reesa moaned again. He realized that she wasn't fully awake as he edged himself free of her and went to the bathroom, returning with a fresh cloth. He placed the cold, wet cloth on her forehead and over her eyes, eliciting another sound from Reesa.

Then he went back to the bathroom to shower and shave. He was finishing up, wiping the last of the shaving cream from his face when he heard her scream. He sprinted from the bathroom into the bedroom. "Reesa!"

"I'm blind!" she croaked, her body splayed on the bed, the sheet barely covering her lower body.

"Darling." Drake barked a laugh, then bent down and lifted the wet cloth from her face.

"Cruel!" She rolled her eyes his way, then closed them quickly, as if in great pain. "That was cruel."

"It was to help your headache."

"No! You were torturing me."

"Trying to help you." Dake barely managed not to laugh.

"That's right. Dance on the grave of a dying woman."

"I think you have it turned around. A dead woman has a grave, a dying woman—"

"Stop trying to confuse me."

"Let me help you up." Dake leaned over her.

"Nooooo," Reesa squawked.

"You'll feel better after a shower."

"No."

"Yes."

"I haven't made out a will." She whimpered as he lifted her into his arms. "I need a lawyer." She groaned against his shoulder.

"You need a shower, strong coffee, and lots of fresh tomato juice." He twirled the cold water spigot and watched her body do a reverse arc, her mouth open to howl.

"You're . . . trying . . . to . . . kill me," she gasped as he held her under the coolish water while she tried to squirm free.

"No, love, trying to make you feel better. Didn't you say you had a rehearsal for a show this morning?" Dake switched the water to warmer, smiling when she sighed with relief.

"I am only able to do the death scene between Othello and Desdemona today," she announced in funereal tones, blinking her eyes against the spray. "It will have a realism never seen before, because I am sure I will be three-quarters dead by four o'clock today." Her black tones seemed to cause her pain and she clutched at her head while still under the needle-sharp shower.

Dake swallowed, his eyes going over her nude body, his heart thundering against his breastbone, his fingers clenching at her waist. She was so delicately made! But so strong! So cleanly curved, but so womanly soft. He dragged his eyes up to her grimacing face, her eyes still closed, her hands still clutching at her head. "Reesa, I know we haven't spoken about this, but you must be aware that the honeymoon from the press is over. Tomorrow when we reach Maria Island they'll be there."

Reesa stepped from under the running water, taking the soap that Dake handed her and beginning to wash. "Are you sure? I didn't think I would have to face them until we reached the mainland again."

"Not a chance. They'll be there. They wouldn't miss something as juicy as this, especially since they know by now I'm aboard the *Windward.*"

"Someone would tell them," she said flatly, applying shampoo to her hair.

"Who knows how they find out anything?"

Reesa's head jerked up and she winced. "Liza and Miguel, Miguelito too—they'll pester them so."

"I'll try to get someone to run interference for them," Dake said, trying to soothe her.

Reesa nodded, not questioning him, knowing that when he decided to do something, it would get done.

"Think you can come out of there now? Do you want me to rinse the lather from your hair?"

"Yes. No," Reesa snapped, turning her back on him.

"Sweet heaven, darling." He caught his breath in a laugh. "The view is wonderful." He leaned down and kissed her buttocks, then turned and strode from the room, his boiling libido making him barely aware of her gasps.

He leaned one hand against the top of the porthole, staring unseeingly out over the rolling blue waters of the Caribbean. What the hell was he to do about her? He wasn't about to let her go. Maybe after she told her story to the authorities—He smacked the metal wall with the palm of his hand. "Stop lying to yourself, Masters. You can't let her go because you still want her, because she has the same hold on you that she's always had." He muttered curses and ground his teeth.

Reesa came out of the bathroom behind him and he turned, feeling a smile lift the corners of his mouth as he stared at the bedraggled Reesa Hawke, film star.

"Stop laughing," she blurted out, trying to dry the wet strands of hair clinging to her head while holding closed his terry bathrobe that hung on her like a sack and trailed along behind her. "I've seen you look worse."

"Never!" Dake let the laughter out when she glared at him. She came at him with one fist raised.

The errant bathrobe tripped her up and sent her sprawling into his arms.

"Great entrance," Dake drawled, lifting her straight up his body.

"Thank you." Reesa sniffed. "Now, if you would just let me get dressed—"

"I'll dry your hair first," he told her, then proceeded to take a hair dryer out of a drawer, plug it in, and begin the process before she could do more than sputter.

His gentleness quieted her. She was glad to sit on the bed, leaning against him, and let him brush and blow-dry her long, thick hair. "I don't remember it being so heavy, so wavy." His voice barely penetrated the noise of the dryer, but Reesa heard what he said and looked up at him. His smile made her heart turn over like a flapjack in a hot pan. She felt the familiar weakness in her knees that his gaze always caused.

"It was a long, lonely time without you," he said when he shut off the switch.

"I didn't feel any of that," she mused. "All I knew was that I didn't want to remember, that there was something in my life that made me unhappy. I was sure I had been a criminal or something awful like that."

"Instead, it was because we had been fighting that night. We both said we were through. Neither of us would back down." His voice had a rawness to it, but his hand didn't falter as he continued the long, slow strokes of the brush.

"Yes," she whispered through lips as stiff as pasteboard.

"I would unsay everything I said to you that night if I could." Dake's voice was just audible.

"I—I think there are some things that can't be unsaid." Reesa felt a tightness in her chest.

"We could try again," Dake urged.

She tried to smile at him when he stepped away from her and rested the brush on the dresser, putting one hand up to massage her temple. "Maybe we could—"

The knock on the door had Dake cursing in round, fluent Saxon terms.

"Yes," he barked through the door.

"Ah, Mr. Masters, it's Consuela. I'm looking for Reesa. You see—"

Reesa walked past Dake to turn the latch and open the door. "I'm here, Connie."

Relieved, Consuela let out a whush of air. "Good. I've looked everywhere for you. Rehearsal is in another half-hour and we—hey, what's wrong with you? Are you ill?"

"You could say that," Dake remarked, standing close to Reesa and gesturing to Consuela to enter the suite. "An illness from a bottle."

Reesa shot him an angry look, then winced when the sharp action caused a pain to ripple through her head. "Damn fool," she muttered when he chuckled and kissed her cheek.

"Hungover? You?" Consuela was slack-jawed for a moment, then she grinned. "All those times you lectured me when Barney and I—" Her smile fell away, her lips trembled.

"What's wrong, Connie?" Reesa took her arm and led her toward the sofa.

"Barney Freedling has taken leave and gone back to Norway, no doubt to marry his Anna." She gulped and abruptly sat down in one of the lounge chairs. "I'll never see him again," she whispered, staring at Reesa. "He'll join the staff of another ship—"

"But, Connie, you don't know that."

The other woman nodded her head fiercely. "I know. I know." She blinked up at Reesa, her gaze sliding past her to Dake. "But Mr. Masters doesn't want to hear my troubles—"

"Who cares what he wants." Reesa's words were harsh, so much did she hate to see the misery on her friend's face.

"Thank you," Dake snarled softly. Her words had shafted right through him! No one in the world could do that to him but Reesa. He was immune to anyone else's words and most of anyone's actions. He had always been a strong, self-reliant man able to turn aside the annoying vicissitudes of life with ease. But with Reesa it was different. She could lay him low with a few words—and he hated it.

Reesa turned around and looked at him, one finger massaging her left eyebrow. "You know what I mean," she said testily. She looked back at Consuela. "You're hurting now, I know, but—"

"No." Consuela surged to her feet. "I will not let him get to me. I'm going to forget he ever existed." Her eyes glittered. "Now, come on, Reesa." She sniffed, then gave a watery laugh when Reesa groaned. "Be brave, sister, bear your burden with grace."

"Don't giggle, Connie, or I may strangle you!" Reesa said, more than a little relieved that Consuela *was* laughing.

"You had better wait here until I bring you some jeans and a blouse." Consuela hastily left the cabin.

When Dake didn't say anything, Reesa looked at him. She coughed. "Ah, I can wait in the hall if you like," she fished, trying to fathom what had put that haughty yet thunderous look on his face now. It had always been like that between them! She never knew what was going to set him off next! And he never even seemed to notice if her feelings were hurt about anything. She fumed to herself. How easy it was for him! He never became involved in earthly beings and their stupid emotions—oooh, her head hurt so much.

"Do as you please," Dake snapped. "And if you want something for your head, try the Bromo-Seltzer in the bathroom cabinet. I have a date to do some skeet shooting with First Officer Tor Renquist." Dake spun away from her and went into the bathroom, slamming the door behind him.

"You won't beat him," Reesa muttered after him, her head thumping like a steel drum. "He is one of the champion shooters in all Norway." She poked her tongue at the bathroom door, then moaned and held her head again. She went over to the door and banged on it. "How am I to get the Bromo-Seltzer if you are in there?"

The door opened. One hand came out holding the seltzer bottle.

Reesa took the bottle. The hand retreated. The door was slammed.

"Capricious jackass!" She held the cool bottle to her forehead and walked to the bar built into a corner of the sitting room. She half filled a glass with water and dropped in some of the crystals. The fizzing sounded too loud. She drank it down without stopping.

She answered the knock on the door, opening it to Consuela, who entered with a small stack of clothing.

"I brought underpants and your sandals too. Is the sleeveless shirt okay?"

Reesa shrugged. "I don't have a bra, but who will be looking?" She dropped Dake's terry robe from behind her.

Consuela gasped and jerked her head toward the closed bathroom door. "What if he comes out?" she whispered.

"What if he does?" Reesa grimaced when her friend looked shocked. How could she explain to Consuela that she was used to being nude around Dake, that they had lived together for years. "Ah, I've known him for a long time."

"Even so—" Consuela began, then gasped when the bathroom door opened and Dake walked out into the room just as Reesa, standing in her fresh underpants, began pulling the sleeveless cotton shirt over her head.

When Consuela saw the way Dake's gaze roved over Reesa, she closed her own eyes.

"What is it, Connie? Do you have a headache now?"

"Not yet," she mumbled to Reesa, then opened one eye to stare at the chestnut-haired giant who seemed frozen in place.

"That vest shows your breasts, darling," he remarked.

"Oh, dear, now the headache *is* coming," Consuela bleated, throwing a quick glance at the door, as though measuring the distance.

Reesa looked down at herself, then over to Dake. "I'm covered." She dragged on her jeans and zipped them. "Thank you for your hospitality," she said to Dake, tugged at the crouching Consuela, and left the cabin.

"You shouldn't attack him like that," Consuela said. "That's like wrestling a jaguar bare-handed." She shivered. "Those eyes turn green and brown and yellow just like a big cat's eyes."

"He has hazel eyes with brown rings around the irises," Reesa informed her. "They seem to change color with his moods," she mused aloud.

"I thought he was going to eat you up with a shrimp fork when he came out of the bathroom and saw you in your briefs, pulling on your shirt. That man is scary, but so beautiful!"

Reesa felt a dart of jealousy.

"How many men like him have you met, Reesa?" Consuela asked eagerly.

None, Reesa thought. There was no other man in the world like David Kennedy Masters. He was a once-struck mold with no copies. "Thousands," Reesa said to her friend. "Filmland is crawling with creatures like him."

"I don't know why you're lying to me, but you are. You're blinking real fast like you do when you're trying to pull something on me," Consuela said serenely, laughing when Reesa grimaced.

"Know-it-all." Reesa sighed. "I have never met anyone like Dake. I hate him, but—"

"I know the feeling." Consuela grinned weakly.

The two women walked in when the rehearsal was well under way. The routines devised by the central office in Miami varied little from cruise to cruise, however, so neither one felt lost about starting rehearsals late.

Reesa was halfway through a routine with Andy when a flashbulb went off in her face and a voice in the darkened nightclub said, "Thank you, Miss Hawke."

She shaded her eyes and stared out beyond the microphone. "Who is it?"

"Wallings from the *Tribune*, Miss Hawke. I was flown out here on a helicopter."

The houselights came up and Reesa stared at the sandy-haired man fiddling with camera equipment hanging from both shoulders and around his neck. He did look familiar. "We've met, haven't we?"

Wallings looked pleased as he nodded vigorously. "Yes. I shot film on you many times. I'm glad you remember me."

"Look, Wallings, would you mind not shooting until we're done with rehearsal? Then you can take plenty of pictures. Okay?"

"Ah, all right Miss Hawke, if you promise me several good shots and an interview?"

"Pirate," Reesa accused mildly, then nodded assent.

"Thank you, Miss Hawke." Wallings beamed before fading to a corner of the darkened nightclub, working furiously with his camera equipment.

"Now, ladies," Zev Lizzman croaked in a smoke-roughened voice, "it would be nice to get on with this."

Reesa thought he was going to say more, his razor tongue well known to most of the staff, but then he looked at her, bit his lip, and came toward her. She rolled her eyes at Consuela. "Now what?"

"He's probably decided on a human sacrifice for the grand finale and you've been chosen," Consuela said from the side of her mouth.

"Thank you, sister dear," Reesa muttered back as the rather harried cruise director approached them.

"Look, ah, Maria, ha ha, I mean Reesa . . . er . . . Miss Hawke . . ." Zev coughed.

"What's the matter with you, Zev? You're behaving as though your pet piranha died." Reesa frowned when he shouted with laughter; other members of the staff looked at them open-mouthed. "What's up?" Reesa snapped.

"Ah, well, you see, ah, Richie Whyte, our comedian, who does the big show, is down with the flu."

"A giant hangover, I'll bet," Consuela muttered.

Zev glared at her, then looked back at Reesa, a

smile appearing on his face. "So I wondered if you would like to sing a few songs for us."

"You always told me I sang like a dying frog." Reesa chuckled.

Zev looked aghast. "No, no, ah, what I meant was you have a soft-pitched voice, and you should sing low—"

"So low you can't be heard—" Consuela chortled, earning another fuming look from Zev.

"So if you would sing for us?" Zev looked back at Reesa.

Reesa shrugged, knowing she would, since her friends needed her. "I'll do it for the Sea Dive Group." She looked right into Zev's eyes. "You couldn't afford me otherwise, Zev."

His forced laugh had the others turning to look at them once more. "Maybe we should get on with the rest of the rehearsal. Would you like to rehearse later? I could get Harry to accompany you."

"I'll accompany myself." It flashed through Reesa's mind that she did play the piano, that she had done so in small supper clubs across the country before she had gotten a part in pictures—a small part, but it had launched her career.

They rehearsed the comedy routine that all of them had a part in, then the rest of the staff wandered away.

When Wallings approached her, Reesa nodded, posed for a few pictures, answered a half dozen questions, then called a halt to it. She was finally alone.

Reesa sat down at the piano. Her fingers seemed stiff and alien as they did some warm-up exercises, first treble, then bass, then both. She sighed, rubbing her hands together, trying to stretch the fingers of each hand. "You are sadly out of practice, old girl."

"But it still sounds wonderful to hear you play," a voice whispered from the darkness beyond the stage.

Reesa didn't look up from the keyboard as she

answered Dake. "As I recall, you played quite well yourself."

"Ah, yes, dear Aunt Minerva thought she had a concert musician at last in the Masters family." Dake's silken voice held amusement.

"Instead, she got a performing seal that fits right into that zoo situation you call a family." Reesa's laugh sounded harsh to her own ears.

"Why didn't you just chuck them all out in the street when they came to our house?"

"It wasn't my house."

"Don't you dare say it wasn't your house." Dake's sibilant hiss menaced the room. "Everything was ours . . . together."

Always, at other times, when they had had this argument, Reesa finally concurred that, yes, everything they shared was equally owned, because the house was in her name as were all the furnishings. Now a balloon of resentment seemed to burst inside of her and different words tumbled from her mouth. "On paper it was mine, but you and yours steamrolled over me as though I weren't there. The highbred, Brahmin discourtesy of your visiting cousins was everywhere, like warm molasses. Your parents were nice to me, that's true." Her head came up and she looked away from the keyboard out into the darkened nightclub, one hand shading her eyes. "I don't want that anymore. I don't want the sham of your family around me, telling me about dear Linda and sweet Cynthia. Climb out of your pit, then talk to me, but don't ask me to lower myself into that morass you call a way of life." She squinted, trying to pierce the blanket of darkness. "Dake? Dake, did you hear me?" She heard a muffled thud and recognized it as the door to the nightclub closing. Dake was gone!

She went through a few songs, accompanying herself, trying to ignore the block of hurt and tears lodged in her chest.

An hour later she left the nightclub and went back to the cabin she shared with Consuela.

Her roommate threw open the door when she heard Reesa's key. "Hurry. Wait until you see." Consuela pulled Reesa's arm, yanking her into the tiny cabin. "Look what Dake Masters sent us." She waved her arm, almost knocking down two dresses on hangers suspended from a ceiling hook.

"Dresses?" Reesa stared at the silks, slowly swaying, then she looked at Consuela, excitement glittering from her eyes. "We have our own clothes," she began, then when she saw her best friend's face begin to crumple, she back-pedaled. "But who wouldn't rather wear something new?"

"I would!" Consuela gasped with laughter, relief spreading over her round face. She reached out and hugged Reesa.

They were still hugging each other when there was a knock.

Reesa opened the door and took a tissue-wrapped flower that Kim, a cabin boy, offered her. She closed the door, shrugging at Consuela. "There's a card . . . oh, the envelope has your name on it, Connie." She smiled and handed the flower to her friend. "I'll wash up first while you look at your gift."

Reesa hurried in the bathroom, knowing that they had costumes to don for the show, so they would have to get there early.

When she came out of the tiny shower room, Consuela was sitting on the stool in front of the vanity mirror, staring at the red rose in her hand.

"It's from Barney Freedling. He's back on the ship and he wants to see me, to talk to me after the show." She looked up at Reesa round-eyed. "What should I do?"

"What you want to do. See him, if you wish, or don't see him, if that's your choice, but make up your own mind." Reesa kissed Consuela's cheek, then pulled her to her feet. "For now, you have to get going."

"Yes." Consuela still stared at the rose in her hand. Then she seemed to shake herself.

"I can put that in water for you," Reesa told her gently.

"No need," Consuela mumbled as she went into the bathroom. "It has its own water holder."

Reesa fluffed her thick, curling black hair with her fingers, staring at the two silk dresses. A cherry-red silk with a ruffled hem was in Consuela's size, and though both dresses were calf-length, the cherry-colored dress seemed to have more substance than the grape-green dress. "It looks like something from the thirties with the halter neck. Oh, dear, it doesn't have a back. I can't wear a bra," she exclaimed, twirling the dress on the hanger. It was a good thing the garment was lined, since she'd only be able to wear briefs with it.

She sat down in front of the vanity mirror, applying moisturizer and blush to her face, outlining her eyes, but doing nothing to her naturally dark lashes and brows. She decided to wear the green quarry-stone earrings that her Indian friend, Figueroa, had made for her, and no other jewelry.

When Consuela came out and began to dress, the two of them were bumping against each other, but finally they were both ready.

"God, don't let my mother ever see you looking like that, Reesa. She'll put you in a convent. I can see your navel and your coccyx," Consuela mused as she turned her friend this way and that.

"How about you?" Reesa laughed. "Barney will go out of his mind."

Consuela blushed and pressed her hands down the front of her off-the-shoulder gown. "Too much bosom showing?"

"Just right. Shall we go?"

"Yes . . . Wait. I want to take my flower." Consuela grinned.

The two women hurried upstairs to prepare for the first show. Afterward, when the second show was over, there would be a party for everyone.

To Reesa's surprise, the people in the first seating were very enthusiastic about her indifferent accompaniment on the piano. They seemed to enjoy her singing as well. She was more confident with that.

At the second show it seemed to be even more crowded, and when it was her time to sing, she felt a choking nervousness that she hadn't experienced since she had played in her first supper club.

She walked over to the piano when the polite applause died, her stomach doing flipflops as she faced the keyboard. She took deep breaths, her hands poised.

"Let me play for you, darling. You stand up and sing. You'll be more comfortable," Dake whispered at her side.

She looked up at him, wondering where he'd come from, not noticing him when she had first sat down at the piano. She stared at him, mute.

"Wouldn't you be more at ease standing in front of the mike, facing your audience, while I played?" Dake asked gently.

"Yes." She gulped, reaching for his hands and grasping them in hers.

He lifted her from the piano bench, smiling at her in the glare of the lights, not seeming to notice the rustling sounds of the audience. He kept hold of her hand as he turned her to face the crowd in the nightclub. "Ladies and gentlemen, Reesa Hawke."

During the applause that rose again, Dake went back to the piano, rolled a few bars, then went into the introduction of the first song she had marked on the sheet.

After the first ballad ended, there was a long

silence. Reesa kept her head down, then lifted it slowly.

Clapping hands and shouts of approval came at her like a wave. She inhaled a deep breath of satisfaction. She turned to look at Dake and he was nodding and smiling.

She sang four songs, and each time she was greeted with roars of approval. The confidence that had become part of her after years of training and hard work began to assert itself once more and she felt a surge of power, of delight in doing what she had always loved to do—perform.

When the applause died away on the last song, Reesa cleared her throat and looked out past the lights to the shadowy faces. "Ladies and gentlemen, this is my first performance as Reesa Hawke in a long time . . . and I hope I've made you as happy as you've made me."

Applause interrupted her and stayed heavy until she held up her hand for quiet.

"I want to sing you one last song, one that I recorded, but to my knowledge was never released." She coughed again to ease the huskiness of her throat. "At the time of my accident there were still problems with the album that included this number. It's a song from a Broadway show of some years back, titled *Annie* and the song is called 'Something Was Missing.'" Reesa backed from the microphone, turning to look at Dake, all at once realizing that he might not know the music.

His smile was a hard slash in his face, his nod of assent curt.

Puzzled, Reesa stared at him for a moment, then looked back at the audience when Dake played the introduction. The poignant words filled her mind and being, pouring from her mouth as the memory of her days with Miguel and Liza and backward to her days with Dake caught her in the tempo and words of the song.

The last note died away and a collective sigh swooshed through the audience. Then they were on their feet clapping and shouting.

Reesa stared at them, unable to move. When she felt the strong arm encircle her waist, she leaned back, relieved.

"You were wonderful. You never sang better," Dake whispered in her ear, his words having a sardonic tinge though. "And your album was released two months ago. It's been a sellout. I tried to prevent it being sold, but I couldn't."

"Why?" Reesa mouthed the word over the clapping, her head still dipping in response to the acclamation of the crowd.

"Because I couldn't stand the thought of listening to your voice wherever I went," he snarled in a low voice.

Reesa jerked back at his fierceness, but Dake drew her back close to him.

"Smile at your audience, darling," he hissed. "I hope you realize that our pictures will be all over the papers tomorrow."

"It won't be the first time," she charged, keeping the microphone away from her mouth.

"No, it won't, will it?" He bit out the words, his hand clenching at her waist.

At last she could move away from the stage, but instead of going behind the curtain, Dake led her down into the audience. "Wait, there's more show to do."

"Not for you. You're exhausted now." His mouth was stiff.

When Zev came out from the back, he followed them down the side of the room between the tables. People called congratulations to Reesa; Dake turned to face Zev, his body crouched, his eyes narrowed, like a big cat on the hunt.

"Ah, Reesa." Zev's laugh was forced. He nodded to the people at the nearby tables. "You want to come back and change into your—"

"No," Dake barked, his voice carrying over the music of the steel band that had just come onstage. "She's tired. And she's through for the night."

"Sure. No problem." Zev grinned weakly, his eyes shooting around him to see if people noticed the fuss. Most did not, but there were a few who kept an avid eye on Dake's wolfish smile, his bared teeth, his body looking ready to pounce. "Ah, staying for the dancing?" Zev asked.

"No," Dake shot back. Then he took hold of Reesa's arm and propelled her in front of him and out of the room.

Reesa waited until they were in the large foyer where there were fewer people, then she clawed at the hand on her arm. "Stop it. I don't appreciate your imitation of King Kong. I should be back there."

"No. If you don't want to go to my suite and lie down, then I'll get you something to eat."

"No need. I'll eat at the midnight buffet. I feel like gambling."

Dake shrugged. "Fine."

Reesa stopped in her tracks. "And you had no right to tell Zev that I wouldn't be in the rest of the show."

"Was there much more?"

"There was a finale and—"

"So you didn't miss much," Dake interjected, taking her arm again. "Let's take a turn around the deck and get some air. You'll feel better."

"I don't feel bad." Reesa was unable to free her arm from his grip.

"You're tired," he said.

"Am not," she answered.

"What did you say?" He put his arm around her,

keeping her steady as the ship plowed through the blue waters of the Gulf of Mexico heading for the Straits of Florida.

"Nothing." She felt his arms go around her, keeping her body back against him as they looked over the railing to the water creaming past the ship to froth at the stern.

"There's Orion," Dake whispered, lifting his arm and pointing.

Reesa nodded, not moving her head from his shoulder. "The stars are so close on the water, so clear," she said softly, her back feeling warm and cosseted as she rested against him. The breath left her body when she felt his palm press on her middle, the hand moving slowly downward. "Dake!"

"Yes, darling." His lips fanned her ear, then fastened in gentle abrasion at her neck. "I'm here."

"I know that," she squeaked. "You shouldn't—"

"Shouldn't what?" He growled softly, his hand pressing lower on her pelvic bone.

"Huh?" Reesa croaked, closing her eyes.

"I've arranged for a plane to pick us up in Miami, then we can fly to Maria Island." His hand whorled from hip to hip, pressing gently, his breathing growing ragged.

"Oh," Reesa responded. Then her eyes popped open. "But Maria Island doesn't have an airstrip."

"Not to worry, darling. It's a seaplane," Dake said in a soothing tone.

"Oh. We have lots of water." Reesa licked her dry lips.

"I figured you might." The velvet amusement in his voice surrounded her like a rope.

"We aren't walking." Reesa took a deep breath.

"What?" Dake kissed her temple, letting his mouth graze down to her neck again.

"You said we would walk on the deck." Reesa gasped.

"So I did." Dake turned her in his arms, his breath rasping her face. "You are one beautiful lady."

"You're pretty too." Reesa giggled, feeling her body break away in chunks and float right off the deck of the *Windward*.

Dake shook her gently. "Did you just giggle?"

"I think so." She looked up at him, her eyes half closed.

"I think I've heard you do that only once before, when we went away on that ski trip to the Laurentians and no one knew who we were."

"We were alone . . . and we talked . . . and walked . . . and skied . . ." She cuddled into the circle of his arm as they walked on the deck, their bodies pressing against each other.

"We'll do it again," Dake said.

"No, I don't think so. We always said we would do it again, but we never did. There was always money to make, another empire to build, industries to buy and sell—"

"Don't," Dake rasped out.

"Isn't it the truth?"

"Yes."

"I've been happy off the treadmill," she mused, feeling his arm convulse around her.

"Have you? I suppose you'd like to stay off it then?"

"Yes, I think I would. Oh, I want to perform now and then, but I don't want to go back to the frenetic lifestyle we had. I just want to earn a good living at what I do best. I won't be eaten up by it again."

"I see." Dake felt as if his insides had shredded and started to bleed. She didn't want a life with him again! She didn't want what they had! "Then we'll have to change what we had, drive down a different road."

"And at a different speed," Reesa said forcefully.

She didn't say she didn't want him in her new life.

His mind ballooned with relief. "We can find a quieter place to live than California."

"I liked living on Maria Island," Reesa offered.

His mind raced like the Silver Streak out of control. "We could live there most of the time. Then we could maybe have a . . . a ranch in California, something off the beaten path."

Reesa nodded. "California is a large state."

"Very large." His ego reasserted itself. His natural self-confidence resurfaced. "We can pick it out together."

"No." Reesa turned and faced him on the deck, her body barely moving as she adjusted herself to the motion of the ship. "You're welcome to visit me on Maria Island at any time or see me at the house that I think I may purchase at Malibu, but you choose your own ranch, whatever you like."

Her clear calm gaze froze him. "Your eyes are very painful *flèches d'amour*, darling." Silky menace emanated from him. "I can't be gotten rid of that easily."

Reesa took a step back, her spine hitting the railing. "I'm not trying to get rid of you. I'm—I'm only trying to assess our relationship realistically."

"You sound like a mail-order psychologist." Dake felt as though his whole body were sweating blood. She damn well wasn't going to open his veins and leave him for dead! She would find out just what kind of adversary she was facing!

"I've looked at myself through murky glasses for months, thinking that what I didn't want to remember was some crime that I had committed. All that while I kept thinking how much I wanted to protect the way of life I was leading." She looked away from him, along the deck of the ship to the stern. "I wasn't ecstatically happy because there was the cloud of not knowing my past, but still I was productive and I had friends." She looked back at him. "I don't want to reenter that tinsel tiptoeing with the so-called elite. I never liked your cousins and I have to assume that the rest of your family is the same way. You never knew mine except my uncle, who is much like your clan. I don't want to move in those circles with the supercilious remarks behind my back." She looked into his eyes. "Your family are bluebloods, but they are rather stupid people." She watched his lips part in surprise. "Oh, yes, they are draped with degrees, from Harvard, Yale."

"Harvard and Princeton," Dake whispered.

"Whatever." Reesa shrugged. "But they are stupid and one-dimensional. They give to charities but they never lend a hand to anyone. They pay lip service to causes, but they truly aid no one but themselves." Reesa shrugged again. "I want to belong to a better class of people, like Miguel and Liza and Consuela and her mother."

"You don't know me or my family." Bitterness filled Dake. She didn't know him at all. They spun on the same world axis, but she didn't understand him, and he was damned if he would explain that he was not like the people she described.

"I don't want to belong to anyone anymore." Tears welled inside her as she sensed Dake withdrawing from her. *I love you, David Kennedy Masters, but I know I can never have you—we are two different people now.*

Seven

Dake had walked Reesa back to the cabin she shared with Consuela, kissed her coolly on the cheek, said good night, and left.

All night she had hugged her pillow to her mouth, trying to smother the sobs that shook her so that she wouldn't waken Consuela, who had come in very late.

The next day she was up early getting ready to collect the latecomers' diving equipment. She had drawn the duty at the Sea Dive desk next to the purser's office.

She talked and smiled with many of the people she had had in her classes and welcomed the diversion so that she didn't have to dwell on Dake Masters.

There was a long lull and Reesa was sure that she was through, when she looked up and saw a beaming Consuela come toward her dragging Barney Freedling by the arm.

"Reesa, look, look." Consuela shoved out her left hand to display a ring. "Barney and I going to be married. He's coming back to Maria Island with me to meet my mother."

"I had no sooner reached the mainland," Barney said excitedly, "than I knew I made a mistake leaving Consuela. I phoned my family to explain that I couldn't marry Anna when I loved Consuela. My grandmother said that I did the right thing. My Connie is wearing only a temporary ring; it is my grandmother's she'll wear as soon as it arrives from Norway." Barney smiled at Reesa, then looked down fondly at Consuela. "I was honor bound to talk to Anna and her family before I could talk to my Connie."

"Yes, of course you were." Reesa felt like laughing and crying when she looked at the stolid Norwegian and the beaming Consuela. "I know you'll be very happy."

"Yes. We will." Barney nodded his head vigorously. "I have saved much money so that I can buy a fishing boat." He nodded once firmly.

"That's nice," Reesa replied, wondering why he felt it necessary to buy a fishing boat when he would be onboard the *Windward* or another ship six or eight months of the year.

"Barney is going to run a tour and charter service. He is very familiar with the weather and the waters in the Caribbean," Connie said proudly.

"Oh. Of course. Miguel does that."

"Yes. I know. I am going to ask him if he would like me as his partner," he announced. "I do not wish for Consuela and me to be away from each other very much."

Reesa could feel her eyes widening as she stared at him.

"I think Miguel will want to," Consuela interjected.

"I hope so," Reesa whispered, but the other two didn't hear her. They turned away with their arms around each other, smiles sliding all over their faces.

"Oh." Consuela said over her shoulder, still held closely to Barney. "We'll be leaving with you and Mr. Masters." She looked back at Barney, then they wandered away.

"Wait," Reesa called, turning a few heads of the debarking passengers. "I might not be going with Dake Masters," she muttered, banging her fist on the counter, not caring when several persons looked her way again.

It seemed to take forever to tie up the loose ends necessary in order that the crew might depart the ship. The *Windward* was due for a good going-over in dry dock, and most of the crew would be switching to one of her sister ships, namely the *Leeward*. For others like Consuela, Barney, and Reesa, it would mean a long-needed rest.

When Reesa finally got down to her cabin, Consuela had already packed and left the ship.

Contrary to her usually neat ways, Reesa threw her belongings in the two canvas sea bags that Miguel had given her, then struggled out of the cabin and along the corridor to the crew's exit area from the ship.

Perspiring from the weight of the two bags, she was about to signal an attendant to help her get her things to a taxi when a liveried man stopped in front of her.

"I'll take your things, Miss Hawke. Just follow me." The man in the black uniform threw her bags over his shoulder and marched away.

"Now, just a minute," Reesa said. Then when she realized that he wasn't stopping to listen to her, she sprinted after him. "Wait! Hey!"

She was still running after the man when he passed through the customs building; he'd slowed to a walk as he reached a limousine standing at the curb. Puffing, she put a hand on his arm to stop him when he opened the trunk and placed her bags inside.

"Darling, you're out of condition." Dake was at her side, sliding his arm around her waist and urging her toward the open door of the vehicle.

"So," she panted, trying to dig in her heels, "you're behind this . . . this abduction."

"How dramatic," Dake drawled, loosening her grip on the door handle where she was trying to brace herself. "Get in the car or I'll toss you in there."

"Don't get tough with me, buster," she snapped.

"Reesa, what are you doing?" Consuela asked from inside the car. "Aren't you coming with us?"

"She is," Dake said, taking advantage of her surprise at seeing Consuela and Barney in the backseat to lift her into the middle seat in front of the other couple. He followed her in and closed the door with a decisive bang. "Step on it. We have a plane waiting," he told the driver, who nodded, closed his door, and roared away from the curb.

"Let me go," Reesa hissed at Dake.

"Damn you, I'm not letting you go. Wherever you step or move from now on, I'll be right behind you," he vowed in a rasping voice.

"You're not my keeper," Reesa said through her teeth.

"We'll just see what I'm going to be in your life." All at once Dake straightened. "Hell. Where did they come from?" He glared at two men with cameras who tried to jump in front of the car. "Lose them, Henry. There's a hundred in it for you if they don't follow us to the seaplane hanger."

"Right, Mr. Masters," Henry answered with a lilt in his voice.

The car leaped ahead like a live thing, careening down streets. Horns blasted, pedestrians shook their fists, but Henry was a man on a mission.

Reesa heard Consuela squeal in the backseat. She gasped when she saw a delivery truck back over a curb, its rear end to a warehouse entrance. "We can't go under the truck," she whimpered, not protesting when Dake wrapped her in his arms.

"We'd die together," Dake murmured.

"Aaagh. Sadist." Reesa tightened her grip on him, burrowing her head into his chest as the car bumped, lurched, and swayed, the sound of over-turning trashcans forcing her to open her eyes and raise her head. "Where did Henry take us?" She sounded out each syllable in a husky voice.

"Not under the truck," Dake stated. "But up on the sidewalk for about two blocks. We've bumped into a few containers and gotten a few dents on the fend-ers." He shrugged, then leaned forward and tapped the driver on the shoulder. "Good work, Henry. I think you lost them."

"I think he's lost more than 'them.'" Reesa glared at the driver and tried to straighten her clothes and push back the hair tumbling about her face.

Dake threw her one narrow-eyed look and contin-ued speaking to Henry. "I'll want the baggage loaded onto the plane as soon as possible, then I want you to go back the way you came, talk to the merchants we passed, and tell them to bill me for any damage. Don't haggle over price."

"Yes, sir," Henry responded, seeming delighted with his morning's imitation of a stuntman in an old Steve McQueen movie.

Reesa leaned over the back of the seat to gaze at a pale-faced Consuela, still held close in Barney's arms. "Are you all right?"

Consuela nodded. "Now I know how it feels to get caught in a video game!" She looked up at her "intended," noticing that his eyes were bright with excitement. "You enjoyed it!" she accused.

"Yes." Barney nodded vigorously. "I would like to have driven the car." He squeezed Consuela. "But I did not like it that you were frightened, *mi cortijo*." He kissed the top of her head.

Reesa's mouth dropped. "But—"

"He is just learning Spanish," Consuela said defensively. "He already speaks French and German."

Reesa closed her mouth and sank down into her seat again. Before she could struggle free, Dake had her in his arms once more, leaning over her, brushing his lips into her hair.

"Were you going to be so unkind as to tell Barney that he just called his loved one a farmhouse?" Dake whispered into her ear.

"I think he meant to say '*mi cortejo*,' meaning my sweetheart." Reesa felt her heart bump against her ribs as his hand closed in a gentle caress over her breast.

"Must be, *mi cortejo*," Dake muttered, a breathless sound to his laugh.

"We're here, sir." Henry stopped the car with a jerk, pulled on the brake, pressed the button to open the trunk, and was out of the car in a flash.

Dake released Reesa with a quick peck on the nose. "We'll continue this a little later."

"Stuff it."

Dake shouted with laughter. "The elegant Miss Teresa Martita Hawke from the old Californio family would never have said such a thing." He jumped out of the car to signal to an attendant to bring a dolly to load the luggage on; then he proceeded to help Henry.

"Of course I said things like that," Reesa mused to herself. Had Dake thought she was stuffy? How could that be? He was the one from the "cashmere-attitude family." For a moment it flashed through her mind what kind of life she had had with Dake. They always dined out, it seemed. They were always dressing to go someplace. Even when they were on the yacht, others were with them, and every day was filled with group activities ending with a formal dinner, followed by a party. Except in bed, they were rarely alone. "I was afraid of him, fearful of the turmoil, the vortex, the whirlpool of his love. . . ."

"What whirlpool, Reesa?" Consuela tugged her overnight case behind her as she slid across the seat to get out of the car. Barney was already out of the car and helping to get the luggage loaded on the seaplane.

"Just thinking out loud." Reesa smiled at the woman who was more than friend, more than sister. "Uh-oh, Dake is waving at us, looking like a bear," She drawled, making Consuela laugh.

"I don't know how you dare pull his tail the way you do. You're so sure of him, aren't you?" Consuela shook her head, smiling, then walked toward the plane, hurrying when Barney gestured to her.

Reesa stood there, her mouth agape. "Me? Sure of him? Dear heaven, you must be joking."

"Rees! Damm it, will you move?" Dake called to her, then moved toward her, his strides long, his face grim.

"I'm coming. I'm coming. Cool your jets," she flung at him, using the slang that was common among the Sea Dive Group.

Dake glared at her. "And you never used to talk in that preppie way either."

"Sawry, dahling," Reesa drawled, flapping her hand, gliding past him, her nose in air. "I shall try to remember to be more Boston-snobbish in the future."

"Bitch," he commented at her back, his hand coursing over her backside, then gently pinching her. "Nice."

Reesa stopped in her tracks, turned around, and kicked him in the shin. It hurt her toe because she was wearing sandals, but it gave her great satisfaction when Dake grabbed his leg. "I've never done that before either," she simpered, batting her lashes at him.

He glared at her, his one leg held up while he massaged it. "I owe you a few, lady, not the least of which were my nights in jail."

Reesa walked to the plane sensing he was beside her but not looking at him. "How could they hold you in jail? The battery of lawyers your family would provide would swamp the police department. Besides, you have about twenty uncles and cousins who are lawyers."

"Twenty-two, but that doesn't seem to matter when there is a question of murder involved, when there is nobody, but a few of my acquaintances onboard the yacht give evidence that you and I have been arguing for two days—"

"Three days, the way I remember it," Reesa interjected, trying to imagine Dake in jail, feeling sick at the picture conjured up in her mind.

Henry stepped up to them and touched his cap. "All set, Mr. Masters. I'll take care of everything at this end."

"Good." Dake turned around and helped Reesa through the door of the plane, the sound of the propeller engines smothering conversation.

Consuela was sitting with Barney, cuddled into the crook of his arm, her eyes going constantly to the ring on her left hand.

When they roared across the water of the channel, they could see the M/S *Windward* anchored on the far side. It had taken them twenty minutes to come around and over the bridge to the seaplane hanger. If they had been able to take a boat across, it would have taken them five minutes.

Reesa stared out the small window of the plane at the *Windward* and wondered if she would ever see it again. The engine of the aircraft revved up; the plane began its surging course to take off from the channel. Then they were airborne and it was quieter.

"Do you think we've lost the reporters?" Dake asked, chuckling.

Reesa's head swirled toward him. "Decidedly!" Suddenly, though, she had a distasteful image of men crawling all over Miguel's small house and fenced-in yard.

"I think so. If Henry keeps his mouth shut . . . and his job will depend on that!"

"How do you know that?"

"I own the limousine service he works for," Dake said.

"Good Lord, when did that avaricious family of yours move into that area?"

"When they found it was easier to get a charter if they owned the airline." Dake shrugged. "Take the sour look off your face, love. You've always known my family has money. Don't turn it into a hanging offense now."

"I despise their arrogance, not their money." She looked back out the small window at the azure sky fluffed here and there with clouds. It flashed through her mind that she didn't know his family that well, that only his cousins had irritated her with their pompous ways, that she had met his parents briefly and they were very courteous.

It was a hand-laundered day, Reesa thought. The weather would be perfect on Maria Island, as usual. She smiled when she thought of the small parcel of land only fifteen miles long and three miles wide that was shaped like a horseshoe. The harbor at Maria was deep and navigable, and many cruise ships like the M/S *Windward* had ports-of-call there.

Reesa wasn't sure when she fell asleep, but all at once the murmurs of Barney and Consuela ceased to penetrate and her eyes closed.

"Wake up, darling. We're just landing," Dake said softly. "Open your eyes."

"Awake . . . I'm awake," she mumbled, moving her

head back and forth, her heavy lids rising at last. She glanced out the window at the island rushing by them as the pilot maneuvered the plane toward the landing pad for seaplanes near the beach. "Home," she sighed.

"Your home is with me," Dake said angrily, pulling her head around. He stared at her for long moments, then he surged to his feet, saying something in a low voice to Consuela and Barney.

Reesa watched him go foward to speak to the pilot, knowing her mouth was hanging slack. "Where the hell does he get off barking at me?"

"Reesa? Did you say something?" Consuela leaned forward against her seat belt as the plane bumped ashore, the small wheels carrying it up the ramp to dry land.

"I said I'm sorry we don't have killer sharks around Maria Island," she fumed.

"Those you can find in deeper waters," Barney informed her.

Consuela took one look at Reesa and pushed her fiancé to his feet, quickly undoing her seat belt and following him. "Hurry."

Barney frowned down at Consuela. "Why are we in such a rush?"

"Hurricane warnings," Consuela said, then pushed past him, pulling him in her wake.

Reesa bit down on the inside of her lip. "I am not going to take my anger with Dake out on everyone else."

"Did you call me, darling?" Dake drawled, his body crouched in the opening to the cockpit.

"No."

"Time to go, love." He came down the narrow aisle toward her, lifted her out of her seat, his mouth sealing hers like hot wax. "I'm looking forward to meeting your new family."

"I won't let you talk down to them," Reesa vowed,

her hands clenching and unclenching on his shirt front.

His hands gripped like a vise for a moment. "Where the hell do you get off talking to me like that? You don't know me at all."

"And you don't know me," she shot back. "I think that's been the problem all along. We don't know each other." She felt as though she had just knifed herself.

He released her with a jerk that made her body sway. He steadied her, his face looking like a stone carving. "Come along. Connie is anxious to get home, and we're riding together in one taxi."

"Tonio's," Reesa remarked, feeling gray and unattractive.

"Who?"

"Tonio has the only taxi service on the island. Sometimes his cousins drive for him in the busy times when a ship has docked, but other times it's Tonio who gets the people where they want to go. He also runs a sightseeing business."

"Great." Dake's lips barely moved.

Consuela was on pins and needles by the time they reached the cab, urging them to get inside so that they could leave.

Tonio grinned as all of them stored some of their gear in the small trunk of the car, then took the rest of it up on the front seat next to him. "You can sit on his lap, Maria." Tonio pointed to Dake. "He will not mind." He nodded his head and smiled when Reesa glared at him.

"Come on." Dake slipped into the backseat and held out his arms to her, pulling at her hand when she hesitated, then settling her on his lap.

At first she sat ramrod stiff, but after a few minutes of Tonio swerving around curves, blaring his horn at the hapless chickens who had wandered out into the road after the fine gravel, she was thrown back against Dake's chest.

His arms closed around her at once and tightened so that she couldn't move. "Comfy?" he drawled.

She didn't dignify his question with a response.

His hand kneaded her backside in tender fierceness, his eyes never leaving her face, her heart thudding against his chest wall. She was so beautiful! And he was becoming very aroused holding her like this.

"Ah, we may be in time to have some of Miguelito's birthday cake," Consuela said happily as the cab screeched to a stop, throwing Reesa forward. But Dake was there to pull her back to him, his teeth nipping at her neck.

"Here we are." Reesa wrestled free of him and almost tumbled out the door.

"Reesa, have you been drinking?" Consuela asked darkly.

"No, I have not—" Reesa began when she heard a shriek of laughter. She whirled to see Miguelito stagger out on the porch, Liza right behind him. "Darling," Reesa exclaimed, and pushed through the gate to run up the path. "Birthday boy!" She swooped him up and his chubby arms went round her neck, his delighted chortle filling her ear.

"If I had known you would have been home so quickly, I would have put off the party until today." Liza smiled and kissed Reesa's cheek, her eyes going in puzzled query to Barney, then to Dake.

"See." Consuela smiled, reaching for Miguelito. "I knew there would be enough cake." She turned when someone called her name. "There is Mama." She looked back at Liza. "This is Barney, Liza. We are to be married."

Mama Diego, a round, smiling woman, heard this as she bustled through the gate to come over to her neighbor's yard. "What is this? Should I not be the first to know? Is he working? How are you feeling, Maria, my child? Such excitement." She panted to a stop, managing to hug Consuela, Reesa, and Barney all at once.

Barney backed off and in his courtly way bowed over Mama Diego's hand. "I am happy to meet you and hope you will learn to like me, for I love your daughter very much."

Consuela burst into tears and hid her face in Barney's chest.

For the next hour there were introductions and everyone was talking at once.

Promising to come over after dinner that evening when Miguel would be home and they could all celebrate together, Consuela left with her mother and Barney.

The silence in the kitchen-living room area was broken by Miguelito's peals of laughter as Dake lay on the floor with the little boy setting up rows of dominoes that Miguelito was allowed to push down again.

Liza looked over the counter-divider into the living area, watching the smiling man and giggling child. Then she looked back at Reesa. "So, Maria, my sister, you are what Miguel and I always thought you to be—a special person. Reesa Hawke! Lord, I've seen you in movies and on television! Why didn't I know?" She shook her head, smiling.

Reesa hugged her. "If I am special, it's because you let me become part of a special family. Nothing is ever going to change that."

"And rightly so." Dake was standing in the opening between the kitchen and the living area, holding Miguelito in his arms. "We'll come back often, darling. Perhaps there is land around here where we could build. The fishing industry has always intrigued me." He smiled at Liza, ignoring Reesa's astonished expression. "I thought I would take him outside unless you have an objection."

"As long as Maria, I mean Reesa, says you are fine, you are okay with me." Liza grinned at him and made kissing sounds at the boy as he looked over Dake's shoulder and waved at the two women. "He is some kind of man. If my Miguel knew what I was thinking, he would wring my neck." Liza laughed and turned away to the sinkful of dishes.

Reesa bit her lip on the angry words that rose in her throat. She smothered the jealous pain she felt and laughed with Liza.

"I see the irritation in your eyes, sister mine," Liza said, placing a rinsed plate on the drainboard. "How you hate loving this man, yet you would strangle me if I made a play for him."

Reesa was indignant. "I would not."

Liza picked up a towel and handed it to Reesa. "No?"

"No. I would probably shoot you." Reesa grimaced when Liza laughed. "What am I going to do? I want to go back to my profession, but I can't have the same personal life I had. It would choke me—" She swallowed and tried to smile.

"Don't worry." Liza dried her hands and put an arm around Reesa. "Take it easy. Do what feels right and discard the rest."

"I want to remain your close friend and come back and stay on Maria Island sometime."

"Of course."

That night when Miguel came home the house rang with laughter and singing and everyone talking at once as neighbor after neighbor stopped by to meet the American who had come to take Maria from them.

Reesa and Miguel walked out in the yard, through the gate and along the dirt road.

"Liza says that you wish to stay as our family, Maria." Miguel grinned at her, not using the name *Reesa*. "That is good, because I was not about to let you go, little sister. Your man tells me that he proposed to buy the Seston estate at the end of the island. I told him the land was for sale." Miguel kicked at a stone. "He has also said that he would like to go into partnership in my fishing business." Miguel stopped walking and looked at her. "And Barney wants this too." He shrugged again. "Perhaps I am becoming a corporation."

She laughed. "Barney told me he wanted to go into business with you." She sobered, then she nodded. "Dake Masters is a principled man and a good businessman. You can trust him, as you can trust Barney."

"But you do not, little sister. You do not trust his heart or your own."

"No, I don't. But I'm going back to performing. I've made up my mind that it would be foolish of me to give up work that I love. Even though I had much satisfaction on the cruise ship, I will go back to acting." She turned, tucking her arm into his. "I will be home to visit at least twice a year, my brother."

"I'm content."

The next morning Reesa packed, leaving a few things behind.

"I'll be back in three or four months," she told the damp-eyed Liza and Miguel; Consuela and her mother were crying openly; Miguelito was laughing and pulling at Reesa's ear.

"We'll both be back," Dake said, giving Miguelito a kiss on the cheek. "I'll look into buying some boats when I'm in California and I'll have a lawyer check out that property."

Reesa opened her mouth to say something, but Tonio pulled up in front of the gate with a squeal of brakes, his broken muffler making the taxi sound like a tractor.

Reesa sniffled, looking out the back window of the taxi, waving until they turned the corner onto the road leading to the beach where the seaplane was hangered.

"Don't cry. We'll be back in three or four months."

"I know, but it was such a quick visit. I had no time to play with Miguelito."

"That's why I've invited them to come and spend Christmas with us in Santa Barbara. Barney, Consuela, and her mother will be coming too. I'll send my own plane for them."

"They're coming?" Reesa was stunned. "We might not even be together in six weeks."

"We'll be together," Dake said through his teeth. "We will also be flying to Boston next week and getting married in the cathedral there."

"Never," she croaked. "Do you want your grandmother to have a stroke? Your mother and father liked Cynthia and Linda. Do you think I would go through with a ceremony with people glaring at my back? It's insane."

"Fine," he agreed mildly. "We'll get married in Nevada, then fly to Boston for Thanksgiving. Very traditional." He stepped out of the cab, hoisted the bags from the trunk with Tonio, and loaded the seaplane. Then he came back to the taxi, leaned down, and peered inside. "Are you coming under your own steam? Or do you want me to drag you out of there?"

"When did you get so bossy? So macho?" she fumed, getting out of the car but not looking at him as she strode to the plane.

During the ride to the mainland not much was said between them. Dake read and Reesa looked out the window.

When they landed at the seaplane base in the harbor at Miami, it was swarming with photographers and reporters.

"Do you think Henry told them?" Reesa shivered inside the plane, dreading her first press stampede in a long time. She had never liked it. Now she hated it.

"No. Henry wants to keep his job." Dake bit out the words, jerking his head to the pilot to open the hatch. "Don't worry, I'll handle them. And remember, I have security people out there who will be running interference for you. Just keep moving until we get to the hanger. Then we'll allow them fifteen minutes. I have our plane waiting at the Miami airport ready to go."

Reesa nodded, blinked at the noise and shouting that assailed her when the door was opened, then she followed Dake down the steps to the ground.

People swelled and surged around her like tidal waves. She smiled and nodded, but said nothing, grateful that Dake kept his arm around her as they fought their way to the hanger.

Once there, the questions were shot at her like missiles.

"Miss Hawke, Wethering of the *Times* here. Is it true that you know nothing about Mr. Masters being charged with your murder? That you didn't know he was held incommunicado in jail? that the grand jury indicted him on the strength of the circumstantial evidence and the testimony of your friend Haddon James, who said that the two of you argued constantly on the cruise?"

"Yes. No. No." Reesa beamed at the reporter, her heart thudding in painful cadence against her chest wall. Oh, Dake, it must have been bad for you, she thought.

"Miss Hawke, do you still harbor fearful feelings about Mr. Masters? Is it true that you fainted when you first saw him?" Another eager face pushed forward, a television camera on the shoulder of the man next to him.

Reesa smiled at each and every reporter, her mind turning over like a computer as she watched the avaricious faces. A sidelong glance at Dake showed that he was facing her, stony and silent, many of the cameras clicking at him.

She cleared her throat. "It's true I fainted when I first saw Dake because my memory returned the moment I saw him. To answer your other question about my fearful feelings toward him, I can only say that I would not, could not, choose to marry a man I feared or distrusted." Her quick glance at Dake caught the widening of his eyes, the slight slackening of his lips. She had surprised him! It gave her a good feeling.

"When are you getting married, Miss Hawke? When did you decide? Are you going to be in all Mr. Masters's productions now?" The questions flew thick and fast.

Reesa kept answering, smiling and waving her hand. When she felt Dake's arm around her waist, she sagged with relief. She had had a moment there when she was sure he would repudiate what she had said.

"Gentlemen," Dake drawled, one eyebrow quirked, telling them that he thought the word a misnomer. "Miss Hawke and I haven't decided yet where we will be married, but it will be before New Year's. Thank you. That will be all." Dake took her arm and led her through the hanger into a room, out through another door to the outside, and into a limousine driven by the redoubtable Henry.

"Let's go, Henry. A hundred if you get us to the plane without anyone following us."

"Yes, sir." Henry gripped the wheel with the zeal of a country preacher heading for a meeting with a thousand potential converts in attendance.

They roared through Miami, but Reesa didn't mind. Her eyes were shut and she was held close to Dake's chest.

"So, my darling, you rescued me," Dake whispered in her hair.

"That doesn't mean we have to marry—" Reesa

began. Then her face was pushed back into his chest again by his hand.

"We are marrying, my sweet, just as soon as I can arrange it. Then we will fly back to Boston for Thanksgiving. Shhh," Dake said when she lifted her head to speak again.

The flight back to California was uneventful. Reesa was aware that Dake was on the phone much of the time, but she was too tired to take note of what he said. She drifted in and out of sleep, even refusing to eat when Dake brought her food.

In her dream she was in the water again, struggling to call out to the yacht, sobbing when she found herself alone. . . .

"Darling, don't! Wake up!" Dake's voice penetrated the blackness of the nightmare.

Reesa blinked her eyes open, clutching at him. "Oh, God, I thought I was back out on the water again." Her breath came out in sobs as she tried to control herself, cold perspiration running down the inside of her arms. "I hate that dream."

"All right, all right." Dake rocked her in his arms. "Tell me about it from start to finish. Maybe that will whitewash your subconscious so that your ghosts won't rise in your sleep."

Reesa sighed. "I hate talking about it, too, but maybe you're right." She sighed again. "You remember we had that flaming argument about Cynthia and commitment and marriage. . . ."

"You were right. I should have told Cynthia that I loved you, that I wanted to marry you." He paused for a moment. "I had actually decided to do just that. I could feel you slipping away from me. Just because I was fond of Cynthia was no reason to allow her to assume that I would never marry again." Dake inhaled a deep breath. "If I hadn't been so angry, I would have told you about my decision, but when you gave me the ultimatum that you would leave me for good if we didn't discuss a change in our lifestyles, it angered me more and I just dug in my heels." His arms tightened on her. "I was a fool, and I paid dearly for my stupidity."

"We were both out of line that night. I just had taken a few shots from Haddon about our relationship and was feeling very raw when I found you in the lounge. . . ."

"Primed for battle . . ." Dake grated.

"The argument seemed to explode," Reesa recalled.

"Like a megaton bomb," Dake whispered in her hair.

"I was so angry, I couldn't see straight. It was enough to make me less steady on my feet than I should have been."

"Anger can do that to you." There was a bitter tinge to his voice.

Reesa took a deep breath. "I went up on deck for just a minute. I had every intention of going to bed just as I had told you, but I needed some fresh air. I was standing on the stern deck when I noticed that one of the dinghy lines had broken loose. I looked around for someone, then decided that I could climb down the stern ladder and fix it myself. I took off my shoes."

"I found them on the deck." Dake's voice sounded hoarse.

". . . then lowered myself down the ladder to the dinghy. It was while I was trying to retie the hawser that I lost my footing and fell over the side of dinghy."

"Lord." Dake moved his mouth over her hair and down her cheek. "When I found your shoes I—I almost went over the side myself. Insane is the best way to describe my actions then. The captain threatened to have me tied and locked in my cabin if I didn't calm down." She pulled back to look at him. "All the fires of hell will not be as punishing as that time for me. We radioed for helicopters to come at first light."

"Miguel found me just before dawn. He was working on his lines. Manuel was at the wheel. Carlito was up the mast. He spotted me, they told me later. I honestly don't remember much of the trip back to land. I was feverish from the blow on the head I'd suffered on falling. It was only the habit of donning a life preserver before I climbed down to the dinghy that saved me."

"If I hadn't been so stubborn and stayed in the lounge—" Dake spat out, clutching her to him.

"We were both stupid that night, and we both paid for it. As happy as I was with Miguel and Liza, I dreaded to find out what nightmare I had blanked from my mind." Her mouth wobbled for a moment. "At times I was sure I had killed someone—or worse."

"I regret very much not divorcing Linda long before I did, and I regret not marrying you the first week I met you, and I know that in some ways, despite what you said about not marrying, you couldn't forgive the stand I was taking."

"Dake." Reesa felt an uncomfortable heat at the truth of what he said.

"You haven't forgiven me, have you?"

"I—I want to. It makes me feel small to be this way, but it isn't a grudge, it's—it's just that I feel we have a low level of trust between us. Disposable relationships are so much a part of the life we had that cynicism is a natural growth on most of the lives around us, including our own. We were caught up in a cycle of failure when it came to personal lives. Most of our friends had failed marriages, failed relationships. Success was a word that went with material gain, monetary excellence."

Dake drew in a sharp breath. "You became quite a philosopher while you were Maria Halcon. Those darts you throw are razor-sharp."

"I lived in a house where people loved each other selflessly. I cherished the feelings I found there. Discovering you're a very poor person emotionally is a sad experience, but even when I didn't know who I was, I realized that my other life was not as fulfilling as Miguel's and Liza's. In part, that was the reason I didn't want to regain my memory, I'm sure."

Dake released her, moving back into his seat and a little away from her.

When she thought he must be angry with her, he took her hand and threaded his fingers with hers. "It's a bitter pill to think that you feel that what we had between us was fluff with no substance."

"No. I don't think that. I think what we had was very powerful, but neither of us was willing to make the sacrifices it demanded to make our relationship great." She smiled at him, feeling her lips tremor. "I claim my share of guilt for our personal vortex. It was easier for me to eschew the responsibilities of marriage as our relationship allowed me to do. Oh, I argued that we should get married, shouted and yelled, too, but I didn't walk away from you, did I? And I should have done that if I really wanted the world to back away, if I desired a home with you." Reesa gulped, her admission tearing at her.

Eight

Staggering into one of the private lounges in the Los Angeles airport, cradled by Dake's arm, Reesa turned to face the reporters who had been allowed by her agent, Ben Secomb, to enter the room and question her.

Ben hugged her, tears in his eyes. "I couldn't believe it for the first twenty-four hours, angel. It's so good to see you."

"Good to see you, Ben." Reesa intercepted the hard look exchanged between Dake and her agent. Neither man had ever liked the other too well, and Reesa sensed that Ben must have been one of the persons who had pushed for an indictment of murder against Dake. "Ah, Dake and I are being married. We had decided that before I fell from the dinghy."

"Oh?" Disbelief flashed across Secomb's face at her words, then dissipated into an expressionless mask. "You were arguing the night you went into the sea . . . and you couldn't remember," Ben whispered, one eye on the converging press.

"Dake and I argue about everything, but he didn't try to kill me, and I resent any and all implications that he might have conspired in my accident." Reesa stared at Ben for long moments.

He inhaled, nodding, understanding her. "All right." He looked at Dake, his eyes glittering for a moment, then his gaze slid back to Reesa. "You don't have to give them a great deal." He jerked his head toward the pushing and shoving crowd of newsmen. "But they will want a few answers."

"Fine. I feel better now." And she did. Her mind seemed to have taken over, reminding her of other interviews, other sessions with the media.

With Ben on one side and Dake on the other she plastered a wide smile on her face and turned to meet the mob.

"Is it true you're marrying Dake Masters? Did you know that many people thought he killed you?"

Tinkling laughter came from Reesa's throat as her adrenaline started to flow. "Yes. That would make a great script. Perhaps once Dake and I are married we will collaborate on a story like that. I think the premise is fascinating."

"Miss Hawke, when will you marry?"

"No date has been set."

The questions came at her like bullets, but she was pleased that she was able to field most of them. Still, it was an ordeal, and she began to feel a quivering in her limbs.

"That's all, gentlemen. Miss Hawke is tired."

Reesa wheeled to stare at Dake when he spoke. "How did you know?" she whispered.

"I know." He looked down at her, not hiding the heat in his gaze. "Let's go home."

Reesa hesitated. She hated going back to the house in Santa Barbara. There were ghosts there that she didn't want to face.

"Not to worry." Dake leaned down to her, ignoring

the clamor of the press for "just one more question, Miss Hawke." "We'll be staying at Bill Hanks's house at Malibu Beach." Dake named the man who had directed Reesa in a few movies and who had worked with Dake more than once. "He's away on location."

Reesa felt relieved that they weren't going to Santa Barbara.

"Reesa." Ben took her arm. "We should talk. The minute the press and folks in the business discovered you had returned my phone has been ringing off the hook. We should discuss it."

"I'll call you when we get settled. You could come out to the house." Reesa heard the hiss of Dake's indrawn breath, but she didn't turn around to look at him.

"All right. Call me." Ben turned to face the crowd with placatory words as an attendant gestured to Dake and Reesa to follow him through a doorway.

After walking along a winding corridor they came to a door leading outside, where a car was waiting. The engine was running in the 1976 Buick, but no one was in the car. The dents and faded paint didn't begin to telegraph what was under the hood.

Reesa smiled at him when Dake opened the passenger side of the car so that she could enter. "Still have Peachy, I see." Reesa referred to the Buick that Dake had sometimes raced in beach derbies. Though he hadn't done it in a few years, he still kept the car in tip-top condition, but the outside could have done with a little care.

"Yes. For something like this, the old girl comes in handy. Who would ever think that the glamorous Reesa Hawke would travel in a jalopy?"

Reesa slid across the leather bench seat in the auto. "They don't know what Peachy is like on the inside then." Reesa rubbed the leather dashboard and gazed at the complicated stereo system underneath.

"Put your sunglasses on, darling." Dake instructed Reesa as he fired up the powerful engine. "Not that we couldn't outrun them in Peachy. We could." His hands clenched and unclenched on the leather steering wheel, his eyes glinting over her in excited amusement. "Fasten your seat belt."

Reesa remembered that Dake would never let her ride or drive without a seat belt. She fastened it, affixed her glasses, then looked at him. "You're looking forward to outrunning the press!"

Dake shrugged. "Not looking forward to it, but I wouldn't mind doing it." He pulled away from the rear of the Quonset-shaped building and drove around onto an access road that led to the front of the airport terminal building. "When in doubt, do the opposite from expected." Dake placed his own dark glasses on his face, then donned a plaid driving cap he pulled from behind the sun visor.

Reesa laughed, then put her hand over her mouth.

"Stop laughing at my driving cap, brat." Dake growled, stopping in front of the terminal at the crosswalk. "Look at them." Dake barely enunciated his words as hordes of cameramen and reporters rushed across the road and into the parking area, not even looking at the battered Buick.

Reesa didn't reply, not even realizing she was holding her breath until it was released in a sigh when the last of the newsmen ran in front of the car.

"Relax, darling," Dake said, his hand reaching out and gripping her knee. "We'll be home before they know where we've gone. In two weeks we'll be flying back to Boston. In one week or less we'll be married."

"Dake, I don't think—"

"We're marrying, Rees. We'll settle our problems after that."

"That seems rather wrong end to, doesn't it?" she snapped, irritated that he would assume that they would have problems, even though an inner voice told her that she and Dake would always have different views on something. They were too volatile to have smooth sailing in any type of relationship. "My family does not believe in divorce."

"You have one uncle, Lionel Hawke, whom you don't see much of anyway. You have no other family. Besides, my family doesn't believe in divorce either—"

"You're divorced," Reesa shot at him.

"So I am," he observed mildly, angling the car over toward the exit that would take them to the coastal route to Bill Hanks's retreat. "*We* will not be—ever. It wouldn't be good for the children."

"Children! What children? Neither of us wants children," she lied.

"We do. Both of us want them. I watched you with Miguelito . . . and I discovered that I want a child with you very much," Dake stated in flat tones. "Robert would like a brother or sister. Besides, my love, I think the matter may be out of our hands."

"What do you mean?" She watched him, feeling like a rabbit in a snare.

"Stop looking as though I'm going to pull over to the side of the road and make love to you. Not that the idea isn't appealing. It's just that I'm willing to be patient until we're home." He grinned, shooting a glance her way when she sputtered in outrage. "My love, were you on the pill while you traveled on the *Windward*?"

"None of your business. I haven't asked you about your love affairs, have I?" Her imagination swelled with thoughts of the women who would have been in his life while she was supposedly dead.

Dake felt as though someone had just inserted a very sharp knife into his chest. It hadn't occurred to him, not really, that she might be having an affair with someone. "Who?" he croaked.

"Who what?" She frowned at him, wondering if he had a pain.

"Don't play games with me, Rees. I don't like it." He slammed his hand against the wheel, his foot jamming down on the accelerator, shooting the car ahead like a meteor. "Who was the man you were involved with before I found you, before your memory returned?" For one hellfire moment, it shot through his mind that she hadn't forgotten anything, that she had not wanted to come back to him because of this man.

"You have no right to ask—" Reesa began, tight-lipped, then she saw his face pale. "No one," she whispered. "There was no one. I dated with a group most of the time. I wasn't close to anyone."

He swallowed three times but still couldn't get words past his constricted throat. He could feel the muscle jumping in his cheek, but couldn't control it. Even after she had gone from him and he suffered such a loss, he hadn't realized the grip she had on him. She was his blood, his tissue, and damn her to hell, he couldn't live without her now.

She leaned toward him. "I wasn't trying to hurt you." Her voice was low. She slipped her hand through the crook of his arm, her heart pounding faster when he squeezed it against his side.

"I'm more paranoid about you than I knew, I suppose." His smile was lopsided. He shot her a quick look. "Were you on the pill, darling?"

"No, No, of course I wasn't. I didn't feel the need of it." She rested her head against his shoulder, removing her sunglasses when they twisted on her face.

"And, remember, I never used anything the night we made love," Dake informed her quietly.

Reesa jerked erect, staring out the windshield. "I could be pregnant," she whispered.

"Could be."

Reesa flattened the palm of her hand on her middle. "My family doesn't believe in abortion."

"Mine either," Dake whispered back.

"Oh, your family believes in anything expedient." Reesa flapped her right hand, her left still pressing her middle.

"True, but they have nothing to do with us. We're a family now."

Reesa stared at him open-mouthed. "Do you think?"

"It could very well be." He breathed a sigh of relief when he saw her bemused smile. "Robbie would be ecstatic."

Reesa chuckled. "Yes he would." Then she sat straight up again. "My picture! I have to finish it now, Ben said—"

"I heard him. We'll work around it somehow."

They turned into a private road that would take them to Bill's place, stopping to identify themselves to the security guard at the gate. Then they were through and driving down the narrow road behind the beautiful homes that sat at long intervals from one another.

"Ben was one of the ones who accused you, wasn't he?" Reesa asked.

For moments the only sound was the purring engine and the surf.

"I know he did, Dake. I could see it in his eyes today. I know you two didn't like each other, but I never thought he would go that far."

"Your agent loves you almost as much as I do! He was reacting out of grief over you and dislike of me." He gripped the wheel with both hands. "But don't expect me to like him. I don't, but I understand why he did it."

Reesa didn't deny what Dake said. She had always known that Ben cared for her, but she had never allowed their relationship to be anything but platonic. She liked Ben and respected his business judgment, but there was only one man she could love, and he was sitting beside her. "I shouldn't have invited him to the house. I'll call and change it to his office."

"No. Your friends and business associates are welcome in our home. I'll just avoid talking to him," Dake assured her.

Reesa promised herself that she wouldn't put Dake through that. How many others had done this to him? Accused him of killing her? Blackened his name! "I guess I didn't realize how many people believed that you hurt me. It must have been horrible. Did your work suffer too?"

Dake shrugged. "I suppose it did, but frankly much of what was said to me and about me went right over my head. I was so miserable without you, I didn't care what went on around me." He stiffened for a moment. "I'm not trying to lay a guilt trip on you, Rees. It's just—"

"I know. I know how it must have been. Because if I thought you were dead, I wouldn't want to live either. I'd be a zombie."

They reached the house and unloaded their bags quickly. Dake put the car into the garage and locked it.

"Groceries!" Reesa groaned as they walked toward the bedroom wing.

"Not to worry. Bill stocked the place. We're set. All we have to do for the next week is swim, relax, talk to each other and discuss where we should be married."

"Nevada." Reesa said, her mouth jumping ahead of her mind.

Dake stopped in the act of swinging a suitcase onto a luggage rack. "That justice of the peace outside Reno who gave us directions when we were looking for Dancer's casino . . ." The suitcase thudded onto the floor. Dake snapped his fingers, then came over to her. "I'll call," he said, and left the bedroom at a run.

Reesa sank down on the bed. "I can't marry Dake," she whispered.

"If you feel that way," her other self said, "go out there and tell him!" "I can't," she answered. "Then stop acting like a fool and accept that you will marry him." Reesa moaned. "I want to marry him. I love him. But how can I be sure it will work?" She rose and began to pace, but still she argued with herself. "Guarantees come with irons and other small appliances, not with weddings," that other self told her firmly.

Reesa tore herself free of the dialogue and walked over to the telephone console by the bedside. She switched to the second line on the phone and dialed.

"Uncle Lionel? Yes, it's me, Reesa. I'm fine. I—" She was appalled when she began to cry. "No, no, Uncle Lionel, I'm fine. I didn't mean to make you sad. Oh, Uncle Lionel, don't. I've never heard you cry. Yes, yes, I'll come for Christmas. Ah . . . Uncle Lionel, I'll be bringing Dake with me. We'll be married soon. Oh . . . thank you. I will be happy. We're going to visit his family in Boston. Good-bye for now. I'll call you when we come back from the East. Good-bye."

Reesa replaced the phone with shaking fingers. She and her uncle had never talked so openly. Dake was right. He had been shaken by the reports of her death. "I will go to see him at Christmas and we'll talk!" Reesa nodded to herself. "Now, if I could believe that I'm doing the right thing in marrying Dake . . ."

"Darling, are you quarreling with yourself?" Dake drawled from the doorway, one shoulder propped against the jamb.

"I'm trying to be sensible," she answered crossly. "It doesn't make sense that we should marry."

"Not to worry. I will give you a written guarantee

that we will have a good marriage for sixty-five years. After that, we'll take our chances like anyone else."

"In writing . . . with witnesses?"

"In writing with witnesses."

"That should work."

"I think so." Dake ambled across the room and leaned down to kiss her nose.

"You can't be too careful these days."

"*Caveat emptor.*" Dake nuzzled her neck.

"Yes. Let the buyer beware." Reesa cuddled close to him. Then she straightened again. "We need a will. I'm leaving my money to you and Robert, but I want some to go to Liza and Miguel and I want money for Miguelito if he wants to go to college."

"Good idea. I'll get Sam on it tomorrow." He pulled her back to him again, cradling her on his chest.

"Yes. I feel better."

"That's why I'm here, to make you feel better."

She smiled up at him, seeing his mouth coming toward her, her lips parting as they touched, her body arching closer to him.

He lifted his head a fraction from hers. "I used to wake up at night, thinking I was holding you like this. It was hell. I finally moved out of the house, but still I couldn't sleep nights. I kept thinking I had to go back to the Caribbean, that I would find you somewhere." He lifted her in his arms and carried her over to a chaise in front of sliding glass doors leading out to a balcony. "When Jazz Leaman called me, I didn't even want to speak to him at first. I thought it was another scam to make me open up about you. The stunts that were pulled were unbelievable, Rees. I found people going through our trash, taking pictures through the windows, accosting me on the street by grabbing my arms and holding me while a partner took pictures and asked questions. . . ."

"My God!" Reesa slipped a protective arm across his chest. "Was there no one to defend you?"

"Lydia Freedman was very supportive." Dake grinned down at her when she pushed back and glared at him.

"She has always wanted you."

"Yes. That's what she told me." Dake laughed.

"Damn her." Reesa laughed, too, but she couldn't suppress images of Dake and Lydia together in bed.

"No, we did not sleep together. I was grateful for her support, but I had a hell of a time relating to anyone at the time."

"You didn't sleep with anyone while we were separated?" Reesa took a deep breath. "Strike the question. It isn't a fair one."

"No, it isn't, but I'll answer it. I slept with a woman when I went on a drinking binge one week in Las Vegas when you had been gone four months. I had been in jail and was feeling sorry for myself. I went to Vegas and started gambling and drinking, staying up all night. Paula was the someone I took to my rooms after I had been there three days. . . ."

Reesa saw the muscle jump in the side of his face. "You don't have to say any more."

"I thought after four months I should have stopped seeing your face at night. Suicide was not on my list of things to do, but I felt like I had already killed myself. I had sex with that very beautiful girl and saw you there instead."

Dake released her to lean forward, his elbows on his knees, his chin resting on his joined hands. "This isn't true confessions, but I want you to know that Paula left me the next day. She said I was a zombie and should find a grave and bury myself." He cleared his throat. "I agreed with her. I sobered up, came back to Los Angeles, and started work on a new picture. We shot most of it up in the Sangre de Cristo mountains. When I came back after three months of relative solitude and fresh air, I felt I was ready to resume my life and begin a court fight to clear my name."

He turned around to look at Reesa as she sat back against the cushions. "I put our house on the market and bought a small beach house not far from here. It isn't as private as this, nor does it have the security guards."

He sat back with a sigh, his hand going to her knee. "That's how Leaman got hold of me. I didn't answer his phone messages on my answering machine, so he came out to the beach house. I was ready to punch him in the nose. But then he convinced me he had seen you. He said that you were thinner, but your voice was the same and he had photographed you so many times that he was sure he couldn't be wrong. The more I listened to him, the more hope built in me—and the more anger that surged through me! Even while I was filled with joy, I was furious too. It was like being sawed in half. I owe Jazz Leaman a great deal and I'm damned well going to see that he has a job with me whenever he wants it."

Dake pushed her knees down, then lowered his head into her lap. "Do you know on the flight down to Miami, then the shuttle out to the Grand Caymans, I was sure it wouldn't be you and I was both glad and sorry. I had begun to come back to life a little, to deal with a world that had no Reesa Hawke. I didn't want anything that would bring back the agony of your loss when I had just relegated it to a painful ache in the back of my mind."

"When I saw you that day . . ." Reesa shook her head, her hands threading through the thickness of his hair.

"For the first blinding moment I thought you had played a macabre trick on me. I exploded at you." His arms curled around her waist and he pressed his face into her middle. "I will never let you out of my sight again. I couldn't stand it."

"All the projects you're involved in will separate us some of the time."

"No," Dake said firmly. "I will let assistants handle anything that would take me away from you." His face nuzzled her stomach. "I had planned to take you shopping for clothes this afternoon after you rested." He pulled up and looked at her, his tiger eyes a topaz flame. "I even made the appointment with Zaza," he muttered just before he pressed his face between her breasts.

"Good idea," Reesa said, breath hissing from her body as his mouth fastened to her nipple through the light material of her dress.

"We could go to bed together." Dake's voice was hoarse.

Reesa stared down at him. "Let's."

"God, woman, you've turned me to water." Dake groaned. Then he heaved his body upward and out of her arms. As his feet hit the floor he turned to her and pulled her from the couch into his embrace.

"For a man who's turned to water, you're not doing bad." Reesa chuckled into his neck.

"Superman, that's me," Dake whispered in her hair. His mouth slipped down the side of her cheek, checking at her mouth, his teeth nibbling there. "Tastes sweet," he observed in slurred tones.

"Thank you," she said in a breathy voice, her hands coming up to hold his head and bring his mouth back to hers.

The kiss went on and on, their mouths searching and clinging as though they must if either of them were to survive.

Reesa felt him unbutton her silk traveling dress, pushing at the shoulders until the garment dropped down her body.

"I love it that you don't wear a bra." The silly grin seemed magnified with marks of lipstick on his mouth and cheeks.

"They told me it was smearproof."

"What?"

"My lipstick is on your face. They told me at the beauty counter where I bought it that it was smearproof."

"Sue 'em," Dake responded, his hands going to her buttocks and lifting her up his body. "I don't think we're going to make it to the bedroom."

"No?"

"No." His face was close to hers. He could see the tiny pores in her clear skin, the tiny bump in the middle of her straight nose where she had fallen from her bicycle as a child and broken it. Her almond-shaped eyes were like lustrous green jade. Her neck seemed almost fragile from her weight loss, yet she looked healthy. "I want you very much. I want you for my wife, for my lover, for the mother of my children, and I won't take no for an answer."

"You might regret it. I tend to be bossy." Reesa brought her face against his so that their mouths and noses were meeting.

"I know that—ouch! You pinched me. You can boss me, push me around."

"Hah! That'll be the day!" Reesa clutched his neck. "The person who is strong enough to push you around has to be a modern-day Goliath."

"That is not a name I'd choose for you, but if you like it, that's what I'll call you—Goliath." Dake's eyes were closed, as though it required supreme concentration to love her body with his mouth and hands. In slow motion he lowered both of them to the beige alpaca carpet, the soft scratchiness of the natural fibers an erotic impetus to their already fired nerve endings. "You have the creamiest skin in the world. It looks as though it would never tan, that it's too fragile for sunlight, yet you tan so beautifully." Dake perused her body, his hand going in light exploration over her skin. "Velvet." He sighed, lowering his face to her abdomen.

"Dake—" Reesa sobbed out. "I do want to marry you." It was as though the confession were wrenched from her as her body arched to meet his.

"Oh, my love, I want that too. I want you now. I'll want you when I'm ninety."

"Please love me always." Reesa clutched at him, bringing his head up her body, fastening him to her. She stared into those hot eyes of his and felt herself melt. "I never knew what sensuality meant until you made love to me, but I deepened my sense of the word when I lived with Miguel and Liza and saw the palpable love between them. I want our physical love, but I want to make love with our minds, too, our spirits. I want it all with you, Dake."

He gulped, feeling years of self-confidence, awareness of his mental and physical ability, love of challenge, all focusing on this fragile yet strong woman at his side. She embodied all that was womanly to him, but he never saw her trade on that. She met people and stumbling blocks head to head, but she had a gentle, sweet touch that made him reel. Her voice was strong and sure. She had incredible business acumen, and she was more feminine than any creature he had ever known.

"What are you thinking?" Reesa ran her fingernails down his back, feeling powerful when he shuddered under her hands.

"I find out new things every day that keep me in a whirl, but all of the old things don't change. You make me weak and strong simultaneously. I don't understand it, yet it is the simplest equation in the world. You and love equal life to me. You put color into the gray of life, you put sound and harmony into a barren world empty of hearing, you put tingle into my numbness, driving feeling throughout my sys-

m." Dake gave a half laugh and buried his face in
er neck. "Your mouth is hanging open."

Reesa could feel the tremor in her hands as she
ıressed the thickness of his chestnut hair. "It
ıocks me that you should be able to put my emo-
ons and responses to you into words . . . such per-
ct words." She cupped his face in her hands. "Have
e too much? Will we lose it?"

"We won't lose it," Dake said fiercely. "Every day
e'll nurture it."

"We can't be selfish. Selfishness dries up love."
eesa lay on her side facing Dake, their bodies
ressed together at thigh, hip, chest and mouth.

"We won't be separated. Being apart causes anxi-
y, makes fears balloon." Dake's tongue entered her
ıouth, touching then retreating.

"We . . . we . . ." Reesa rolled her eyes, then gripped
is neck with both hands. "My mind's blank."

"Mine's on fire." Dake groaned, his hand prying her
ıighs apart gently.

"Please love me."

"That's my intention," Dake intoned solemnly, slid-
ıg down her body again and taking hold of one foot,
is mouth caressing each toe, his tongue coursing
own the sole of her foot.

"Aaah!" Reesa moaned. "Don't . . . oh, my. My skin
; falling off." Reesa babbled as he ministered to her
ody in absorbed tenderness.

Not one inch of her form was ignored. Dake felt his
ulse jump out of control, his blood pump harder and
arder. Sensations coursed through his system until
e felt he had been remade, that he was brand-new.

Reesa couldn't stand the loving torment. Her
ands and mouth began a discovery of their own.

The lovemaking between them had always been
lectric and satisfying, but within moments it went
eyond that. Each of them felt pulled apart and

rebuilt as one. Love cemented them together, glue them elbow to elbow, knee to knee, heart to heart.

They slept afterward; no words were possible.

Later in the night Dake woke and tried to orien himself. For a blinding, painful moment, he though he was back in the house alone, that Reesa was gone dead. Black horror engulfed him for that second grief tearing him apart. Then her felt her warmt next to him. Though reason told him she was there his side, that life was no longer the pit it had been, h reached over and turned on one of the track light near the stereo system. Then he stared down at he as she cuddled close to him for warmth. His body ha been her blanket until he moved. Now she whimpere in her sleep and tried to push closer to him agair "Not to worry, my angel. I'm here." Dake gathered he to him again. He was going to lift her and carry he into the bedroom where they would have the warmt of the bed in the slight chill of night, but he indulge himself for a few moments, studying her at his lei sure, letting the light play over her face and body. Sh was thin! God, her beautiful body was delicate. "Yo will need taking care of, my precious. I am just th man for the job." He was still staring at her when a unwelcome thought intruded. "Are you too slende for good health? What if you are pregnant now—an you shouldn't be? Damm it, why didn't I use some thing!" He could feel cold perspiration coat his bod at the thought of what a long, arduous labor could d to her. "You are going to the doctor this week, befor we marry even."

Reesa moaned in her sleep, her hands pulling a him.

At once Dake's blood pounded through his system He kissed her neck, then pushed himself up Kneeling at her side, he lifted her up his body. "Yo will damn well abort a child if you are pregnant, my lamb. I will not lose you now."

Reesa's eyes fluttered open, her smile hazy and sleep-filled as she looked at him. "Are we going out?"

"Not like this, darling. We are going to bed."

"Good. Let's make love there now."

"Darling." Dake groaned, holding her high in his arms, his hands clenching on her satiny skin.

"Please." Reesa blew in his ear, her words still slurred from sleep.

"You need your sleep," Dake said, but already knew he had weakened.

"I need *you*."

He walked through the master suite to the bedroom and lowered her to the bed. "You have me. In all ways it is possible for a human being to have another, you have me."

"Good." She raised her arms up to him, her body sprawled in sensuous comfort on the bed.

"Reesa, Reesa." He sat down on the bed, his hand making lazy whorls on her pelvic area, loving the feel of the soft hair on his palm.

"I want us to be happy."

"We will be."

"Happiness has to be given away before you get to keep it." Reesa sat up on the bed, leaning forward to kiss his chest.

"Then you must have given a great deal to me, because I am a happy man."

Reesa laughed out loud.

"What's so funny?" Dake sank down beside her.

"Nothing. I just feel like laughing." She raised her hands over her head, clasping them together, prayerlike, then moving in a sinuous motion in front of him as she sat yoga fashion facing him. "And I feel like seducing you."

"That might be the easiest thing you've ever accomplished," Dake said hoarsely, his eyes following her every movement.

"Do it. Imitate what I'm doing," she whispered.

Dake lifted his arms and began to move as she was, his eyes glued to her.

"You're making me very sexy, David Kennedy Masters." A sleepy excitement ran through Reesa.

"Tell me about it." Dake felt as though all his vital signs had gone wild. He was swept away by the wonder of the woman facing him. He needed to possess her, to care for her, shield her from all harm.

"Do you think this is a good way to exercise?" Reesa asked, her lips dry as she watched his muscles glimmer in the glow of the lamp as his body swayed and dipped in sensuous accompaniment to hers.

"Must be. I'm feeling like Tarzan and Superman all rolled into one. If I start thumping my chest and leaping tall buildings at a single bound, you will understand, won't you?"

"Of course." Reesa inhaled a deep breath.

"You're beautiful, Rees."

"You're gorgeous, Dake."

"Thank you, but if you take a close look at me, ma'am, you will see that I am at the end of my tether." He smiled at her, grinning when she looked at his arousal, then up at his face again.

"No self-control."

"None." Dake reached for her, bringing her to him as he fell backward on the bed. "I will never have control where you're concerned, my love." His mouth met hers, imprisoning her very smug smile.

study. "Are you sure you want to go through with this marriage? You—"

Reesa held up her hand, palm outward. "I won't listen to anything bad about Dake. I've heard enough—and from people who were supposed to be his friends."

"I was never his friend," Ben said abruptly.

"No, you weren't." Reesa looked down at the script in her hand, then up again to stare at her agent. "And you are certainly free to sever our contract if you feel that Dake, as my husband, will be a thorn in your side."

Silence stretched between them as they stared at each other. They had been friends as well as business associates.

"The lines are drawn," Ben said finally.

Reesa nodded.

Ben rose. "I understand. We'll let things stand as they are. If we find that it's too uncomfortable for us, we'll talk again." Ben nodded to her and picked up his briefcase. At the door he paused, his back to her. "I wish you every happiness, Reesa. I always have."

"I know." Reesa's voice was barely audible.

After he left she sat for a long time looking out the floor-to-ceiling windows that faced the ocean. For the past few days she had been getting phone calls with just the same veiled suggestion that she not go through with her marriage to Dake. "Perhaps you are a fool, Reesa Hawke, but your path is set."

Dake had had business meetings and she did not expect him back before dinner. After that they were flying to Reno in his private jet and would spend the night in a cottage at one of the casinos. They would marry the next morning with a judge and two witnesses supplied by the magistrate. She spent the rest of the afternoon on the beach with the script, familiarizing herself with it again.

She must have fallen asleep, because a sudden

coolness of a shadow had her blinking upward trying to make out who was the dark silhouette looking down on her.

Dake hunkered down on the sand beside her, his finger scoring down her cheek.

Unaccountably she shivered.

He pulled his hand back as though he'd been scorched. "Listening to the many warnings, Reesa?" He stood, looking out at the waves rushing to the shore. "Secomb been filling you in on all the lurid details of what could happen to you if you married me?" He spat the words into the ocean breeze.

Reesa struggled to a sitting position, shading her eyes with a hand as she looked up at him. "Ben said something. . . ."

"Oh, I'm sure he did. If you don't mind, I'd rather have the news when we're in the house rather than on the beach." He swiveled away from her and stalked over the sand, a sputtering Reesa looking after him.

"Fool." She slapped her hand down on an errant sheet of manuscript that was not weighted down as well as the others. Then she gathered her things together and followed him back to the house, kicking at the sand and considering a watery grave for the aloof Mr. Masters. "Just assume that I listened to the stories! Don't bother hearing what I have to say! That would be too sensible, too intelligent!" she muttered as she made her way into the shower room under the wooden deck on the main floor of the house. She stripped her clothing from her body, flinging the articles every which way, then stepped under the warm spray of water. "Arrogant bastard!" She ground her teeth as she shampooed the salty stickiness from her hair. "I have a good mind not to marry you!" She fumed as she dried herself then wrapped a towel around her head. She draped another towel around her body and left the shower room to go up the inside stairway at the back of the house that would take her to the kitcen area.

Dake was there fixing himself a pitcher of martinis.

"Don't you think that's a bit out of line if we're flying to Reno tonight?" she snapped when he turned to look at her, one eyebrow raised.

"Are we flying to Reno this evening?"

"That was the plan. Are you changing it?" she challenged him.

"No." He handed her the pitcher of martinis. "Here. You drink these. I'm going for a walk. Would you like me to put a casserole in the oven?"

"No." She took the martinis from him. "I would rather have a salad, then eat something when we reach Reno." She bit her lip when he nodded then turned away to go down the spiral staircase leading to the shower room.

She went to the window to watch Dake walk rapidly up the beach; then she ducked back inside and got a glass of juice for herself.

She touched the towel on her head, knowing that her hair would have to be dampened again before she could comb it. The thickness of it felt too heavy in her hands as she braided it in front of the dressing room mirror, then twisted the coil on top of her head. Wisps of silky black hair trailed on her cheek and neck.

She pulled a suede skirt out of the closet, the jade color the same as her eyes. With it she wore a matching vest in the same color and a silk blouse. Her ankle-high boots were of the same green suede.

"You look beautiful." Dake was standing in the doorway of the dressing room rubbing his hair with a towel, another around his waist.

"Thank you. I'll go make the salads."

They ate in relative silence, straightened the house, and packed the last of their things in the same quiet. They locked the house, then stashed the key in the earthen jar in the storage house where they had found it, left, and drove to the small airfield where Dake's jet awaited them.

"You're nervous." The amusement in Dake's voice fired her temper.

"Yes," she said, then clamped her lips shut.

"Would you like a drink?"

"I had juice, thank you. Dake, did it ever seem to you that we fought the most after we had worked too hard?"

"Yes." He gripped the headphones, then asked for instructions for takeoff.

In moments they were aloft, and Reesa was experiencing heart-jerking nervousness she always felt on takeoff.

"Stomach doing flipflops, love?"

"No." Reesa gulped.

"Pretty, isn't it?" Dake pointed to the orange and purple tinge to the ground cover below.

"Yes." She nodded.

Their conversation was as desultory as it had been while they ate and packed, but somehow it was more relaxed.

In little more than an hour the Learjet brought them into the airfield near Reno in the fading light of day.

"There's a car waiting for you, Mr. Masters." The mechanic pointed across the field, but his eyes made an avid perusal of Reesa.

"Thanks." Dake glowered at the man, then took Reesa's arm and led her toward the car, his long legs covering the distance in seconds.

"Stop." Reesa gasped, pulling at the hand that held her above the elbow. "These are low heels, but I just can't run that fast in them. So stop it."

Dake looked down at her, one corner of his mouth

twisting upward. "Sorry, darling. I just wanted to get you away from there before I punched his face in."

Reesa looked at him, her mouth agape. "I'm still not used to you being like this."

"I'm not too used to it either, but I can't help it."

"It never used to bother you that much when men looked at me." She gulped air even though they were moving at a slower pace.

"I always hated men looking at you. I learned to mask it. I damn well can't and won't mask it anymore. If I find someone looking at you, I'm going to paste him one."

Reesa skidded to a stop next to the car, glaring up at him. When the giggle escaped her lips she put a hand to her mouth. "I'm mad at you for acting like such a caveman, but I can't stop picturing how the scenario will go. You'll be hitting men left and right. In our business, being a lecher is being ordinary."

Dake studied her for a minute, then as he helped her into the car, telling the driver their destination, he grinned at her. "No more so than in any other industry, I suppose. Perhaps we are a little more overt."

"A little?" Reesa laughed, sinking against the plush upholstery.

Dake lifted her left hand to his mouth, his lips caressing the emerald-cut diamond he had put there not two days before. "I will try for a little self-control . . . since my dreams are coming true tomorrow."

"Are they?" Reesa looked at him through the curtain of her lashes, his caressing hand a balm, her nerve ends unknotting because his shoulder was pressed to hers.

"Oh, yes. They are. The first evening I took you out I was ready to be your husband. I knew, but I smothered that feeling with sophisticated excuses."

"Cynthia's heart condition was real." She took deep shuddering breaths, aware she spoke the truth.

"Your remarriage could have caused her to have an attack."

Dake's face contorted. "Yes. Sometimes it was like being in quicksand. I—I couldn't take a chance on killing a woman who had been like a mother to me."

She slipped her hand into his. "I liked her that one and only time I met her . . . and somehow I think she knew about us."

Dake squeezed her hand. "No doubt. She was sharp, but I was afraid to take the chance." He took a deep breath. "It's over now."

And now it's time for you to have a little happiness, Dake. The thought surprised her, but she knew it was true. He had had much success in everything he'd turned his hand to, except his personal life. Now, it's my turn, she thought, filled with a sudden delight that she could be the one to turn Dake's life around, to bring him a measure of the joy of living.

That evening she and Dake went to gamble in the casino, but Reesa was so nervous about the next day that they left early and went back to the bungalow.

"I never thought you would be nervous about getting married," Dake chided her as he held her in his arms after making love to her.

"God. Neither did I, but I am." Reesa wrapped her arms around his neck and buried her face in his chest.

The next day she was trembling so that Dake had to fasten the tiny buttons of her peach-colored silk ensemble, the strapless dress beneath her Chanel-type jacket hugging her body, the invisible inverted pleats from knee to calf showing only when she walked.

"There," Dake informed her. "I've buttoned only the bottom two buttons, the rest we'll leave open since it will be warm outside."

"Cold," Reesa bleated, following him in her stocking feet when he went to the bathroom.

"I'll be out in a minute, darling," Dake assured her.

Reesa nodded, but didn't move from her place in front of the door, her eyes on the doorknob.

When Dake opened the door she stepped close to his chest, wrapping her arms around him and pressing her face into his middle. "I've changed my mind. Let's just live together. Marriages break up all the time."

"Not ours." Dake freed himself from her hold and went to get his suit coat. "Ready?"

Reesa nodded, mutely reached for the nosegay of salmon-pink roses Dake had had sent over for her.

"Shouldn't you put on your shoes?" he asked, going over and getting peach peau de soie slings from the shoe section of her luggage.

"Can't wear them," Reesa told him in a hoarse voice. "Feet are swollen." One tear rolled down the golden satin of her skin.

"Not true." Dake kissed her, prying her cold fingers from their death grip on the nosegay. "I'll carry your flowers until we reach the chapel. Now, sit down in that chair and let me see if I can fit your shoes on your feet."

"Can't." Reesa moaned. "My feet swelled by two sizes. I tried to get them on after I showered. Can't."

Dake maneuvered her into the satin dressing room chair, then hunkered down in front of her, the shoes in his hand. He looked at the shoes, then reached inside each one, pulling out cotton wadding that had been used to keep the delicate shoe in shape while packed. "That's why they didn't fit, darling. You didn't remove the wadding." He reached up and kissed her cold lips, feeling the trembling in her foot when he raised it to fit the shoe to it. "See. Doesn't that feel good?"

Reesa nodded, watching him. "Divorce is out." She licked her dry lips.

He looked up at her, placing the other shoe on her foot, his smile warming her. "Divorce will never be discussed between us, nor will separation. When we argue, we'll settle it as soon as possible and hopefully without hurting each other."

"No hiding how much we love each other"—the words seemed dragged from her throat as she scrutinized his features—"be-because the rest of our circle of friends think that's the way it should be."

"We'll make new friends if we must, but no matter who it is, new friend or old, no one will dictate our relationship except us."

Reesa drew in a shuddering breath and nodded. When Dake reached for her hand to pull her to her feet, she was smiling, even though she still felt shaky. "I can't really describe why I'm nervous. I want to do this. I need to marry you, but it's as though we were carrying a very fragile object between us and the least movement could destroy it."

Dake led her from the bungalow to the car parked on the winding drive, the liveried chauffeur holding the door. "All marriages are fragile, angel," Dake said. "Working hard at shoring them up is what makes them strong. It's a day-by-day, hour-by-hour job, and you can never let up for a minute. I never felt the need to protect or nurture the relationship I had with Linda. Neither did she. We married out of expediency and it was stupid for both of us. We are marrying for love and want to work at building and maintaining our life together."

"Thank you." Reesa put her head on his shoulder, feeling calmer, even though some of the butterflies did return when they alighted in front of the chapel where they would be married.

The ceremony was short, but Reesa listened to

every word, delighted when Dake pronounced his vows in a strong, sure voice.

It startled her when there were photographers outside taking pictures, questions flying thick and fast.

"Damn. I thought we wouldn't get into this." Dake managed to field most of the queries while keeping Reesa moving toward the limousine that would take them back to the casino.

"Not to worry," the chauffeur whispered to Dake. "I have it all figured. We'll drive back to the casino, then when you get out, you go through the casino to my boss's office, out the back door to a car there. All your luggage will be in it."

The charade worked and it made Reesa gleeful when they arrived at the airport with no reporters on their tail.

Ten

At Logan Airport they were able to avoid the press; another car was waiting there to whisk them away.

"I think you'll like the house where I was born, Rees," Dake said as they sped along. "It's big and dates back to Revolutionary days. In front of the property the Charles River takes a bend. There's enough land around the house so that we can go cross-country skiing if you like, and there's a pond nearby that freezes over. We used to skate there as kids."

"I haven't skied much, and I've never skated, but I'll try. You love Boston, don't you?" Reesa leaned against Dake.

"Yes, I do. And thank you, darling."

Dake turned her in his arms, his tiger eyes liquid with love. He kissed her deeply, then pulled back. "You're apprehensive about being with my family, aren't you? But don't worry. Tonight is our wedding night and we'll spend it in my private apartment in my parents' house. If you decide you don't care for my family, we won't even spend Thanksgiving with them. No, no, don't protest, sweetheart. Now that we're man and wife, I'm not about to do anything to endanger our happiness in our life together. If my family irritates you—"

"Don't say that!" Reesa gasped. "I met your mother and father once when we were on location in New York. They were very polite."

"But very distant." Dake nodded. "I know. When I was young I thought that they cared about each other, about me, but when I grew older I realized it was the business that was the glue between them, not love. You see, my mother came from a very old Back Bay family steeped in tradition. She married my father against her family's wishes, but"—Dake shook his head—"the 'but' was a big one—my father's family had a great deal of money though his name was not quite as old and blueblooded. Since my mother was an only child and my father the oldest son of his family, they coupled her name and his money and came up with the Masters conglomerate."

"You have a sister, don't you?"

"Yes, but we don't see each other that much." Dake shrugged, then grinned. He pointed out the window at a brick house sitting upon a knoll.

"It's beautiful," Reesa exclaimed. "It looks like an old-fashioned Christmas card."

"It was one once. An artist came and painted the scene, then sold transparencies of the painting to a card company. Father bought the original from him. It's hanging over the mantel in the living room."

"I thought a painting of your mother when she was a young married woman would have pride of place over the mantel."

"No. My mother's painting hangs over the mantel in the library, where my father does most of his work now."

It crossed Reesa's mind that it seemed a strange place to hang a painting of his mother if neither parent cared for the other, but she didn't say anything because the car had traveled the circular drive and was pulling to a halt.

The front door opened and an older man came down the steps, a retriever at his side. "Welcome home, Dake."

A young boy, his jacket hanging from one shoulder, his tiger eyes so like Dake's, rushed down the steps, almost falling in his eagerness. "Reesa! Reesa!" He flung himself at her, his face pushed into her, his arms going around her waist. "I prayed, Reesa, I prayed." The tremolo voice was muffled into her middle.

"Oh, darling, Robbie, Robbie darling, how I missed you!" Reesa said.

They stood there swaying together, their words lost in tears and laughter.

"Now I'm your boy, if you want me." Robbie grinned at her.

"Oh, I want you all right." Reesa gave a teary chuckle.

"I knew you would," Robert said with the smugness of the young. "This is Acme, my grandma's retriever, but he likes it when I come here to visit. We play."

"Good for you." Reesa kept her hold on him as they entered the huge foyer.

"Darling, this is Jesse. He runs the household."

"Hello," Reesa said, a little out of breath, grateful to be away from the icy wind coming off the river.

"How do you do, Mrs. Masters. Best wishes on your marriage." Jesse smiled at her and shook hands with Dake. "And congratulations to you. You always were the lucky one."

"I am, aren't I?" Dake drew Reesa close to his side, pressing his mouth to hers, not seeming to mind that Jesse and Robbie watched them. He lifted his head and grinned at his son. "Well, I brought her home to you."

"Thanks, Dad." Robert still clung to Reesa's hand.

"David Kennedy!" The voice carried down the circular stairs, resounding in the octagonal foyer. "Welcome home and felicitations." A graceful woman, taller than Reesa, glided down the staircase. Her dove-gray chiffon dress was a shade deeper than her hair; her skin, though wrinkled, was taut at the throat; her figure was slim. "Robert dear, can't you release your stepmother?" She smiled gently at the boy, her smile widening when he shook his head.

"Thank you, Mother. Come and meet my wife." Dake held Reesa close as they walked to meet his mother at the foot of the stairs. "You are a little overdressed for the afternoon before Thanksgiving, aren't you?" he kissed her cheek, then brought Reesa forward.

The two women shook hands, each making a veiled assessment of the other.

"My dear, you are lovely." Priscilla Lynch Cabot Masters looked back at her son. "You didn't give me a chance to tell you that the whole family will be here for the weekend in honor of Reesa's arrival. The cocktail party begins in thirty minutes."

Reesa inhaled, her actress's training allowing her to conceal the surprise she felt.

"Fine," Dake said. "We'll be ready. Excuse us, won't you, Mother?"

"Ah, David Kennedy, will you let Jesse show your wife to your quarters? I would like to speak to you for just a moment."

It looked to Reesa as though Dake were going to refuse his mother. "Go ahead, Dake. Jesse and Robert will show me. I'll see you in a moment." She kissed Dake and felt his tongue tease hers. Then she pulled away and hastily started to climb the stairs.

Dake followed his mother into the library. "Father is showering," she explained as she shut the door. She turned, looked at her son, and didn't mince words. "Why did you marry a woman who has caused you so much pain, Dake?"

"I loved her, Mother, then and now. I will love her until I die and beyond—" Dake broke off at the sight of tears in his mother's eyes. That shocked him. He did not remember her ever showing much emotion, and certainly she had never before cried in front of him. "Mother, don't!" The love for her that he had kept buried surfaced, and he took her in his arms. "I hate to see you cry. Please try to be happy for me even if Reesa isn't the sort of person you might have wished to have in our family."

"My boy, my boy," his mother sobbed. "I have always loved you, but I thought you could be happy married to someone like Linda whom you didn't love. Love cripples a person, Dake."

Dake held his mother back from him. "Mother, because you didn't marry for love—"

"Oh, but I did." Priscilla took a lace hankie from her sleeve and dabbed at her eyes. "I love your father very much. That's how I know love cripples. He married me for my name. He always assumed that I married him because of his money, but I didn't."

Dake stared at his mother for long moments, then he shook his head. "You've wasted all this time because of pride. Why not put it aside for once and go upstairs and tell him you love him?"

"Just like that?" His mother smiled, pulling back from him.

Dake took her into his arms again. "Just like you told me you loved me. Something I wanted to hear you say all my life because *I* love you, Mother."

She hugged her son, then withdrew.

"I've got enough Yankee courage to tell your father! Of course I do!" She flapped her hands at her son and crossed to the door. Still with her back to him, she spoke again. "I'm not rescinding what I said though.

When you love someone, you get hurt. I don't want to see you hurt, David Kennedy."

"Mother, I will never suffer any greater hurt than I did when I thought Reesa was dead. I'll chance anything else as long as I have her."

Priscilla nodded, then opened the door and walked from the room.

Reesa and Dake ended up staying in the shower too long, then hurrying to dress.

Reesa chose to wear a green velvet gown that was not new, but it had always been one of her favorites. It had been tight on her when she last wore it. Now it was loose. She took the time to move the hook and eye that was the only fastening in the back of the strapless garment. The dress hung straight from under her breasts, the soft folds at the hem pulling into a demi-train at the back so that with every movement she made, the heavy material hugged her form, delineating every curve. With it she wore the rings that Dake had given her for her engagement and marriage, and old-fashioned teardrop emerald earrings that had belonged to her grandmother. She wore no wrap on her shoulders or jewelry on her neck or arms.

Dake came through from the dressing room looking devastating in a black silk tuxedo and matching bow tie. The pleats in his white silk shirt had been hand sewn with gold thread, the same color as his eyes. He paused, looked her up and down, and whistled softly. "You are lovely. I've seen you in that dress when you were heavier and you were beautiful, but now you're ethereal, angelic." He shook his head. "You have made me one happy man by marrying me, but I find I still feel jealous at the thought of other men seeing you like this."

Reesa laughed, feeling the whirlwind of his love surround her. "It's strange," she murmured, taking his arm as they left the room, "I felt the same vortex sensation when we met on the *Windward* as I do now, but now I feel so safe in the eye of the hurricane, not tumbled out of control."

"That's because we're there together," Dake told her, lifting her hand to his mouth, then tucking the hand under his elbow before leading her down the circular stairway.

A tall, graying man, Robert at his side, came into the foyer and looked up at them.

As they reached the marble-floored foyer Reesa held out her hand to her stepson.

"Father, I want you to meet my wife," Dake said.

Kennedy Masters kissed Reesa on both cheeks and edged her away from Dake. "You are lovely, my child, and as your father-in-law I claim the right of introducing you to our family."

Reesa was dazed by the number of people she met, not expecting half that number. Her actress's training did her good service by helping her remember the many names.

She was standing next to Dake's mother being introduced to a cousin by the name of Lowell when she noticed Dake speaking to his father. Shortly the two left the room.

"Oh, dear, where do you think David Kennedy and his father are going? Isn't the football game tomorrow?" Priscilla grimaced when Reesa laughed.

They didn't come back for a while, Reesa noticed, and when they did, Dake's father had a grim expression on his face. He walked right to his wife's side.

Dake ambled over to Reesa. "Well, as you suggested when I told you about Mother's 'little confession,' I talked to Father. I don't think he believed me." He slipped his arm around her waist. "But I'm glad I followed your advice and said something." He shook his head. "He seemed stunned at first that I would speak to him in such a fashion. Years of being closed to each other, that damned restraint that is considered breeding, makes it hard to communicate." He looked down at her, his eyes caressing her, lingering on the swell of breast above her dress. "I thank God for what we have, Reesa Hawke Masters."

Reesa lifted her face to him, delighted when he bent to kiss her.

"Good Lord, Priscilla, can't you speak to David Kennedy?" A relative by the name of Sinclair raised his voice, bringing heads around to stare at Reesa and Dake.

"Why should she speak to him?" Dake's father interjected. He put his arm around his wife and pulled her close to him, smiling down at her when her mouth fell open. "We approve, don't we, my love?" He leaned down and kissed his wife.

"Oh, yes, we approve," Dake's mother said a few seconds after her husband's lips released hers.

"You are getting very silly," another relative volunteered.

"Just getting smart. Come along, sweetheart, time for dinner. Robert, you sit next to your stepmother at dinner." He turned back to those following him and Priscilla. "If any of you have plans for playing bridge after dinner, please don't include Cilla and me. We're retiring early so that we can go skating with our daughter-in-law tomorrow. It will be her first time on skates." He leaned down and kissed his wife again, smiling at her. "You want to go to bed early, don't you, love?"

"Yes."

"Priscilla," Sinclair whined. "We always play bridge."

"Not tonight," Priscilla said in a breathy voice.

"I don't understand. This household is fast becoming unstable." Sinclair glowered at Lowell and told him to leave the canapes and come to dinner.

Dinner was a noisy affair.

"I thought proper New Englanders were silent at

dinner," Reesa said to her father-in-law as she sat at his right hand.

"They're neither proper nor silent." Kennedy smiled at her. His eyes narrowing, he bent closer to her. "I was prepared to hate you for all the trouble that Dake had with the police after your accident, but I think I must thank you for giving me back my son. He had become so cynical married to Linda. From the moment he met you some of the hardness of him began to fall away, but after your accident he became worse than he had ever been. I think he hated being alive." Kennedy sighed and nodded permission to the maid to remove his empty soup plate. "His mother and I went out to California often to see if we could help him, but he was as closed with us as we were with each other." He shot a glance at Reesa. "I love my wife."

"I can see that," Reesa murmured.

"I loved her from the moment I lifted her from the ice where she had fallen, but I hid that from her out of pride. That sort of foolishness gets to be a habit, and I'm afraid we imparted that habit of—of coldness to our children."

"I think we all want to protect ourselves from love. It's instinctive to hide ourselves from hurt." Reesa felt a great affinity for this man who looked like an older version of her love.

"Dake tells me he is hoping that you are pregnant."

Reesa gasped. "He told you that?" She could feel the blood filling her face.

"Would you like a child, my dear?"

"Very much, but—but I don't know that I—"

Kennedy Masters patted her hand. "Of course you don't, but I must say, I never thought I'd see my son so excited over such a nebulous project. He even told me that he wants a girl who will look exactly like you."

Laughter escaped Reesa. Her father-in-law laughed with her.

Heads turned their way.

After dinner there was music from the stereo and some of the younger cousins danced in a corner of the large living room where the Persian rugs could be pushed back.

"Reesa, dance with me." The owlish Lowell came and stood in front of her, where she sat with her mother-in-law drinking coffee from Sevres cups.

"Ah." She looked around her at the gyrating couples on the dance area of the floor and recalled the many times she had danced to rock and roll with the Sea Dive Group.

"Dake doesn't mind. I used to dance with Linda all the time, and that didn't bother him."

Priscilla gasped. "Lowell."

"Well, he didn't," he said truculently.

"Come along. We'll dance." Reesa wanted to save her mother-in-law from any more uncomfortable moments.

Lowell belonged to the jack-in-the-box type of dancer. He bounced, cavorted, and swung his arms, his body energetically moving to the music. "You're pretty good, Reesa," Lowell panted.

"Thank you." She ducked as one of his arms came around like a windmill.

Reesa suddenly felt herself lifted backward out of range of the lethal Lowell.

"What the hell are you thinking of, Lowell? Are you trying to maim her?" Dake asked.

"You never minded when I danced with Linda!" Lowell glowered back.

"You can dance with anyone you damn well please, except my wife. I'm not going to have her marked up by your clumsy motions."

"Reesa is Dake's love, Lowell. You must understand that," Priscilla remarked, glancing shyly at her husband, who had come up to her side and taken her hand.

"I want to dance, but not to that," Kennedy announced, putting his arm around his wife. "Put on a waltz, Gibson," he said to Dake's uncle.

Despite the groans from the younger members of the family, there were quite a few who did waltz, including Dake and Reesa.

It was Dake who first suggested they should go to bed since they would be rising early to skate.

Reesa barely had time to say good night to everyone before he whisked her from the room. She cooed at him as they reached the second floor and walked down the hallway leading to their apartment.

"Darling—" Dake gulped. "When you look at me like that I feel like my kneecaps just fell off." He opened their door, picked her up into his arms, carried her through, then locked the door behind them.

They undressed each other in record-breaking speed, making love as though it were the first time, with gentle sweetness, but at the culmination of their love, at the apex of the peak they had climbed, the love force took them into the roaring vortex, wiping away the control, making them one and alone in the world.

Much later Reesa remembered the conversation with her father-in-law. "What's this about telling your father you hoped I was pregnant?" she asked Dake. "Aren't you rushing it a bit?"

"Yes and no. I want a baby, but I want you all to myself. You said you wouldn't mind having a baby. Still, I want to be sure you're healthy."

"I am healthy. And wrong—I said I would *love* to have your baby, silly."

They fell asleep, face to face, their mouths touching, their arms around each other.

The next morning they woke and made love again. Afterward, Reesa tried to convince Dake that she should stay in the house while the rest of them went skating.

"Never."

"You'll hate dragging me behind you. Besides, I don't have skates."

"I had some delivered to the house for you when I knew we were coming east."

"You did?"

"Yes." Dake grinned at her like a small boy. "I'll get them for you."

"Help," Reesa whispered when he left her, imagining her body flying in four directions when she tried to skate.

Twenty or thirty persons were already twirling and dipping in graceful figure eights and spins when Dake and Reesa arrived at the pond.

"Oh, glory, I'm cold already," she muttered as Dake laced up her fleece-lined skates. "Umm, they are comfortable," she observed when she stood and her ankles stayed firm.

In minutes Dake was leading her out onto the ice.

"Aaaagh! It's slippery!" Reesa's left leg went west, her right leg east, but Dake held her erect.

"Not to worry, darling, I have you. Now, hold it. There. Now you're balanced with my arm around you. Push your foot forward. That's it. Now glide."

Reesa felt her body buckling and slipping, but Dake kept an iron grip on her.

When they'd gone once around the area, Reesa was puffing, but she liked it more than she thought she would despite the aches in her legs from trying to keep her legs firm.

"Darling," she urged Dake, "please go and skate. I'm going to finish a hot chocolate, then see what I can do on my own just at the edge of the pond."

Robert came up then, urging his father to join him on the ice.

Dake hesitated, but Reesa was adamant since she'd detected the gleam in his eye when he watched the other skaters. "All right. For just a minute, then I'll be right back." He pushed off, the blades of his skates sending up sprays of ice as he shot around the pond, Robert right behind him.

When Reesa finished her hot drink she pushed herself to her feet, waited a moment to balance herself, then began a slow, scraping progress at the edge of the pond.

She was congratulating herself for not falling when she paused to watch a younger group of Dake's relatives whirl around the frozen water.

Someone yelled, "Whip! Whip!" Then they grasped hands in a long line.

Reesa smiled and lifted her hand to wave at Lowell, Dake's cousin, as he skated by in the snake of people.

A young man at the end of the line spun near her and grasped her outstretched hand, pulling her behind him.

"Nooooooo!" Reesa called, her scream floating out behind her like a banshee's.

"Isn't it great?" the man with the death grip on her hand shouted to her.

"Reesa!" Robert called to her, his mouth open as he watched her go past him.

"Noooooo!" Reesa saw blurs of faces and forms, becoming aware that many of the skaters had paused to watch the snakelike group of people that was increasing its speed as it came to the far end of the ice, where it would turn and go back in the opposite direction. Reesa caught fuzzy glimpses of her in-laws standing near a wood fire, then she heard Dake roar.

"Reesa. No. Stop. Damn you, stop that whip!"

"Ohhhhhh!" Reesa felt her body gain momentum as it came around in the wide circle. She was the caboose at the end of the train of people. She wobbled, then seemed to be flying, her mouth and eyes wide open. Her hand became unhooked from the stranger's and she flew toward the sidelines, where a group of skaters in varying acts of putting on and taking off skates watched her in fascinated horror.

"Reesa!" Dake bellowed, then caught her around the waist. Her speed and his momentum were too great to be stopped, but he managed to aim them toward a monstrous pile of snow, which they crashed into full tilt. Dake's body protected hers. He spat snow from his mouth, swiping at his face to clear his eyes.

"Darling, are you all right?" He reached out and wiped her face, feeling his mouth drop as he saw her laugh, snow clinging to her cheeks and brow. "You're not hurt." He let out a long sigh of relief.

"No . . . oh, Dake, I was scared . . . but it was like flying. I couldn't stop!" She choked, laughing even more. She looked past him at Priscilla and Kennedy, who were fast approaching. Reesa was a little envious of her mother-in-law's graceful motions on skates.

"Reesa, my dear, are you all right?" Priscilla reached down to wipe more snow from Reesa's face. "Richard must be out of his mind to have pulled you behind him on that whip." She bit her lip as Kennedy pulled Reesa to her feet, then watched when her son rose from the snow, his lips tight, his hands balled into fists. "Now, David Kennedy, stay calm."

"I am going to very calmly kill him." He fired the words from his mouth, making the others blink.

"Darling, don't be that way. He's your cousin and he didn't mean any harm. He was just trying to be friendly," Reesa said in a placating tone.

"You could have been killed," Dake barked. "There he is," Dake pronounced in a doomsday voice as his gaze riveted on his youthful cousin.

"Darling, I do feel a little woozy." Reesa blinked her eyes, trying to get Dake's attention away from his cousin.

"What?" Dake swiveled to her, his hands reaching

out for her and sweeping her up in his arms. "You're pregnant," he announced in a voice that carried.

"No, I'm not!" Reesa hissed at him.

He picked her up and strode swiftly up the hill to the house, not bothering to remove her skates or his, his parents panting in his wake.

"Reesa, dear, there is no need for you to hide it. We are delighted, aren't we, Kennedy?"

Kennedy Masters chortled at the look on Reesa's face as she stared over her husband's shoulder. "Don't worry, child, we are willing to wait for grandchildren." He put his arm around his wife. "Maybe we should try for another child ourselves, Cilla."

"Kennedy!" Mrs. Masters shot a look at Reesa, then she put her arm around her husband's waist. "Shame on you. We're too old."

"Maybe not, love."

"Dad, you old dog." Dake gave a hard laugh, then tightened his grip on Reesa as they crossed the circular drive and went up to the front door. "I'm going to take Reesa up for a hot shower and a nap. We'll see you at dinner—maybe."

"But David Kennedy . . ." his mother began as they entered the large foyer, Dake's skates marring the floor.

"Let them alone. They can always have sandwiches," Kennedy said.

"Sorry about the marks, Mother," Dake called down to them as he ascended the stairs.

"You shouldn't have done that." Reesa moaned as he carried her down the corridor toward the wing where their apartment was. "There's nothing wrong with me. Take off those skates."

Dake set her down on the bed, then knelt in front of her to loosen the laces of her skates. "When I saw you at the tail of the whip I almost went into cardiac arrest. Never again will I let you out of my sight."

"Darling!" Reesa watched him remove his own

skates, then come back to undress her. "I didn't get the least bit hurt."

His head snapped up and he glowered at her. "Reesa, I almost lost you once. I lived in the middle of a fiery vortex, the torment never ending. Do you think that I am going to risk losing you again?"

"No, of course not, but—"

"No buts. I will not chance it." He stared up at her as he knelt in front of her, pulling off her socks, then standing her on her feet to remove her outerwear. "I love you. The only vortex I want is the one with you in it. It can be painful, joyful, happy, sad—all those things. I know that without you, my love, life is a gray hole."

"My sweet one," Reesa sobbed as he pushed her back on the bed. "I do love you, but you shouldn't have said I was pregnant. I'm not."

"You don't know that. You haven't kept a calendar, and neither have I. Even so, I don't want anyone endangering you," he crooned into her neck. "I need you so much. It excites the hell out of me that today is Thanksgiving Day and you and I are sharing it as man and wife. I won't let anything hurt you."

Their lovemaking was as volatile as always, but there was a new dimension that each of them sensed, a new depth to the love they gave to each other. They strived harder to give each other joy, fulfillment. When they crested together, whirled as one in the vortex, there were no more questions, no more doubts. There was only the whirlwind of love.

THE EDITOR'S CORNER

Please be sure to turn to the back of this book for a special treat—an excerpt from the novel **CHASE THE MOON** by a marvelous British author, Catherine Nicolson. I hope the short sample of this extraordinarily romantic story will prompt you to ask your bookseller for the book next month when you get your four LOVESWEPTs. And, of course, we believe those four LOVESWEPTs are real treats, too!

It astonishes me at times how our authors continue to top themselves book after book. They're all talented authors who are devoted to expanding their imaginations and developing the skills of their craft. And I know how hard they work. Still, I'm often surprised at the high level of creativity they are able to maintain. And no author demonstrates better those qualities of originality and ingenuity in superb romantic storytelling than Kay Hooper.

IF THERE BE DRAGONS, LOVESWEPT #71, is one of Kay's most emotionally touching romances. The surprises you expect from a Kay Hooper book are abundant in this story of lovely Brooke Kennedy whose rare gift has kept her a virtual prisoner of loneliness. But, thanks to that delightful meddler Pepper, a golden knight comes to her rescue. Cody Nash, Thor's best friend in **PEPPER'S WAY,** enters Brooke's world and brings her the warmth and light of love. I'll never forget Brooke and her dragons, Cody and his virile tenderness . . . or a very special "wild" creature who contributes a unique and heartwarming dimension to this wonderful story.

(continued)

Sandra Kleinschmit makes her debut as a published author next month with a nifty romance, **PROBABLE CAUSE,** LOVESWEPT #72. Jami Simpson isn't playing cops and robbers when she detains a man she suspects of breaking and entering. She's a police officer all right, but Lance Morgan is hardly a burglar . . . or is he? He assaults Jami's emotions and tries to steal her heart in a love story that's sensitive and fun. We hope you'll join us in giving this brand new author the warmly enthusiastic welcome you've given the other talented writers we've been so pleased to be able to publish for the first time.

And speaking of new talents, here comes BJ James again with **MORE THAN FRIENDS,** LOVESWEPT #73. BJ's first book, **WHEN YOU SPEAK LOVE,** was vibrant with dramatic tension, though touched with humor; her second romance shows her versatility in a work that's full of charming lightheartedness, though touched with dramatic tension. The heroine of **MORE THAN FRIENDS** is pocket-sized Jamie, the sister of six brawny males. She's grown up in a household devoted to competitive sports and has always been in the thick of rough and tumble football games and fierce races, never asking for privilege because of her sex or size. Then she literally tackles a gentle giant named Mike Bradford and he tries to turn her life around. You'll be as appalled—and impressed—as Mike is by Jamie's foolish physical courage . . . and her confusion about the conflict between competition and independence. What a love story!

Ah, it is such a delight for me to tell you about **CHARADE,** LOVESWEPT #74, by Joan Elliott Pickart. This sensual love story is spiked by some of the most amusing exchanges it's been my pleasure to read. (One line in particular struck me as so side-splittingly funny that my son ran into the room where I was reading to see if I was choking!) **CHARADE**, as the title suggests, is a merry romance in which heroine Whitney assumes a false identity . . . and gets trapped (hmm, quite deliciously) in her role by one of the most captivating of all possible heroes. The marvelous cast of secondary characters—from a soap opera heart-throb to a babbling would-be vamp—truly enrich this tale. Watch out for the hero's dear old gray-haired Aunt Olive. She has a surprise or two up her sleeve!

Enjoy! And do continue to write to us. Your comments are so helpful and so interesting!

Warm good wishes,
Sincerely,

Carolyn Nichols

Carolyn Nichols
Editor
LOVESWEPT
Bantam Books, Inc.
666 Fifth Avenue
New York, NY 10103

Dear LOVESWEPT reader:

CHASE THE MOON is a one-in-a-million book, the kind of story that won't let you rest until you've finished it, and then won't fade from your heart and mind for months. Set apart from other novels in the romance genre by its unusual blend of the richly exotic and the touchingly innocent, CHASE THE MOON is a fairy tale for grown-ups, created of mystery and magic, beauty and sensuality, fantasy and fulfillment. And next month it will be available from your bookseller.

The heroine's name is Corrie Modena, alias Columbine. A naive, lonely orphan whose stunning musical talent drives her in search of fame and fortune, she has confided her secret dreams to only one man—an enigmatic stranger she knows only through letters signed Harlequin. Although they have never met, theirs is a perfect, trusting love . . . until the night that Corrie meets Guy de Chardonnet at the opera. The magnetic attraction that Corrie and Guy feel is immediate and fierce, although they are constantly at odds with each other. But Corrie is torn between Guy and her burning ambition, an ambition that Harlequin, in his letters, urges her not to betray. Corrie determines to leave Guy, realizing that Harlequin is right—for how can she know that the man to whom she's lost her heart is the steadfast keeper of her soul?

The storyline is magical, but what makes CHASE THE MOON truly unique is the extraordinary way in which the story is told. The writing is exquisitely sensual, skillfully evoking the sights, smells, tactile experiences, tastes, and sounds of the world Corrie and Guy share—a world of light: an apricot moon hanging in the still azure sky above the Riviera; sunlight; stage lighting; the dazzling spangles and sequins refracting light on costumes; the play of shadow and moonlight spilling into the nighttime ocean. Even Corrie's voice is described as having the deep and dark quality of "L'heure bleue," the strange blue hour between summer twilight and summer night. Dusky, fragrant, and everchanging, the world of CHASE THE MOON is memorable and magical, even to its elusive characters: the "real" Guy and Corrie, the fantasy Harlequin and Columbine. And CHASE THE MOON could perhaps only have been written by Catherine Nicolson—a lovely woman from Great Britain who possesses abundant charm and talent.

CHASE THE MOON is spellbinding . . . a world of romantic fantasies come breathtakingly true— where two lovers have no secrets from each other . . . except their names. It was a special delight for me to be Catherine's editor on this book. I hope the excerpt on the following pages will captivate you so much that you'll be sure to ask your bookseller for CHASE THE MOON.

Carolyn Nichols

Chase the Moon

by Catherine Nicolson

He had invited her to Paradise to enjoy oysters and peacocks . . . and she'd been unable to resist.

She turned, slowly. He looked different, younger. Against the white of his suit his skin was lightly tanned, with a satiny evenness that disturbed her. His hair, touched by the late sun, had reddish hints. Only his ice-gray eyes were unchanged. She felt suddenly confused. Perhaps in these few short weeks he had grown younger and she had grown older, perhaps they were growing together, like herself and the Balenciaga . . . She halted the thought. It didn't make sense.

"You don't seem surprised." She spoke abruptly to hide her confusion.

"Should I be?" He smiled at her, a lazy, self-assured, mocking smile.

"I might not have come."

His smile deepened, touched his eyes briefly.

"I knew you would come. You wouldn't be able to resist it. The oysters or the peacocks would persuade you, one or the other. And curiosity. All women like the same things."

"Really?" She spoke with some asperity. She was not and would never be like all women. "What might those things be?"

He smiled down at her lazily, shrugged.

"Silk. Paris. Compliments. Surprises." He offered her his arm. "Besides . . ." His tone was gently conversational. "I always get what I want."

"Always?" She was uneasily aware of the warmth of his skin through the soft material of his sleeve.

"Almost always."

Ceremoniously he escorted her back to the table overlooking the garden. She felt strange, as if she were in a dream. The restaurant was still deserted, they had the whole gallery room to themselves. It made her feel unreal, timeless, as if they were both on a stage, acting out a kind of play for an unseen audience. A waiter materialized out of the wings. She noticed for the first time that there was no menu.

Guy nodded in response to the waiter's inquiring glance. Not a word was spoken. The waiter disappeared as silently as a fish.

"I hope you're hungry." She was conscious of his eyes on her face.

"I'm always hungry."

"I know, I remember." He smiled. She felt a blush coloring her cheeks and refused to acknowledge it. The past meant nothing, she could rise above it.

"And you . . . Are you always late?"

"Touché." He spoke mildly, offering neither explanations nor excuses. She felt a fleeting tinge of admiration. His effrontery rivaled her own, though she had to admit his had a degree more style.

The waiter reappeared, with a large tray in his arms. As he set it down carefully Corrie saw to her astonishment that it was filled from edge to edge with small shallow bowls, each containing what seemed like no more than a mouthful of different dishes. Guy dismissed the waiter with a nod of approval. Corrie stared at the table. There was scarcely a spare inch of tablecloth to be seen.

"What is this?" She looked up to find Guy studying her with that annoying hint of irony.

"You told me you wanted everything. Well, here it is. Something from every single dish on the Belvedere's not inextensive menu." Her eyes widened. "There's more to come, but there wasn't enough room on the table." His smile was limpidly ingenuous. "Eat up, or it will get cold." He handed her a small silver dish. "I suggest you begin with the smoked oysters."

The unmistakable challenge in his eyes was irresistible. Corrie instantly resolved to do justice to the feast or die in the attempt. She'd show him what it meant to be hungry.

Manfully, she set to work. He watched in growing astonishment as she polished off dish after dish, chasing the last drops of sauce with catlike delicacy. Lobster bisque and *consommé madrilène*, *chateaubriand printanier*, *suprême* of sole, artichoke hearts, soft carps' roe, lamb cutlets, veal escalopes with apples and cream, flamed in calvados, crab claws dressed in pistachio nut oil. Invisibly the empty dishes were whisked away to be replenished with tiny spring vegetables, duckling with green pepper and brandy sauce, wild strawberries, brandied peaches, chicken stuffed with braised fennel roots, shrimp soufflé . . . Recklessly she mixed sweet with savory, fish with fowl, red meat with white. It was a cornucopia of delights, a Roman orgy. White Burgundy followed red, Nuits St. Georges chasing Pouilly Fuissé, and capped with a rainbow assortment of different ice creams.

"Are you quite sure you've had enough?" His tone was elaborately solicitous as she pushed away the last ice-cream dish and patted her lips with a napkin. She nodded, so full she could barely speak.

"Yes, I think so." She glimpsed a remaining petit four and downed it with relish. "For the moment."

He shook his head in mock astonishment. "You'll be sick."

"I'm never sick. I have the digestion of a camel."

"So I see. How do you manage it?"

"It's quite simple. All you have to do is eat with your spine." She took a deep breath. "And there's something else."

"What's that?" He was regarding her with as much polite interest as he would have shown a real camel in a zoo.

"Motivation."

"Motivation?" He frowned, puzzled.

"Perhaps you've never heard of it." She allowed a slight trace of sarcasm to enter her tone. "It's called hunger."

"Indeed." He seemed unmoved, just faintly curious. "You interest me, Miss Modena. Why should a woman in your position . . ." his eyes rested lazily on her bare shoulders—"ever have to suffer such an indignity? Surely your patron cannot be such an ogre? Or is it . . ." Here his eyes took on a mocking gleam. "Can it possibly be that he prefers slender women?"

Corrie drew herself to her full height and with an heroic effort choked back her anger at the implied insult.

"M. de Chardonnet." She spoke with dignity, as befitted a widow recently bereaved. "I no longer have a patron."

"Oh." He seemed surprised, even concerned. She gritted her teeth, disguised her fury behind demurely cast down eyes. Doubtless he couldn't imagine how a young woman could survive without the support and protection of a man such as himself. "Are you no longer at the Savoy?"

"From tomorrow, no." She thought about coaxing a tear, decided against it. She was bereaved, but brave.

"Because of me?"

The effrontery of the man! He didn't seem in the least abashed—if anything he sounded pleased, almost gratified. He assumed, of course, that she'd been dismissed by her patron because of one eve-

ning spent in another man's company. Such arrogance . . .

"You could say so." She sighed deeply.

"My deepest sympathy." He was smiling a small,
knowing smile, as if now at last he had her in his
power.

"I don't want your sympathy, thank you very
much!" A trace of tartness entered her tone. His
smile broadened.

"Perhaps another petit four?"

"Certainly not." She folded her hands primly in
her lap. He was still looking at her with that
disturbing, assessing gaze. He gestured at the
waiter to clear away the remaining dishes.

"At least you enjoyed your meal."

The touch of irony in his voice brought a blush
to her cheeks. A healthy appetite hardly became
the grieving widow . . . But it was too late now.

"It was delicious." Belatedly she remembered
her manners. "Thank you." A thought struck her
suddenly; she frowned in puzzlement. "But why
has no one else come to eat here? They don't
know what they're missing."

He smiled patiently.

"Because I've engaged the entire restaurant."

"What?"

Now he really had managed to surprise her.
"Just for us?" It was an extraordinary extrava-
gance, it almost made her feel ill.

"Of course."

"Do you mean . . . they've cooked all these different dishes . . . just for me?"

"Of course."

"You mean, there's a whole rack of lamb back
there, and I've just had one mouthful?"

"I've no idea. I should imagine so. It hadn't
occurred to me."

He smiled indulgently. "I could ask for it to be
put in a bag for you, if you like. We could take it
with us."

She leaned back in her chair, half amused, half appalled. He and she were worlds apart. She couldn't even begin to imagine what it must be like to live as he did, to spend as if money were a mere toy for his own amusement. And yet he himself had barely touched a mouthful of the feast.

"Why didn't you eat anything?"

He shrugged. "As you say, it is a question of . . . motivation. I preferred to watch you."

She blushed again. It hadn't been the sort of performance she'd intended. She stared at him. The light from the gardens outside was deepening infinitesimally into blue, flattering, softening, making outlines unreal.

"Now, Mademoiselle Corrie, you have done ample justice to the oysters. It is time for peacocks."

In a dream she took his proffered arm. She could no longer remember whether she liked him or not, she was too full of good food for logic. As they emerged into the air she saw there were no other people in sight. A thought struck her.

"You haven't hired the whole of the park as well?"

"No." He laughed, the deep spontaneous laugh which she was beginning to like, to try and prize out of him. Slowly they walked up toward the ornamental garden. Around them she felt the faintest stir of breeze, bringing with it the hypnotic scent of newly mown grass. Sunlight glinted off the little clocktower with its turquoise copper roof and golden ball. The old rose bricks of the arcade leading to the orangery were soft in the sunlight, the shadows violet beneath the murmuring trees. He was right. It was as near as man could get to Paradise.

Beneath the trees, in the emerald green shade where the grass bloomed with an underwater intensity, rabbits browsed while on the high old walls peacocks strutted and bowed, saluting the evening with their harsh haunting cries. Everything around them was poised timelessly on the brink of summer, every rabbit soft and fat with plenty, every peacock with its hen.

Against her will, she was drawn into the fairytale. She couldn't resist the peacocks. Their voices had the authority, the aching, soulful penetration of a prima donna soprano. Those slender necks and tiny heads didn't look capable of producing such a noise. And they moved so slowly, sure of their charisma, milking their audience. The last light was brilliant on their opalescent plumage. How much she wanted to be a peacock.

They halted, mesmerized. A peacock eyed them motionlessly with its malachite gaze. His snakelike neck, insufferably blue, waved, searching, swelling. He emitted a superb, spine-shaking shriek. And then slowly, like a magician, he produced his tail, spreading it like a moonscape, a heaven full of dancing planets. He stayed there, quivering for enough time to stun them, then shuffled his feathers back with a businesslike air, squawked once and stalked away.

It was a revelation. They looked at each other with a sort of awe. They had been privileged, it was as if royalty had stopped to speak to them in the street. They had shared something irreplaceable, unrepeatable.

"What was that?" Her voice was a whisper. She hardly dared to break the silence, but she wanted to spread her own plumes for him, tell him her plans and dreams, flaunt her secret inner world.

"Serendipity." He turned to her, his white suit dappled under the shimmering leaves. "I never realized . . ." His voice was soft, like someone woken from a deep sleep. "Your eyes are so blue, violet, actually."

They stared at each other. The image of the peacock's tail still seemed to be imprinted on her retina, a dazzling mist of color. She couldn't see, couldn't think.

"Come with me." His voice was low. "Come with me to Paris. Now, tonight."

Paris, Paris, Paradise . . . It sounded so easy. It would be easy. She could float away and never be heard of again, supported by him and his money, like a swimmer in the Dead Sea. But it wasn't enough, it couldn't be enough for her.

She shook her head. The peacock's plumes were fading, the moment was lost. She couldn't go to Paris with a man who'd only just noticed the color of her eyes.

Dear Harlequin,

What's happening to me? Why can't I stop thinking about him? He's nothing special, just a collection of cells and corpuscles like me, and yet I think if I saw him in the street I'd throw away everything, all the future we've planned, just to hear his voice again . . . Does that sound crazy? I wish I knew how long this was going to last. Some days I think I'm cured, I hardly think about him at all, and then at night he comes alive again as soon as I fall asleep, and I wake up crying.

I was such a fool, I don't know how I came to fall in love with him of all people. You know how I feel about rich men—surely I should have been immune?

Please, tell me I've done the right thing.

Columbine

#1 HEAVEN'S PRICE
By Sandra Brown
Blair Simpson had enclosed herself in the fortress of her dancing, but Sean Garrett was determined to love her anyway. In his arms she came to understand the emotions behind her dancing. But could she afford the high price of love?

#2 SURRENDER
By Helen Mittermeyer
Derry had been pirated from the church by her ex-husband, from under the nose of the man she was to marry. She remembered every detail that had driven them apart—and the passion that had drawn her to him. The unresolved problems between them grew . . . but their desire swept them toward surrender.

#3 THE JOINING STONE
By Noelle Berry McCue
Anger and desire warred within her, but Tara Burns was determined not to let Damon Mallory know her feelings. When he'd walked out of their marriage, she'd been hurt.

Damon had violated a sacred trust, yet her passion for him was as breathtaking as the Grand Canyon.

#4 SILVER MIRACLES
By Fayrene Preston
Silver-haired Chase Colfax stood in the Texas moonlight, then took Trinity Ann Warrenton into his arms. Overcome by her own needs, yet determined to have him on her own terms, she struggled to keep from losing herself in his passion.

#5 MATCHING WITS
By Carla Neggers
From the moment they met, Ryan Davis tried to outmaneuver Abigail Lawrence. She'd met her match in the Back Bay businessman. And Ryan knew the Boston lawyer was more woman than any he'd ever encountered. Only if they vanquished their need to best the other could their love triumph.

#6 A LOVE FOR ALL TIME
By Dorothy Garlock
A car crash had left its marks on Casey Farrow's beauty. So what were Dan

Murdock's motives for pursuing her? Guilt? Pity? Casey had to choose. She could live with doubt and fear . . . or learn a lesson in love.

#7 A TRYST WITH MR. LINCOLN?

By Billie Green
When Jiggs O'Malley awakened in a strange hotel room, all she saw were the laughing eyes of stranger Matt Brady . . . all she heard were his teasing taunts about their "night together" . . . and all she remembered was nothing! They evaded the passions that intoxicated them until . . . there was nowhere to flee but into each other's arms.

#8 TEMPTATION'S STING

By Helen Conrad
Taylor Winfield likened Rachel Davidson to a Conus shell, contradictory and impenetrable. Rachel battled for independence, torn by her need for Taylor's embraces and her impassioned desire to be her own woman. Could they both succumb to the temptation of the tropi-

cal paradise and still be true to their hearts?

#9 DECEMBER 32nd . . . AND ALWAYS

By Marie Michael
Blaise Hamilton made her feel like the most desirable woman on earth. Pat opened herself to emotions she'd thought buried with her late husband. Together they were unbeatable as they worked to build the jet of her late husband's dreams. Time seemed to be running out and yet—would ALWAYS be long enough?

#10 HARD DRIVIN' MAN

By Nancy Carlson
Sabrina sensed Jacy in hot pursuit, as she maneuvered her truck around the racetrack, and recalled his arms clasping her to him. Was he only using her feelings so he could take over her trucking company? Their passion knew no limits as they raced full speed toward love.

#11 BELOVED INTRUDER

By Noelle Berry McCue
Shannon Douglas hated

Michael Brady from the moment he brought the breezes of life into her shadowy existence. Yet a specter of the past remained to torment her and threaten their future. Could he subdue the demons that haunted her, and carry her to true happiness?

#12 HUNTER'S PAYNE
By Joan J. Domning
P. Lee Payne strode into Karen Hunter's office demanding to know why she was stalking him. She was determined to interview the mysterious photographer. She uncovered his concealed emotions, but could the secrets their hearts confided protect their love, or would harsh daylight shatter their fragile alliance?

#13 TIGER LADY
By Joan J. Domning
Who *was* this mysterious lover she'd never seen who courted her on the office computer, and nicknamed her Tiger Lady? And could he compete with Larry Hart, who came to repair the computer and stayed to short-circuit her emotions? How could she choose between poetry and passion—between soul and Hart?

#14 STORMY VOWS
By Iris Johansen
Independent Brenna Sloan wasn't strong enough to reach out for the love she needed, and Michael Donovan knew only how to take—until he met Brenna. Only after a misunderstanding nearly destroyed their happiness, did they surrender to their fiery passion.

#15 BRIEF DELIGHT
By Helen Mittermeyer
Darius Chadwick felt his chest tighten with desire as Cygnet Melton glided into his life. But a prelude was all they knew before Cyg fled in despair, certain she had shattered the dream they had made together. Their hearts had collided in an instant; now could they seize the joy of enduring love?

#16 A VERY RELUCTANT KNIGHT
By Billie Green
A tornado brought them together in a storm cel-

lar. But Maggie Sims and Mark Wilding were anything but perfectly matched. Maggie wanted to prove he was wrong about her. She knew they didn't belong together, but when he caressed her, she was swept up in a passion that promised a lifetime of love.

#17 TEMPEST AT SEA
By Iris Johansen
Jane Smith sneaked aboard playboy-director Jake Dominic's yacht on a dare. The muscled arms that captured her were inescapable—and suddenly Jane found herself agreeing to a month-long cruise of the Caribbean. Jane had never given much thought to love, but under Jake's tutelage she discovered its magic . . . and its torment.

#18 AUTUMN FLAMES
By Sara Orwig
Lily Dunbar had ventured too far into the wilderness of Reece Wakefield's vast Chilean ranch; now an oncoming storm thrust her into his arms . . . and he refused to let her go. Could he lure her, step by seductive step, away from the life she had forged for herself, to find her real home in his arms?

#19 PFARR LAKE AFFAIR
By Joan J. Domning
Leslie Pfarr hadn't been back at her father's resort for an hour before she was pitched into the lake by Eric Nordstrom! The brash teenager who'd made her childhood a constant torment had grown into a handsome man. But when he began persuading her to fall in love, Leslie wondered if she was courting disaster.

#20 HEART ON A STRING
By Carla Neggers
One look at heart surgeon Paul Houghton Welling told JoAnna Radcliff he belonged in the stuffy society world she'd escaped for a cottage in Pigeon Cove. She firmly believed she'd never fit into his life, but he set out to show her she was wrong. She was the puppet master, but he knew how to keep her heart on a string.

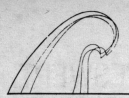

LOVESWEPT

Love Stories you'll never forget by authors you'll always remember

LOVESWEPT

Love Stories you'll never forget by authors you'll always remember

☐	21630	Lightning That Lingers #25 Sharon & Tom Curtis	$1.95
☐	21631	Once In a Blue Moon #26 Billie J. Green	$1.95
☐	21632	The Bronzed Hawk #27 Iris Johansen	$1.95
☐	21637	Love, Catch a Wild Bird #28 Anne Reisser	$1.95
☐	21626	The Lady and the Unicorn #29 Iris Johansen	$1.95
☐	21628	Winner Take All #30 Nancy Holder	$1.95
☐	21635	The Golden Valkyrie #31 Iris Johansen	$1.95
☐	21638	C.J.'s Fate #32 Kay Hooper	$1.95
☐	21639	The Planting Season #33 Dorothy Garlock	$1.95
☐	21629	For Love of Sami #34 Fayrene Preston	$1.95
☐	21627	The Trustworthy Redhead #35 Iris Johansen	$1.95
☐	21636	A Touch of Magic #36 Carla Neggers	$1.95
☐	21641	Irresistible Forces #37 Marie Michael	$1.95
☐	21642	Temporary Forces #38 Billie Green	$1.95
☐	21646	Kirsten's Inheritance #39 Joan Domning	$2.25
☐	21645	Return to Santa Flores #40 Iris Johansen	$2.25
☐	21656	The Sophisticated Mountain Gal #41 Joan Bramsch	$2.25
☐	21655	Heat Wave #42 Sara Orwig	$2.25
☐	21649	To See the Daisies . . . First #43 Billie Green	$2.25
☐	21648	No Red Roses #44 Iris Johansen	$2.25
☐	21644	That Old Feeling #45 Fayrene Preston	$2.25
☐	21650	Something Different #46 Kay Hooper	$2.25

THE BRIDES OF BELLA LUCIA

A family torn apart by secrets, reunited by marriage

When William Valentine returned from the war, as a
testament to his love for his beautiful Italian wife Lucia,
he opened the first *Bella Lucia* restaurant in London.
The future looked bright, and William had,
he thought, the perfect family.

Now William is nearly ninety, and not long for
this world, but he has three top London restaurants
with prime spots throughout Knightsbridge and the
West End. He has two sons, John and Robert,
and grown-up grandchildren on both sides
of the Atlantic who are poised to take this small
gastronomic success story into the twenty-first century.

But when William dies, and the family fight to
control the destiny of the *Bella Lucia* business, they
discover a multitude of long-buried secrets, scandals, the
threat of financial ruin—and ultimately two great loves
they hadn't even dreamt of: the love of a
lifelong partner—and the love of a family reunited…

Read the first two books of this compelling
new miniseries, and meet twin sisters…

Rachel Valentine, in
**Having the Frenchman's Baby
by Rebecca Winters,**

and Rebecca Valentine, in
**Coming Home to the Cowboy
by Patricia Thayer.**

THE VALENTINE FAMILY

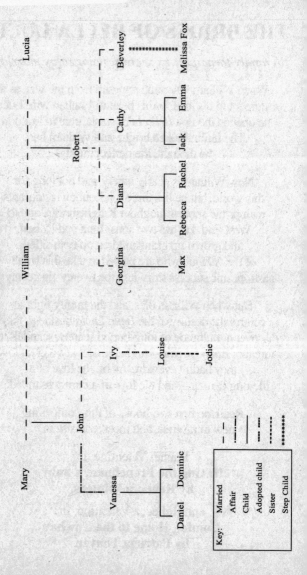

Key:
Married ————
Affair —·—·—
Child ————
Adopted child —··—··—
Sister ————
Step Child ********

COMING HOME
TO THE COWBOY

BY

PATRICIA THAYER

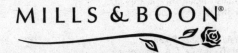
MILLS & BOON®

All the characters in this book have no existence outside the imagination of the author, and have no relation whatsoever to anyone bearing the same name or names. They are not even distantly inspired by any individual known or unknown to the author, and all the incidents are pure invention.

First published in Great Britain 2006
Harlequin Mills & Boon Limited,
Eton House, 18-24 Paradise Road, Richmond, Surrey TW9 1SR

© Harlequin Books S.A. 2006
Special thanks and acknowledgement are given to Patricia Thayer for her contribution to *The Brides of Bella Lucia* series.

Standard ISBN 0 263 84917 1
Promotional ISBN 0 263 85132 X

Set in Times Roman 10½ on 13¾ pt.
02-0806-38128

Printed and bound in Spain
by Litografia Rosés, S.A., Barcelona

THE BRIDES OF BELLA LUCIA

A family torn apart by secrets, reunited by marriage

**There's double the excitement in August—meet twins
Rebecca and Rachel Valentine**
Having the Frenchman's Baby—Rebecca Winters
Coming Home to the Cowboy—Patricia Thayer

**Then join Emma Valentine as she gets a
royal welcome in September**
The Rebel Prince—Raye Morgan

**Take a trip to the Outback and
meet Jodie this October**
Wanted: Outback Wife—Ally Blake

**On cold November nights catch up
with newcomer Daniel Valentine**
Married Under the Mistletoe—Linda Goodnight

Snuggle up with sexy Jack Valentine over Christmas
Crazy about the Boss—Teresa Southwick

**In the New Year join Melissa as she heads
off to a desert kingdom**
The Nanny and the Sheikh—Barbara McMahon

**And don't miss the thrilling end
to the Valentine saga in February**
The Valentine Bride—Liz Fielding

To the Valentine Ladies, Rebecca, Helen,
Ally, Linda, Teresa, Barbara and Liz...
Thanks for showing the new kid the ropes.
I've enjoyed working with you all,
especially my twin, Rebecca Winters,
for giving me your time and expertise.
I value your friendship.

PROLOGUE

SHE had run out of time.

Rebecca Valentine stood at the large window overlooking Central Park. She'd worked hard to gain this big office and the junior partnership at the Pierce Advertising Agency. That had been her goal since college. It had taken ten years but she'd achieved it. In the meantime, she'd lost something she wanted even more.

She reread the official report from her recent medical tests. "The buildup of scar tissue caused by advanced stages of endometriosis… This condition highly decreases the ability to conceive. Surgery recommended."

In layman's terms, there would be no babies in her future.

Not that her OBGYN, Dr Shields, hadn't warned her for years to have a child early. And not that Rebecca had deliberately put it off. She just hadn't found a man to be a suitable father, and, of course, her career had contributed to the delay. But thirty-three shouldn't be too old to have a baby.

Deep down inside she'd wanted children. She wasn't sure she'd be good mother material, but now she'd never have a chance to find out. She'd never get the chance to feel a life move in her womb, nourish a baby at her breast, and give her child all the love she knew was so precious.

A tear escaped, and she wiped it away. Dr Shields had also informed her she was anemic and needed to slow down, get away from the stress of her job. The prescription had been for her to take some time off. How was she supposed to do that when she was responsible for no fewer than ten accounts? They were all important to her, especially now since all she had was her career.

There was a sharp knock on her office

door and Brent Pierce poked his head in. The good-looking son of the agency's owner always had a smile for her. "Hey, Beck, have I got a proposition for you."

"Unless it involves relaxing on a beach somewhere for the next two weeks, I'm not interested. I'm overdue for a vacation."

"You, go on vacation?" He shook his head. "You'd be bored within two days."

"Brent, I've been working nonstop for the last six months. My doctor said I needed to take some time off. I'm anemic." That was all she was going to tell him.

He came into the room and sat on the edge of her desk. "So you'll eat a lot of red meat. I need you on this one, Rebecca. It's a new account for free-range beef." Suddenly his eyes brightened. "You know, I think there's a way we both can get what we want. You can still handle this new account and have your vacation, too." His smile widened. "How do you feel about ex-changing a beach for a ranch in Wyoming?"

CHAPTER ONE

REBECCA looked out the window of the Cessna at the vast miles of majestic Rocky Mountain range. The brilliant May sun was reflecting off the dew-covered emerald-green pastures below.

Suddenly the plane dipped lower and she got a better look. The Tucker ranch came into view. Pristine white fences lined the road that led to a sprawling brick and white clapboard house trimmed with dark green shutters and surrounded by a perfectly manicured lawn. Her attention shifted to the outer buildings, several brightly painted red barns. In a large corral two beautiful white and black leopard-spotted horses, Appaloosas, ambled back and forth.

So this is Mitchell Tucker's Wyoming empire.

Rebecca felt the familiar stirring of excitement at the prospect of a new client. The chase and proving her talent were her favorite parts of the job. Her record was impeccable when it came to landing the premier accounts. She wasn't going to give this millionaire rancher the opportunity to consider any other agency to promote his new business, free-range beef.

The pilot tapped her on the shoulder and motioned that they were going to land.

"I'm ready," she called and drew a calming breath. This might be partly a vacation, but she planned to work her tail off too. It was the only thing she knew how to do. Besides, what else was there to do in Wyoming?

Waiting for the plane to land, Mitch Tucker leaned against his black Range Rover. His kids stood beside him at the end of the private landing strip. He was still wondering if he'd needed his head examined to agree to contact a New York ad agency. He'd relinquished that part of his life two years ago when he'd sold off all his international holdings. His focus was on business close to home in Wyoming. He'd resisted getting involved again with that old fast-paced lifestyle. He'd hoped to do everything locally, while being hands-on with the whole operation.

He glanced at his eleven-year-old daughter. Greta Caroline not only looked like her mother, blonde and fair-skinned with rich sapphire-blue eyes, she was also just as stubborn when she wanted something. His daughter was the one who'd practically taken over his idea to raise free-range beef.

Greta had spent hours on the Internet researching marketing agencies for this project. And after he'd done some of his own research he knew they needed the right promotion to make their venture profitable. Not that he needed to worry about money. Working together with his kids was what mattered most. This was the first thing Greta had taken an interest in since her mother's death. He couldn't deny her this.

If it hadn't been for his children, losing Carrie would have finished him. At the time of their mother's death, Greta was nine and Colby was only three. Someone had to take care of them. That alone made Mitch drag himself out of bed every day, put one foot in front of the other and keep moving forward.

Two years later, he'd long since stopped his travel and gotten more involved in the ranching operation. But always in the center of everything were his kids. They were the reason he was standing here waiting for a New York executive to help promote his new beef program. This was just the beginning of his new life. Someday, he wanted to give his kids a complete family again.

"Please, Daddy, promise you'll be nice."

He looked down at his daughter's worried face. "This is business; you can't always be nice. I'll be polite."

"But you can be…intimidating."

"In business, that's not a bad way to be, Greta."

She sighed dramatically. "You said you'd give this a chance. I've researched this, and we need the right kind of advertising, the right market to promote our beef. Please, just listen to Ms Valentine's ideas."

He forced a smile. "I said I would, and you know I don't go back on my promises." *How in the hell is a New Yorker going to know anything about ranching in Wyoming?* "I talked with Brent Pierce and he's assured me that Ms Valentine is the right person for this job."

Greta nodded enthusiastically. "Rebecca Valentine is one of their top agents and a junior partner. She's worked for the Pierce Agency since college when she graduated Summa Cum Laude ten years ago—"

"Whoa, where did you get all this information?"

She looked up at him, showing off the pretty smile that was going to do him in. "I did my research like you taught me."

Before he could say anything more, Colby began jumping up and down, pointing to the other end of the runway as the plane touched down. "They're here, Dad."

When the plane stopped taxiing, Mitch took his son's hand and the three of them hurried onto the runway. He would give this a chance, just as he'd promised, realizing he had to be crazy to invite a career-driven female into his home. Ms Valentine wasn't the type of woman he planned to expose his kids to, or the type who would be content living on a cattle ranch.

Mitch paused next to the Cessna as his pilot and his ranch manager, Wally Hagan, walked around and popped open the passenger door. The first thing he saw of the New York agent was a pair of black high-heeled shoes that were attached to long, shapely legs. A sudden dryness in Mitch's throat made it difficult to swallow when bare knees and part of a thigh made an appearance.

Holding Wally's hand, the passenger

finally made it out of the plane. Clearing the wing, she stepped into the sunlight and Mitch couldn't catch his breath. Rebecca Valentine was a tall woman with golden brown hair that was drawn back into a bun, except for a few wayward curls that circled her pretty face.

A smile touched her full mouth, but it was her light blue, almost gray eyes that he was drawn to. He didn't realize he'd been staring until his daughter nudged him.

"Ms Valentine…I'm Mitch Tucker," he said and held out his hand. "Welcome to Wyoming."

She had a firm handshake. "Please, call me Rebecca."

"And I'm Mitch." He quickly moved on. "This is my daughter, Greta."

She took the girl's hand. "Greta, it's good to finally meet you."

"I'm glad to meet you, too, Ms Valentine."

"Since we'll *all* be working together, please call me Rebecca."

Greta turned to her father and he nodded his permission.

Mitch gathered his small son in front of him. The five-year-old was already dirty and his dark curly hair unruly. "And this is Colby."

She leaned down to look in his eyes. "Hello, Colby."

Colby smiled, showing off his missing bottom tooth. "Hi, Rebecca, I'm five." He held up his spread fingers.

"My, that's old," she said. "I bet you go to school."

He bobbed his head. "This year I start kindergarten."

Mitch motioned to the SUV. "Well, let's take you to the house and get you settled in."

Wally helped Mitch load the suitcases and the kids climbed in back. He came around the passenger side to find Rebecca attempting to climb into the high seat. Her narrow skirt rose up dangerously, threatening Rebecca's modesty, and Mitch's sanity.

"SUVs and short skirts don't mix," she

said. "I guess I didn't think about this outfit being impractical. I should have worn pants."

"Jeans might even be better," he offered. "If you'll allow me to help, we can get going."

"Sure."

She gasped as he scooped her up. He dropped her in the bucket seat, but not before he caught a whiff of her scent, and felt the enticing curve of her small waist.

"Like I said, pants will make it easier...for all of us." He grimaced, knowing his words were too revealing.

Hell, he'd been widowed for two years. Just about anything would set him off.

The house was even more impressive close up. Rebecca eyed the small details of the fence and flowers that hung from the front porch. Mitch pulled the car into the circular drive and continued around the structure to the back.

"We live pretty simply here and the back door is closer to everything," Mitch told her.

"I know," Rebecca replied. "I spent a lot

of time at my grandparents', we always used the back door."

For some reason she was just chattering away. She knew Mitch Tucker hadn't been exactly thrilled about calling in a New York company, but a good businessman should want the right promotion for his product. She just needed to convince him that she was the best person to do that for him.

Once parked, she opened the truck door and got out without any help. Mitch grabbed her bags and went up the step to the small back porch. Colorful pots filled with flowers were arranged against the house, making the place look homely and welcoming.

Mitch opened the glass-paneled door and motioned her in. She walked into a mud room with a washer and dryer; several pairs of boots were lined against one wall. She crossed another threshold into a bright yellow kitchen with maple cabinets and white-tiled counters. A trestle-table sat in front of a row of windows that overlooked a view of the ranch.

"This is lovely," she said as Mitch walked through, carrying her bags down a hall.

She started to follow him when Greta stopped her. "Yellow was my mom's favorite color," the girl said.

Colby pulled a chair out and climbed up on it. "She died when I was really little," he announced as his brown eyes glistened.

"I'm sorry." Even though Rebecca knew the Tucker family history, she wasn't prepared to deal with this. No child should have to be without a mother.

"She loved us a whole bunch," the boy added.

"I'm sure she did," Rebecca said, fighting the urge to wrap her arms around this child.

"Do you have any little boys?" Colby asked.

Her chest tightened with the familiar pain. "No, I don't."

"Any little girls?"

Rebecca swallowed. Unable to speak, she shook her head.

Greta stepped in. "Colby, Rebecca is a

career woman and she flies all over the country for her job."

Colby put his hands on his hips. "I know that, but she can have kids, too."

Mitch returned. "Hey, can't you two at least stop arguing until Rebecca gets settled? You don't want to scare her off."

The children's eyes widened. "We're sorry, Rebecca," Greta said.

Mitch pointed to the hall. "Why don't I show you to your room so you can rest?"

Rebecca was tired and her stomach was a little unsettled after the long trip into Denver, and the flight to the ranch. "How about I rest a while, then later we'll discuss some ideas?"

"You rest today. Tomorrow is soon enough," Mitch said.

Before Rebecca could argue, he was escorting her down the hall. He led her to a doorway off the main floor and opened double doors leading into a large bedroom. The walls were painted a pale blue with white crown moldings and off-white carpeting. A mahogany four-poster bed was adorned with an ecru satin comforter.

"Oh, this is a beautiful room." She sighed. "I think it's bigger than my entire apartment back in New York."

He smiled and she felt the jolt all the way to her toes. "Land is more plentiful here and I hope it stays that way." He waved to the full-sized bathroom. "There should be plenty of towels in the cabinet. If there's anything else you need let me know. Our housekeeper, Margie, is away for a few months on family business. So the kids and I are handling things on our own this summer."

"You are a brave man," Rebecca said without thinking.

His piercing brown eyes held hers, and he folded his arms against his broad chest. The man was big and gorgeous with thick, wavy dark brown hair. She couldn't help but enjoy the total package. Her gaze swept over the blue Western-cut shirt tucked into the narrow waist of his fitted dark denim jeans and on to his feet encased in snakeskin boots.

He could be an ad as the perfect cowboy.

"Are you saying I can't handle a hundred and forty sections of cattle ranch, a horse-breeding business, and two kids?"

Rebecca raised an eyebrow. "If your kids were just run-of-the-mill kids, but those two…" She nodded toward the kitchen. "They're scheming for a takeover."

That brought a wide, sexy grin. "You could be right." He took a step toward her. "So tell me, Rebecca Valentine, are you here to join forces with them, or save me?"

Two hours later, Mitch moved around the kitchen preparing an early supper, admonishing himself for flirting with Rebecca Valentine. This was business, and no matter how attractive she was he couldn't mix the two. Not that he wanted to. No. Even though he was attracted to her, he'd be crazy to get mixed up with a New Yorker, a career woman. No, this wasn't the woman he needed…

Mitch ran his hand over his face in frustration. He'd better get it together because she was going to be here a while, right under his roof. He just needed to think about what was good for Greta and Colby.

Okay, he could handle it. He went to the oven and checked on the enchiladas. Thanks to Margie, they had several prepared dishes in the freezer.

Margie Kline had been working for the Tuckers part-time since Colby was born. Then after Carrie's death, the widowed grandmother moved in to stay. She'd become a part of the family, and helped Mitch keep his sanity.

So when Margie had asked for a few months to stay with her sister during her hip surgery and recuperation, he hadn't been able to turn his housekeeper down. Besides, it gave him more time to spend with the kids. Of course, now he had a house guest.

Rebecca Valentine could stay in town, but he'd spend too much time driving her back and forth. This seemed to be the best solution, especially since he was needed here and she had to familiarize herself with the operation.

Greta came in and immediately began to take the dishes from the cupboard and set the table. "Do you think we should eat in the dining room? We have a guest."

"No, Greta. Rebecca is here to learn how we do things. She's going to get dirty just like the rest of us." Did she have clothes to wear on a ranch? Visions of her trying to get around in a short skirt had his body suddenly stirring to life.

"Is there anything I can do to help?"

Mitch glanced up to see Rebecca standing in the doorway. She had changed into a pair of gray pleated trousers and a wine-colored, short-sleeve blouse. She looked a lot shorter in her flat shoes, but that didn't take away from her appeal.

"Sure, you can pour the milk for the kids and iced tea for us," he told her. "It's in the refrigerator."

Rebecca went to the cupboard and found glasses. "Something smells wonderful."

"Enchiladas," Greta said.

"Did you make them?" she asked.

Greta smiled. "No, I can cook some things but these are Margie's specialty. She left us a lot of food in the freezer."

"We won't starve," Mitch said.

"I'm not worried," she told him. "Give me some lettuce and tomatoes and I'm happy."

He stopped opening the tortillas. "Please, don't tell me you're a vegetarian."

Rebecca enjoyed seeing the panicked look on Mitch Tucker's face. "No, I'm not. If I could I'd eat steak and burgers all the time. I just have to watch my weight."

She felt his intense gaze roam from her head down to her toes, spreading heat in its wake. She had never been able to obtain that lean look that was so popular. Rachel had gotten all the thin genes.

"You look fine," he told her.

"Those great-smelling enchiladas aren't going to help," she said as she took the milk and pitcher of iced tea from the refrigerator and placed them on the table.

Mitch put on oven mitts, took out the covered baking dish, and brought it to the table. Just then Colby raced into the room and jumped into his seat.

"Oh, boy," he cried, looking hungrily at the food.

"Did you wash your hands?"

A pair of big brown eyes widened as if deciding what to say. "I did this morning."

Mitch frowned and pointed to the door. "Go and wash."

"Okay." Colby got up.

"I should go with you," Rebecca said. "I forgot to wash mine, too. Will you show me the way?"

Colby perked up. "Sure. Come on. I have this cool soap that foams up and smells like bubble gum."

"Wow. I've got to see this." She glanced over her shoulder. "We'll be back shortly."

It wasn't long before there was laughter coming from the bathroom. There was nothing sweeter to Mitch's ears.

Finally the twosome returned and sat

down at the table. Soon both his children were vying for Rebecca's attention. Mitch decided it wasn't that odd. Besides Margie there hadn't been many women in the house since their mother's death.

"Hey, Dad," Colby called. "Did you know that Rebecca knows how to ride? Her grandpa owned horses."

"Is that so?" he said, somewhat surprised. "Where was their farm?" He dished out a helping of enchiladas and handed it to her, then filled Colby's plate.

"Outside of Lexington, Virginia," Rebecca said. "My grandfather bred and trained Quarter Horses and European Warmbloods, all disciplines—hunters, jumpers and dressage. It was a small operation."

Mitch finished serving everyone. "Did your family move to New York?"

Family? That was something she'd never had. Not unless you counted the mismatched union her parents had called a marriage. "No, just my mother and sister;

my parents divorced when I was pretty young."

For all their sakes, Robert and Diana Valentine had called it quits after a few years, but the bitterness had continued until her mother's death a decade ago. It also had caused their twin daughters to choose sides. That was how Rachel had ended up in the UK with their father, and Rebecca living in the States with their mother.

"Our mother moved us to Long Island to work. But I spent summers in Virginia, but once I started college it was too difficult to get back. And by then Poppy Crawford retired and sold the horse farm."

Mitch checked to see that Colby was eating, and took a bit himself. "You and your sister didn't want to follow family tradition?"

"My sister now resides with my father's family," she said, recalling since their mother's death just how many years it had been since she'd seen Rachel. Along with her other family members, Grandfather

William, her father, half-brothers and -sisters.

"She works in London. Our father is British."

"Wow! Do you go to London?" Greta asked.

"I haven't been back there in years."

Rebecca wondered how they'd side-tracked her. She wasn't used to revealing so much family history. There was only one person she'd ever shared the Valentines' sins with; her friend, Stephanie Ellison.

"These enchiladas are great," she said. "Margie is a great cook."

Mitch must have seen her discomfort. "Kids, why don't you finish eating? You have other chores."

They groaned.

"All right, if they don't get done today, then you can't ride out to see the herd tomorrow."

"Okay," Greta said. After they cleaned their plates Colby helped his sister carry their plates to the sink.

Once they were out of earshot, Mitch

turned back to Rebecca. "I apologize for all the questions."

"They're curious."

"Do you think you can handle them for the next few weeks?"

The kids weren't going to be her problem. Rebecca smiled. "One thing about kids: they're open and honest for the most part. I find that refreshing."

"It can get stale pretty quick." He turned serious. "If you ever feel they're infringing on your privacy, just let me know."

She laughed. "As big as this house is, I can't believe we'll get in each other's way. Besides, it's very gracious of you to invite me to stay here."

He got up and took down two mugs from the cupboard. "Coffee?"

At her nod, he did his task. As he walked back to the table she couldn't help but be aware of his powerful presence—but at the same time how comfortable he seemed waiting on her.

"This is a pretty rural area. One of the

reasons I have my own plane is to get in and out fast. The winters can be treacherous."

"They can be in New York, too." She took a sip of coffee. The kids were on the other side of the kitchen doing dishes, chatting away. A good-looking man was sitting across from her as they shared coffee.

Yes, she used to see herself in this life with a man and children. Now…

"Rebecca…"

She turned toward Mitch's voice. "Sorry," she said, embarrassed. "I guess I drifted off."

"I'd say it's more likely jet lag. You've flown a long way. I doubt you slept much in the last twenty-four hours."

"If you don't mind, I think I will call it a day."

"I don't mind at all," he told her. "I want you rested when we ride out tomorrow. There's a lot to see."

It just dawned on her that she'd probably landed this account because she was the only one in the firm that could ride a horse.

Was this all-too-good-looking cowboy waiting to see if she could keep up? She'd been crazy to think she could relax.

"I'll be ready."

CHAPTER TWO

REBECCA woke up to a soft knock at her door. She rolled over in the big bed, fighting sleep.

"Rebecca," a man's muffled voice came through the closed door.

Mitch. She sat up, trying to clear her head. "Just a minute," she called as she threw the blanket back and grabbed her robe off the end of the bed. She walked to the door, jabbing her arms through the sleeves. Belt tied, she ran her hand over her hair to tame the wild curls and opened the door.

There stood Mitch Tucker, dressed in a pressed tan Western shirt and a pair of faded jeans. He had a smile on his clean-shaven face, not looking the least bit apologetic for waking her at this ungodly hour.

"I'm sorry, did I oversleep?" she asked, looking over her shoulder at the darkness outside her window.

"I didn't really give you a specific time." He leaned against the doorjamb. "It's six and we usually have breakfast at six-thirty. Can you make it?"

"Sure," she lied. "That'll give me plenty of time."

He nodded, but didn't move to leave. "Are you sure you're up for riding today?" His voice was husky and low, causing a shiver along her spine.

She could only manage to nod.

"We could get there in the four-by-four."

She was touched by his concern. "No need. I can ride, but just take into account that I haven't ridden in years."

He smiled, and Rebecca couldn't breathe. "You should be fine," he assured her. "Besides, we'll have Colby and Greta with us so there's no rush. I thought I'd pack some sandwiches for lunch, make an easy day of it. There's a lot of pretty country to see. It might give you some ideas on the marketing campaign."

"I'll be sure to take my notepad."

All at once Rebecca was too aware of the cozy silence in the house, and the gorgeous man standing just outside her bedroom. How was she supposed to concentrate on business?

"Do you have some jeans and a pair of boots?" he asked.

"I brought some. So…I'd better get in the shower if you want me ready on time."

"And I'll go start breakfast."

"Bye," she said and closed the door. *Great, I come to Wyoming and let a man distract me.*

Over the years, she had perfected the "this is strictly business" look when it came to clients wanting more from her—not that Mitch wanted more from her. But whenever the man came near her, she wasn't sure she knew her own name. Worse, thirty seconds ago, she hadn't cared.

"Well, you better care," Rebecca scolded herself. She yanked fresh underwear and a pair of jeans from the drawer, then a blouse from the closet. She headed for the tumbled-stone-tiled bathroom, and turned on the shower.

Somehow she had to regain her footing on this, or she was in big trouble. This was her career. She couldn't mess this up.

It was all she had left.

At six-thirty on the dot, Rebecca walked into the kitchen. Mitch couldn't help but stare. He wasn't sure he'd seen a woman in a pair of jeans look so good…so sexy. A white oxford-cloth blouse was tucked into her small waist. But it was her hair pulled back with clips, hanging free and curled against her shoulders, that had him blink.

"Good morning," he said to her.

"It will be as soon as I find some coffee," she said and walked toward the pot.

"Help yourself," he told her as he removed the rest of the bacon from the skillet and placed it on a paper towel. "How do you like your eggs?"

"However you're having them." She gulped some caffeine and her expression changed to immediate pleasure.

It made him wonder what else pleased her, causing a jolt to his body. He quickly diverted those thoughts. "Have a seat."

"No, I'll help you." She took another sip and set her mug on the table, then went to the cupboard and found the plates, arranging four place settings at the table. "Where are Greta and Colby?"

"They're still asleep." He leaned against the counter. "A parent needs some quiet time."

"So that's your secret."

He glanced out the window toward the rising sun. "Early morning was always when Carrie and I got to spend time together, especially since I traveled so much back then. I guess I still like it."

"You shouldn't feel as if you had to invite me for breakfast if you'd rather be alone."

"I didn't." He was too aware of her. "I wanted to share breakfast with you," he said, then rushed on to say, "I mean…

maybe we could run over some ideas without…interruptions."

She blinked and nodded. "Sure. If that's what you want."

What he wanted could get him into trouble. "Why don't we enjoy the peace and quiet first?"

The moment ended with a thundering sound on the stairs. They smiled. "I guess that was wishful thinking."

"Dad, Colby didn't make his bed," Greta announced as she walked in.

"I did, too," the boy argued. "It's just not made her way."

"Greta, Colby," he said. "Remember your manners."

Both children mumbled their good mornings.

"Now, sit down before you drive Rebecca back to New York."

The children took their seats. "Sorry, Rebecca," Greta said.

"Yeah, sorry, Rebecca," Colby repeated. "I hope you stay with us."

"I'd like to," she told them. "I wouldn't want to miss the ride today."

Their eyes widened. "Are we going for sure?" Greta asked.

Mitch glanced over his shoulder giving them both his best stern look. "I'm still thinking about it." He turned back and poured eggs into the skillet.

That was when he heard Colby whisper, "That means yes."

Over the next hour, Rebecca helped pack sandwiches and drinks. Then everyone headed out the door toward one of the barns. She couldn't help but be impressed by the obviously well-run ranch. There were several ranch hands at work doing their assigned chores.

Wally and another young man had four horses saddled and waiting for them next to the barn. Suddenly Rebecca was both excited and fearful.

The forty-something ranch manager tipped his hat. "Good morning, Rebecca."

"Good morning, Wally," she returned the greeting. "Are you going with us?"

"No, ma'am," he said with a smile, causing tiny lines to crinkle around his hazel eyes. "I'm sorry to say I have work to do." He glanced at Mitch. "You enjoy yourself, though. It's a pretty ride. And you'll have a great mount here with Ginger."

"Dad, Rebecca's going to ride Ginger?" Greta asked.

Mitch exchanged a glance with Wally. "I thought she'd be the best mount for her." He went to the chestnut mare and patted her neck. "You can trust her; she's gentle," he assured her.

"Mom used to ride her," Colby said.

Rebecca felt odd. How could she ride Carrie Tucker's horse? "Are you sure?"

"Ginger, here, is getting a little stocky." The horse shifted at Mitch's insult and everyone laughed. "The ride today will do her good."

"This is my horse, Rebecca." Greta went to a small Appaloosa mare, brown with a sprinkling of small white snowflake-like spots. "Her name is Snow Princess. Dad gave her to me for my birthday."

"That's quite a present."

As if not to be outdone, Colby spoke up. "When I'm ten, Dad says I can have my own horse, too. Right now, I'm riding Trudy." His mount was a small bay mare. Rebecca knew enough about horses to recognize that this mare had been around for many years. She was as docile as a family pet.

"Dad's got the best horse, White Knight," the boy said.

Rebecca's gaze went to the impressive stallion, a white Appaloosa with four black stockings, mane and tail. This animal was the most spirited.

She was drawn to the beautiful beast. She knew about Mitch's Appaloosa breeding program. "Is he one of your studs?"

"Not much any more." Mitch patted the horse's neck and the animal bobbed his head and whinnied. "His male offspring have taken over for the most part. If you're interested, I can show you around my breeding operation."

Keep focused on business. "If you have time," she said and went back to her horse while Mitch assisted his kids up on their horses.

"Need some help?" he called to her.

"Not unless the way you mount a horse is different now than when I was a kid," she said teasingly as she tugged the borrowed straw cowboy hat lower on her forehead. She took the reins, put her foot in the stirrup and began to pull herself up when she felt Mitch's hands on her waist. She bit back a gasp as he helped and lifted her into the saddle.

"I could have managed."

"Just thought I'd help," he said with a wink. "How do the stirrups feel?"

"They're a little long," she told him.

Mitch immediately adjusted one, then the other. "How's that?" he asked. His hand on her leg was more disturbing than she'd like.

"It's fine." Rebecca backed away, putting the unfamiliar horse through a few basic commands. She was pleasantly surprised at the easy ride.

Mitch nodded when she finished, then he strolled to his horse. His easy gait let her know he was comfortable in this element. And he had a great-looking backside in a pair of jeans. She watched as he took the reins and swung his leg over the horse's back into the saddle.

"Let's go." He turned and started across the yard to the gate. A ranch hand held it open until they went through. The four of them ambled along the trail in pairs, Colby and Mitch, followed by Greta and Rebecca.

Although it was May, the morning sun promised to heat up the day soon enough. And with a three-mile ride, it was going to take some time.

Before long Rebecca got into a rhythm with her horse. She leaned back and began to enjoy the ride.

Greta was quite the tour guide, pointing

out landmarks. The Rocky Mountains made a proud backdrop against the rich blue sky, white billowy clouds scattered around as if in a painting. Rows of aspen trees moved with the gentle breeze.

"You should see the aspens in the fall. The leaves turn bright gold and red," Greta explained as she pointed toward the mountains. "And see the pine trees? At Christmas we get to go up there and find a really big tree and cut it down. That was my mom's favorite time of year."

"Mine, too," Rebecca said. "I love New York at Christmas time with all the lights and decorations." She also remembered an earlier time as a child in England with her mother and her father…and sister. She thought about her grandfather William. What was he now—ninety? As a child, he'd always smiled and hugged her a lot. Even though those holidays had been stiff and formal in William's London home, they meant family to Rebecca. Besides the grandchildren had always been able to escape upstairs where there had been a special room loaded with books and toys.

She smiled. "It's good to have memories."

"Hey, you two," Mitch called. "Try and keep up."

"Yeah, try and keep up," Colby echoed his father.

"He's such a brat," Greta said.

Rebecca smiled again. "One day, when you grow up, the two of you can be good friends. Just don't lose touch with the people you love."

The young girl looked concerned. "Did you lose touch with your sister? Is it because England is so far away?"

"That's one of the reasons," Rebecca admitted. "But even being twins, we were very different."

"You're a twin." Her companion's blue eyes widened. "What's her name?"

"Rachel."

"Rachel and Rebecca," Greta said. "That's so cool. Does anyone ever call you Becca?"

Emotions rushed through Rebecca as she

remembered her dad's pet name for her. "Someone did once. A long time ago."

Rebecca couldn't help but smile. Her body actually began to relax. She could get used to this. It might be the best medicine for what ailed her. Well, that wasn't quite true, but it was a start.

Mitch tried to keep an eye on Rebecca to see how she was handling the ride. Maybe he should have driven them up here to see the herd. Three miles wasn't far if you were used to being on horseback. This New Yorker wasn't.

He dropped off the trail and waited for Greta and Rebecca to catch up. "Greta, go ride with your brother for a while."

"Okay, Dad, but he better mind me."

"There's no reason to boss him. Just stay on the trail and I'll be back in a few minutes." He patted the horse's rump and Princess moved up to Colby's mount.

Mitch fell in beside Rebecca. "How are you holding up?"

"Pretty good, but I have a feeling that I'll know better tomorrow." She shifted in the saddle. "Please don't worry about me. I'm truly enjoying the ride. I haven't seen this much open land in years. You have a gorgeous ranch, Mr Tucker."

"I know." He smiled as he glanced around. "It's not everyone's taste, but it is mine. Feel free to enjoy." His gaze settled on her. He liked her hair down. Made her look younger, more relaxed, as if she belonged here. But she didn't. "We'll be in the valley in another mile."

"No hurry," she assured him.

Mitch didn't switch places with Greta. He was enjoying the view right where he was. He couldn't help but watch Rebecca. She sat on a horse with ease and grace, but she was also in control.

"Did you train horses with your grandfather?"

She smiled. "If you mean exercise them, and muck out stalls, yes. Poppy said I had to earn my way up. By the time I was old enough, my time there was limited. But, yes, I did get to help some. I rode jumpers. Believe me, I've fallen off my share of horses."

"That's better than getting bucked off. I spent some time trying to rodeo. Decided I could find easier ways to earn money."

Rebecca laughed and he found he liked the sound. They rode for a while in silence before Mitch asked, "Do you miss being around horses?" He stole a glance at her. "I mean, I've done a lot of business in New York—the pace can be grueling."

She sighed. "I agree, but I need to be in New York for my line of work. I've gotten used to the pace and madness."

"I guess you're right," he conceded. "I just noticed how relaxed you look right now."

"I can relax in New York, too," she said.

He started to disagree when Greta called to him. They reached their destination. In the clearing was a large grassy valley surrounded by a barbed-wire fence.

"Welcome to Freedom Valley. It's fenced

in to keep the cattle in the pasture that's free of any pesticides." He directed the riders up along the fence.

"The herd consists of over a hundred and fifty head of Angus mix," he told her, and remembered that this was supposed to be a new beginning for his family. He'd been planning and preparing this project for quite a while.

"This isn't exactly a new way to raise cattle. It's going back to the old way of free-range beef."

"They don't look any different," Rebecca said.

"But they're being raised differently. They're fed for eighteen months on only grass, then they're transferred to feed lots and grain-fed for another hundred and twenty days. No hormones, antibiotics, pesticides, or animal products."

"I guess, for a steer, it can't get any better than that."

They continued to ride and came up to one of the Angus calves. A black-faced yearling made a bawling sound at them. Greta pointed. "Look, Dad, it's Blackie. He remembers me."

"Greta, you know you don't name cattle. They aren't pets."

"He's the only one, only because he got tangled up in the fence and we had to call the vet. Remember I got to take care of him for a few days."

Mitch looked at Rebecca. "I know it sounds cruel, but it's better for the kids, rather than have them cry their eyes out when the animals go off to the slaughterhouse."

"I'm not disagreeing with you," she said and glanced at the calf. "But look at that face…"

Mitch groaned, but he was finding he enjoyed their easy banter too much. "Okay, who wants lunch?"

Rebecca was too lazy, but she'd get up just as soon as she gathered the strength. Lying on a blanket under the shade of trees, next to a trickling stream, was only something written about in books. Places like this weren't real life.

"Rebecca, are you asleep?" Colby asked.

She opened her eyes. "No, of course not. I'm just resting my eyes." She sat up and smiled at the boy. He had peanut butter on his cheek and his shirt was dirty. He was adorable.

"That's what Dad is doing, too."

She glanced at the man stretched out on his back on the other side of the blanket. His legs were crossed at the ankle, hands folded on his chest, and his hat covered his face. "Well, he works hard. He deserves some rest."

Colby leaned close to her and whispered, "I think he's playin' possum. He's not really asleep." The boy's hand was over his mouth to hold back a giggle. He leaned closer to his father. Suddenly Mitch reached out, grabbed the child by his waist and wrestled him to the ground.

Colby laughed and finally cried out, "Uncle! Uncle!"

His father released him. "That will teach

you to sneak up on a cowboy." He ruffled his son's hair and grinned at Rebecca. His own hair was messy, his dark eyes piercing into hers.

"Did you get enough to eat?"

"More than," she said and grabbed her backpack. "I was thinking maybe we should have an impromptu meeting."

Mitch lay on his side and propped his head up on his hand and turned those deep-set brown eyes on Rebecca. Colby sat down beside her, and Greta was next to her father.

"Okay," Mitch said.

Suddenly she wasn't so sure of herself. "I was thinking that we should have a company slogan for your website."

"I think we should use our family name," Greta said. "People know it." The young girl looked at her father. "I mean, Great-Grandpa and Grandpa Tucker have raised cattle in Wyoming for a long time. That should mean something to people."

"That's good, Greta," Rebecca encouraged. "People like and trust family-run businesses." She jotted it down, eager to prove her worth to Mitch Tucker and that she was prepared for this job. "My assistant in New York is working on a nationwide list of specialty grocery stores that carry free-range meats." She smiled. "Even I was surprised how many there are, or how in demand free-range beef is. I'll have the list for you in a few days." She looked down at her notes. "I understand that you're going to be processing your own beef."

Mitch nodded, and reached over to put his hand on her tablet so she couldn't look at any more notes. "How about we renew this discussion tomorrow at the meeting?"

Rebecca recognized his determination. And she liked the challenge of this project. It was hard for her to stop when she got started on something, but he was the boss. She nodded. "Sure. Tomorrow."

He moved his hand. "I have no doubt you're good at your job, but we got to take time to relax."

"I don't have trouble relaxing, it's just not when I'm working."

"I don't do business the usual way any more. I'm not on deadline." He smiled at Greta and Colby. "Not any more. Right, kids?"

"Right, Dad," they said in unison, then turned to her.

She'd be the first to admit she didn't take time for herself, and this trip to Wyoming had been supposed to be part vacation. But she was never good at relaxing, especially when she started a new project.

"Come on, Rebecca," Mitch began. "It's a great afternoon, enjoy it."

"Yeah, Rebecca," Colby said as he stretched out beside his dad.

Mitch pointed toward her notebook. "Here's something you can write down," he told her as he rolled on his back, but his gaze didn't leave her face. "I'm going to have to teach you how we do things in Wyoming. First thing is how to enjoy a lazy afternoon."

CHAPTER THREE

"OKAY, son, we're home," Mitch said.

Colby didn't fight him as the boy slid out of the saddle into his dad's waiting arms. "We had fun."

"We sure did," he said as the child dropped his head against his shoulder. "Maybe we should rest."

"I'm five…I don't take naps any more," Colby murmured.

"I know, but maybe we can just lie down for a while."

Greta climbed off Princess. She also looked a little fatigued. "I feel fine, Dad."

"And you did great today, sweetheart. Thanks for all your help."

"Rebecca did great, too," his daughter said. "She's a good rider."

Mitch looked toward the last mount. Wally took hold of Ginger's reins as Rebecca climbed down. He didn't miss the grimace on her face, but she quickly put on a smile when Wally said something to her. "Yes, she is." He hadn't found much about Rebecca Valentine that she couldn't do. "Let's head up to the house and out of the heat."

Rebecca walked toward them carrying the backpack. "Looks like we lost one," she said, reaching out to push away the dark hair off Colby's forehead.

"He held up better than I expected." He shifted his son a little higher. "Let's go up to the house. This guy is heavy."

Rebecca handed the backpack to Greta. "If you wouldn't mind, I'd like to take care of Ginger. It's been a while since I've groomed a horse."

Mitch frowned. "Are you sure?"

Rebecca nodded. "You said I could have the rest of the day off."

Before he could say anything, his daughter appeared.

"Dad, can I stay and help, too?" Greta asked. "I mean, I should take care of my own horse."

Wally came up to the group. "Not to worry, Mitch. I'll take care of the ladies."

"I'm sure you will," Mitch said. Not having a choice, he headed off toward the house.

Wally Hagan was more than just Mitch's ranch manager and his pilot. Divorced for years, he'd worked for the Tucker ranch for years. Wally had watched over Mitch's family as if they were his own, and he'd been the one who called him about Carrie's automobile accident. He had flown to get him so he could see his wife in the end.

Wally was a good man. He'd known him to have an easy smile and quite a way with the ladies.

Did he have his eye on Rebecca?

Mitch found himself feeling something he didn't like. Jealousy? How could that be?

The last thing he needed was to get involved with a career woman.

After Rebecca finished with Ginger, she made it back to the house, showered and changed into clean clothes. She braided her damp hair and left her bedroom in search of Mitch. She'd had second thoughts about not working the afternoon.

She came down the hall, but instead of going into the kitchen she wandered into the great room. The high ceilings, along with the huge brick fireplace, made it look bigger than it was. The hardwood floors glistened with high polish. There was a big-screen television, a cocoa-colored leather sofa and two matching overstuffed chairs. Oval patterned rugs covered the seating area. In the corner sat an overflowing toy box. This was definitely a family-friendly room.

She went into the front hall and found a carved oak staircase that curved upward and around the open second-story hall. A cut-glass chandelier hung over a round antique pedestal table in the center of the marble floor. She glanced into a parlor that had more of a feminine touch with the Victorian-style furniture. Over a tiled fireplace hung a portrait of the Tucker family that drew her in for a closer look.

Mitch looked handsome and a little younger in his dark Western suit. The beautiful blonde next to him had to be his wife, Carrie Tucker. She was a slender woman with startling blue eyes and a warm smile. On her lap she held a dark-haired toddler. Rebecca couldn't help but smile at the cute Colby. In between her parents was a younger Greta with her curly blonde hair and light eyes that were so much like her mother's.

The perfect family.

A feeling of envy came over Rebecca. The Tucker family represented everything Rebecca wanted and couldn't have—a man like Mitch and…children.

She turned and walked out. Passing Mitch's study, she paused, hearing movement behind the closed door. Suddenly she wasn't in the mood to talk business. She kept walking until she reached the louvered doors that led into a sun room.

The late-afternoon sun shone through the row of windows and Rebecca took a seat on the padded bench below and stared out at the mountains.

She hadn't had a day like today in years, hadn't ridden since she was a teenager, and she wasn't half bad at it. With a proud smile, she relaxed back against the overstuffed cushions and closed her eyes. She stretched to relieve the stiffness in her back.

It wouldn't hurt to rest here for a minute, then get up and help Mitch with supper. Warmth spread through her as she thought about the combination sexy cowboy and dad. He was a pleasant surprise for her... too pleasant.

Mitch searched the house, but couldn't find Rebecca anywhere. He'd even called down to the barn, looking for her. Wally seemed amused that he couldn't locate his house guest.

Finally he peeked into the sun room. That was where she was, curled up on the bench. He watched her even breathing and knew she was sleeping. His gaze moved to her slightly parted lips, then to her hair, mussed just enough to look sexy. Man, a hundred things began to run through his head, none of which he wanted to analyze. Why did this woman get to him? The obvious answer was Rebecca Valentine was a beautiful woman.

In the twelve years he and Carrie had been married, he'd never looked at another woman. His wife had been everything to him. But it was so long since she died. So long…

He stole another glance at Rebecca as she slept peacefully. A long braid hung over her shoulder, and strands of curls clung to her cheek. She didn't have on any makeup, exposing tiny freckles across her nose. Otherwise, her skin was flawless.

Feeling his body stir, Mitch sank into the wicker chair across the room. What was he doing looking at this woman as if she were dessert? He knew better. She was running his campaign. If that weren't bad enough, she was staying in his home. If anything he should run in the other direction.

He started to get up when he heard her moan and shift again. She blinked her eyes and finally looked at him. "Oh, Mitch," she whispered hoarsely.

That got his heart beating even faster. "Sorry, I didn't mean to disturb you."

She sat up and pushed back her hair. "I must have fallen asleep. What time is it?"

"A little after five," he said, checking his watch. "You needed to rest after today." He nodded. "I must say you were a real trooper and pretty good on horseback."

"It was fun. As I said, it's been a while since I rode." Her smile widened. "It brought back memories of my sister and me going riding at the farm. Rachel was a natural, even did a little competive riding."

"You two were close?"

She shrugged. "We were until after college she wanted to return to the UK."

Mitch heard the sadness in her voice. Suddenly he made a connection with her name. "Would your grandfather happen to be William Valentine of the Bella Lucia restaurant?"

"Afraid so," she said.

"I can believe it. It's one of my favorite restaurants. Whenever I had business in London, I made sure that I dined there."

"My grandfather would be happy to hear that. And before you ask why I live and work in New York, and not London for the family business, let me say that our mother was American. And after my parents' divorce, Mom brought Rachel and me back to the States." She glanced away. "I never had much desire to go back to the UK, not like Rachel... She enjoys working with our father."

Mitch figured there was a lot more to this story. "Your sister went into the family business and you chose something else to do, and somewhere else to live. I'm sure your mother is happy that she has one of her daughters here," he said.

Once again Rebecca realized how easily this man got her to talk—about her family, no less. Why stop now? Her gaze locked with his. "Mother died about a year after we graduated college."

"I'm sorry. That's tough."

"She had been sick a long time. As they say, it was a blessing in the end."

Mitch's expression didn't give much away. "It's never a blessing for those who are left behind."

"I'm sorry, Mitch. I didn't mean to bring back memories…"

"You didn't bring them back; they're with me all the time." He patted the spot over his shirt pocket. "The kids had it bad for a long time. Hell, so did I. But we got through it." He drew a shaky breath. "If I've learned one thing from losing Carrie, it's never to take anyone or anything for granted. That is why this project is so important to me. I want to build something with Greta and Colby."

Rebecca swallowed back the lump in her throat. All she'd ever known were broken families. A father who'd never had time for her; a mother who had been bitter over a man. All men. But the love for his family shining in Mitch Tucker's eyes brought tears to hers.

He looked at her and a half-smile moved across that sexy mouth. "Now you know my secret."

She blinked. "What secret?"

"I'd rather watch a Disney movie with my kids than travel the world, or handle acquisitions in the boardroom."

She raised an eyebrow. "And what will you pay for my silence?"

He held her gaze a long time. "How about you go riding again…?"

"I'm listening," she said, realizing she could easily become hooked on the activity.

"I'll show you more of the ranch, but this time without the kids."

"Won't we be playing hookey?" It wasn't a good idea to get too personal with this man, but...

He leaned forward. "I bet you haven't had a vacation in years. And I can guess that your blood pressure is a little high. You drink too much caffeine and probably eat every lunch at your desk."

She gasped. "How—?"

"I used to be you," he said. "Everything I did was to build an empire. All the long days...and nights, I thought were so important, didn't mean squat in the end. If I had it to do all over again, I'd have a dozen more kids and stay right here on this ranch." He leaned back. "It took a while but I managed to slow down." His eyes brightened. "Kids will do that for you."

Of course he wanted more kids, Rebecca thought painfully. And he had that option. But what did she have besides work? "I still have a job to do."

"I know, but you don't have to live it twenty-four seven. Pace yourself. There's time. I'm paying your agency enough that you can afford to stay here for as long as it takes."

She couldn't stay here indefinitely. "What about my other clients?"

Darn the man if he didn't grin like a devil. She could see the tiny lines around his eyes, the only thing that gave away his age at forty-two. "Have you ever heard of delegating?"

"That's all well and good, but how would you feel if I delegated this job?"

He raised an eyebrow. "I thought Brent Pierce was going to handle my account, but he said you were the one for the job. I trusted him to know what was best." He nodded. "He did know, because he sent me you."

The way he'd said it, she felt as if she'd been awarded to him as a prize. *Don't dwell on those thoughts.* "I truly can't see Brent Pierce on Ginger." She giggled. Rebecca couldn't even picture the man out of his Hugo Boss suit. "Thank you for your confidence."

"I can't wait to hear your ideas."

"And we should get back at it bright and early tomorrow."

The sound of Greta's voice drew their attention.

"We're on the sun porch," Mitch called to her.

Both children appeared. Colby's face and hands were washed and he had on a clean shirt. Greta had probably had something to do with that.

"Hi, Dad and Rebecca," she said. "Dad, who's going to fix supper? I'm hungry."

"I'm doing it."

"That doesn't seem fair," Rebecca said, drawing all the Tucker family's attention. "Wouldn't it be easier if we took turns? We could make up teams. I'll partner with Greta, and Mitch, you partner with Colby. How does that sound?"

The three looked at each other, and Mitch said, "Rebecca, are you sure about this?"

She nodded. "You've all been gracious enough to open up your home to me. Please,

I'd feel better if I help out some, especially since your housekeeper is away."

"Well, if it means that much to you," Mitch said, "then the kitchen is all yours."

She stood. "Okay, Greta, it's the girls against the guys. We'll take tonight."

"You're on, girls." Mitch gave his son a high five.

"We'll win, right, Dad," Colby said.

Rebecca placed her arm around Greta's shoulders. "Not when there's all this girl power." They turned and left the room, hearing the muffled words of a declared war behind them.

This was a war for Rebecca. A war to stay focused on her objective. She needed to win here, because she had to come to terms with what she was losing once she returned to New York.

"That was a great meal," Mitch said, tipping his chair back from the table.

"You know it was one of Margie's casseroles," Greta admitted. "But we made the salad and bread."

"Everything was delicious." He leaned across the table and kissed her forehead. He looked at Rebecca. "You, too. It was nice to have a night off."

"For me, it's a pleasure to cook. I don't do it often. I can only make a few dishes. Cooking for one isn't much fun."

"What about your boyfriend?" Greta asked.

Mitch glanced at his daughter. "Rebecca's private life isn't our business."

"But, Dad, she knows all about us," Greta said, then turned back to Rebecca.

"I don't mind answering," she told him. "No, Greta, there isn't a special man in my life. Not that there haven't been a few over the years."

"Anyone famous?" Greta asked with growing interest.

This time Rebecca did smile. She looked young and carefree. "Well, I didn't date anyone famous, but I've met a few. Let's see… Oh, I went to a movie première for *Spiderman*."

Colby's eyes rounded. "Wow, you saw *Spiderman*?"

Rebecca nodded.

"Who else have you met?" Greta asked.

"There was Russell Crowe…Tom Hanks and Hilary Duff. Some Broadway stars you wouldn't know. A few New York Yankees—"

"The Yankees?" Mitch sat up. "Who?"

"Well, let's see, there was Derek Jeter and Gary Sheffield—oh, and Joe Torre."

"You've met Jeter and Sheffield?" he demanded.

She nodded. "That was a few years ago. Our firm did some PR work for a charitable organization."

"Your job is so cool." Greta pouted as she began to clear the table. "We *never* get to meet anyone famous here."

"I didn't at your age, either," Rebecca assured her as she got up and carried dishes to the sink.

Mitch watched the two together at the sink. Rebecca was talking to his daughter, soothing her sulky mood. Then finally the two began to laugh. Greta came back to the table to gather more dishes.

"Dad, do you want some coffee?"

"No, thank you." He stood. "Why don't you take Colby upstairs and start his bath? I'll finish the dishes."

She looked up at him and smiled. "Sure. Come on, Colby."

His son looked suspicious of his sister's sudden sweetness. "Can I play with my army men?"

Greta sighed. "Okay, but only for a little while." She took her brother's hand and they started out of the kitchen. Greta paused at the door. "Rebecca, thanks for going today. It was fun."

Rebecca smiled. "It was fun for me, too. Remember, tomorrow I want more of your input on this campaign. We'll work on it first thing."

"I'll see you in the morning." Greta tugged on Colby's arm and they left.

Mitch stood and brought glasses to the sink where Rebecca was rinsing them and placing them in the dishwasher.

"Okay, tell me what you said to Greta that made her laugh."

She shrugged. "Not much. We just talked. Adolescence is a rough time. You're not exactly a kid, but you're not quite a woman."

Mitch groaned. "Please, not my baby girl. I'm not ready for that change yet."

Rebecca would have given anything for this kind of concern from her father, but Robert Valentine hadn't had the time for her. "It'll happen sooner than you realize, so you'd better get ready. Greta is a beautiful girl. Before you know it she'll be dating—"

"They'll have to go through me first," Mitch insisted. "Teenage boys have one-track minds."

Rebecca bit back a smile. "I didn't know

it was just teenage boys whose minds worked that way."

"I suppose we can all be jerks."

"Okay, I have to admit, I've met my share." She wouldn't put Mitch Tucker into that category. "Still, not all men are jerks."

He rewarded her with a crooked smile. "It's nice to know that a few of us are salvageable." He rested his hip against the counter and folded his arms across his broad chest. "What do you look for in a man?"

The question surprised her. It had been so long since she'd taken time to date, she wasn't sure what she wanted in a man. "I guess the basics. No games. Honesty. Treats me with respect."

Mitch leaned in closer. "That should go without saying. You should try Wyoming men. They know how to treat a woman."

Was he flirting with her? Oh, brother, she was in bad shape if she didn't even know that. "Wyoming men, huh?"

"Of course, we live a slower pace here. We take time with…everything." He was so near she could feel his breath against her face, and his dark eyes were locked with hers.

"That would be nice," she managed to say. "I have to say, I haven't had much time to think about a relationship."

"That's a lonely existence," he said. "I know… sometimes…it's nice to have another person just to talk to." His gaze moved over her face, causing her heart to pound against her ribs.

"It would be nice to share your day with someone," she added.

He sighed. "Yeah, I think I miss that the most." His hand rose toward her face, then Greta called from the top of the stairs. Mitch pulled back. "I better go check on them."

"Go on, I'll finish up the kitchen," she told him. "Then I'm going to turn in."

After Mitch walked out, Rebecca finally let out a long breath. What was she doing? She was here on a job, not to audition for the role of the second Mrs Mitchell Tucker. She was going to get her heart broken if she wasn't careful.

She took the sponge and wiped off the counters. If she let herself, she could fall and fall hard. That wouldn't do. They had different plans for the future. She had her career. He was into kids, and she couldn't have any. With him or anyone else.

That painful truth was going to keep her on track.

CHAPTER FOUR

THE next morning, Mitch glanced at the kitchen clock. It was after seven, and Rebecca hadn't appeared for breakfast. He poured a second cup of coffee, knowing he had to leave soon.

The kids had gone into town with Jimmy to pick up some supplies so they were taken care of until about noon. That gave him the opportunity to handle business with Jake Peters at the breeding corral. Mitch's stallion, Kid Knight, was scheduled to cover Jake's mare, Dancer's Lady. But right now Mitch's mind wasn't only on equine breeding.

He recalled last night, and how he'd nearly stepped over the line. He always prided himself on being able to keep his business and his personal life separate. Now he'd brought one big temptation right here into his own home. And after only two days, he couldn't stop fantasizing about Rebecca.

Was she sore after yesterday's ride? He probably should have offered her the use of his Jacuzzi tub last night. He drew in a quick breath. No. All he needed was to picture Rebecca Valentine naked in bubbling water and he'd never be able to go into his bathroom without thinking about her there.

Mitch took another sip of coffee and decided to leave her a note, then she walked into the kitchen. She was dressed in a pink tailored blouse and khaki slacks. Her hair was pulled back into a ponytail. Today, she looked as if she belonged on a ranch.

"Good morning."

She nodded and walked to the coffeemaker. He was ahead of her, poured a full mug, then handed it to her. After a few sips, she finally smiled. "Good morning." She glanced around the kitchen. "Where are Colby and Greta?"

"Jimmy took them into town on some errands." Mitch retrieved a covered plate from the stove and brought it to the table. "They'll be back in a few hours so enjoy the peace while you can."

"You didn't have to fix me breakfast." Rebecca wasn't used to people waiting on her. She looked at the scrambled eggs and sausage and realized she was hungry. "This is nice." She sat down and started to eat.

"Glad to see you have an appetite."

"I've always had an appetite."

"Well, after all the physical activity yesterday you need to eat."

Mitch sat down across from her. She looked at his crooked smile and bedroom eyes. The scar on his chin, and the laugh lines that bracketed his mouth only added to his appeal. She could get used to mornings like this.

Whoa, slow down. You're here for the free-range beef ad, not the sexy Wyoming cowboy.

"Did you want to continue our discussion from yesterday?" she asked.

Mitch checked his watch. "Can't now, I'm due down at the breeding pen. Kid Knight is scheduled to cover Dancer's Lady. I need to be there."

Rebecca tried to hide her disappointment that she wasn't able to go with him, recalling the years on her pop's horse farm. "Then you go. I'll clean up here and get some work done."

She carried her plate to the sink, thinking she should call Brent and run some ideas by him. She could use this quiet time to her advantage.

Mitch came up beside her. "I don't have a problem if you'd like to go with me."

She stared at him. "You won't mind?"

His eyes met hers. "You know how to handle yourself around horses."

"I would like to see your breeding operation," she told him.

Mitch tossed the towel on the counter. "Then let's go."

Together they left the house, and strolled to the barn. Rebecca was determined to forget about work and enjoy this time. Yesterday she'd realized how much she missed being around horses. Maybe when she returned to New York she could find a stable and do a bit of riding on the weekends. It would be good to have something else in her life.

Mitch escorted Rebecca into the cool barn where six mares were housed in spacious stalls. The wooden gates were painted cream with hunter-green trim, as was the outside of the structure.

All dozen stalls, the tack room and feeding bins were immaculate, just as she expected them to be. It was obvious the mares boarded received the best of care. No doubt their owners paid top dollar to be covered by one of the Tucker studs.

"This is impressive."

"I'm pretty proud of the operation myself. It's a lot of work, but I'm sure you know that."

A high-pitched whinny drew their attention. "I think Kid is getting anxious."

"Yeah, he knows there's a pretty filly waiting for him."

Mitch directed Rebecca along the aisle until they reached the corral where the beautiful stallion was prancing around a holding pen. No doubt he'd caught the scent of the mare. A warm breeze blew strands of Rebecca's hair against her face. Mitch reached out and brushed them back, his finger caressing her cheek.

"Will you be okay waiting here?"

She nodded. "Go on, before Kid breaks down the pen."

Just then Wally walked up. He tipped his hat. "Morning, Rebecca. I see Mitch brought you to see the operations."

"He was nice enough to let me look around." There was another whinny from Kid. "I promise to stay out of everyone's way."

Mitch glanced at his foreman. "Is Jake here?"

Wally nodded. "He's with his mare in the corral."

Suddenly Mitch wondered what he'd been thinking to bring Rebecca here. She was a distraction just being close by. Hell, she could be at the house and still bother him.

"Let's get going, then," Mitch said. He and Wally approached the corral. The mare's hind legs were hobbled and her tail wrapped. Lady was young and he couldn't risk his stud getting kicked. He shook hands with Jake, and went to get Kid.

Mitch needed to concentrate on handling his young stallion. Although he wanted nature to just take its course, he needed to lend a strong hand. Neither owner wanted any harm to come to their animals. While two ranch hands held the mare, he and Wally helped make the mounting go smoothly.

Once the act was successfully completed, Wally took charge of Kid and led him from the corral. Dancer's Lady was escorted back to her stall. There she would reside a few weeks to verify she'd been impregnated before returning to her owner's ranch.

Mitch removed his gloves and shook hands with Jake before he walked off to join Rebecca standing at the fence. His heart tightened at the sight of her. It had been a long time since he'd had a woman waiting for him.

"So what do you think of Kid?" he asked, trying to ignore the feelings she aroused in him.

"He's a magnificent animal," she said excitedly. "I hope you have him on your website."

Mitch couldn't hide his pride or his grin. "Of course. I'll show it to you later." He led her back toward the barn. "For now, I think we should take advantage of Greta and Colby being gone. I love them to death, but sometimes it's nice to be by myself, or with another adult."

"I don't mind the children," she admitted. "But what about the ad? Shouldn't we use this time to work on it?"

That was the last thing on his mind. "Is that all you think about?"

"It is, when I'm getting paid to do a job."

"Well, since I'm the one paying you, I say we take the morning off. Besides, you'll need to see the operation. Instead of by horseback, we'll take the truck. Come on, Rebecca. I know you want to."

She raised an eyebrow. "Do you think it's a good idea?"

Mitch wasn't going to think about what was good or bad. He didn't want to think at all. He just wanted to spend a few hours alone with this beautiful woman.

It was as simple as that...and as complicated as that.

Twenty minutes later, the beat-up Jeep bounced over the uneven ground, jarring Mitch and Rebecca in their seats. Mitch glanced toward the passenger seat. Rebecca had a tight grip on the safety handle as she looked around.

He downshifted and steered the Jeep into the steep climb up the hillside. Finally he reached the top and parked along the ridge.

Turning off the engine, he leaned back in his seat and looked out at the view.

"Well, what do you think?" he asked her, finding he wanted to impress her.

She was silent for what seemed like a long time. "It's amazing. The view is incredible."

"Glad you like it." Mitch looked in one direction where the ranch compound was neatly laid out below them. In another direction rose the powerful Rocky Mountains range where pine trees dotted the landscape and the green valley below much like a plush carpet.

"Look, Mitch," she called, pointing out her open window. "There's your herd."

He leaned toward her and caught a whiff of her hair, reminding him of wild flowers. He pulled back from the temptation.

"That's Freedom Valley, all right," he told her. "Since it's been free of all chemical fertilizers we thought that name seemed to suit it."

Rebecca smiled. "I like it."

"I have to confess, it was Greta's idea."

"She's a clever girl."

He didn't want to talk about his kids. "So, do you like my backyard?"

Once again Rebecca took in the panoramic view. "Let's see, the Rocky Mountains, lush green valleys and an endless blue sky." She sighed. "It's incredible! How do you ever get any work done?"

"That's the best part. I get to be outside all the time. There's a downside, too. It's pretty cold in the winter. In fact we usually get snowed in at least once a year."

"Sounds like fun to me," she said. "Of course, you have to have heat and food."

"We try to stay prepared." He definitely hadn't been prepared for Rebecca Valentine coming into his life. "We have generators, and if those fail we all just hover around the fireplace." He sighed remembering the last time. Carrie had just discovered she was pregnant. He'd been so worried about her delicate condition, but Carrie had only wanted to make love in the firelight. Then suddenly his idyllic life had ended when another snowstorm had taken his wife and unborn child from him.

Rebecca leaned back against the seat drawing his attention. "That reminds me of Poppy's and Nana's farm. Virginia isn't nearly as cold as Wyoming, but storms can take out the power." She closed her eyes. "We had fun sleeping in front of the fire."

Suddenly the picture of Rebecca snowed in with him formed in his head. Both of them wrapped up in blankets in front of a fire, using their body heat to keep warm. Damn. That was a daydream to stir a man's blood.

Mitch shook away the thought. "Are your grandparents still in Virginia?"

"No, they sold the farm years ago, and both passed away a few years back. Nana died after complications from a stroke, and Poppy soon followed. I don't think he could handle being alone." Her voice grew soft. "They were the most loving couple I ever knew." She turned to Mitch. "What about your parents?"

"Oh, yeah, they're alive and well, thank

goodness. They've been living in Florida for the past six years. Mom couldn't take the cold weather any more. Years before Dad turned the ranch operation over to me. So there wasn't any reason for them not to spend the winters in the sunshine state. Lately, they've just stayed all year round." He sighed. "They wanted to move back here when Carrie died to help with the kids, but I told them I needed to do it on my own."

"That was nice of them."

Rebecca smiled at him, reminding him again that he was alone in a car with a beautiful woman. It had been a long time since he'd had such strong feelings for the opposite sex. He hadn't seen it coming, and he wasn't sure it was a good thing. He just knew he liked the feeling.

"You're doing a good job with Greta and Colby."

"Thanks. Being an only child, I always wanted a houseful." Mitch blinked. "Speaking of kids, I nearly forgot." He checked his watch. "Jimmy will be back with mine soon."

"Then you should be there," Rebecca said. "You must know how much Greta worries about you."

"I know. She's becoming quite the mother hen." He started the Jeep. "There's a short cut back, but it's pretty rough terrain."

She raised an eyebrow. "You think I can't handle it?"

He caught her mischievous look. No doubt she could, but he was more concerned about himself. Was he going to survive Rebecca Valentine?

"Buckle your seat belt, darlin'," he told her as he started up the Jeep. "Let's see what you New Yorkers are made of."

The following afternoon, Mitch sat behind his desk in the den. The last thing he wanted to do was spend the afternoon inside. But he'd promised Rebecca they'd go over some ideas.

He'd rather have a repeat of yesterday. Take a lazy ride around the ranch in a Jeep with a pretty woman, a woman who was genuinely interested in the ranch operation. He smiled to himself. Remembering the roller-coaster ride home, he wondered how she had ended up in New York City when she seemed to love open spaces.

Suddenly Colby scurried into the room followed by his sister. "I get to come to the meeting, too, don't I, Dad?" the boy asked as he went to the oak desk where Mitch sat.

Mitch came out of his reverie. "Of course you do, son. But remember what I said. You have to sit still and only talk when it's your turn."

"Dad!" Greta gave an exaggerated sigh. "You know he's just going to cause trouble."

"You both sit down and stop arguing." He directed them to the chairs beside the desk. "Greta, I know you've spent a lot of time on this project, and I appreciate all your work, but I'm going to run the meeting." Whoever thought he'd have to say that to his eleven-year-old daughter? What had happened to his baby girl?

When Greta opened her mouth, he raised

his hand. "Although we are partners, I'm still the parent here," he said. Why didn't he sound convincing? "Now, you can sit in on this meeting, and are allowed to give me your opinion, but in the end I make the final decisions."

Colby was already losing interest, but Greta just looked more determined. "Do you agree?" he asked.

"Sure, Dad," Colby told him, pulling his favorite Hot Wheels car from his jeans pocket, the red one with the white racing stripe. Greta took out a small tablet, ready to take notes.

There was a soft knock and he glanced up to see Rebecca standing in the doorway.

He stood. "Rebecca, please come in."

"Thank you," she said.

She was dressed in dark pleated slacks and a white blouse and with her hair pulled back into a bun. She was definitely back in business mode. He recalled her yesterday with her hair blowing free as they rode over the hillside. She was smiling and laughing as the Jeep bounced her up and down in her seat. Never once had she complained. He preferred that woman.

"Hi, Greta and Colby," she said as she placed her slim portfolio on the desk. "Is everyone ready?" she asked.

"Sure." He pulled over a chair to the group. "Please, sit down."

As she took the chair he offered he caught another whiff of her soft scent. He moved behind the desk, out of the line of fire. He needed a clear head for business.

Rebecca drew a breath to ease her tension. She'd been trying to get an official meeting together since she'd arrived here three days ago. Now that it was happening, she found she was nervous.

"First, let me say I enjoyed riding out to see some of the ranch and the free-range herd. I also hope I can come up with an ad campaign that you all like."

"Are you going to take pictures of our steers?" Colby asked.

"If we decide that's what we want to do," Mitch said. "Son, please don't interrupt."

"I don't mind questions," Rebecca said as she turned to Mitch. "If it's okay with you?"

Mitch nodded.

"Although I've done extensive research on free-range beef, this is my first time on a cattle ranch. I'll need your help with where we should direct our marketing."

"The Internet," Greta said.

"That was my thought, too," Rebecca agreed. "I found several websites for free-range beef that you can order right online. We'll also have to direct our focus to soliciting food stores and fine restaurants." She opened her folder and started thumbing through her notes, realizing her hand was trembling. Why was she so nervous? She did presentations all the time. She stole a glance at Mitch and found him watching her. "I worked on the ideas we started on yesterday." She began to read when Colby raised his hand.

Mitch turned toward to the boy. "What is it, son?"

"Dad has a website for his stallions, Kid

Knight and Stormy Knight," Colby volunteered. "He has their pictures and pictures of their foals. They're all over the world."

Rebecca felt herself blush as she recalled Kid Knight in action yesterday. "Then maybe we should do the same thing for the beef."

"Wow, are we going to sell our beef all over the world, too?"

She smiled at the child. "Maybe we'll start closer to home, Colby. There's a large market in cities like New York and San Francisco. There are restaurants that specialize in free-range beef. Of course, your herd is still young," she said and glanced at Mitch. "When will the first steers be ready to market?"

"Next week we're rounding them up and moving them into the feed lot. It'll be early winter before they go to slaughter."

"That gives us time to get together a target client list. Mitch, I'm sure you realize how much your business connections are going to help with the promotion of your product. And people will recognize the Tucker name. That list of contacts will help us."

"I'll see what I can come up with," he told her as he wrote something down.

"Good." Rebecca opened her folder and pulled out a rough mock-up of an ad. All three of the Tuckers leaned forward to have a closer look.

"Since you've decided to use the family name, I came up with some more ideas that I wanted to run by you." She pointed to the bold print. "'Tucker, a name you've trusted for years. Three generations of Tucker beef. Tucker's Best Beef.' And a slogan maybe something like: 'We'll stake our family's name on an unrivaled quality product.'"

There were empty spots for pictures of the family and ranch. "Greta's suggestion to use the Tucker name is a good one. It will be a great ad for the website. You will need to hire a promotion staff to make contact with buyers for specialty stores and restaurants." She waved her hand. "But that's down the line. We need to lay the groundwork now."

"Tucker's Best Beef," Mitch repeated. "Not bad."

"I think it's cool, too, Dad," Colby said. "Can I go play?"

"Sure, son." Colby took off and Mitch looked at his daughter. "How do you like it, Greta?"

"I like it a lot," she said, her blue eyes wide. "Maybe we can use Blackie in some pictures for the website."

Mitch groaned. His clever daughter had managed to work the calf in. But he had to admit it wasn't a bad idea. "I knew you were going to make a pet out of that steer."

She stood next to Rebecca. "Daddy, if Blackie is in the pictures, we have to keep him around. He's like our trademark."

Mitch looked at Rebecca and tried to act stern. "Did you two cook this up?"

Rebecca caught on to Mitch's teasing. She admired the way he connected with his children. "No, but I like how Greta thinks." She slipped her arm around his daughter. "We girls have to stick together."

"Dad, we should vote on making Blackie our mascot."

"Ranchers don't have steers as mascots," he said, but his expression softened. "Okay, I'll think about it." He stood. "I better go get Colby. It's our turn to cook. I'm a little tired of casseroles, so I thought I would grill some steaks for supper. Unless you ladies have a problem with that."

Greta raised an eyebrow. "As long as it isn't Blackie."

Mitch threw up his hands in mock defeat. "Blackie's safe for now. But when he outgrows that cute stage, he's history." He walked out.

The father/daughter banter made Rebecca smile. Mitch Tucker was handsome, sexy, a nice guy and a great father. It was the latter that drew her to him the most. And it was the best reason for her to stay away.

That evening, Mitch stood at the large stainless steel grill on the backyard deck, enjoying the peacefulness of dusk. He checked the steaks, making sure that they weren't overcooked. An easy task unless

your mind was on something or someone else.

Rebecca Valentine.

She'd distracted him since the day she'd
arrived. And as the days passed it seemed to
be getting worse. His thoughts turned to
Carrie.

From the moment he'd met her in college,
Caroline Colby had been the love of his life.
After they'd married Carrie had been more
than willing to help him when he'd taken
over the family business from his father.
They'd had a good life and she'd traveled
with him until Greta. Both being only
children, they'd wanted a large family, but
it had taken a while for her to conceive
Colby. His business obligations might have
had a lot to do with it because he'd had to
travel a lot and that had cut into their time
together. He'd tried to slow down, but he'd
needed to travel to be successful.

Mitch turned the steaks.

For the rest of his life, he'd feel guilty that
he hadn't been home when Carrie had been

involved in an automobile accident. He'd only arrived at the hospital just in time to tell her how much he loved her.

Carrie had known she wasn't going to make it. They'd cried together, but she'd made him promise to go on with his life, to take time and enjoy the kids, and not to mourn her long, but to find someone else to love. He'd thought she was crazy at the time. He'd never be able to replace her; he'd never be able to want another woman. But it had been a lonely two years and too many in front of him to live alone. And there was that longing to have more kids.

Mitch looked heavenward. What would Carrie think of Rebecca? He heard his son calling him and glanced at the door.

"Hey, Dad, how much longer? I'm hungry."

Mitch smiled. "You can't rush the chef. Should be about five minutes."

That seemed to appease the boy, but Colby didn't go inside. Instead he sat down in a lawn chair. "Hey, Dad. Do you think Rebecca's pretty?"

He was caught off guard by the question. "Sure, she's a pretty lady."

"Do you think she's as pretty as Mom?"

"I thought your mother was the prettiest girl in Wyoming. But you've seen pictures of her. What do you think?"

Colby shrugged. "It's different in a picture." Those dark eyes bore into Mitch's. "I can't remember what Mom looked like." The boy's voice cracked.

Mitch's chest tightened as he knelt down in front of his son. "I know. You were so young." He took Colby's hand. "You have to know that she loved you and Greta a lot."

He nodded. "I know." Colby remained silent for a long time, then asked, "Is it okay if I like Rebecca?"

He'd expected this. His son had always gravitated toward females. No doubt it was their soft voices and touch, and their instinctive nurturing ways. And he'd witnessed the special attention that Rebecca had given his son and daughter.

"Yes, it's okay to like Rebecca," he said.

"It's hard not to. But, son, she's going back to New York in a few weeks."

"I know, but I want her to be my friend anyway." His eyes brightened. "Maybe she can come back for a visit."

Mitch knew it was unlikely the career woman would return, but found he wanted the same thing. "Maybe."

In bed, Rebecca rolled onto her side and pulled her legs up hoping to ease the cramps. Nothing had worked, not even the strong pain medicine the doctor had given her. She glanced at the clock. It was after midnight.

She sighed and finally got up, thinking some hot tea might help. Since all the Tuckers were in bed she wouldn't be disturbing anyone. She grabbed her robe and headed down the hall. Once she reached the kitchen she saw the light over the stove and the tea kettle. That was when she noticed the shadow by the window.

The figure was tall with wide shoulders. "Mitch," she whispered.

"Rebecca. What are you doing up?"

He stepped into the light and she saw he was only wearing a pair of jeans. She couldn't help but stare at his bare, well-developed chest and those muscular arms and shoulders. "I…thought I'd get a cup of tea, but I don't want to disturb you." She turned to leave when he took her by the arm.

"Rebecca, you don't have to leave. I guess we both had the same problem. I couldn't sleep, either."

Suddenly her stomach clenched and she nearly doubled over.

"Rebecca, what's wrong?"

She tried to wave him off. "It's just cramps."

"It doesn't look to be just cramps." He took her by her arm and led her into the family room. "Here, lie down."

"Mitch, you don't need to worry about this. Hot tea should help."

He sat her down on the sofa. "I know I'm just an insensitive male, but I was married for a dozen years. I know a few remedies that might help. I'll be right back."

He left and, in too much discomfort to argue, Rebecca stretched out on the cushion. Soon Mitch returned with a heating pad and placed it on her stomach and plugged it in, then left her again. This time he came back with two steaming cups of tea.

"I hope you like Earl Grey?"

"I'm half English. I'll drink any kind of tea."

Mitch sat on the edge of the coffee-table, close to her. Too close. She pushed herself up but her feet were still curled under her. He watched her sip from her cup, and drank his own.

"How's the heating pad doing?"

She patted her stomach. "It's helping. Thank you."

With more tea she felt herself relaxing until she caught Mitch staring at her.

Placing the cup on the table, Rebecca smoothed her hair back as best she could. "I know I look a mess."

To Mitch, the moonlight shining through

the window only emphasized her beauty. "You look fine. Besides, just worry about your...condition." He reached for the blanket off the back of the sofa and covered her. "Just rest and let the heat relax your muscles." Instead of resuming his seat on the table, he moved to the edge of the cushions. He knew he was too close, but he couldn't seem to back away. Their eyes connected, and his throat went dry. She had to feel the heat between them.

"I feel better," she breathed. "Thank you."

"No problem." Oh, but there was a big problem. The way she made him feel whenever he got close. The way she kept him awake at night, dreaming about what it would be like to touch her...to kiss her...

"I think my medicine is kicking in."

Something was kicking in with him, too. "Good. And tomorrow morning, I want you to sleep in."

"Oh, there's no need for that."

"Just take the morning for yourself. In the afternoon, we'll all drive out to the feed lot, and, if there's time, to the construction site for the meat-packing plant."

"I'd like that," she said with a bright smile. "Have I told you how much fun I'm having doing this job?"

He was excited by her obvious pleasure. "I think you're enjoying being out of the rat race."

"Could be," she admitted. "The quiet here is soothing. And being with Colby and Greta has been nice."

"What about me?" he asked. "Do I live up to my reputation as a tyrant?"

She gasped. "I never heard that…"

He began to laugh. "I'm not the easiest man to work with."

"I haven't found that," she admitted. "You've been fair and open to new ideas, and you're not a bad cook."

"You haven't been hard to take, either, Rebecca Valentine." He leaned closer. He could feel the side of her hip against his. "I thought for sure that a gung-ho woman would arrive who wouldn't want to step foot out of the house, let alone ride a horse. Little did I know that you grew up on a farm." His voice lowered. "To say the least, you were quite a surprise."

"I was?"

He couldn't help it. He touched her cheek. Her skin was as soft as he imagined. "A beautiful surprise," he repeated. His head lowered and his mouth caressed hers gently.

Rebecca sucked in a breath, but that didn't stop him. He went back and took more. He burrowed his fingers in her wild hair. When she didn't resist, he settled his mouth on hers, parting her lips in the process. He groaned and his arms wrapped around her, pulling her close.

A surge of need seared his body like a hot poker. When her fingers locked behind his neck and clung to him, he almost lost it. His pulse was pounding in his ears as he savored the taste and feel of her. Finally the air was gone from his lungs and he broke off the kiss.

They were both breathing hard. Oh, Lord,

he wanted…nothing more than to carry her upstairs to his bed. But, somehow, common sense prevailed and he released her.

"I'm not going to apologize for the kiss, but it would be best if I say goodnight." He got up and walked away.

It was the last thing he wanted to do.

CHAPTER FIVE

SHE was a coward.

Rebecca paced her bedroom trying to get up the courage to face Mitch. How was she supposed to act after her client had kissed the living daylights out of her last night, and, worse, she'd kissed him right back? Her stomach tightened at the thought of being in Mitch's arms, having his mouth on hers.

"Stop it," she ordered herself as she shook away the memory. This wasn't helping the problem. How should she act when they'd both gone over the line?

Well, first thing was not to make too much out of it. Right. Her career was everything to her, and she wasn't going to mess that up. Besides, she was returning to New York so there was no future for them.

She glanced at the bedside clock. It was nearly eight o'clock. Maybe her immediate problem wasn't so immediate. He'd probably already gone down to the barn to start his day.

"Well, for sure I can't stay in my room all day."

Squaring her shoulders, Rebecca opened the door and headed down the hall. "He kissed me. So what?" she murmured. "If anyone should be embarrassed, it should be him."

With renewed courage, Rebecca walked into the kitchen but was disappointed to find the room empty except for Greta.

The girl got up from the table. "Good, you're awake. Dad said to let you sleep because you weren't feeling well last night. Are you better today?"

"Much better," Rebecca told her, realizing she did feel pretty good. "Where is everyone?"

"Dad and Colby are down at the barn waiting for the bus."

"What bus?"

Greta smiled. "First eat breakfast, and I'll take you down so Dad can tell you." The girl went to the stove and brought back a plate of food and put it on the table.

Rebecca needed coffee. She turned to the coffeemaker, poured a cup and took a drink. "Help do what?"

"It's a surprise, but it'll be fun. So eat."

Rebecca glanced down at the heaped plate of bacon and eggs. "Your dad needs to stop feeding me like this."

"Dad always cooks too much." Greta giggled. "Just eat half of it and we'll go."

The girl's excitement was contagious. "Give me a hint."

"Well, let's just say it has to do with kids. You like kids, don't you?"

"I'm crazy about kids." That was her problem.

Mitch kept looking toward the house, for a sign of Greta. Maybe Rebecca still wasn't feeling good, or she'd decided she didn't want to come down. Maybe she regretted last night. No. Not the way she'd kissed him back.

Maybe he'd had no business kissing her. Except for the fact that he hadn't been able to resist any longer, and, if she was as willing as last night, he planned on kissing her again.

"Dad, the bus is coming," Colby yelled from his perch on top of the corral fence.

"Okay, son," Mitch said as he turned toward the row of his gentlest horses, saddled and ready for their young riders. Nearby were a half-dozen ranch hands who had volunteered for this task.

"Dad, we're here," Greta called as she and Rebecca hurried toward him.

Mitch's focus was on Rebecca. His heart did a funny skip as he saw how natural she looked in jeans and boots, and how her beautiful hair was down, held away from her face by silver clips.

"Hi," he managed, wondering if she had lain awake half the night remembering what had happened between them.

"Hi." She placed a straw cowboy hat on her head.

"How do you feel this morning?" he asked.

"Much better, thank you." She glanced at the horses. "What's going on? Greta was very mysterious."

Mitch smiled. "In about two minutes there'll be a dozen kids here, eager to ride. I was hoping I could count on you to help out."

She blinked those big blue-gray eyes at him. "Sure, but I'm not qualified to teach—"

"There's no teaching involved, Rebecca. These kids just want to ride a horse around the arena. They're kids with special needs. So basically you'll help us get them in the saddle and lead the horse around the corral. You can handle a horse."

She nodded. "Of course. Whatever you need me to do."

Mitch could see she was distant and he had to find out why. "Rebecca, can I have a quick word with you?" Before she could answer him, he led her away from the kids. "About last night…and what happened between us… I never want you to feel uncomfortable around me. If I took advantage of the situation…"

"Mitch, we both were responsible for what happened. I want you to understand that I'm usually more professional than that; I haven't let my personal feelings get in the way of business."

"I never thought you did. Rebecca, you did nothing wrong, and neither did I."

"We overstepped, Mitch. I'm here to work—"

He'd opened his mouth to argue when the bus's horn sounded. He looked up to see the small yellow school bus coming down the road, kicking up dust in its wake.

"We'll talk about this later," he told her, not giving her a chance to protest. "But just one thing, Rebecca: I'm not sorry I kissed you. And I think you enjoyed it as much as I did." As a matter of fact, he wanted to kiss that shocked look off her face, right now, but he hadn't the time to do it justice. "Now, we've got to help the kids."

She followed him. "Mitch, wait. You can't say that and walk off." Her voice lowered. "Whether we enjoyed it or not isn't the question. It can't happen again."

"We'll talk about it later," he said.

Rebecca was fuming, but she followed Mitch. He welcomed the teachers as they came off the bus, then turned to help the excited kids down the steps.

"Hi, Mitch," several of the children called in greeting as they lined up.

He went to them and gave high fives and hugs all around. "Hey, kids, I want you to meet a friend of mine. Her name is Rebecca and she grew up on a horse farm. She's going to help you ride today."

"Hi, Rebecca," they chorused.

"Hi," she said, then Mitch introduced her to two teachers, Kathy Sanders and Peggy Anderson.

Rebecca was assigned to a beautiful five-year-old boy named Matthew. The boy didn't speak to her, but his blue eyes told her of his excitement. She took his hand and together they walked to the spotted mare.

"Magic," Matthew said.

A ranch hand, Neil, was holding the horse's reins. "That's right, Matthew, you're riding Magic today." He handed a helmet to Rebecca. "He needs to wear this."

She secured it under his chin. "Okay, Matthew. Let's get this strapped on." The child stood patiently until she finished. Neil lifted the boy into the saddle and strapped him in with a safety harness. Rebecca stepped back, until the task was completed, focused on the big grin on the five-year-old's face.

Neil handed her the reins. "You take the lead, I'll spot him." At her nod, he moved to the side of the horse's rump.

"You ready for a ride, Matthew?" she asked.

"Ride…" Matthew said. "Go…Magic."

Rebecca smiled as she tugged on the reins and joined the circle of horses walking around the corral. She stayed close to the boy, making sure he was holding on, then watched the other leaders and riders.

In the front of the group was Wally, walking Colby's horse, Trudy, with a little girl perched in the saddle. One of the teachers was at the rider's side, and behind them came Greta and Jimmy. Greta led the horse, but her eyes were on the young ranch hand. It was obvious that the girl had a crush on the handsome teenage boy.

Rebecca's attention turned to the next rider, Mitch's charge, an older boy of about eight, whom Mitch had charge of. He was showing the child how to do commands for his horse. Then he walked the horse to the center of the arena, where several colorful stuffed animals sat on top of the closed barrel.

"What's the command, Tim?" Mitch asked.

"Stop, Rudy," the boy called out. The horse stopped next to the barrel.

"Red, Tim."

The boy paused a moment, then reached down and picked up the red squirrel.

"Good job, Tim," Mitch said.

The boy's face beamed, his pleasure obvious as Mitch walked the horse to the other barrel.

Rebecca glanced up at Matthew to see he was watching the activity. "Matthew, do you want to do that?"

The boy pointed. "Monkey."

"Well, let's go get the monkey." With Neil's help Matthew retrieved the stuffed animal. The next hour passed quickly, but it wasn't until the kids headed for the bus that she realized her fatigue.

She helped Matthew onto the bus. He looked at her and said, "Bye, Becca."

Her heart melted, and tears pricked her eyes. "Bye, Matthew." She waved and stepped back as the teachers strapped the children in their safety seats, and the bus drove off.

She felt Mitch's presence as he came up behind her. "They tug at your heart," he said.

"How long have you been doing this?"

"A few years, but only from May through October," he said as leaned back against the fence. "With the weather and round-ups, there isn't more time."

"I'd say it's pretty incredible for you to open your ranch for the time you have."

He smiled. "It's easy. I'm crazy about kids, but I can't take credit for the project. Carrie started it about three years ago. Her cousin's boy is autistic, and when she saw how much he responded to horses at her parents' ranch in Cheyenne, she decided to help other kids with special needs locally. It was Carrie's dream to have a summer camp here."

They both were silent, watching the ranch hands lead the horses back to their stalls. Colby and Greta hurried after Wally into the barn.

"What a great idea," Rebecca finally said. "Maybe we can work the plans so some profit from the beef can go to support the camp."

Mitch's gaze locked with hers. As much

as she tried to glance away, he wouldn't allow it. "Rebecca… you're the first woman I've kissed since Carrie died."

She tried to act unaffected, but it didn't work.

"It's not that there weren't opportunities," he went on. "I just haven't wanted to. Until last night. Until you."

"It still shouldn't have happened, Mitch." She felt the tremble in her voice. "I'm here on business—"

"Can you just forget about business for a minute? We kissed, Rebecca, and I want to kiss you again. I also know that we have to work together."

"And I'll be returning to New York soon."

His mouth twitched. "Not that soon."

Rebecca's heart was pounding hard. It would be so easy just to let this happen, but she couldn't. In the end, she would only get hurt. She couldn't dream about a husband and a family. It was too late for that.

"I have a job to do, Mitch. My career is important to me."

He grew serious as he pushed away from the wall and stepped in front of her. "Take it from me, Rebecca—don't let it be everything. You need to have something else in your life." He released a long breath. "Fame and fortune don't mean anything unless you have someone to share it with." A smile appeared across that handsome face of his. "Be warned, Rebecca Valentine, as long as you're here, I'm going to try and convince you of that."

As hard as she tried, Rebecca couldn't put Mitch's words out of her head. She decided she would spend less time with the Tucker family. Then, Mitch announced that no one was cooking tonight—he was taking them all into town for supper.

Rebecca tried to beg off, but when Colby asked her to "Please, come," she couldn't turn him down. The kids climbed in the back of the Range Rover and Mitch held the door so she could get in the passenger seat. This time she wore dress slacks so she didn't have to worry about exposing too much leg.

"I've decided pants are more practical for SUVs."

Mitch's eyes gleamed as he leaned closer. "I'm a little disappointed," he whispered in her ear. "You've got great legs."

The huskiness of his voice sent a shiver down her spine. Before she could say anything he walked around to the driver's side and took his seat. The thirty-minute ride into town focused on the kids, the movies they wanted to see and other activities. Rebecca enjoyed listening to the easy banter between parent and children.

It wasn't long before they pulled into the parking lot of the local family-style restaurant, The Country Kitchen. Inside was cozy, with café-style curtains in the windows and checked tablecloths on the tables. Colby hurried to one of the red-vinyl booths beside the large window. Greta slid in next to him, leaving Rebecca and Mitch to sit side by side.

A slim waitress of about forty walked over. She was dressed in a starched white blouse and dark slacks. Her color-treated blonde hair was pulled into a French twist and her name tag read "Wanda". She set down four glasses of water and smiled.

"Well, if it isn't the Tucker family. What brings ya'll into town? A special occasion?"

"Hi, Wanda," Greta said.

"Hi, Wanda," Colby echoed. "Dad's treating us 'cause we're tired of cooking."

Dancing hazel eyes turned to Mitch. "So you ran out of Margie's casseroles."

"No," Mitch said. "We just decided to come into town and show Rebecca around."

"Well, it ought to take about fifteen minutes," she teased and held out her hand to Rebecca. "Hi, I'm Wanda Shaw. I went to school with Mitchell here, but it seems he forgot his manners about introductions." She sighed. "I guess I'm gonna have to tattle to his mother in Florida."

Rebecca got a kick out of seeing Mitch blush. "I'm Rebecca Valentine. I'm here to help market the Tuckers' free-range beef project."

"As if Wanda doesn't know all about what goes on in this town," Mitch accused. "I'm sure Greta and Colby told her all she wants to know."

Wanda straightened. "Well, people expect to come in here and know what's going on."

"Since you know everything already, you can bring us each a Calvin's burger with all the trimmings." He looked at Rebecca. "Is that okay with you?"

She nodded. "And I'll have a diet cola to drink."

"Dad, can we have soda, too?" Greta pleaded.

He looked thoughtful, then nodded.

They cheered and Colby said, "I want orange soda, please."

"And lemon-lime soda for me, please," Greta said.

Mitch turned to Rebecca. "You could have ordered something besides a hamburger. Cal has great specials."

She inhaled the scent of his aftershave. He was too close. "No, I like hamburgers."

"They're my favorite." Colby frowned. "But I hate onions. Greta doesn't like them either 'cause it makes her breath stink and she can't kiss boys."

Greta gasped. "That's a lie."

"No, it's not," Colby argued. "That's what you told Sarah Peterson."

A blush spread across Greta's cheeks. "You were listening at my door. Dad!"

Mitch raised a hand. "We're not going to discuss this now, but Colby, what you did was wrong. I'll be talking to you at home."

The boy hung his head. "Okay, I'm sorry, Greta. I won't do it again."

"You better not," his sister fumed.

"I don't know why anyone would want to kiss a girl anyway," the boy muttered. "It's dumb. I'm never gonna do that."

Rebecca could barely contain her laughter. Then Mitch turned toward her, but he wasn't smiling.

"When you get older, son, you'll think differently." His gaze held hers for a long time, then finally he turned away and looked at his daughter. "Since when are you kissing boys?"

"Dad…I'm not…" Greta's wide-eyed gaze sought Rebecca for help.

Rebecca reached for Mitch's hand to stop the interrogation. "I remember when I was Greta's age, my sister and I used to talk about boys all the time. But that's all it was, just talk." Surprisingly, Rebecca felt Mitch's hand grasp hers. "That's what girls do. We dream, we fantasize…"

"I was only thinking about fast cars and horses at Greta's age," Mitch told her.

Rebecca laughed. "That's because boys don't mature as quickly as girls."

"Yeah, Dad," Greta said. "Maturity-wise, girls are ahead of boys." She giggled. "But at about twenty-one you guys finally catch up to us."

Mitch couldn't believe this was his daughter talking. Where did she get this stuff? "Twenty-one? How do you know this?"

The preteen rolled her eyes. "In Sex Ed."

Before Mitch could respond, Rebecca squeezed his fingers under the table and Wanda arrived with the drinks. Rebecca released his hand and he immediately hated the loss of contact, but wasn't going to let her keep pulling away for long.

Rebecca hadn't laughed so much in years. She truly liked being with the Tuckers. It had been a long time since she'd felt like a part of a family. Not since she and Rachel had spent summers with her grandparents.

She stole a glance at the man seated next to her. Mitch Tucker would be a hard man to forget, along with his kids. No matter how unwise, she couldn't seem to keep her distance from him.

Mitch tossed down money for the check and tip when someone called to him. He turned around and saw Mildred Evans, his mother's friend, coming toward him. Biting back a groan, he plastered a smile on his face as the older woman approached. He stood and greeted her.

"Mrs Evans, it's good to see you."

She smiled. "Good to see you, Mitchell." She looked down at the children. "Oh, my, you've all grown so much. This can't be Colby. Well, aren't you getting handsome? Just like your father." Her attention moved to his daughter. "And this is little Greta," she gushed. "Such a young lady, and the image of your beautiful mother."

"Thank you, Mrs Evans," Greta said.

"I'm only speaking the truth. We all miss Carrie so much." The older woman finally glanced Rebecca's way. "And who is this?"

"Mrs Evans, this is Rebecca Valentine. She's from the Pierce Agency and is helping with my free-range beef project. Rebecca, this is Mrs Evans. She's a friend of my parents."

"Nice to meet you, Mrs Evans," Rebecca said.

The woman gave Rebecca the once-over,

and Mitch knew that his mother in Florida would get a full report in the morning.

"It's nice to meet you, Ms Valentine. I'm sure you feel like a fish out of water in our small town."

"It's a nice change of pace. And I've enjoyed staying at the Tucker ranch."

Mitch could see the older woman's mind clicking away. "It's so nice that Mitch opened his home to you."

He needed to end this, before the kids fed her any information. "Well, we should get going if we want to watch a movie before bedtime. It's been nice to see you, Mrs Evans."

Mitch quickly gathered the kids and Rebecca, and they were out the door and in the car without any further incident. All the way home, Rebecca was silent, probably because of what Mildred had said.

As promised, they watched a movie in the family room. Mitch wasn't sure which Disney movie it was, because he couldn't stop watching Rebecca. Ever since Mrs

Evans' appearance tonight, she had pulled away from them, into what seemed like her own little world.

When the movie ended, Colby had fallen asleep. When Mitch scooped him up, his son protested and said he wanted Rebecca to go, too.

Rebecca agreed and followed the group upstairs. Mitch carried Colby to his room, stripped him down and put on his pajamas. Rebecca came in, but stood back.

She felt out of place. She'd never put a child to bed before. Not that she hadn't wanted to; she'd just never had the chance.

"Rebecca," a sleepy Colby called her, "I'm glad you went with us tonight. It was fun."

"I had fun, too."

Mitch finished dressing the child, and put him under the thin blanket.

"Dad, did you have fun with Rebecca?"

Mitch looked at Rebecca. "Yes, I did," he told his son and kissed his forehead. "Now, go to sleep, kiddo."

Rebecca came closer and couldn't resist

brushing back the child's hair. "See you in the morning, Colby."

She followed Mitch out of his son's room. "If you don't mind, you better come with me for Greta."

She wanted nothing more, but this was the wrong direction if she was going to keep her distance. "Okay."

He tapped on the door. "Greta, you ready for bed?"

"Come in, Dad," she called.

Opening the door, he walked in. Rebecca decided to remain in the doorway.

The girl's room was all pink with a canopy bed and stuffed animals lining the top shelf of a bookcase. Greta sat on her bed, leaning against the headboard with a book. Her father went to her and leaned down to kiss her cheek.

"Don't stay up too late, honey."

"I won't, Dad," she said, then looked over at Rebecca. "Rebecca, I'm glad you went with us tonight. I had a good time."

"Yes, so did I," Rebecca said, even if

she was getting too involved with her client's family.

"Maybe we can do it again." Greta glanced at her father. "Dad, why don't we go riding tomorrow?"

"As nice as that sounds, I have things to do. You know, I run a ranch."

"I thought Wally did."

"Someone has to tell him what to do. Besides, I have an appointment with a mare's owner. Goodnight, now, Greta."

"Goodnight, Greta. I'll see you in the morning. It's my turn to fix breakfast."

Mitch kissed his daughter, then walked out and closed the door. "You don't have to cook for my children," he said when Rebecca reached his side.

"And you don't have to wait on me, either," she said, trying to keep her voice down.

Mitch grabbed her hand and pulled her with him down the stairs, away from prying ears. "I told you, I'm fixing meals for myself and the kids so it would seem silly…" He paused. "Why are you suddenly acting like this?"

She glanced away. "I just feel that we've gotten off track a little…"

"So we took today off." He studied her for a moment with those incredible dark eyes. "But you're still thinking about the kiss."

"It shouldn't have happened," she said. "And maybe going out to dinner tonight wasn't wise either."

"You kissed me back, Rebecca." He moved in closer, forcing her back up against the banister. He placed his hands on either side of the railing. "You could have stopped me."

"I know," she whispered. "And I should have."

"Admit it, Rebecca, you didn't stop me because you wanted it as much as I did then, and we both do now." He slowly lowered his head to her. Try as she might, she couldn't seem to force out any words to deny it.

CHAPTER SIX

REBECCA shouldn't want this man, but she did. In fact she was starved for him. For his touch…his kiss, the feel of his body against hers.

"Come here, Becca," Mitch said in his husky voice. He reached for her and pulled her into his arms. She resisted for a moment, then relented, her arms sliding around his neck.

He tangled his hands in her hair, shifting so her body was flat against his. Then he closed his mouth over hers. A bolt of raw sensation knocked the wind right out of her lungs. But who needed to breathe?

Mitch shuddered as Rebecca moved against him. He was so close to the edge, it wouldn't take much to push him over. And she felt so good, smelled so good…tasted like heaven.

Unable to control his need, he widened his stance and eased her in closer. She whimpered and clutched at him. Mitch opened his mouth against hers, feeding on the hunger between them. Trying to regain some control, he buried his head against her neck. "You can't tell me that you don't want this," he whispered.

"That still doesn't mean it's right," she said breathlessly.

Mitch shifted against her. She couldn't help but feel what she did to him. "It feels pretty damn right to me." He captured her mouth once again and slipped his tongue inside to taste her. Hearing her whimper, he repeated the action. When he finally released her, his heart was pounding in his chest like a drum.

Rebecca grasped at the last of her common sense. She couldn't keep doing this. She was an emotional wreck, reacting to the moment, using Mitch for comfort. "We have to stop," she begged.

She moved out of his embrace. Unable to look at him she murmured goodnight and hurried off toward her bedroom. Once the door was closed, she walked to the bed and sank onto the mattress. She had no control when it came to Mitch Tucker.

And she had too many things to think about other than having an affair with him. Her hand covered her stomach, feeling the cramps that plagued her midsection, reminding her that she couldn't have it all. It was just a shame she hadn't realized sooner that a family was the most important thing of all.

The next morning, Mitch was up early and out with Wally, who was getting ready to move the herd. It would take most of the day to get the steers into the feed lot and make sure they were settled for the next four months.

And he wanted to go along, but he couldn't leave the kids alone. So he got Jimmy's seventeen-year-old sister, Kelly, to come by for the day. He knew Greta would throw a fit, but he had no choice. This way, Rebecca could concentrate on getting some work done.

Rebecca. He'd thought about her all night. He shouldn't have pushed the situation with her. Whether or not she had feelings for him, it was clear she was struggling with her own demons and he was doing the same thing. He'd loved Carrie a long time. Now suddenly he had the hots for another woman, and it was quickly turning into more than that. And his kids were getting just as attached to Rebecca.

Was he ready for what came next?

Rebecca checked the clock again. It was after nine and Mitch hadn't returned to the house for breakfast. Not that she was anxious to see him, but she needed to talk to him. He needed to know her plans.

The back door opened and her heart began to race. She released a long breath as Mitch walked into the kitchen. He removed his hat and hung it on the hook. She couldn't help but stare at the good-looking man in the worn jeans and Western shirt. Who would have thought that she'd fall for a Wyoming cowboy?

She plastered on a smile. "Good morning."

"Good morning," he returned and went to the coffeepot. "Where are the kids?"

"I asked Greta to take Colby outside."

"I'm sorry. Were they bothering you?"

"No, they've never bothered me. This is about you and me. Last night…what happened between us wasn't wise."

He leaned against the counter and took a sip of coffee. "Because we're working together?"

"That's most of it. But being in your house, with your kids… I don't feel right about starting something."

He set down his mug and came to her. "Look, Rebecca, I'm so rusty at this. I've forgotten all the rules. I haven't even taken the time to date anyone." His dark eyes bored into hers. "But I do know I'm attracted to you, and I believe you're attracted to me. Isn't that a good beginning?"

"No! You're my client."

"And that's interfering with what?"

"Everything!"

"Is there someone else in your life?"

"No!"

He looked relieved. "Okay," he began. "I'll back off because we need to get this project going."

"And my returning to New York for a while will help."

He frowned. "You're leaving?"

"I want to get things set up with our art department. And I need to touch base with my other clients." She also had a doctor's appointment she couldn't cancel. "I should be back in a week or so."

Suddenly a loud scream drew their attention. Then the back door slammed, and Greta rushed in with Colby. His leg was cut and bleeding.

"What happened?" Mitch lifted his crying

son and seated him on the counter. Rebecca went to the sink, grabbed a clean towel and ran water over it.

Greta's face was flushed. "He was climbing on the wood pile… I told him to get down, but he didn't listen to me." Tears streamed down her face. "He fell off and got caught on a nail."

Rebecca came over and handed Mitch the towel. "No, you do it," Colby begged her.

With her own heart pounding in panic, she saw the strained look of a worried father. "Go ahead, you can handle it." He handed her the cloth.

Rebecca tried to soothe the boy. "It's going to be okay, Colby. Just take a deep breath and blow it out."

The child did as she asked, and she began to clean the big gash in his leg. She looked at Mitch and spoke softly. "I think he should see a doctor."

Mitch nodded. "Let's go." He scooped up his son.

Rebecca followed with Greta. In the car

she sat in the back seat with Colby while Mitch phoned the doctor. When they reached the small emergency room, Dr Walters was already waiting for them.

Rebecca stayed with Greta in the reception area trying to concentrate on the TV and not what was happening to a little five-year-old boy.

Seeing that Greta was upset, Rebecca slipped an arm around her shoulders and said, "What happened to Colby was an accident."

"He never listens to me," Greta said. "I tell him things all the time and he just does what he wants."

"That's a little boy for you. The big boys are the same way."

They both laughed, then Greta quickly sobered. "Do you think he's hurt really bad?"

Rebecca shook her head. "The cut wasn't too deep, but he needed stitches. Colby will have a scar to brag about."

Great groaned. "I'm going to have to be his slave for ever."

"Well, he'd do the same for you."

The girl grew serious. "I know I act like I don't care about Colby much…but if something bad happened…"

Rebecca hugged her. "I know. You love him." She thought about her sister. All the years they hadn't spoken. Her heart ached. Maybe she should contact Rachel…

Mitch came out of the room, pushing a smiling Colby in a wheelchair.

"I got six stitches and a shot. And I didn't even cry." He cocked his head upward. "Huh, Dad?"

"No, you didn't." Mitch turned to Rebecca. He looked less stressed then he had when they'd brought Colby in. "He was a brave boy."

The boy grinned. "So how about we go get hamburgers?"

Greta looked at Rebecca. "See, he's already getting everything. Oh, I'm not going to be able to stand living with him."

Rebecca and Mitch exchanged a glance. She had an urge to hug him. But no. She was a visitor here. This wasn't her family.

* * *

The rest of the day, everyone catered to Colby's every wish. By the time the boy was put to bed they were all exhausted, including Greta, who had gone to her room.

Rebecca was in her bedroom when she decided she wanted a cup of tea. She wasn't the only one. In the dimly lit kitchen she found Mitch sitting in the dark, looking out the window. She started to leave, but when she heard his sob it tore at her heart.

She knew that desperate feeling of being totally alone. Against her better judgment she went to him.

"Mitch…"

He quickly wiped his eyes before he turned to her. "I thought everyone was in bed."

"I came for a cup of tea." She frowned. "We've all had a rough day and it took a lot out of us."

He nodded. The moonlight through the window showed his red eyes. "I felt so helpless today."

"You weren't, though. You called the doctor and got Colby to the hospital." She stepped closer to him, unable to keep from touching him. He needed someone. He needed her.

"Oh, Becca," he whispered, his head rested against her breasts. "I don't know what I would have done if something…"

"Shh… Don't borrow trouble, Mitch. Colby is all right."

"Damn, it's rough doing this alone." He stood and drew her close. "I wish you weren't leaving."

She weakened. "I guess I don't have to go right away. I can postpone my trip until Colby gets his stitches out."

He pulled back and looked down at her. "Are you sure?"

No, she wasn't sure of anything, any more. She nodded. "I'll need more time in your office."

"Tell you what, if you watch Colby in the mornings, I get Wally and the crew working for the day, and I'll take over for you in the afternoon. How does that work for you?"

"Just fine. But there's something else. We can't let this get any more personal."

"You mean no more kisses?"

She nodded.

He sighed. "You drive a hard bargain, lady. But if it's the only way to keep you here… So when does this new rule begin?" he asked as he drew her to him.

She was in big trouble. "Tomorrow," she breathed just as Mitch lowered his mouth to hers.

The next morning, Mitch hurried back to the house. He knew keeping his son in one spot for long was nearly impossible. Besides, he didn't mind seeing Rebecca.

His thoughts turned to the kiss they'd shared last night. There had been several last kisses. One had led to another and another, until he'd finally begged for mercy and given Rebecca a shove toward her bedroom.

The last thing he wanted to do was mess this up. He wanted Rebecca Valentine to stay so they could find out where these feelings were going. And he was going to do everything possible to find out, which might be the craziest thing he'd ever done. What if this didn't work out? No, something told him that Rebecca wanted more than her career.

He already knew she was great with his kids. She was a natural mother. Suddenly, he pictured Rebecca pregnant with his child. He stopped short trying to catch his breath. Had his feelings for her gone that far? He climbed on the porch, opened the back door and headed for the family room where he heard his son's favorite Power Ranger video playing. Colby sat on the sofa with his warrior figures in his hands.

Mitch glanced across the room. Rebecca sat at the table, looking over some papers. She had on jeans and a red polo shirt. Best of all, her glorious hair was hanging loose.

Colby finally spotted him. "Hey, Dad! What are you doing here?"

"I thought I'd check on you. I have a few

minutes before going into town," he said, and went to ruffle his son's hair. He glanced at Rebecca. "Then I need to go with Wally to check on the herd. I might be a little late getting back."

"That's okay," Rebecca said.

"No, it's not, but I'll make sure that Greta is here to sit with Colby."

Rebecca smiled. "And I'll be close by if there's any trouble. But I doubt there will be. Your daughter is very mature for her age."

"You mean nearly twelve going on thirty." Mitch grew serious. "Sometimes I feel I stole her childhood from her. She suddenly had to grow up when Carrie died."

"It's hard losing a parent so young… At any age it's hard. Greta is an amazing young lady."

Mitch couldn't help but see a lot of the same traits in both females. "She really seems to relate to you," he said. "I feel I'm not going to be able to keep up with her."

"Just keep talking to her, make her feel special."

Mitch wondered if Rebecca's father's living in England made it difficult for them to have a relationship. "Every woman should be treated special. Was there someone who made you feel special when you were Greta's age?"

She glanced away. "In some families, when there's a divorce, the focus isn't on the children. But that's past history. You better get going. I'll let Greta know the arrangement." She stood and walked out of the room.

Rebecca wasn't real subtle about avoiding his asking questions about her family situation. There was so much about this woman he wanted to know. Especially who'd hurt her so deeply.

The week passed faster than Rebecca could imagine. Colby healed perfectly with a nice scar to show all the kids in kindergarten in the fall. Mitch got the herd into the feed lot and she toured the site for the slaughterhouse and meat-packing plant. Another six months and it would be up and operational.

Mitch Tucker got things done, or he figured out a way to work around them.

The morning of her departure, Greta fixed breakfast while Rebecca packed her suitcases. After rechecking all the drawers to see if she'd forgotten anything, she headed to the kitchen. It was going to be tough to say goodbye. She wondered if she should even return here. Maybe it was better for everyone if she didn't. Cut her losses before someone got hurt, namely her.

She met Mitch in the kitchen, but he wasn't alone. He'd played the kid card, and both Colby and Greta looked adorable, and very sad that she was leaving.

"I don't want you to go, Rebecca," Colby said.

"But I need to be in my office for a while. I've been away for nearly three weeks." The children were others that could be hurt if she started something with their father, started a relationship that couldn't lead anywhere. She had no future with a man who wanted a houseful of kids.

After she hugged them both goodbye, Mitch helped her into the Range Rover. Then he instructed his daughter to watch Colby until he returned. He started the truck and pulled away. Rebecca watched the two kids waving, looking forlorn. Why did she feel she was abandoning them?

In a sudden moment of panic, Rebecca wanted to call it off, reveal her feelings to Mitch and confide that she wanted to stay and see where this would lead. But she couldn't saddle him with her problem. She had to go this alone, as she'd had to do since she was a kid.

Mitch kept the conversation light until he pulled up at the landing strip. He climbed out and Wally gave him the thumbs-up from the Cessna that he was checked out to go.

Mitch wasn't ready to let Rebecca go. He helped her from the passenger side, but blocked her path until he said what he needed to say. "Think about us while you're gone."

"Of course, but, Mitch…" She closed her eyes a second. "When I come back, it has to be different."

He relented, realizing if he didn't, she might not return. "Okay, if that's what you want, I'll keep us business. But you agree that after we get this project going, we'll see what happens—where this can lead."

She didn't get a chance to answer. Wally came over, took her bags from the back and loaded them into the plane.

"I should go, so I can make my connection in Denver."

Finally he leaned down and kissed her, a soft kiss that offered tenderness. He pulled back. "Have a good flight, Rebecca."

"Goodbye, Mitch," she whispered and started for the plane.

He called to her and she turned. "Just so you know, whatever you're fighting, you don't have to go it alone. You have me."

After a week back in New York, Rebecca sat at her desk in her nice office. For years this had been everything to her. Her life. She'd worked day and night for it.

Now, all she could think about was how Colby and Greta were doing. How was Mitch handling the ranch and the kids? She shook away the thoughts. She had to stop this. What had happened in Wyoming was over. It was time to get back to reality.

Reality had hit her hard after she returned home. Yesterday had been the anniversary of her mother's death and she had been to the grave to find the flowers from her sister. Then today she'd received the phone call from Rachel asking if the roses had been placed at the graveside.

Rebecca wanted so badly to bridge the gap between them. But the call had ended before she could tell Rachel about the D and C the doctor had performed just days before, or that it was only a temporary solution. It wouldn't solve her problem. He'd wanted to schedule a hysterectomy in a few months.

Rebecca hadn't told her twin any of those

things. She would handle them as she always had, alone. Tears welled in her eyes as she thought about Mitch.

He'd always wanted a houseful of kids, he had said.

So how could Rebecca go back to Wyoming? She couldn't hide her feelings for Mitch…for his kids. And if something more developed between them, she couldn't handle his pity. He needed a younger woman who could give him a home, more children. That wasn't her.

There was a knock on the door, and Brent swung into the room, but he wasn't wearing his usual smile.

"Hey, Beck, we've got to talk." He sat down in the chair and stretched out his long legs.

"What's the problem?" she asked, taking her chair behind her desk.

"It all depends on what you define as a problem. How do you feel about returning to Wyoming?"

She tensed. "Come on, Brent. You know

I can't." She hadn't revealed everything to her friend, but enough for him to know that things could easily stray from business. "I've committed my time to the Newman project. You promised you would finish the free-range beef project."

Brent raised a hand. "And I will—would, but Mitch Tucker has other ideas. He wants you and only you."

Rebecca breathed in and out to control her anger. "He doesn't need me to finish this. I've done all the groundwork. Anyone can handle the rest."

Brent looked concerned. "Tucker has threatened to go to another agency if you don't return to finish the job."

Rebecca sucked in a breath. "Can he do that?"

"According to our legal department he can. Dad is adamant about this, Beck. He wants you to return to Wyoming."

Why was Mitch doing this to her? Maybe he was so used to getting what he wanted that he'd decided he wasn't finished with her. Well, she was finished with him. "Fine, I'll go, but I'm not happy being railroaded."

"Thanks, I owe you." He walked to the door and stopped. "Come on, Beck, it's only a few more weeks. When you get back home we'll celebrate."

"I may not survive till then," she murmured.

He arched an eyebrow. "I think you protest too much." He studied her for a long time. "If I didn't know better, I'd say this Wyoming cowboy was getting to you."

"That's crazy," she denied. Mitch Tucker had already gotten to her.

CHAPTER SEVEN

"OKAY, I'm back," Rebecca announced as she marched into the den and tossed her portfolio on the desk.

Mitch looked up at her, pretending he didn't care. But he did care. Very much.

He'd known Rebecca had landed thirty minutes ago but had decided to let Wally bring her to the house. He'd even asked Greta to help her get settled in her room, saying he had to take a conference call and couldn't be disturbed. There'd been no call. Not that Rebecca seemed to care if he were busy or not when she barged into his office.

"It's nice to have you back," he commented. But his eyes ate her up. He'd been starved for the sight of her this past week, not being able to see her every day. Even her black business suit worn like armor, and her beautiful hair pulled back and captured in a tight bun, didn't detract from her appeal. He had to fight to keep from coming around the desk and kissing her until she admitted how much she'd missed him, too.

His tactics to bring her back to Wyoming might have been a little underhanded, but desperate times called for desperate measures. He leaned back in his leather chair. "I want to continue moving forward on this project, and you and I worked together well."

She folded her arms "That's beside the point. You bullied me into coming back here. More importantly, you threatened my job at the Pierce Agency. It's my career."

Mitch worked to maintain his calm. He wasn't used to people questioning his decisions. "First of all, I would never threaten your career. I just didn't want to waste time bringing someone else up to speed."

Had he made a mistake about her feelings

for him and his children? He knew he was taking a big risk, but hopefully it was worth it.

"Any one of my qualified associates could have handled your…needs. I would oversee things from New York."

At the sound of a horn, he glanced out the window to see the familiar school bus, then turned back to her. "Well, I'm the client here, and I want you on this project, and I want you here."

Rebecca reached for her portfolio. "Okay, let's get started…"

"Sorry, right now isn't a good time."

Her jaw tightened, revealing her irritation. "When would be a good time? I've prepared a presentation."

"It's going to have to be later today. No, tomorrow would be better. The kids are here to ride." He stood and started across the room, but paused. "If you're interested, I could use your help."

At his suggestion, her whole demeanor softened. "Of course, if you need me."

"Oh, I need you, all right," he said. "Later, I hope I get the chance to tell you—tell you how much it means to me that you've come back."

"You didn't give me a choice."

Even after changing into her jeans and boots, Rebecca still fumed over Mitch's arrogance. But as soon as she arrived at the corral and saw the kids her anger disappeared.

She was assigned to Matthew again. Today the boy let her take his hand and she walked him to Magic.

"I'm glad you came to ride, Matthew. Maybe today you can see if Magic will do some tricks."

"Magic," he murmured.

"Yes, you're going to ride Magic," Rebecca said, seeing his head was tilted toward the sun, a blank look on his face.

When she'd returned to New York, she'd done some research into the condition, learning that too many things going on at the same time could cause sensory overload. The autistic child withdrew or had a meltdown, indicating his anger or frustration.

Right now, Matthew seemed focused on getting on his horse. With some help from their spotter, Jimmy, Rebecca got the five-year-old in the saddle. She picked up the reins and they'd begun the journey around the corral when Mitch approached. He reassigned Jimmy and began to walk next to the horse.

"Hi, Matt." He patted the boy's leg.

"Hi, Mitch…"

Those dark brown eyes turned to Rebecca. "And how are you really doin'?"

She shrugged. "I can handle it," she told him. *It's you I can't handle,* she cried silently. "If you have to oversee other things, Matthew and I will be fine." Then she tugged on the rein and started off. She couldn't let this man get to her, but she knew he already had.

Mitch stared at her as he walked beside the horse. Rebecca Valentine had a big heart when it came to kids. He'd seen her share it with his children, and also with these kids. She fit in so well here.

She just didn't want anything to do with him.

Mitch motioned Jimmy to come back and spot for him. "I'll let you finish taking Matthew around." He checked his watch. "There's about another twenty minutes before we finish up." Before Rebecca said anything more, he strolled away.

Wasn't that what she wanted? For the man to leave her alone? She'd come here on business and as soon as she was finished she would return to New York and no one would get hurt. Her life would go back to normal.

Right. She closed her eyes for a moment. Nothing in her life had ever been normal. *Not when your family is named Valentine.*

Pushing aside her own problems, she smiled at Matthew.

"Okay, let's go." She tugged him toward the barrel in the middle of the corral, and the game began.

When the twenty minutes were up, Jimmy helped Matthew off the horse and Rebecca walked him back to the bus behind the other children.

One of the teachers took his hand. "Bye, Matthew," Rebecca said.

"Bye, Becca," Matthew called without looking at her.

Every time this child spoke to her, tears stung her eyes. Every small accomplishment was so huge.

Greta and Colby came up beside her. They waved as the bus pulled away and drove along the road until it disappeared from view.

"I'm glad you're back, Rebecca," Colby said. "I missed you."

"I'm glad I'm back, too." It was the truth. She'd missed these two kids more than she ever could have imagined. That was also one of the reasons she hadn't wanted to return. Leaving them again would only cause her more heartbreak.

She glanced toward the corral and saw Mitch walking toward them. His lazy swagger looked as if he had all day, but his six-foot-two height ate up a lot of ground. He was so appealing in those jeans and that fitted Western shirt, with a black cowboy hat sitting low on his forehead. Then he smiled at her. That all knowing, you're-crazy-about-me smile. She released a long breath. She was in deep trouble.

"Hey, how does everyone feel about pizza tonight?"

Colby jumped up and down. "Oh, boy. I love pizza."

"Me, too," Greta said.

They all turned to Rebecca. If she said no, then she was the bad guy. "Sure, pizza sounds good."

"Good," he said. "You kids go and get cleaned up."

Greta walked off with Colby, but Rebecca hung back to talk with Mitch. "I thought we were going to concentrate on the project."

"We will, but it's your first day back and the kids are tired of eating my cooking."

"Of course, but tomorrow I would like you to look over the artwork I've come up with."

He nodded. "Sure, I have the afternoon free." He studied her for a long time. "I missed you."

Rebecca felt a blush rise to her face. "Mitch, please," she begged. "I told you I can't work on this project if you make it personal."

"Rebecca, from the moment we met it's been personal between us."

"That doesn't mean we have to act on it. And you have Greta and Colby to think about."

That seemed to get to him. "Okay, maybe we should tread carefully, but first I haven't welcomed you back…home." He reached out and cupped the back of her neck and lowered his mouth to hers. Although the kiss was a mere brush of his lips against hers, the impact was still powerful. By the time he released her, she was dazed and breathless. A condition she was in a lot when she was around this man.

* * *

Rebecca rolled over in bed and glanced at the clock. It was after one a.m. and she couldn't sleep. Maybe that was because she'd slept in every morning until she knew that Mitch was gone from the house.

But she hadn't really slept. She'd heard all the sounds of a household waking up: Colby running down the stairs, Greta arguing with her brother, Mitch asking about breakfast. Rebecca had ached to join in, but that was a dream she dared not dream.

To stop her thoughts she got out of bed, slipped on a robe and walked to the kitchen. Relieved to have the solitude, she heated some water for tea, and then carried her cup and saucer into the sun room. She loved this part of the house. It was so cozy and private.

She sat down on the window-seat, breathed in the earth-scented night air and suddenly childhood memories of living with Poppy and Nana came to mind. Those days on the farm had been the best. For her and

Rachel. They'd both been happy then. What had happened to them? Was her sister happy in England? Rebecca didn't even know that much about her twin. There was more than an ocean that separated them. That still separated them.

Rebecca sighed and took a sip of her tea. It wasn't that she hadn't wanted to resolve their problems, but over the years she had found it easier to put things off. She thought back to Rachel's phone call. She could sense that her sister had wanted to say more to her.

Now, after the e-mail she'd received from Stephanie earlier today, telling her of Grandfather William's poor health, she wondered if that was what Rachel wanted to tell her.

"Rebecca, are you okay?"

She swung around to find Mitch in the doorway. He was wearing a pair of black sweatpants and nothing else. His hair was mussed and she could tell he'd been in bed.

"I'm fine. I just got some tea, and was enjoying the peace and quiet."

He gave her a lopsided grin. "So you did miss what we have to offer when you went back to New York."

"I have to admit, I did." She stood, not wanting to deal with her feelings, or the look on his face. "I'll go back to my room."

"Please, I don't want to chase you off." He paused and raked his fingers through his hair. "I couldn't sleep, either. So why not keep each other company?"

She hesitated. "I could make you some of my tea."

"Cures all ills, huh?" He went to her, took her cup in his large hand and sipped. "Not bad."

The intimacy of his action sent her pulse racing. "A friend sends it to me from the UK."

"I don't think tea will solve my problem." He stared out into the starlit sky. "We've lost two calves this week."

"Oh, no. How?"

"The tracks show it's most likely a mountain lion."

She sucked in a breath. "A mountain lion."

"Don't worry. You and the kids are safe here. But the herd is vulnerable, so I've increased the night patrol."

"Will they catch it?"

He shrugged. "That would be nice, or if the cat would go back to feeding off the deer population. If not, we'll have to go after it."

Mitch didn't want to talk about cats; he was concerned about Rebecca. "What about you? What's got you up?"

"Oh, I was on the computer earlier." She sighed. "I just needed to unwind a little."

"Rebecca, you can't do business twenty-four seven."

"I was actually e-mailing my friend, Stephanie. It's difficult to call each other since she lives in London."

"It's good you stay in touch," he said, watching the dim light reflecting off her hair.

She smiled. "Stephanie and I have been

friends since college. Whenever she comes to New York we get together."

"And since your family is in England, you must get to see her when you go there."

She glanced away. "I haven't been in a long time."

"What about your family? When do you see them?"

She hesitated a second. "When you're a product of divorce you don't always come out with a whole family. After our mother brought us to the States, we only went back a few times. Of course, Rachel returned to London after college. I decided to stay with our mother."

Mitch wanted to know everything about Rebecca. Just seeing the pain in her eyes and the loneliness in her voice tore him apart. Only his promise to her kept him from taking her in his arms. "What about after her death? You could have gone back…for a visit."

She shrugged and looked down into her almost empty cup. "By then I didn't feel like I fit in." Her voice was soft and hesitant. "Grandfather William always seemed to favor Rachel. Not that it was that obvious, but they've always gotten on so well."

Mitch's heart ached for her. How could anyone not love this woman? "What about your father?"

A half smile transformed her face. "Let's see…at last count, Robert Valentine has had a total of four marriages, and six children. The shame is, I don't think he's ever gotten over our mother. Diana Crawford Valentine was the love of his life."

"I'm sorry." He tried to reach out to her, but she stood and her teacup rattled as she moved away.

"Don't worry, Mitch. I got over my father's lack of interest a long time ago. I've made a life and career in New York."

He came toward her. "We don't get over needing family. If you had, it wouldn't bother you so much that you haven't seen your father and sister in—what…ten years?"

"We talk now and then," she offered. "We've just never been close."

Mitch didn't believe her casual attitude for a second. "Maybe after this project is finished, you can go see your friend, Stephanie, and let your sister know you're there."

He could see she was thinking about it. "So now you're a travel agent?" She laughed.

He smiled. "I'll even fly you over there."

She raised an eyebrow. "In your Cessna?"

"I also have a Lear jet in Cheyenne. Since I've retired I haven't used it much."

"Thank you for the offer, I'll consider it. I guess I should get to bed," she said as she started for the door.

"There's no need to run off." He came toward her. "I promised I wouldn't pressure you and I'll keep my word."

"I know." She swallowed. "I just need some sleep."

He took a step closer, getting into her space so he could inhale her sweet scent. "Darlin', I haven't been able to sleep since you came to Wyoming. And it's been the sweetest suffering I've ever endured."

The sweetest suffering I've ever endured.

The next morning, Rebecca tried to get some work done, but Mitch's words kept distracting her. She finally tossed her pen down on the desk and looked out the window.

That was when she saw Mitch. He was leading four saddled horses toward the house. The mounts were the same they'd ridden out to see the herd when she'd first arrived at the ranch.

Her attention turned to the two kids running out the door. Their father said something to them and Greta went back into the house. It wasn't long until she appeared at the office door.

"Rebecca," she said, "I know we're not supposed to bother you when you're working, but Dad, Colby and I want to know if you'd like to ride with us out to Horseshoe Pond. We're going swimming."

Rebecca found she was as excited as

Greta. The last thing she wanted to do was stay here all day alone.

"I'd love to go." She came around the desk. "Just give me five minutes to change." Rebecca started out of the room, and Greta reminded her to bring a swimsuit if she had one.

Once in the bedroom, Rebecca dug through the pockets of her suitcase where she always packed a simple one piece suit to use at hotel pools. It took two extra minutes to put it on under her jeans and T-shirt. She grabbed her hat off the hook as she walked out the back door, and hurried down the steps. Colby and Greta were already on their horses.

Smiling, Mitch held out Ginger's reins to her. "I'm glad you could make it."

"Thanks for inviting me."

He suddenly sobered. "I planned this day for you, Rebecca. Just so you could see there are other things in life besides work. I plan to show you how to relax."

"Come on, Dad, Rebecca," Colby called impatiently.

Barely managing to tear her gaze away from Mitch's, she went to Ginger and swung up into the saddle. This time Greta took charge of her brother and they led the foursome along the path.

"You know we can only play hookey for so long," Rebecca said.

He smiled. "I'm the boss, so I say when we work. Besides, it's too nice a day to work. What will it hurt if we take a little break?"

It could be very dangerous, she thought.

He glanced up at the cloudless sky. "There's plenty of time during the Wyoming winters to hang around the house."

Rebecca felt a stab of regret. "I won't be here this winter."

He sighed and gave her a sideways glance. "I guess I'll just have to think up another project to keep you here."

What was he trying to do to her? "That would be an expensive endeavor."

His eyes locked with hers, stirring up all sorts of sensations. "You're worth it."

She didn't know how to answer, so she didn't even try as they continued to follow the trail.

Over the next twenty minutes Mitch kept it light with stories of his childhood. Rebecca talked about her time on the horse farm. There was such an easy banter between them that she was surprised to find they'd reached their destination. A group of trees at the base of the foothills sheltered a small pool of water.

Colby was the first to slip off his horse. "Dad, can we go swimming now?"

"Just let me take care of the horses." Mitch climbed off his mount and Rebecca followed. The summer sun had caused the temperature to climb and the water did look inviting.

Mitch took the horses to the edge of the pond for a drink, then into the shade and dropped their reins so they could graze. He untied the blanket from his saddle and with Greta's help, spread it on the ground.

The kids plopped down and quickly

pulled off their boots, next came their T-shirts and jeans, revealing their swimsuits underneath.

"My dad used to swim here when he was a kid," Colby volunteered. "He skinny-dipped." The kid grinned. "That means he was naked."

"Too much information, son," Mitch said. He glanced at Rebecca. "You probably didn't have a suit with you… I wouldn't go in but there's a deep end to the pond and I need to play lifeguard."

Colby screamed as he jumped into the cool water. Mitch sat down and pulled off his boots, socks and jeans, revealing a pair of navy boxer-style trunks. "It's a shame you can't go in."

Rebecca felt giddy as she tugged off her boots and stood up. "But I hear you don't need a suit here." She unfastened her jeans and began to lower the zipper…slowly. She bit back a smile, seeing Mitch swallow as she tugged her pants downward. "I guess if you can skinny-dip, so can I."

The tables were turned as she saw a rush of excitement and desire in his eyes.

"You're playin' with fire, darlin'," he said in his best cowboy drawl. "If you want me to keep my hands off you, you'll need to cooperate." Slowly a wicked grin appeared. "No, on second thought, don't stop on my account."

Rebecca swallowed hard and her hand began to shake as she pushed her jeans off, revealing her long legs.

Mitch watched her every move. "Damn, if I knew you were hiding those beauties, I'd…"

Suddenly Colby called to him. He stood and yanked off his shirt. It was her turn to stare. The man was built, and she didn't think he'd been aided by any gym work.

"I'll meet you in the water," he told her, then ran off toward the kids. She watched as he picked up Colby and dunked the giggling child into the water.

Rebecca removed her blouse, and walked to the edge where Greta was waiting for her. Together they sank into the cool water.

Mitch's father had lined the bottom of the pond with rocks and sand, making it a nice place to swim. It took a few minutes, but Rebecca soon adjusted to the water and began to swim with Greta. Colby started making a commotion at the far end where there was a large tree and a long knotted rope. Mitch climbed out of the water, and, with his kids egging him on, he stood on a big rock and grabbed hold of the rigging. With a loud Tarzan cry, he swung out over the water, then let go and landed with a big splash.

Colby and Greta cheered their father's antics. But when he didn't surface immediately, Rebecca was worried, until she suddenly felt hands on her waist. She gasped as he raised her up out of the water and tossed her back in.

Rebecca came up sputtering. "That wasn't nice." She brushed her thick hair out of her eyes.

Mitch moved toward her. "I'm sorry. Are you okay?"

Catching him off guard, Rebecca used her leg for leverage, and shoved him backward into the water. He came up surprised, but smiling.

"So you want to play?"

"You started it." She backed away.

"And I always finish what I start," he said, moving toward her. "After that little striptease of yours…" he kept his voice low "…how do you expect me to keep my hands off you?"

She swallowed. "I didn't mean…"

Mitch was half mad for this woman. The simple nylon suit showed off every curve of her sexy little body. "Rebecca, you made me crazy just looking at you." His gaze wandered down over her curves. "In that suit you should be illegal."

She tried to move away, but he grasped her arm.

"Don't run away, Rebecca. I know you're afraid, but you can't deny what's happening any more than I can."

Tired of being ignored, Colby and Greta called to them.

Mitch knew he had to go. "This isn't the time or place to discuss this, but I'm not letting it go. Not unless you tell me to." He searched her face. "If you want me to stay away, I will, but I don't think it is what you really want."

"We can't always get what we want," she said weakly.

"Do you want me to kiss you right here and prove you wrong? I care about you, Rebecca Valentine. Now, I need some honesty from you."

Her beautiful blue-gray gaze widened, her breathing was ragged. He released the hold on her arm. "Say it, Becca."

She closed her eyes momentarily. "Okay. Yes! I care about you. I don't want you to stay away."

He smiled, and glanced toward his kids. "Just hold that thought until about nine o'clock tonight."

CHAPTER EIGHT

SHE was playing with fire and she might get burned.

Rebecca paced the sun room while Mitch was upstairs with Colby and Greta, making sure they were settled in for the night.

She clasped her hands together. She had no idea what Mitch expected from her when he came downstairs. No, that was a lie. Of course she knew. He wanted her…in the biblical sense. And she wasn't any good at this. The only two relationships in her life had consisted of one short-term boyfriend in college that had been the typical see-what-sex-is-like experience.

She hadn't been impressed.

Then, in her early years at the Pierce

Agency, she had shared a brief fling with Brent during a business trip. Luckily, they'd remained friends after that disaster.

Now, there was Mitch Tucker. What category did he fit into? He'd been married for years. He was definitely a for-ever kind of guy. A family man.

She closed her eyes. If only he'd come into her life five years ago. Not now, not when her life was in turmoil. Not when she had to face a life-changing decision—and not with a man who wanted more children. That above everything else tore at her.

Her chest tightened with emotions she'd never felt before. "I could so easily love you, Mitch Tucker."

"Rebecca…"

She swung around. The man in question was standing in the doorway. He was handsome, sexy… with dark, piercing eyes that seemed to see right through her. A warm shiver moved down her spine as she remembered how it felt to have his skilled hands on her. A lazy smile curved his mouth and suddenly she couldn't breathe.

He walked toward her and drew her into an embrace. "Are you all right?" he murmured against her ear.

Unable to resist him, she wrapped her arms around his waist and snuggled into the welcoming warmth of his chest. "I'm not sure," she admitted. "But don't let me go."

Rebecca wished she could block out the world, but too many people were involved, including the two kids asleep upstairs.

"I wasn't planning to any time soon," he told her. He cupped her face and touched his mouth to hers in a whisper of a kiss so tender she felt light-headed. How could being with Mitch seem so right and yet be so wrong?

Mitch needed to slow things down. He didn't want to push too hard. If he hadn't insisted that she return to Wyoming, she would be out of his life. That realization tore him up.

He pulled away, and rested his forehead

against hers. "Rebecca, I'm trying to tread slowly with you… but when you're in my arms it becomes damn difficult." But, unable to help himself, he kissed her again. This time he showed her his hunger and she responded to him. His hands moved over her body, finally bringing her against him. With Rebecca it was more than a physical thing. He needed *her*. Her smile, her heart…

She broke off the kiss, her face flushed and her lips swollen. She stepped back. "Mitch…this is happening too fast…" Her shaky hand brushed back her hair. "We don't know each other…"

"Better than most, since we've lived in the same house for the past month," he insisted.

She arched an eyebrow. "Not the same thing. Besides, I'm going back to New York soon. You live here."

"Do you have to go back…right away?"

"Yes, my life, my career is there. Those things are important to me."

"I'm not asking you to give them up," he said calmly. "Just take some time…to see about us. There are other things in life, Rebecca," he said. To prove it, he captured her mouth in another passionate kiss.

When he released her, she stumbled backward. "Is that your answer to everything?"

"If you were honest you would admit it's the same for you."

She groaned and turned away. "I can't do this."

"Do what? Just act on your feelings? Stop hiding behind your job, Rebecca."

Her eyes blazed. "I'm not hiding anything. I came here to do a job, and if that's not enough I can be gone in the morning."

"Rebecca, that's not what I meant. You're doing a great job," he said, but it was obvious that she'd already tuned him out.

The phone rang. Mitch cursed as he went to the table and grabbed the receiver. "Hello," he barked.

"Mitch, it's Wally. I'm sorry to bother you so late."

"Not a problem. What's up?"

"Neil just radioed in. We lost another calf."

"Damn." He turned away from Rebecca. "Did he see anything?"

"Yeah, he heard a commotion and got there just as a big cat took off toward the foothills above the south pasture. He also found some tracks. Charlie Peterson got hit, too. Last night. He wants to go after the cat—tonight."

"Okay, Wally. Get together a couple of the men you want to take with you."

He felt Rebecca's hand on his arm. "What happened?"

He covered the mouthpiece. "The mountain lion got another calf. Wally's going to take some men and go after it."

"What about you?" she asked. "Don't you need to go?"

He shook his head. "I can't leave Greta and Colby."

"You won't be leaving them alone. I'll be here."

He studied her. How could she say she

didn't want to get involved when she already was? "It's not fair to ask you—"

"Is it fair that a mountain lion is killing off your herd?"

"I don't know how long I'll be gone," he told her.

"I'm not going anywhere."

But she was. She'd be leaving soon. Without taking his gaze from her, he removed his hand from the mouthpiece. "Wally, there's a change of plans. I'll be going along. Just give me ten minutes." He hung up. "Come on, we can talk as I get ready." He took her hand and pulled her along with him.

Rebecca wanted to refuse to go, but she suspected that Mitch wanted to instruct her about the kids. Together they climbed the stairs and walked down the hall through double doors that led into the master bedroom. Rebecca was taken aback as she glanced around at the soft green walls and plush ecru carpet. A dark armoire and dresser matched the straight lines of the king-size bed that was adorned with a rust-colored comforter.

It was definitely a man's room, except for the glow that came from the lit candles. She suddenly realized that he'd planned to bring her here.

Mitch quickly extinguished the burning wicks. He went to the dresser, pulled out a pair of jeans and a T-shirt, then went to the closet and took out a black sweatshirt. He dumped the clothes on the bed, then disappeared into the connecting bathroom. When he returned he was carrying a small case.

"I needed a toothbrush." He tossed the toiletries on top, then rolled up the clothes. His eyes met hers. "As you can see, I had different plans for tonight."

Rebecca didn't want to rehash what had happened between them. "It's better things didn't go any further."

He nodded. "Maybe. I don't think I need to instruct you on how to handle Greta and Colby. Just tell them I love them, and I'll be back as soon as I can. I'll have my cell phone. Call me if you need anything." He released a long breath. "Are you sure you want to do this?"

She nodded. "I'm sure," she said. "Now, you better get going."

For a moment they stood very still, staring into each other's eyes. When he came toward her, she held her breath. "You could sleep in here so you're close to the kids. Of course, I might not be able to concentrate on tracking the cat if I'm picturing you in my bed."

She wouldn't be able to sleep, either. "I'll just stay in my room and leave the door open. You should get going."

He reached for her. "I don't want to leave you, Rebecca. Not now, not when I need to convince you to give us a chance."

"Please, Mitch. You need to go."

"Then kiss me, Becca," he said in a low, husky voice. "Let me know that you'll miss me."

She rose up on her toes and pressed her lips gently against his, but Mitch wouldn't settle for gentle. Tipping her head back, he parted her lips to taste her. He caught her around the waist and tugged her roughly against him, letting her feel his desire.

When he released her, his dark gaze held hers. "Think about me when I'm gone." He kissed the tip of her nose. "I've got to go."

She nodded. "Be careful."

"Always," he said, then grabbed his things off the bed and headed for the door. "I had this room redone last year. You're the first woman who's been here. You're the first woman I've *wanted* here."

With Mitch gone the kids were handling the separation in different ways. Even though Greta tried to hide her fear with grumpiness, Rebecca knew the girl was worried about her dad's safety.

Colby was excited by the idea of his father being a hunter, and couldn't wait until he brought back a trophy.

And last night Rebecca had slept in her

own room, but she'd been tempted to move to Mitch's bed if only to feel closer to him.

That would have been foolish. She had to keep reminding herself a future between them was impossible. They were too different. She lived in New York; he lived here. Her career was everything to her—the only staple in her life. She'd been able to depend on her work. It was what she fell back on when she had nothing else.

But that didn't stop her from dreaming of a family.

With her mother and Nana and Poppy Crawford gone, she didn't have any family close. Her blood relatives were in the UK, but they really didn't count. Her own father never had time for her—not once over the years had he asked her to come for a visit.

And Rachel. Rebecca knew she'd been partly to blame for their estrangement. Maybe she should have tried to repair the problems between them. They'd been apart for so long now. It was too late—too late for a lot of things.

She absently touched her stomach and thought about her condition. She had to concentrate on that rather than having a man in her life.

Mitch was going through a transition, too. He hadn't dated a single woman since his wife's death. A virile man like Mitch Tucker needed a sexy, exciting woman in his life.

Not…not half a woman.

She heard Greta's agitated voice and headed to the family room. Colby had a toy rifle and was pretending to shoot it.

"Get rid of that stupid rifle," Greta insisted.

"I don't have to," he argued. "I'm practicing so when I get older enough I can go hunting with Dad. I'm going to kill a wild animal and hang the head on the fireplace."

"That's gross. You're gross," Greta said. "Dad is only shooting the mountain lion because it's hurting our calves, not for a trophy."

"It's okay to hunt, Dad said, 'cause there's too many animals."

Greta jammed her fists on her hips. "You don't have to be so happy about it." Tears flooded her eyes. "You know Dad could get hurt…"

That took the air out of Colby's sails and he went to his sister. "Okay, Greta, I won't shoot my gun any more…in the house."

Rebecca crossed the room. "Colby, why don't you go get your pajamas on and then you can watch a movie before bed?"

The boy grinned. It was already his bedtime. "All right," he cried and dashed out of the room.

Rebecca turned to Greta. "Honey, I know you're worried," she said. They all were. Rebecca had gotten a quick call from Mitch, just checking on the kids. "But your dad will be careful."

"I know, but what if the cat…?" The girl turned away.

Rebecca took Greta in her arms. "Your dad is with a dozen other men."

"I know, but he's all we have…"

Rebecca understood how the girl felt. "Not

so. You have Margie, your grandparents in Florida, and Wally. And you have me." Rebecca found she meant that and wished it could be more. "Now, I don't want your father to come back and find your glum faces."

Greta looked up at her and smiled. "I'm glad you came to Wyoming."

"I am, too," Rebecca admitted, even though she would be leaving soon.

"I am too. What?" a familiar voice asked.

The three turned to find Mitch standing in the doorway. Rebecca ate up the sight of him. He looked tired and dirty, but no less than wonderful to her.

"Dad," Greta yelled and went running into his arms. Then Colby arrived to get a hug.

"Hey, Dad, did you kill the cat?" the boy asked.

Mitch was so glad to be home that he didn't want to go into the details of the hunt. He just nodded. "We didn't have any choice, son."

Colby jumped up and down. "Are you going to get it stuffed?"

"Colby, no." Greta folded her arms. "I'm not going to live in a house with dead animals."

"Neither am I," Mitch said and caught Rebecca out of the corner of his eye. She was wearing jeans and a rich blue Western-style blouse and looked as if she belonged here. He liked that.

"Hi, Rebecca," he said.

"Welcome back, Mitch."

"It's good to be back." His gaze moved to her hair. She wore it down in waves. He itched to get his fingers in the silky strands.

"I hope these two weren't too much of a handful."

"No, Dad. We were good," Colby said. "Rebecca took us into town and we got school stuff, and we had lunch at the café. And Greta wanted to buy a really short skirt, but Rebecca said it wasn't a good idea. That a girl needs to leave a little mystery." He wrinkled his nose. "What does that mean?"

Mitch couldn't help but smile. "I'll explain it in about ten years, son."

"We worked, too, Dad," Greta added. "We even talked about the idea for the kids' camp. Rebecca came up with the name Carrie's Camp. In honor of Mom."

Mitch's throat tightened. His deceased wife's dream, a reality. He looked at Rebecca. "It seems you've been busy."

"I thought the kids might like to be involved with the planning stage."

He wanted nothing more than to walk across the room and take this woman in his arms. Later, he told himself. "Kids, I think it's time you both should be in bed."

"But I want you to tell us about the cat," Colby begged.

"In the morning," Mitch said, unable to think about anything except being with Rebecca. "Greta, will you take your brother upstairs? I'd like to talk with Rebecca."

Greta glanced between the two adults, and smiled. "Sure, Dad. Come on, Colby." She tugged at her brother. "I'll read you a story."

Left alone, Mitch walked across the

room toward the woman he'd thought about all during his time on the range. Now he was certain he wanted her in his life. "I missed you."

"I'm glad you're back…safe."

He took another step. "Since I've been away all I've thought about is…this…" He caught her head between his hands, leaned down and took her mouth. Hit with a rush of feelings, he nestled her closer, vowing to do whatever it took to keep Rebecca with him.

He finally broke away. "I have to smell like an old goat. I'm going to take a shower and say goodnight to the kids, then I'll be back so we can have some time together. I plan to convince you that we belong together."

Thirty minutes later, Rebecca still wasn't thinking clearly when there was a knock on her bedroom door. She answered it to find Mitch, clean-shaven, and his hair still damp from his shower.

When he took her in his arms he made her

forget about common sense. And she'd always prided herself on thinking things through. But this man made her want to feel— feel his mouth on hers, his hands on her body.

He finally broke off a kiss, but didn't release her.

"I like the way you say hello." His dark eyes locked with hers. "If you only knew how much I missed you. How much I want you." He brushed his lips over hers, nibbling, tasting, teasing her. "Damn, I can't get enough of you. I don't want to let you go."

She hated herself for her weakness, but she couldn't let him go, either. Not yet. "I don't want you to," she confessed.

He froze and his gaze searched her face. "Be sure, Becca."

Rebecca blocked out everything but this night, and being with the man she loved this one time. She didn't want to love him but she couldn't deny her feelings any longer.

"I am sure."

The words were barely spoken when he

captured her mouth in a demanding kiss, then released her to lead her into her room. Once the door shut, he leaned her up against it and his mouth came crushing down on hers again. His hunger was evident as he parted her lips and slid inside, deepening the kiss. It wasn't long before Rebecca was caught up in the sweet pleasure.

Mitch moved from her lips to her cheek, trailing kisses until he reached her ear. "You're driving me crazy, and I think you like that," he breathed. "Be warned, Becca, I'm going to return the favor." Then he proceeded to whisper in her ear how he planned to love her and she shivered.

Just this once, she told herself. Just once she wanted to know what it was like to love…and be loved.

Sliding her hands up his broad back, Rebecca pressed her breasts against his chest. "So far, you're all talk, cowboy."

That was all she got to say as Mitch swung her up into his arms and carried her across the room. He kissed her as he set her down on the floor next to the bed. "I'm going to make you pay for that."

Mitch felt raw as he cupped his hands under her chin, and tilted her head toward him. Inhaling unevenly, he covered her mouth with a soft, searching kiss. He drank from her, savoring the taste of her, trying to relay what she was doing to him, the feelings she drew from him. It had been so long since he'd felt anything like this, if ever.

He quickly worked the buttons on her blouse, then stripped it off her shoulders and let it drop to the floor. Her pale skin glistened in the dim light, and he hesitated to touch her, less he lost all control.

She tugged at his T-shirt, and he finished the job, pulling it off over his head. Then she reached out and ran her fingers over him. Next, he watched as her shaky hands unclasped the lacy bra and let it drop to the floor. "Love me, Mitch," she whispered. "Love me tonight."

He sucked in a breath. "I plan to, oh,

Becca, I plan to." His mouth covered hers as he gathered her into his arms and pressed her back into the bed. Then he began to fulfill his promise.

CHAPTER NINE

JUST before dawn, Mitch lay on his side watching Rebecca sleep. Facing him, her hands tucked under her cheek, she looked so innocent. He wanted to wake her up and repeat what they'd shared throughout the night. His body stirred as he remembered how Rebecca had come alive under his touch. He preened a little, knowing how he'd pleasured her, and she'd returned it in so many ways.

Rebecca whimpered his name as she shifted in her sleep, and Mitch leaned down and placed a soft kiss on her lips. She didn't respond. So she wasn't so easy to wake up, he thought, recalling her need for morning coffee. He didn't give up easily and returned to her tempting mouth.

Rebecca arched into the warmth as skilled hands caressed her body, making her tingle. She wanted more. Fighting sleep, she blinked and tried to adjust to the dim light.

"Well, hello." Mitch's voice was low and husky.

She froze as their night together flashed in her head. "Mitch, what are you doing here?" she asked, a little too harshly.

He blinked. "I guess if you have to ask, I didn't make an impression." He sighed. "I'll just have to show you." He reached for her and she pulled away.

Sitting up, she bunched the sheet against her breasts. "I mean…I thought you'd be gone…because of the kids." Oh, Lord, she couldn't face him now.

"Greta and Colby are still asleep." He sat up, and the sheet fell to his hips, revealing that he was naked.

She turned away. Why hadn't she thought about the morning after? "Maybe you should leave anyway."

Mitch didn't move. "Becca, what's happening here? What's changed since last night?"

Everything! She was trembling. "It's just that I don't want to answer a lot of questions…from impressionable kids."

He didn't say anything for a long time, then she felt him get up and heard the sound of him pulling on his jeans. He came around the bed and handed her a robe. "Put this on, and we'll talk."

That was the last thing she wanted to do, but she didn't have a choice. She managed to slip on the robe, tie the belt, and move to the other side of the room. For what she had to say, she needed to be as far away from him as possible.

He spread his hands. "Did I do something wrong?"

She shook her head. "Oh, no…last night was wonderful." She couldn't believe how tender and loving he'd been with her. "But it can't happen again, Mitch. It wouldn't be wise. I'm returning to my life in New York, and you and the kids have your life here."

She couldn't catch her breath as she stared at the tall gorgeous man, his broad shoulders and chest and that slim waist. Wranglers hung on his slim hips, the top button undone. Desire shot through her.

"There's got to be some middle ground… some way to work it out. If we're both willing to give a little… To compromise…" He started toward her. "That's what couples do when they fall in love."

Oh, no, don't let him say love. Fighting tears, she held up her hand. "Please, Mitch. Don't make this difficult."

"Oh, darlin', I plan to make it very hard for you to leave me."

She had to get him out of there before she broke down. "Well, I'm not going to listen," she said as she started for the door and opened it. "You need to go. I refuse to argue with you about this."

He stood, rooted to the spot, then finally relented and headed for the exit just as the phone rang.

Mitch went to the extension in the hall

and picked up the receiver. "Hello," he said. "Yes, this is the Tucker Ranch. Yes, she's here. One moment please." He held out the phone to Rebecca. "It's your sister."

Rachel? Rebecca's heart raced. Why would Rachel be calling her? She took the receiver from him. "Hello, Rachel?"

"Rebecca, Stephanie helped me locate you. It's Grandfather William. I—I'm afraid he's dying."

She heard Rachel draw a breath. "He's asking for you, Rebecca."

Rebecca's chest tightened. It had been so many years since she'd seen her grandfather, but that didn't mean she didn't love the man. "He's dying?"

Rebecca tried to take it all in as her sister told her it was only a matter of time, and begged her not to miss this last opportunity to see him. Worse, Rebecca heard the tremble in her sister's voice as she revealed how much she regretted not being there when their mother died. "I should have been there, Rebecca. I should have been there for you, too. Don't miss this chance to say goodbye to Grandfather."

Rebecca could barely speak, let alone make a split-second decision. Then she felt a hand on her shoulder and turned to find Mitch beside her. He took the phone from her.

Not taking his gaze from her, he spoke the words she couldn't manage. "Rachel, this is Mitch Tucker," he said. "I'll make sure your sister gets on a plane." He paused, listened, then looked at Rebecca. "Yes, she needs to be there with her family." He hung up, but only to make another call.

Rebecca walked back to her room in a trance. She closed the door, but that wouldn't keep Mitch out. How dared he make decisions for her? She knew she had to go to the UK, but how could she face the group of strangers who called themselves her family?

She needed someone with her. Taking her cell phone from her purse, she punched in Stephanie's number. After a minute or so she reached her close friend in London and informed her of her impending visit. Stephanie offered her a place to stay at her apartment. Rebecca promised to let her know when she would arrive at Heathrow Airport, and hung up.

There was a soft rap on the door, then it opened and Mitch walked in. "Rebecca, I don't think you should go alone," he said. "I want to go with you."

It took everything she had to shake her head as she pulled out her suitcase and began emptying out the dresser drawers. "No, I'll be fine," she said simply. She went into the bathroom and returned with her personal items. "This is my family. I'll handle it on my own." Right. Just as she'd handled everything so far, by simply ignoring it.

"Okay, but let me at least get you back to New York. I've already notified a pilot in Cheyenne. He'll bring the Lear jet here."

Before she could argue, Mitch left her to finish packing. It was better this way. The faster she got away from Mitch, the faster she could start forgetting him.

An hour later, Rebecca's bags were in the Range Rover and she was ready to leave. But was she? She was leaving Mitch and the kids. They were waiting for her outside. She slowly opened the door to see them lined up on the porch.

"I'm sorry about your grandpa, Rebecca," Greta said.

"Me, too," Colby added.

"Thank you." She hugged them both, then looked at Mitch. "I better get going."

"The plane is here." He opened the door.

She drew both children in her arms, desperate to hold back her tears. It was hard enough giving up Mitch, but these two... These children were her heart.

"I love you, Rebecca," Colby said.

"I love you, too," Greta echoed.

She was dying. "And I love you, back," she whispered over the lump in her throat as she hugged them both.

"Please come back soon," Greta pleaded.

Mitch stepped in. "Kids, Rebecca needs to catch a plane."

He escorted her to the passenger side, and walked around, climbed in and started up the truck. Surprisingly, Mitch didn't talk to her during the ride. He left her alone to look out the window at the mountains she'd come to know and love.

Finally they arrived at the air strip and Mitch parked. "Jerry Driscoll is my pilot. He'll get you to New York." He reached into his pocket and pulled out an itinerary. "I reserved a seat for you out of Kennedy with British Airways."

She wanted to argue that she could have made the calls, but she couldn't. "Thank you."

He helped her out while Wally took her bags from the back. Now all she had to do was leave Mitch and she'd be home free. "Thank you for everything. Goodbye, Mitch." She stole a glance at him. Bad idea.

He reached for her. "If you think I'm

going to let you walk out of my life like this, you don't know me."

"Mitch, we've talked this to death," she said. "We're not right for each other."

"After what we shared last night, how can you say that?"

"I won't talk about this now." She glanced toward the small jet on the runway. She had to get away. "I need to leave."

But he still wouldn't let her go. "I can't let you go until you at least understand how I feel. I love you, Rebecca. Just give this a chance, we can make it work."

Her heart pounded hard. "We can't."

"You're wrong," he argued. "You love my kids. And I'd love nothing more than to be with you, to marry you, to have a child with you. Hell, I'd love to have a half-dozen more."

The pain was tearing her apart. "No, I can't do this."

"Why?" His eyes searched hers. "I've seen you with Greta and Colby and the way you treat Matthew. I know you care about them." He lowered his voice. "Becca, you were meant to have children."

There was another sharp pain that tore through her heart, nearly staggering her. "Just let me go, Mitch. Please…"

"Then tell me why you wouldn't give us a chance?" He kept at her. "Tell me why not?"

Finally the tears broke loose and ran down her face. "Because, Mitch, I can't have your baby! I can't have any man's baby."

She backed away when she saw the shock on his face. He finally started toward her and she couldn't stand to hear the regret or pity in his voice. "Oh, Rebecca…"

The pain was worse than she ever could imagine. "I've got to go. Goodbye, Mitch."

Rebecca turned and took off running. She didn't stop until she got onto the plane. Once the jet took off, she gave in and sobbed her heart out. She'd gotten the truth out. And she had finally gotten Mitch Tucker out of her life. For ever.

Now if she could just get him out of her heart.

* * *

The next morning, Rebecca handed the fare to the taxi driver and climbed out in front of the black wrought-iron fence surrounding William Valentine's white Georgian villa in London.

She stood on the sidewalk, exhausted. She hadn't slept in what felt like days. First that flight to New York, then racing to her apartment where she'd repacked her suitcase, grabbed her passport, and headed out to the airport to catch her flight into Heathrow. Stephanie had met her, and after she'd dropped her bags off at her friend's apartment and freshened up, she'd come here.

Rebecca's grip tightened on the book in her hand. *Sleeping Beauty*. Grandfather William had presented Rachel a copy of *Black Beauty*, and she'd received a copy of *Sleeping Beauty* when they'd left London to move to the States over twenty years ago.

Before she'd left her apartment in New York, she'd found herself reaching for her favorite fairy tale, and reading as she'd crossed the Atlantic. It also saddened her that it had been so long since she'd seen her grandfather and had spent so many years away from a place that had once been her home.

Rebecca stepped through the gate and walked toward the huge double doors. She lifted the knocker and dropped it against the brass plate. The door was opened by an attractive, smiling middle-aged woman.

"Miss Valentine, it's so good of you to come. I'm Margaret Jordan. I work for your grandfather. Please come in, your sister is expecting you."

"Thank you, Margaret," Rebecca said and followed the woman inside. Suddenly childhood memories began to bombard Rebecca.

The floor of the grand entry hall was made up of large squares of marble tiles. The room was painted a deep taupe and trimmed with decorative bright white moldings and original artwork lined the walls. To her right was the formal parlor, painted in a sky blue with huge windows and high ceilings. A grouping of oversized furniture was centered in front of the fireplace.

Margaret waited for her at the bottom of the carpeted staircase, while overhead a crystal teardrop chandelier hung overhead from the twenty-foot ceiling.

She couldn't take it all in. More memories came as her hand moved over the carved handrail along the winding staircase. At the top, Rebecca hesitated. She and Rachel had played hide and seek here, going in and out of the many rooms. There also had been the special room Grandfather had decorated and filled with toys for his grandchildren.

A deep sadness overtook her thinking of William Valentine dying. She should have come back sooner. She should have had the chance to get to know her grandfather as an adult.

Margaret stopped at her grandfather's bedroom. She gave Rebecca a gentle smile.

"He'll be so happy to see you." She knocked and opened the door.

Rebecca's pulse raced. She drew a calming breath, moved into the dim room and directed her gaze to the bed, at the frail man under pristine-white sheets.

Holding vigil next to the bed was Rebecca's twin, her beautiful sister. Rachel was tall and elegant, the picture of the professional woman with her dark brunette hair combed in a sleek style just brushing her shoulders. Rachel turned toward her and surprise and joy registered in her blue-gray eyes. She held out her hand.

All at once the years melted away, and Rebecca saw the loving look, mixed with some regret for all the lost years. She walked toward the bed and reached across for her sister's outstretched hand. They held tight to each other as if gathering strength for what was to come.

Rachel leaned closer to the thin man lying in the bed. An oxygen tube threaded through his nose.

After a moment her grandfather's eyes blinked open. Seeing the familiar steel-gray eyes, she smiled. "Hello, Grandfather."

William Valentine's gaze found Rachel, then Rebecca. Tears poured down his withered cheeks. "God heard my prayers. My two beauties together at last."

Rebecca stood on the white-railed balcony that overlooked Hyde Park. Stephanie's apartment above the Bella Lucia was a fringe benefit of her job as manager of one of London's finer restaurants. It was the second of three that the Valentine family owned in the area, all having been named after the love of her grandfather's life, his second wife, Lucia.

It seemed as if most family members worked in the business. Rachel was the wine buyer. Her half-sister, Emma, was a chef. Her father, Robert, and her half-brother, Max, managed the charter restaurant in Chelsea. Her uncle, John Valentine, managed the one in Mayfair. Now that

Grandfather was gone, who would keep the peace between the rival brothers?

Rebecca had been ten years old when she'd left London, yet it seemed like yesterday. Except her grandfather had died, and he'd been buried just the day before. Thankfully she hadn't had to handle it on her own. Rachel had been there for her.

Suddenly, her thoughts turned to Mitch, as they had so many times since leaving Wyoming. And like the other times, she tried to push away all memories of the man. She couldn't deal with them right now.

Healing her relationship with her sister was her number one priority, and that had begun when she and Rachel had left Grandfather's sick room and taken the time to sit down and talk. Talk about the insecurities that their parents' divorce had caused. How they had both thought they had to choose sides, and in the process they had lost each other. Now they'd finally found each other again Rebecca was not going to let this chance get away from them.

Rebecca heard Stephanie's voice behind her and turned to smile at her friend. "How are you feeling?" she asked Rebecca.

"I'm fine."

Stephanie was tall and slender with wild red hair she continually tried to tame. There were very few people who knew the secrets behind those green eyes, or all the physical and emotional pain she had endured in her short life.

"Emma is bringing us lunch over from the restaurant."

Rebecca sighed. "I haven't had much of an appetite, but I'd like to spend time with her."

Emma was another family member Rebecca barely knew. Her younger half-sister was her father's daughter from Robert's marriage to his third wife, Cathy, a marriage that had ended the same year Rebecca's mother had died.

Stephanie nodded. "She's nice, and a fabulous chef for Bella Lucia."

"Then I look forward to sampling her food."

They both walked back into the spacious apartment. It was decorated with oriental influences, and contemporary art hung on the gold-colored walls. In the dining area, there were four place settings. Before she could ask about the other guest the bell rang and Stephanie opened the door to both Emma and Rachel.

A cheerful Emma carried the food containers into the apartment. "I talked our sister into coming, too," she said.

Rachel smiled, but Rebecca saw the sadness behind her sister's high spirits. Grandfather's death had been difficult for her. They'd been so close.

"I'm glad you did." She hugged her twin. "We've all been through a lot, and it's time we enjoy some time together before I have to leave."

"Oh, no, please tell me you aren't going back to the States so soon?" Rachel pleaded.

"I can't stay much longer; I have a job," Rebecca said. But did she? She'd walked out on the Tucker account. Told Mitch she wasn't coming back, and she hadn't really had a chance to talk to Brent since.

They all sat down and had a great lunch, but kept the conversation light. Eventually, Emma left to go back to the Bella Lucia in Chelsea and Stephanie disappeared into her bedroom, leaving the sisters alone.

"Rachel, I hate to see you so…down," Rebecca said. "How are you feeling?"

"I'm fine." Rachel brushed away her concern.

"Have you thought about what we talked about that day at Grandfather's?"

Her sister lowered her eyes. "I really haven't had much time to…" She got up and walked out onto the balcony.

Rebecca followed her. She had to tread gently, but didn't want Rachel to brush this away. Her sister had confided that she'd fallen in love with a French winemaker, Lucien Chartier, and she was carrying his child.

"Rachel, I know that I haven't been there for you in the past, but I'd like to help now…with the baby."

Tears welled up in Rachel's eyes. "Oh, Rebecca, I've made such a mess." She broke down. "I love a man who…doesn't love me back."

Rebecca wrapped her arm around Rachel's shoulders and held her as she sobbed. She felt her sister's misery as deeply as if it were her own. "Has he told you that?"

Rachel shook her head. "No, but Luc's mother says he's still in love with his ex-wife." She dabbed at her eyes.

"His mother shouldn't interfere in this; she doesn't speak for Luc. It's between you and him. You need to make some plans."

"I know, and I have." She wiped away her tears. "I'm going to leave my position at Bella Lucia. I can't work with Father any longer. So, I need to ask you for a favor… I want to come to New York and look for a job managing a restaurant." She smiled hesitantly. "Would it be possible to stay with you for just a while?"

Emotions clogged Rebecca's throat. "Oh,

Rachel, I'd love to have you stay with me." She gripped her sister's hands.

"Are you sure?" Rachel asked. "I know this is going to be difficult for you."

The day she'd arrived in London, Rebecca had updated her sister about her own medical problems. "Not as much as losing you again. This baby is a blessing. You and your child are welcome to stay with me for as long as you like. I want to be a part of my niece's or nephew's life."

Yes, Rebecca thought. She would need family with her, because she wouldn't have Mitch. Fresh thoughts of him rushed through her head of their night together. How she wished for some kind of miracle, a miracle that she had been able to conceive his child. It was natural that he would want more children. She just wished she could be the one who gave them to him. She couldn't.

Rebecca pulled herself out of her reverie. "Rachel, there is one condition before you come to New York. You have to tell Luc. He deserves to know about his child."

Her sister paused, then finally nodded. "We've certainly gotten ourselves into messes, haven't we?" she said. "But here we are. We found each other."

They hugged.

Rachel pulled back. "Okay, now what about you?" she asked. "You're ready to hand out advice, but you're not taking any. You need to talk to Mitch, too."

Rebecca shrugged. "My situation is different. He's not my man."

Her sister didn't look convinced. "We're talking about the man who flew you to New York in his private jet. And the same man who answered the phone at the ranch and within seconds put you on the line. You two were in pretty close proximity at five in the morning…for him not being your man."

She sighed. "Okay, I let things get out of hand. And I fell in love with Mitch, but I can't burden him with my problem."

Rachel's look showed concern. "Seems you did the same thing I did. You ran away."

Rebecca frowned. "All right, I did. But he

wants more children and when I told him I couldn't have any, he let me walk away." She fought her tears, but lost.

The sisters embraced again. "I wish there was something I could do to help."

Rebecca pulled back. "I'm fine, really. We'll both get through this, because we have each other again."

Just then Stephanie appeared in the doorway. "I hate to interrupt, but your father just called. He wants Rebecca to go to Grandfather's home."

Rebecca wasn't crazy about spending time with her father, any more than he was with her. "Did he say why?"

Stephanie raised an eyebrow. "It seems there's a Mr Mitchell Tucker waiting to see you."

CHAPTER TEN

MITCH sat in the large sitting room at William Valentine's home. He'd been waiting too long, and was impatient to see Rebecca. He'd resisted coming until her grandfather's wake and funeral were over before he flew to London to pour out his heart to her. Now, he had only a short time to find the words to convince Rebecca of his love. Let her believe that they belonged together. He refused to leave London without her.

Mitch got up and began to pace. For some reason Robert Valentine had decided his daughter's guest needed company. Of course it was the courteous thing to do, but Mitch knew too many things about Rebecca's father to want to be anything more than civil to the man. And after years in the corporate world, Mitch could see right through an opportunist.

"As I've told you, Mr Valentine, I'm no longer associated with Tucker International. I sold all my assets over two years ago. My family and the Tucker ranch is what I concentrate on now."

Robert Valentine was a tall man with black, brooding eyes, and hair just as black with a sprinkling of gray. He raised an eyebrow. "A man never leaves the corporate world. I hear you are in free-range beef now. Our restaurants just may be interested in doing business."

The last thing Mitch wanted to do was talk business right now. He had to see Rebecca. Nothing else mattered.

"It's going to be a while before we're operational," he told Valentine.

"Then we'll need to keep in touch." Robert smiled. "Since you are…working with my daughter—"

"Mr Valentine," Mitch interrupted. "My trip here has nothing to do with business. My reasons for wanting to see Rebecca are personal. And until I speak to her, I don't really give a damn about much else." He drew a calming breath. "So, please, don't let me take you away from your busy schedule."

Robert opened his mouth to say something when the sound of voices echoed from the entry. Anxiously, Mitch looked toward the doorway and froze when Rebecca appeared. He searched her face. She looked tired, yet beautiful. Her usually wild, sun-kissed brown hair was secured into a bun, but some wayward curls still had escaped. She wore a navy skirt that showed off her long legs and a blue sweater that brought out her eyes. He tried to gauge her reaction to his coming to London. She wasn't smiling.

"Hello, Rebecca," he said.

"Mitch, what are you doing here?"

Not what he wanted to hear, but what did he expect? He'd let her walk away when she'd dropped the bomb about her inability to have children. The news had broken his heart. Not for himself, but for her.

"I came to see you," he told her as he searched her face. Right now, he'd sell his soul to see her smile. "I was worried about you. The last time we spoke…"

She glanced at Robert. "Father, would you excuse us, please?"

Robert nodded, and said, "Why don't you go out to the garden? It's such a lovely day."

Rebecca recognized that familiar gleam in her father's eyes. A man like Mitch Tucker was someone that—despite the fact he was an American—Robert would consider a good prospect for his daughter, and for the Valentine family.

"Fine," she said, not caring where they went. She just wanted to get this over with. Somehow, she had to make Mitch leave. Then, and only then, she could begin to move on with her life.

On the way over to her grandfather's she'd practiced what she would say, but she'd had no idea that seeing him again would cause such an impact on her emotions. She couldn't remember a single thing.

The already handsome man looked even more so in his navy pinstripe suit with a snowy white shirt and burgundy tie. His hair was cut and styled perfectly, like the man himself. *Just get this over with and he'll leave.*

She crossed the room to the French doors, praying she could get through this. She opened the doors and stepped into the fragrant garden. There were dozens of colorful tea rosebushes lining the slate-covered terrace. As a child she had come here and many times walked the maze of stepping stones through the flowers, counting each one.

She shook away the memory. "Mitch, you shouldn't have come."

He followed her. "Oh, yes, Rebecca, this is where I should have been all along. I never should have let you handle all this on your own. If it weren't for the kids, I would have climbed on the plane with you."

She closed her eyes momentarily. "No, Mitch, we've said all we have to say. I'm not coming back to Wyoming. Nothing you say is going to change my mind, not even if it costs me my job at the agency."

He frowned. "Do you really believe I would cause you to lose your job?"

She could see she'd hurt him. "No, you wouldn't. But we can no longer do business together. I'll give your account over to someone else."

"If that's what you want." He sighed. "It's a shame since you've put in so much work on the project. I've looked over more of your ideas, especially the one for Carrie's Camp."

"How did you know…?"

"I found your portfolio in my office. I figured you wanted me to see it."

She was shocked that she'd forgotten something so important to her. "Well, you paid for it."

"I paid for your ideas on my business endeavor." His gaze locked with hers. "What we shared that last night together was very special to me. I thought it was for you, too." He stepped closer and she backed away.

"Of course it was, but it's over," she said. "I'm going back to New York."

"What if I asked you to return to Wyoming again?"

It seemed as if her heart stopped, then it began to race. "Mitch, we've been through this. Our lives are too different. I have my work."

"Will you stop hiding behind your job? I'm not buying that act any more."

"It's not an act," she argued, but she knew it wasn't convincing. "I've worked hard to make a career."

"I don't doubt that, Rebecca. At one time I did too, but I discovered that my wife and kids were more important. I think if you had a choice, you'd pick a family, but you think you can't have that. I'm here to convince you otherwise."

Rebecca felt a huge lump lodge in her throat. "I told you when I left Wyoming… I can't…" She turned away. "Please, don't put me through this again. Just go."

"Why should I make it easy for you? You're making things damn difficult for me. I came all this way to tell you that I love you. That my kids love you. And you won't even look at me."

Her chest grew painfully tight, but he was persistent as he took her by the arm and turned her around to face him. His eyes were dark and searching.

"I love you, Becca," he breathed. "I never thought I could care for another woman…" He took a breath. "When Carrie died I wanted to die. I pulled myself together and went on because of my kids. Then you walked into my life." He lowered his head, brushed his mouth against hers and heard her gasp.

"This isn't fair, Mitch." She wanted what he offered, even ached for it, but she was sure he would resent her later. "I only want you to have your dream."

"Rebecca, you are my dream."

She raised her eyes to meet his dark gaze. "But you…want more children. A houseful."

He pressed his forehead against hers. "Yes, I wanted you to have my baby, but that would have been a bonus. It's you I want. You I need in my life…in my kids' lives. I want to grow old with you."

"But—"

"Don't interrupt," Mitch said. He was doing everything he could to convince her how much he loved her. "I love you so much, Rebecca. And I know you love me, too, or you never would have let me make love to you."

"That was wrong."

"No, it was right. We belong together." He pulled her into a tight embrace, dipped his head and covered her mouth with a long, searching kiss. When he came up for air, they were both breathless.

"I could kiss you for ever," Mitch breathed. "And it's distracting me." He took her hand and led her to a small wrought-iron bench in between the roses. "Tell me about your medical problem. Why is it you can't conceive?"

Mitch placed an arm around her shoulder and drew her against him as she explained about her endometriosis from adolescence and her prognosis for the future. "I have to return to New York and schedule surgery," she ended.

"Well, you aren't going alone. I'm going with you. But first we're getting a second opinion."

She raised her head. "Mitch, that's just it—I can't let you get your hopes up."

Mitch cupped her face. Somehow he had to make her realize how important she was to him. "I love you, Rebecca Valentine. Of course, I'd love to give you a child, but you are all I need. As for children—I know they aren't babies, but there are two kids in Wyoming who want you to be their mom." He felt tears sting his eyes. "They made me promise to bring you back."

"Oh, Mitch...if I thought for a minute that..."

"Rebecca, all you have to do is tell me you don't love me or my kids, and I'll walk out the door and you'll never see me again."

When she tried to look away, he grasped her chin. "I know a lot of people have let you down in your life, but I'm not going to. I promise I will be there for you, Becca. Always. Just tell me that you want me with you, that you love me." He needed to hear those words more than he needed air to breathe.

"I do," she whispered. "I love you, Mitch. So much."

"I'm glad that's settled." He slid off the bench and down on one knee. "Rebecca Valentine, I want nothing more than for you to do me the honor of being my wife and the mother of my children."

With a shaky hand, Mitch reached into his suit jacket and pulled out a velvet box. He opened it to reveal an antique-styled ring with a three-carat, round diamond in a platinum setting.

"Oh, Mitch," Rebecca gasped. "It's exquisite. I've never seen anything so beautiful."

He removed the ring from the box. "Give me your hand, Rebecca. Trust in my love for you. Starting now." He waited, his heart pounding so loudly he thought the world could hear. "Let's be a family."

She trembled as she placed her hand in his and he slipped the ring on her finger. "A perfect fit." He looked at her. "Just like we are." He stood, drew her into his arms and kissed her. When he broke off, he asked, "Is there anywhere we can go to be alone? I want to show you how much I've missed you."

She pulled away with a smile. "I'm afraid that isn't possible. You are marrying a woman with a rather large family. And I bet my sisters and my father are standing on the other side of that door wanting to know your intentions."

He grinned. "I'll tell them my honorable ones and then we can make our escape. Boy, a wedding better take place soon."

At the word "wedding" she bit her lip.

"It's going to be okay, Rebecca. We're going to have a wonderful life together," Mitch said. "We'll even work in some time for your career."

"My career isn't as important as you and the kids. Of course, I want you guys to continue sharing the chores."

Mitch leaned in and brushed his mouth against his future bride's. "That's all up for negotiation."

She placed her arms around his neck. "I have a feeling there's going to be a lot of negotiating in this marriage." She placed her mouth against his and began working on the terms.

EPILOGUE

LESS than two hours before her wedding, Rebecca was in the master bedroom at the ranch trying to remain calm. Her sisters, Rachel and Emma, along with Stephanie, had flown in to be here for her special day. Over and over again they'd told her they were going to handle everything. Rebecca hadn't realized how much work it was to put on a wedding. Even holding it at the ranch, with less than a hundred guests, there was a lot to do.

Mitch wanted her to have this day. Rebecca wouldn't have cared if they went to a judge, as Rachel and Luc had done.

Rebecca studied the beautiful diamond that Mitch had given to her in London. Who would have thought when she'd left New York in May that she'd be having her wedding within the year.

She glanced at her dress lying on the bed. It was a copy of her Grandmother Lucia's wedding gown. She ran her hand over the antique white satin with the intricately beaded scalloped neckline. When Mitch discovered how much she loved her grandmother's dress, he'd had a designer recreate it for her.

Rachel came in dressed in her rose pink bridesmaid's dress, her stomach protruding slightly with her pregnancy.

"How are you feeling?" Rebecca asked her sister.

"Stop worrying, I feel fine. I just wish you and Luc would stop asking every five minutes."

"We don't want you to overdo things." Rebecca was glad that her sister was so happy. It had turned out that Luc did love Rachel and had been eager to marry her, though it had just taken a few weeks for the stubborn Frenchman to confess his true feelings for her.

Rebecca would always be grateful that Mitch had been willing to risk coming for her, to convince her that they belonged together. And Greta and Colby had welcomed her with open arms. Oh, yes, she was lucky beyond belief.

Emma walked in. "Rebecca, I'm sorry, but it looks like Father isn't going to make it." Her younger sister traded glances with Rachel. "He just called to say something came up."

"Oh…" was all Rebecca could manage to say. She'd never asked much of Robert Valentine, but she'd thought that he would at least make it to her wedding.

A familiar nausea suddenly hit her. She ran into the connecting bathroom to be sick. Rachel and Stephanie helped her clean up and back into the bedroom.

"Don't let Father get to you," Rachel offered. "He's done this all our lives."

"It's just nerves," Rebecca said. "It's been going on all week. I can't wait until the wedding is over and my life gets back to normal."

Once again, Rachel and Emma exchanged a look.

"What?" Rebecca asked.

"This has been going on all week, you say?" Rachel asked. "Anything else, like… are your breasts tender?"

"Why, yes, they are, but…" Her heart skipped a beat as she thought about the possibility. "No… I can't be…pregnant. The doctor said that the scar tissue…"

"We need a pregnancy test," Rachel said.

Rebecca jumped up. "I can't take a pregnancy test. I'm getting married in an hour."

Mitch adjusted his tie again and smiled as he greeted the arriving guests, then he checked his watch. It should be about time to start. He was still angry to learn that Robert Valentine wasn't coming, only because he wanted this day to be perfect for Rebecca. Thinking about his bride, he smiled. How did he get so lucky to find her?

"Hey, Dad," Colby called as he tugged on his hand. "Is it time to get married yet?"

"Soon, son," Mitch said. "This is the bride's day and she may be running late."

"She's not going to change her mind, is she?"

"No, she isn't." He knelt down to his son's level. "What's bothering you, Colby?"

"I was just wondering if it's okay if I call Rebecca Mom. I mean she is, kinda…"

"Son, I think that will make Rebecca real happy. She loves you and Greta so much. She just wants you to be sure it's your choice."

His big brown eyes widened. "I decided I want to. You think I should ask her first?"

"How about right after the wedding?"

"All right!" Colby cried and high-fived his dad.

Mitch looked up. Stephanie and Emma were coming toward him. "Sorry about the hold-up, but we're ready now, so everyone should take their places." Emma smiled. "The bride needs an escort. Colby, how would you like to walk Rebecca down the aisle?"

Colby puffed out his chest. "Sure!" he crowed, and took off with the bridesmaids.

The guests sat in rows of white wooden chairs along an ivy-trimmed aisle. A white runner made a path for the bride. Mitch and his best man, Wally, stood next to the minister as the bridesmaids came toward them, a beautiful, beaming Greta leading the way. The music changed and everyone stood as Rebecca appeared with Colby.

Her gown was simple. The antique-white satin draped over her shapely body, tucked in at her waist, then flowed into a circle skirt to the floor, with a train in the back. It was an elegant nineteen-forties-style dress. Perfect for her. Perfect for his bride.

Her hair was pulled back with a ring of flowers woven through the strand and her veil was attached at the base of her neck. She carried a bouquet of pink roses. When she smiled Mitch's heart swelled.

They made their way up the aisle to him, and Colby gave Rebecca's hand to his dad. "She said yes, Dad," he whispered. "Rebecca said she'd love to be my mom."

That brought some chuckles from the

guests as Colby took his place next to Greta. Mitch couldn't take his eyes off his bride. "You are beautiful."

"You don't clean up so bad yourself, cowboy."

He wanted to kiss her right there, but instead he tucked her arm in his and they turned to the minister.

Twenty minutes later, they were pronounced husband and wife. Mitch got his wish and pulled Rebecca in his arms and kissed her. He didn't release her until applause from the guests reminded him they weren't alone. They made their way up the aisle together.

After stealing another kiss, he whispered, "Hello, Mrs Tucker."

"Hello, Mr Tucker." She smiled. "Would you mind coming with me before we head into the reception?"

"Haven't I proven I'd follow you anywhere?"

While everyone else headed to the patio, Rebecca took Mitch by the hand and led him to the sun room. When they closed the door, he pulled her into his arms and kissed her again.

"This is a great idea, but everyone is going to notice we're missing and come looking for us."

"I just wanted to give you your gift before we got too wrapped up in the reception. I couldn't wait," she admitted. She went to the table and picked up a small box tied with a simple bow.

He peered into her face. She was flushed and nervous. "You know I'm going to love anything you get me."

"Well, this is something we both wanted, but didn't plan on."

He pulled off the bow and opened the box to find a long white plastic stick. He recognized what it was immediately. And in the stick's window was a pink +. His heart raced. "You're pregnant?"

Rebecca trembled as she nodded. "I've been sick all week and Rachel said I needed to take a test. I called my doctor in New

York. He said it was possible. That was why the ceremony was late getting started," she went on. "Emma drove into town to buy a test. I had to be sure." She sank into the window-seat. "I know this is a shock. We didn't plan this."

When Rebecca saw Mitch's grin she relaxed a little. He came and knelt down in front of her. "I'm just amazed. We spent one night together…and we made a baby." He blinked away the tears. "I'm humbled, to say the least."

She wanted so much to give Mitch a child. But was he ready for parenthood right now? "But happy?" she asked.

He gathered her into his arms. "My Becca," he breathed. "I don't even have the words to express what I'm feeling at this moment. I didn't think I could love you any more than I did, but I do…and I already love our child." He kissed her tenderly, gently, but with even more fervor. She'd never felt so cherished in her life. When he released her, he rested his head against her forehead.

"Let's not tell the others for a few weeks," she said. "I want to keep this just for us for a while." Tears glistened in her eyes as she touched her stomach. "This is our miracle."

"Our love is the miracle."

Rebecca knew the real miracle had been finding Mitch, and the family she'd always dreamed of.

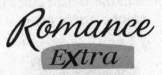
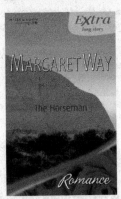

The child she loves…is his child.

And now he knows…

HER SISTER'S CHILDREN BY ROXANNE RUSTAND

When Claire Worth inherits her adorable but sad five-year-old twin nieces, their fourteen-year-old brother and a resort on Lake Superior, her life is turned upside down. Then Logan Matthews, her sister's sexy first husband turns up – will he want to break up Claire's fledgling family, when he discovers that Jason is his son?

WILD CAT AND THE MARINE BY JADE TAYLOR

One night of passion doesn't make a marriage, but it could make a child. A beautiful daughter. Cat Darnell hadn't been able to trample on her lover's dream and kept her secret. Joey was the light of her life. And now, finally, Jackson Gray was coming home…was going to meet his little girl…

On sale 4th August 2006

www.millsandboon.co.uk

"I was fifteen when my mother finally told me the truth about my father. She didn't mean to. She meant to keep it a secret forever. If she'd succeeded it might have saved us all."

When a hauntingly familiar stranger knocks on Roberta Dutreau's door, she is compelled to begin a journey of self-discovery leading back to her childhood. But is she ready to know the truth about what happened to her, her best friend Cynthia and their mothers that tragic night ten years ago?

16th June 2006

FREE

4 BOOKS AND A SURPRISE GIFT!

We would like to take this opportunity to thank you for reading this Mills & Boon® book by offering you the chance to take FOUR more specially selected titles from the Romance series absolutely FREE! We're also making this offer to introduce you to the benefits of the Mills & Boon® Reader Service™—

- ★ **FREE home delivery**
- ★ **FREE gifts and competitions**
- ★ **FREE monthly Newsletter**
- ★ **Books available before they're in the shops**
- ★ **Exclusive Reader Service offers**

Accepting these FREE books and gift places you under no obligation to buy; you may cancel at any time, even after receiving your free shipment. Simply complete your details below and return the entire page to the address below. You don't even need a stamp!

YES! Please send me 4 free Romance books and a surprise gift. I understand that unless you hear from me, I will receive 6 superb new titles every month for just £2.80 each, postage and packing free. I am under no obligation to purchase any books and may cancel my subscription at any time. The free books and gift will be mine to keep in any case.

N6ZEE

Ms/Mrs/Miss/Mr.......................................Initials ....
BLOCK CAPITALS PLEASE

Surname ....

Address ....

....

....Postcode ....

Send this whole page to:

The Reader Service, FREEPOST CN81, Croydon, CR9 3WZ